ONE FINAL BREATH

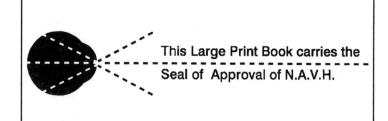

This Large Print Book carries the
Seal of Approval of N.A.V.H.

DIVE TEAM INVESTIGATIONS

ONE FINAL BREATH

LYNN H. BLACKBURN

THORNDIKE PRESS
A part of Gale, a Cengage Company

LIBRARY OF CONGRESS CIP DATA ON FILE.
CATALOGUING IN PUBLICATION FOR THIS BOOK
IS AVAILABLE FROM THE LIBRARY OF CONGRESS

ISBN-13: 978-1-4328-7191-8 (hardcover alk. paper)

Published in 2019 by arrangement with Revell Books, a division of
Baker Publishing Group.

Printed in the United States of America
1 2 3 4 5 6 7 23 22 21 20 19

To my parents, Ken and Susan Huggins, for teaching me to love Jesus and to love stories, and for showing me how stories are often the best way to convey truth. Every book I have written has pieces of you — your sacrifices, your struggles, your joys, your myriad examples of forgiveness and grace — threaded throughout. Thank you for your unwavering love and support . . . and for pretending not to notice when I kept reading for an hour after I'd asked for "just one more chapter." I love you!

ACKNOWLEDGMENTS

Endless gratitude to . . .

Mecina Hapthey and Angelina Zimmer — thank you for letting me pick your brains about Yapese culture and missionary families!

Shawn and Bridget Clarke — for being enthusiastic and creative brainstorming friends from the very first book. Your insights into the ways to contaminate the water supply were invaluable. And to Bella and Cayla for being some of my favorite readers and for being active participants in our crazy conversation!

Jennifer Huggins Bayne — my sister and favorite nurse practitioner for not being concerned by my questions about drugs and how to stab someone without killing them. You're the best! I love you!

Sergeant Chris Hammett — your willingness to talk to me and answer my endless questions gave all of my homicide investigators, including Gabe and Anissa, a depth they wouldn't have had without your input. Thank you!

Mike Berry, Master Underwater Criminal Investigator (UCIDiver.com) — for giving me direction on my diving scenes. All mistakes related to diving and underwater criminal investigation procedures are mine.

My sisters of the Light Brigade — for once again praying me through another book I didn't think I could write.

My critique group — for helping me brainstorm and for talking me off the ledge on a regular basis.

Lynette Eason — for letting me borrow Brady St. John and, you know, for everything else.

Tamela Hancock Murray — Agent Extraordinaire. Thank you for your continual encouragement.

Andrea Doering — It has been a true

privilege to work with you to bring this series to life.

Amy Ballor — for once again editing this manuscript and blowing me away with your ability to catch my mistakes.

Sandra Blackburn — for continuing to hold the title of "Best Mother-in-Law" in the world. And for doing a lot of laundry and dishes at my house when I'm on a deadline.

Ken and Susan Huggins — I couldn't do it without you.

Emma, James, and Drew — for being so patient when Mommy goes to her office to work, and for being excited every time a new book releases. You three make the real world my favorite place to be.

Brian — for so many things, but specifically for this book for saying, "Why don't you go to the beach to write?" I'm beyond blessed to have your support and encouragement and love.

My Savior — the Ultimate Storyteller — for allowing me to write stories for you.

Let the words of my mouth and the meditation of my heart be acceptable in your sight, O LORD, my rock and my redeemer.

~ Psalm 19:14

1

It didn't get much better than this. At least not on this side of the world, anyway.

A light breeze flirted with her hair as homicide investigator and dive team captain Anissa Bell popped a peanut butter M&M into her mouth and gazed over the deep blue that was Lake Porter, the crown jewel of Carrington County. Even as midnight crept closer, the July air held much of the day's warmth and she considered going for a quick dip before driving home.

Or maybe she'd ask Leigh and Ryan if she could crash on the large porch swing under the deck. The crescent moon could be her night-light, the water lapping the shore her lullaby.

Maybe she'd get a good night's sleep.

Or not.

She shook off the gloomy thought. Tonight was a night for celebrating.

Most of the investigators in the Carrington

County Sheriff's Office were on call every sixth weekend, but members of the dive team could be called in at any time to perform an underwater search. With the summer tourism season in full swing in central North Carolina, the dive team had been called out six weekends in a row to look for everything from suspected drugs to stolen merchandise. But miracle of miracles, there'd been no calls today — not even for Investigator Gabe Chavez, who was on call for the homicide unit — and they'd been able to enjoy a Saturday on the water.

The home Leigh had inherited from her parents, which she now shared with her husband, Ryan Parker, sat on a beautiful lakefront lot. Perched on a small point, the house was positioned so that depending on where you stood, you had views of the open water or of a cozy cove, some of which remained undeveloped.

Ryan had recently created an outdoor patio space, complete with a fire pit, on the very edge of the point. The views were fabulous.

Anissa turned to Ryan, her second-in-command on the dive team and a fellow homicide investigator. "You may regret doing such an amazing job on this patio. If you thought it was hard to get rid of us before, you'll never succeed now."

The others around the fire pit chuckled in obvious agreement.

"She's right." Dive team member Adam Campbell leaned forward in his Adirondack chair but kept his arm around his fiancée and the department's resident computer expert, Dr. Sabrina Fleming. "And thanks a lot for setting such a high standard. Leigh says she'd like to have a patio and a fire pit by the lake, and one month later here we are. How am I supposed to compete with that?"

"There's no competition." Sabrina smiled at Adam. The professor had loosened up a lot since she started hanging out with this crew, but public displays of affection weren't her style. Adam had no such issues. He kissed her temple and whispered something in her ear that sent a flush over her cheeks.

Ryan pecked his bride of three months, nurse practitioner Leigh Weston, on the tip of her nose. "Whatever she wants, she gets."

A loud groan came from the opposite side of the fire pit. Gabe put his hands over his eyes. "Make it stop. Please."

Leigh batted her eyes at Ryan for a few seconds before dissolving in laughter. "Sorry, Gabe. But you make it sound like I'm the only one who thought this was a good idea. As I recall" — she glanced around the circle — "all of you were in agreement with this plan."

"Of course we were." Gabe poked the dwindling coals in the fire pit. "Partly because you're very difficult to argue with but mostly because it was a great suggestion." He waved the poker toward the pavers that lined the ground in a large swath near the shore of Lake Porter. "Although if I'd known how heavy these things were — and how many of them you planned to use — I might have rescinded my offer of assistance."

Ryan tipped his Coke can in Gabe's direction. "Couldn't have done it without you, bro. You were crucial to the success of this mission."

Gabe narrowed his eyes at Ryan. "You're buttering me up. Why?"

"Can't I say a simple thank-you? What makes you think I have an ulterior motive?" Ryan almost sold it, but right at the end his eyes widened a bit too much and the game was up.

Gabe turned on Leigh. "Don't tell me you have a new project brewing."

Leigh had a look of pure innocence. "It wasn't my idea. It was Sabrina's. We're thinking we should put a covered area over there." She pointed to the left of the patio.

"We could hang a few swings and hammocks and those of us with fair skin could enjoy the lake without burning to a crisp." Sabrina smiled sweetly at Gabe.

"It would be lovely during a thunderstorm," Anissa added. The girls had to stick together.

Gabe fell back into his chair and ran his hands through his hair. "You women are going to be the death of me."

Their laughter filled the space. If they weren't careful, they'd get a phone call from the neighbors for violating a noise ordinance. That would be the kind of thing a reporter would have a field day with.

One reporter in particular.

Paisley Wilson had shown up at Anissa's last three crime scenes. She never spoke. Never asked a question. Stayed behind the tape. But she was digging. No doubt about it.

The question wasn't if she would find what she was looking for, but when.

"Smile, Bell." Gabe's soft remark pushed back her negative thoughts. She didn't think anyone else had heard him — the two couples were murmuring to each other — but just the same, she forced a smile.

"Fake. Fake. Fake." Gabe shook his head

in mock sadness.

As corny as it was, Gabe's overdone drama elicited a real smile from her. He didn't comment. Just returned it with one of his own — and a knowing look — before resuming his teasing of Leigh.

Gabe Chavez. He'd gotten under her skin for years, but lately he'd gotten inside her head. Ever since he'd talked her off the ledge a few months ago after she'd been forced to kill a man in order to save Sabrina's life, she'd been unable to shake him. She didn't have many close friends and it was unnerving to think that Gabe might be the only person in eight thousand miles who had any idea what made her tick.

Their shared history was . . . complex. She'd tried to keep her distance, but he kept showing up. On random Saturdays when she went for a run. On Tuesday nights when she stayed late to finish paperwork. And unlike the way he was with the group — loud, flirty, the life of the party — when it was the two of them, he rarely spoke. He was just — there. With her. Not asking for anything, but present. Available.

She could almost think it was a coincidence that he'd decided to work late the same night or run on the same path.

But she didn't believe in coincidences.

The wind had picked up and a gust blew an almost empty bag of chips into the yard. Gabe scrambled after it as lightning illuminated the sky. A long rumble of thunder followed. "I guess we'd better call it a night." Adam stood, pulling Sabrina with him. "We have to go to the early service tomorrow so we can make it to Sunday dinner at Grandmother's. We've missed the last two."

"Oooh." Leigh put on a show of concern. "Have you ever missed two in a row? You might get disinherited."

The Campbell family owned half of Carrington, and their Sunday lunch protocol was well known. If you were a Campbell and you were in town, you showed up. The only exceptions were contagious illness — confirmed by a physician — or legitimate work situations.

"Nah." Adam laughed. "I'm safe. Grandmother adores Sabrina."

Adam's grandmother adored him, too, and they all knew it. She just had a unique way of showing it.

Maybe Gabe would go ahead and leave and she could ask Leigh about staying over without him hovering. "I bet you could sweet-talk Anissa into coming up with some sort of mandatory training exercise if you

19

want to get out of it," Ryan said.

"Don't even try it, Campbell." Anissa grabbed a few more M&M's. "Your grandfather cornered me at the Pancake Hut last week and asked if I was intentionally keeping you from lunch. He was kidding, I think. But you won't get any help from me."

"Family dinners aren't so bad." Sabrina picked up a bowl of salsa from the small table. "Aunt Margaret even smiled at me last time. And Adam's parents are in town, so they'll be there."

Ryan clapped Adam on the back. "Come over tomorrow when you're done. We'll take Sabrina to the diving platform and let her practice."

Sabrina and Adam were planning a tropical honeymoon and Sabrina wanted to be able to dive with Adam rather than staying on the beach while he spent the day underwater. But the truth was, she was terrified and they all knew it. They'd started her in a pool where she could see everything and touch the bottom. They'd spent a couple of months working her up to diving in the lake. The last time they went, she said she was almost able to enjoy it.

Sabrina's anxiety baffled Anissa. She'd grown up underwater, free-diving off the small Micronesian island of Yap, and she often was more at home underwater than on land.

"I notice you haven't invited me to come tomorrow." Gabe let out an exaggerated sigh.

Ryan snorted. "It doesn't matter whether I invite you or not. You have your own keys. I'm more surprised when the boat *is* here than when it isn't."

Gabe acted like he was considering Ryan's comment, then shrugged. "True."

Gabe made sure there were no embers in the fire pit. The others gathered the chips, cooler, cookies, and cups and headed toward the house.

Anissa hung back. As much as she loved this wacky group that had become like family, she needed a few moments of peace.

A bolt of lightning lit the night sky. The storm was coming fast. But then another sound — one that did not have a match in nature — split the atmosphere.

Anissa ducked. Was that — ?

She turned to look at the others. Gabe was by her side, bent low, weapon in his hand.

Ryan had pulled Leigh to the ground. Adam had done the same with Sabrina.

She hadn't imagined it.

Shots fired.

"Maybe someone's drunk . . . being stupid." Adam didn't sound like he believed his own words.

"Should we do something?" Sabrina's voice quavered.

Anissa pulled her phone from the back pocket of her shorts. "I'll call it in. Get some patrol officers —"

A scream bounced off the water. Then another.

Then a single terrified word.

"Help!"

Gabe ran for the dock.

He went straight to the back of the boat. No surprise to see Anissa untying the front end while he worked on the back. Ryan jumped on board and cranked the engine, with Adam following right behind him.

The engine stuttered, then started. Gabe caught Anissa's eye and they shoved the boat away from the dock, climbing on board as Ryan slowly backed them away from the dock and Adam continued to shout instructions to Leigh and Sabrina. "Both of you, get inside. Bri, call me and stay on the phone with me. Leigh, grab your medical kit and be ready in case we need you." Both women ran toward the house as Ryan pushed the throttle forward.

"Do you have a spotlight on here?" Anissa yelled over the engine. Ryan pointed to a waterproof box behind the driver's seat.

Anissa jerked it open and handed the spotlight to Gabe. She joined him in the front of the boat and he knew she was scanning the water for any sign of life.

Adam was at the back of the boat, Anissa's phone pressed to one ear, hand pressed to the other as he talked to the dispatcher. She must have handed it off when she ran for the boat. "Investigators Campbell, Bell, Chavez, and Parker responding to a distress call on Lake Porter. Shots fired. Someone, possible female, calling for help. We're on the north side of the lake off Porter Trail, but we're headed toward the south side."

Ryan cut the throttle and they bobbed in the water.

Listening.

Water lapped against the sides of the boat. Night bugs buzzed. Thunder rumbled. But nothing human spoke to them from the darkness. Were they too late?

"I didn't dream that voice." Anissa spoke in a whisper.

A splash.

Could have been a turtle or a fish, but —

"Help!"

The voice was much weaker this time, but

also much closer. "Keep talking to us!" Anissa called out over the water. "We're with the sheriff's office. We can help you."

"Please!" This time the voice had a distinct gurgly quality. "I don't think I can hold him much longer." A girl. Maybe a teenager. And she wasn't alone. How could she have gotten to the middle of the lake?

Ryan put the boat into a slow forward creep in the direction of the voice. But voices carried over the water in weird ways. A fat raindrop hit Gabe's arm. Then another. Great. The storm was here. "Anything, Chavez?" Ryan asked.

"I see a light! Hurry! I don't want to drown!"

They were getting close and now had to be careful not to run over her. "Hang on, sweetie. Keep kicking. Don't try to swim toward us. Just keep kicking." Anissa leaned over the side of the boat and called encouragement as Gabe swept the spotlight across the surface of the water, looking for —

Another sound split the night.

Gabe grabbed Anissa's arm and pulled her with him until they both knelt on the floor of the boat, their arms resting on the seats. He checked behind him. Adam was in a similar position at the back of the boat. Ryan knelt behind the wheel.

Was someone shooting at them or at the girl?

Or taking advantage of the thunder to target practice. At midnight? Unlikely.

"I think the shots are coming from the other side of the cove. We're sitting ducks out here." Ryan pointed to the shore opposite Leigh's house. "Stay low. He could be reloading."

Anissa peeked her head above the rail. Gabe joined her with the spotlight. Both of them kept as low a profile as possible while still scanning the water.

"There!" Gabe held the light steady on the place he'd seen a flash of white face. "She's gone under. I think she may be holding another kid."

Ryan turned the boat in the direction of the light. Anissa slid out of her shoes, her shorts, and the cover-up she'd been wearing over her bathing suit. Adam continued to relay information to the dispatcher. The rain came harder. Faster. If they didn't find them soon . . .

Gabe prayed. *"Ayúdanos por favor. Ayúdanos."*

"Amen," Anissa whispered.

He hadn't realized he'd said the words aloud. Or loud enough for anyone to hear them.

A bolt of lightning split a tree on the other side of the lake and illuminated the night for a few critical seconds. Anissa grabbed his arm and pointed. A head. And another. They were close.

Anissa dove in.

She shouldn't have jumped in without a life ring, but Gabe understood why she did. Anissa was an incredible swimmer and would be able to get to the girl much faster without it. And they were running out of time.

He saw the girl's head break the surface. "Stay on that path, Anissa. You're almost there."

Ryan continued to move the boat toward them.

"I can't hold him!"

The terror in the girl's voice pierced Gabe's heart. What should he tell her? Let the boy go? What if he was still alive and they could save him? But she shouldn't drown trying to keep him from sinking.

Adam joined him at the front with the ring.

"Trade ya." Gabe took the ring and handed the light to Adam. Then he dove in after Anissa.

They had to get these kids out of the water.

And all of them off the lake.

"I've got you." Anissa reached for the girl.

"Not me. Jeremy! Take him. I can swim."

Anissa didn't argue with her. "Okay. I've got him."

Gabe swam up beside them with the ring. "Give it to her," Anissa said. "I can pull him in." Gabe pushed back the desire to stay with Anissa. The boy was limp in her arms. She could handle it.

Another crack — not thunder. They needed to get out of the water. Now.

Ryan idled the boat beside them. Adam lowered the ladder. "Come on. Right here." Gabe stayed with the girl — she couldn't be more than sixteen — as she swam to the ladder. She'd refused the life ring, but she'd been right. She could swim. Quite well. She reached for the ladder but paused before pulling herself out of the water. "Does she have him?" she asked through chattering teeth.

"She does," Gabe said without even looking. "She'll get him on board. Let's get you up so I can help her with your friend. What's your name?"

"Brooke." Her entire body trembled as she pulled herself up the ladder. Gabe stayed behind her. The way she was shaking, she could lose her grip and fall back into the water. "Brooke Ashcroft."

Ashcroft? Was she related to — ? Gabe stopped the thought in its tracks. It didn't matter.

Adam reached for Brooke's hand and helped her into the boat and Ryan wrapped a towel around her shoulders. The rain would soak it through soon, but maybe it would provide a little warmth.

No one brought up how her bathing suit was covered in blood.

Gabe could hear Adam as he settled Brooke on the floor at the front of the boat. Anissa reached the ladder with the boy and didn't appear to be out of breath. Probably wasn't. Sometimes he thought she might be part fish. She definitely had all of them beat when it came to cardiovascular endurance.

Both Adam and Ryan joined them and the four of them maneuvered the young man onto the back of the boat. As soon as he was on board, Anissa and Gabe scrambled up the ladder while Adam and Ryan laid the young man on the floor between the seats. Gabe knelt over Jeremy. No pulse. No breaths. He swiped the boy's mouth and opened up his jaw enough to drain the water from his throat.

Adam pulled the ladder out of the water and Ryan gunned the engine.

Gabe blew into Jeremy's mouth twice.

No response.

Gabe started compressions.

One . . . two . . . three . . . four . . .

"Leigh's dock?" Ryan shouted the question.

Adam shook his head. "The ramp at the end of Porter Trail. The ambulance is almost there."

Anissa wrapped her arms around Brooke. The poor thing was shaking so violently it looked like Anissa was holding on to an out-of-control washing machine.

Adam joined Gabe on the floor of the boat.

"He shot Jeremy." Brooke yelled the words over the roar of the engine. "Why would anyone shoot Jeremy?"

The bullet had entered the upper left half of Jeremy's torso, but Gabe couldn't think about that right now.

"Brooke." Anissa's voice carried over the storm and the engine. "Have you been drinking? Doing drugs? Anything like that? We need to know so we can help Jeremy."

"No! Nothing! We don't do that stuff. It was a race. To see who could swim across the fastest."

Twenty-seven . . . twenty-eight . . . twenty-nine . . . thirty.

Adam did two more breaths.

Gabe continued compressions. Adam continued breaths.

The boat slowed, shouts and lights trickled through Gabe's consciousness, but he kept going. He might not be able to save this boy, but he was sure going to try. He didn't look at his face. He focused on doing the one thing he could do. Arms straight. Steady rhythm.

Nine . . . ten . . . eleven . . . twelve . . .

The boat bumped against the dock.

Paramedics jumped onto the boat. Anissa filled them in.

Gabe didn't stop.

Twenty-two . . . twenty-three . . . twenty-four . . .

2

Anissa brought up the rear of their somber crew as they each nodded at Bill, the security guard in the Carrington Memorial Hospital emergency department.

He gave them a sad nod in turn and reached his hand toward Anissa as she approached. "You okay, hon?"

All she could do was shrug.

No, she wasn't okay. She'd dragged a dead boy out of the lake tonight and then watched Gabe try to force life back into him, even though he had to have known the boy — Jeremy — was already gone.

The lake patrol unit had joined them at the Porter Trail boat ramp and once the paramedics left with Brooke and Jeremy, the dive team members had taken the lake patrol unit back to the scene. Not that there was much anyone could do in a thunderstorm in the middle of the night.

Or anytime.

No one could bring Jeremy back. He was currently on life support, but it was only a matter of time. The family was waiting on his sister to arrive from Georgia in order to give her a moment to say goodbye before they would allow the machines to be disconnected.

And the girl — Brooke — had been checked out and cleared by the emergency department staff but had categorically refused to leave the hospital. When the Littlefield family arrived they had allowed her to say goodbye to Jeremy. She was now waiting in the private room set aside for the family during this difficult time.

That poor girl would need a lot of help coping with his death. She would be convinced it was all her fault. She would beat herself up over this one stupid mistake — and the consequences that she would live with for the rest of her life. She would wish — a million times a day — that she'd died instead.

Anissa wasn't speculating. She knew. She'd lived it.

She pulled in a couple of quick breaths. Blinked back the sudden moisture in her eyes. She could not fall apart. Not now.

She was a professional.

But it would be a lot easier to be a professional back at the sheriff's office.

"You okay, Bell?"

Anissa caught Ryan's concerned remark. Ryan didn't mind being there. Since he'd married Leigh, a nurse practitioner in the emergency department, the hospital had practically been his second home.

He was following behind Gabe and Adam and didn't look in her direction as he slowed his pace to match hers. He spoke in a soft murmur and Anissa knew he was trying not to call attention to the way she lagged behind the others. They all knew she didn't like hospitals, but the way Ryan had asked her if she was okay sparked a question of her own. "Did Leigh tell you?"

"Are you kidding? Leigh believes you are bound by some sort of confidentiality agreement and doesn't seem to think anything you say to her is any of my business. But she did text me a minute ago and ask me to make sure you didn't pass out."

Awesome. She was going to strangle Leigh.

Ryan caught her eye and winked.

Anissa punched his arm. "You're messing with me? Now?"

"Just trying to defuse the tension."

"Keep it up, Parker. I'll make you dive with Stu." Kelly Stuart was the newest member of the dive team. She was . . . eager.

Ryan shuddered. "Sorry, boss." His grin faded. "You've got this."

He picked up his pace and came even with Adam, leaving her to bring up the rear.

She studied the square tiles, not registering anything around her. They wound through the wide hallways, often alone, sometimes stepping to the side as groups of nurses or physicians passed.

Anissa knew Ryan thought her anxiety was due to her deep-seated distaste for hospitals — growing up in a culture where people went to the hospital not to get better but to die would do that to you. And none of them were happy that they were coming to check on Brooke Ashcroft and talk to the family of Jeremy Littlefield.

No one ever wanted to meet grieving parents. The Littlefields had been out of town and had only arrived at the hospital a few hours earlier. Jeremy's father, George Littlefield, had been on the same basketball team as the sheriff when they were eighteen-year-old boys, and the sheriff had requested that the dive team make themselves available to the Littlefields.

She understood. This wasn't her first experience with heartbroken parents.

The difference was that the first time,

she'd been the friend who survived.

The image of her friend — four days dead — forced its way into her mind. She couldn't stop the shudder that dominoed from her shoulders to her knees.

A strong hand closed over her elbow.

She didn't need to look to know it was Gabe. When had he gone from the front of the group to the rear? And why did he have to make his move at the same moment her body betrayed her stress? And why did her stomach do that weird floppy thing it only did around him?

Even as her mind scrambled for answers, it recognized the gesture and the next few breaths came a little easier.

That same hand, in that same place, had gotten her through the early days after the shooting last winter. But until the events of tonight, it had been a while since he'd touched her in any way other than a professional manner on a dive.

Valentine's Day. That had been the last time. They'd both worked late even as others tried to get away for a romantic evening with their dates. As they'd walked to their cars well after 9:00 p.m., he'd squeezed her arm, just like he was doing now, and said, "Maybe next year we'll leave early too."

They'd both laughed at the ridiculousness

of the idea.

She didn't bother to process why she remembered that. It wasn't like it mattered if he touched her.

Or didn't.

"Can you do me a favor?" Gabe's question drew her attention to his face. His eyes were glued straight ahead, his mouth set in a tight line.

It was the most un-Gabe-ish expression she'd ever seen. "What's wrong?"

"Nothing. But I may have to take myself off this case and I need to know if you want it."

"Why don't you want this case?"

He met her eyes for a brief second. "I didn't say I didn't want it. I may not have a choice. But I don't want to throw you under the bus by handing it off to you if you don't want it."

Gabe wasn't making any sense, but the tension in his voice, the set of his jaw, gave Anissa pause. Almost everything was a joke to Gabe, and over the past few years she'd learned to pay attention when he took things seriously.

And clearly this was no joking matter.

Did she want this case?

Honestly? No.

Would she take it? Yes.

But only if she had to.

"I'm next on the rotation, and yes, I'll take it if I have to. But I think you'd be the best person for it." She thought this for reasons she didn't want to get into right now.

Gabe quirked one eyebrow. "I guess we'll see."

They entered the private waiting area. A tall man, gray at the temples, in track pants and a T-shirt, rose to greet them. "George Littlefield." He shook each of their hands. When he reached Anissa, the tears that he'd been blinking back spilled over. "Thank you" — he drew a tortured breath — "for not letting my boy sink to the bottom of the lake."

Sobs rocked through him and Anissa did the only thing she could do. She put her arms around him and he clung to her like a drowning man.

Anissa had no idea how long they stood there, but Mr. Littlefield eventually stepped back. "Thank you," he said again. "If you'll give me a moment, my wife wants to speak to you as well." He waved an arm in the direction of the door and he looked so lost. So broken. "She didn't want to leave Jeremy."

He rubbed his hand across his face and exited the room.

When the door closed behind him, Anissa scanned the room. A much older couple, probably the grandparents, spoke in soft murmurs to a youngish man who she'd guess was their pastor. The only other person in the room was Brooke Ashcroft, huddled in a chair, staring unblinking at nothing.

The door opened, sooner than Anissa had been expecting, and she braced herself for the emotions sure to come from Jeremy's mom.

But it wasn't Jeremy's mom who entered the room.

It was Paisley Wilson or, as she was better known, "This is Paisley Wilson, reporting live from Sky9."

What was she doing here? Surely the families wouldn't want a nosy reporter —

Paisley didn't look around the room as she scurried to Brooke's side. "Was that fast enough?" The words were spoken with kindness and compassion and Brooke leaned against Paisley with the kind of ease that only came from an established relationship.

Paisley draped her arms around Brooke and kissed the top of her head. Only then did her gaze bounce around the room and an uncomfortable awareness filled her expression as she made eye contact with Anissa.

Then her eyes widened, her face paled. She swallowed hard and fast.

Anissa turned to see what had caused such an obvious reaction in the typically cool-as-a-cucumber reporter.

Paisley Wilson was looking straight at Gabe.

Paisley Ashcroft Wilson.

The resemblance between her and her younger sister was slight, but when they were sitting side by side it was unmistakable.

Gabe refused to be the first one to break eye contact.

He'd done nothing wrong. But he'd paid for her mistakes.

Paisley Wilson had nearly gotten him killed.

Her desire for the big story had resulted in the death of a young man who'd been trying to get out of the gang life. She'd blown Gabe's cover so thoroughly he would never be able to go undercover again — at least not in Carrington.

And Paisley knew it. It was there. In the way her breathing hitched. The way her face had gone so white that he'd had a split second of concern that she might pass out. But now her face burned with the heat of spewing lava.

A few rapid blinks and she dropped her gaze to the maroon carpet squares.

He continued to stare at the top of her head, almost daring her to look up again, until Anissa's face filled his vision. Her cheeks were still damp from the tears she'd shed with Mr. Littlefield. Her hazel eyes brimmed with understanding.

Anissa's head bobbed. One quick nod was all he needed and he knew if it came to it, she would take the case for him.

Not that he intended to hand it over.

But he wouldn't put anything past that obnoxious reporter. It wouldn't surprise him if she started bad-mouthing him to the Littlefield family before their son was officially dead. Poisoning their thinking. Questioning whether he could find their son's killer.

And when she finished with the family, she'd do a story about it on the local news. Complete with a grainy photograph of Gabe — probably from his undercover days so he would look as disreputable as possible.

Paisley Wilson was no friend to the law enforcement community in Carrington.

And they were no friends of hers.

The door opened again. This had to be Mrs. Littlefield with her puffy face and a tissue clenched in each hand. She walked straight to Anissa and pulled her close. "Thank you." She had no tears. Probably because she had none left.

She glanced at Gabe, then at Adam and Ryan. "Thank you all." With a dry sob, she turned and all but ran to the door.

Ryan blew out an audible breath — probably in an effort not to hit something. Adam pinched his lips together, nostrils flaring, anger simmering. Anissa turned around and this time there was something different in her eyes.

Panic.

She bolted past him and out the door they'd entered, leaving Ryan and Adam looking as confused as he felt. She'd been acting weird since they'd pulled Brooke and Jeremy from the lake. Not that any of them were okay with what had happened, but this was different.

Almost like it was personal.

Fragments of past conversations clicked into place in his mind. Comments about stupid mistakes. Words that hadn't meant much at the time took on new meaning.

Anissa had secrets. He knew something in her past haunted her. He had no idea what it was, but he had a feeling he was about to find out.

"I'll check on her." He didn't give Adam or Ryan a chance to respond. He went through the same door Anissa had taken. Once in the hall, he scanned left and right, but she was nowhere to be seen. Where had she gone? The signs hanging from the ceiling pointed to different areas of the hospital.

The elevators were to the left. The chapel to the right.

He went right.

The tiles and paint shifted from shiny and new to faded and worn as he left the newer section of Carrington's hospital and entered the part that had been around for close to fifty years. He didn't rush. He wasn't trying to catch Anissa. He was . . . what? Was worried about her? Why? She could take care of herself.

But . . . he didn't want her to have to handle this, whatever this was, alone.

It took five minutes of left and right turns before he caught a glimpse of stained glass set into an ornate wooden door.

He eased the door open and stuck his head through.

Anissa knelt before a cross, bent over so that her head almost touched the floor. Her shoulders shook. Her hair had fallen around her face, but Gabe had no doubt that tears were splashing on the wooden planks beneath her.

He pulled back into the hallway.

Should he go inside? Would she want to know that he'd seen her in this moment?

Anissa wasn't private about her faith. She'd grown up in a missionary family and her faith had always been a public part of her persona. But there was a big difference between telling everybody that Jesus changes everything and having someone seeing you sobbing in prayer.

He waited outside the chapel. *Lord, do I go in? Do I stay out here and wait for her? Do I walk away and pretend I never saw anything?*

He was on shaky ground with Anissa as it was. They'd met seven years ago on a dive. At the time, he was working undercover so often that he almost never made a training dive and responded to calls even less. But he'd loved the once or twice a year that he'd managed to sneak in a dive, and their former dive captain had been okay with that.

The day he met Anissa, he'd been thrilled to get in on the last exercise of the day. Anissa had been his dive buddy and he'd been impressed with her skills.

She hadn't been impressed with him.

She hadn't cared how good a diver he thought he was. As far as she had been concerned, if he couldn't show up for training, he shouldn't be on the team. They'd argued about it off and on over the next couple of years, but he hadn't realized how serious she'd been until their dive team captain retired and she became captain.

Her first order of business had been to kick Gabe off the team. He'd said some pretty awful things about her, both behind her back and to her face. It didn't matter to him that her reasons had been valid, if a bit rigid. What mattered was that she'd taken the one good thing from his normal work life that he'd clung to, even as his undercover life pulled him deeper and deeper into a darker world.

They hadn't spoken to each other again — well, except for that one night when she was undercover with him — until his cover was blown by none other than Paisley Wilson. The captain moved Gabe to the homicide unit and suggested Anissa allow Gabe back on the dive team.

She hadn't taken his suggestion well.

Gabe owed Ryan for smoothing things over with Anissa, but those first few weeks and months had been . . . challenging.

By unspoken but mutual consent, they'd

never spoken of that night. That kiss. It was as if it had never happened.

And the version of Anissa who that night had laughed and flirted and smiled at him like he was the only man in the world? She was long gone. Real-life Anissa was impervious to his charms. His good-natured teasing, which had worked to disarm gangbangers, bounced off her as if she were surrounded by an impenetrable force field.

But then he and Ryan found that body in the lake.

And Leigh almost died.

And for the first time, Gabe felt like he and Anissa were on the same team. She didn't glare in his direction anymore. Sometimes she even cracked a smile at his jokes.

Then last fall when his buddy Brady St. John called in a favor, Anissa had asked him two questions. "He's a friend of yours? You trust him?"

When he said yes to both, he'd expected her to say something smart like "Then why should I trust him?" but instead she'd said, "What do you need?"

They'd saved a life that night, and when it was over, something in their relationship shifted. Anissa had trusted him and that one act had reframed years of antagonism and frustration.

Then a few weeks later she'd had to take a life in order to save Sabrina's.

Anissa had never killed anyone.

But Gabe had.

Suddenly he was the only person in their small circle who had been where she was. Waking up in the middle of the night, mind racing. Knowing there was no other option but ripped apart by the act. The guilt. The doubt.

Now, seven months later, he considered himself to be a close enough friend to follow her all the way to the chapel door.

But was he close enough to go inside?

3

Anissa had no more tears. No more words.

She rested her forehead in her hands and allowed her heavenly Father to hold her heart.

The door opened behind her, a whisper in the sacred silence of the small space. Hesitant footsteps approached.

She wasn't ashamed to be found kneeling before the cross. Broken.

But she braced herself for the questions. Whoever had been brave enough to join her in this moment would be brave enough to ask her what was wrong.

Instead of offering words, the person knelt beside her.

Gabe.

She knew it was him without looking. He had a masculine scent. Clean. Outdoorsy. She'd never been able to figure out if it was his soap or his shampoo or his laundry detergent. Or maybe it was the combination of all three that gave him his own unique signature smell.

He was close enough that his shoulder brushed against hers, but he didn't speak. When she glanced in his direction, his eyes were closed, head bowed.

Praying for her?

Something about that stirred emotions she didn't want to explore. Not now. Not ever.

She sat back on her feet. "I'm okay, Gabe," she said in a raspy whisper. She cleared her throat. "Really."

He opened his eyes and inclined his head toward her. "I'm not buying it, Bell."

Why did it have to be Gabe who managed to see right through her? Although to be fair, it wouldn't take a PhD in psychology to come to the conclusion that her overreaction was indicative of a deeper dilemma.

She glanced at the cross. A symbol of what Jesus had done. A visual reminder that because of his sacrifice and her acceptance of it to cover her sins, she was uncondemnable.

Even though she condemned herself for what she'd done, God didn't.

But would Gabe?

"You don't have to tell me, Anissa. But I'll listen if you want to talk."

His phone buzzed. He pulled it out of his

pocket and groaned.

"Later?" Anissa couldn't pretend she was sorry she didn't have to dredge up the gory details right now, but she knew he would find out sooner or later. Knowing him, he'd go digging for it. And the press had been brutal. If he thought he had reason to hate the press . . .

Gabe stood up and extended both his hands toward her. She took them and he pulled her to her feet. Her legs were stiff and she stumbled into him. His arms wrapped around her as he steadied her, and for a brief second she rested against his chest before they took simultaneous steps away from each other.

He shook his phone back and forth. "Ryan says they need us back in the family room." He grabbed a tissue from a box on the small pew behind them and handed it to her. "Ready?"

He waited for her to go first, then reached around her to open the door. The antiseptic air and ever-present beeps and tones of the hospital assaulted her senses as they reentered the hallway. She hoped whatever awaited them in the family room wouldn't take long, because she needed to get out of this place.

"I know you recognized Paisley Wilson."

Gabe said her name like he was tasting poison.

"I did. You knew Brooke was her little sister as soon as she said her name last night, didn't you?"

"I did."

Anissa couldn't believe she'd ever thought Gabe Chavez was a self-absorbed spoiled brat determined to get his way no matter what. Not that it was Brooke's fault her sister was anathema to the sheriff's office, and to Gabe personally, but he hadn't just been kind to Brooke, he'd been compassionate. He'd treated her the way he would want his own sister to be treated, even knowing Paisley would have a field day with him when it was all over. He'd fought for Jeremy's life even though he had to have known it was a losing battle and had to have been thinking Paisley Wilson would find some way to blame him for the boy's death.

"You're a good man, Gabe."

Gabe stopped walking. Anissa turned to face him. He was staring at her like she'd said the sky was marigold.

"You are. And if that twit of a reporter thinks she can screw up your life again, she's got another thing coming. We won't stand for it. You won't be alone this time, Gabe. I've got your back. Ryan and Adam do too.

It won't be like before when no one could defend you without blowing their own cover."

He continued to stare at her for a few seconds before he whispered, "Thank you."

"You're welcome. Now, let's go see what's going on."

A hint of a smile crossed his face as they continued to the family room. He nudged her elbow, and this time he was grinning at her. "I'd kind of like to see you take on Paisley Wilson. I bet we could sell tickets."

"Stop it." She shoved him away but couldn't stop the laughter that bubbled up at the mental image Gabe's words had generated.

The lightness of the moment evaporated as they neared the family room. "Ready?" she asked.

"After you." Gabe opened the door.

Ryan and Adam leaned against the wall nearest the door. Paisley sat alone. Brooke was no longer in the room.

"What's going on?" Gabe asked Ryan.

Ryan nodded in Paisley's direction. "Ms. Wilson wanted to speak to you without Brooke present."

"Where is Brooke?"

Anissa had directed the question to Ryan, but it was Paisley who answered. "She's with Jeremy's family. They're very close. They've been best friends since kindergarten."

Paisley stood. "Investigator Chavez —"

Adam stepped forward. "Gabe, do you want us in here?"

"It's fine with me," he said. "I haven't done anything wrong."

Good for him. Set her straight from the beginning.

"I'd prefer that you stay as well. All of you. I —" Paisley paced around the small room. "Look, I know you hate me. I know I blew your cover, Investigator Chavez. And I know —" She pulled in a shaky breath. "I know you believe my aggressive reporting got that boy killed."

"It did." Gabe didn't say the words in a harsh manner. But his calm, statement-of-fact approach was almost harder to hear.

It pierced Anissa's heart. Whatever friendship she had with Gabe wouldn't survive the truth about what she'd done.

Paisley dropped her head. "I'm not going to try to convince you otherwise." When she looked up, her eyes shone with tears. "I just want to know who's been assigned to the case."

"I was the investigator on call. Unless there are mitigating circumstances that I'm unaware of, it will be mine. Anissa will run point on any underwater investigating we need to do." Gabe nodded toward Ryan. "We all work together when necessary. I'm sure Ryan will be involved in some way. Depending on what we discover, Adam could be pulled in as well. We aren't lone wolves in this sheriff's office. The goal is to find out who killed Jeremy and see that he or she is prosecuted."

Paisley smiled. It wasn't a friendly smile, but it wasn't hostile either. "I told the Littlefields you were the man for the job." She nodded toward Ryan and then Anissa. "No offense to either of you. But Investigator Chavez hates me enough to dig deep and hard into both my family and the Littlefields'. He won't hold back and I'm okay with that."

Anissa wasn't sure if she believed Paisley. Time would tell.

Brooke burst into the room and ran to Paisley as her sobs reached the point of hysteria. "He would still be alive if I hadn't dared him." She sagged in Paisley's arms. "It's all my fault!"

Anissa couldn't stop herself. She put an arm around Brooke, and by necessity around Paisley. "It isn't your fault, Brooke.

You didn't do this. You didn't pull the trigger."

Anissa didn't care if Paisley Wilson aired some sort of exposé about Anissa's past failures. This child needed comfort and Anissa wasn't going to hold her at arm's length because of her sister.

Another arm wrapped around her and Brooke. "She's right, Brooke." Gabe crooned the words like a lullaby. "I know it doesn't feel like it right now, but you didn't do this. You are not responsible for his death. Don't take that burden on yourself, *querida*."

"We see more death than most people, Brooke." Ryan joined their circle. "You can trust us on this. We know where the blame lies and it's not with you."

"My little brother died in a car accident when I was seventeen." Adam's whispered words settled over them. "I had insisted we switch seats because there was more legroom on the other side and he didn't need it. If I'd been sitting where he was, I would have died that night. Or maybe I would have been able to recover from the trauma of the accident. Either way, he would have survived. It took me a long time to understand that it wasn't my fault, but, Brooke, it wasn't my fault then. And this isn't your fault now."

Brooke's sobs slowly gave way to shudders and moans.

"Thank you," Paisley whispered. It sounded like she meant it.

One by one, they stepped back. "We'll be in touch," Gabe said. "Let us know if you need anything."

It was a standard thing to say to anyone involved in a homicide. But saying it to Paisley Wilson had to have been one of the hardest things he'd ever done.

Ryan held the door for Anissa, then Adam, and finally Gabe. They left the room and made their way down the long hallway toward the exit.

No one spoke until they were outside, huddled out of the slashing rain and under the covered walkway in front of the building.

"How long are these storms supposed to last?" Ryan glared at the sky before facing Anissa.

She could tell what he was thinking. "I know." A long rumble filled the air and three lightning bolts stabbed at the earth. "The odds of finding any evidence on the shore are decreasing exponentially with every drop."

55

■ ■ ■ ■

Monday mornings were bad enough when they didn't start with an autopsy. And it wasn't like the autopsy had given Gabe any information he didn't already know. Dr. Oliver had sent the routine samples off for tox screens, but Brooke Ashcroft had insisted that she and Jeremy hadn't been drinking or doing drugs of any kind, and Gabe was inclined to believe her.

Jeremy Littlefield had been a healthy seventeen-year-old boy.

Cause of death?

The bullet that pierced his heart.

And thirty-six hours after Jeremy drew his final breath, Gabe had no clue who had killed the boy.

Concerned neighbors in the cove where Leigh and Ryan lived had willingly shared surveillance footage and practically begged them to have Forensics examine their shorelines and docks for intruders. But the likely location for the shooter was a decrepit dock on a mostly undeveloped plot of land across the cove.

One of the residents had been out in a shorefront gazebo during the incident. He'd reported a shooting on Saturday night before they had Jeremy and Brooke off the water. He'd also said he'd gotten a glimpse of someone on the old dock and told the dispatchers he thought the shooter had tossed the gun into the lake.

Gabe had no trouble getting search warrants for the property, but the rain that had chased them off the lake Saturday night had made the shoreline a muddy mess by the time Forensics got there Sunday morning. Forensics did the best they could — he owed those guys some donuts or something — but so far their search had come up with exactly nothing.

Not a single footprint. Not even a piece of trash. The property had an old cabin on it, several hundred yards back from the shore, and it appeared to be lived in but barely. A few eggs and lunch stuff in the fridge. Cold coffee in the pot.

Forensics had taken prints and DNA samples. The lab would run everything as fast as it could. They might get a hit off the fingerprints today. The DNA would be weeks, if not months.

Gabe's phone buzzed as he walked into the sheriff's office.

Anissa.

Maybe she'd found something. The dive team had met at nine this morning to search the lake for evidence.

"Got some good news for me, Bell?"

"Not exactly." Anissa sounded like she was forcing herself to say the words.

"What's wrong?"

"Um . . . how are you feeling today?"

That was weird. "If you must know, I feel horrible. I just came from the autopsy. But otherwise I'm fine."

"I'm sorry, Gabe."

She took a deep breath. Then another. What was her deal? "Spit it out, Bell."

"I need your help."

Anissa was asking for help? From him? "Anything."

"You may change your mind when you hear what I need."

"Not likely, Nis. What's going on?"

"I don't know." Anissa's frustration punctuated every word. "Everyone's sick."

"Who's sick?"

"Ryan, Adam, Sabrina, ten other people from the office."

More weirdness. Ryan, Adam, and Sabrina had been fine Saturday. "Define sick."

"Well, to put it delicately, none of them can get out of the bathroom."

Gabe didn't like the sound of that. "Yuck."

"Yeah," Anissa said. "It must be some nasty stomach bug, but there's no way they can dive. And I can't search the lake unless . . . I mean, this isn't a training exercise. We can't afford any mistakes."

He understood what she didn't say. Their team was already undermanned, and while the newer dive team members were young and eager, they were also inexperienced. And if she sent any of them to search, she would always wonder if they'd missed something. "When do you want to go?"

"I know you don't have time for this."

He didn't. He didn't usually have time to sleep during the first forty-eight hours after a homicide. But he needed this search done, and more importantly, he needed to have confidence that it had been done correctly.

Then there was the added issue he tried not to acknowledge but couldn't completely ignore. He didn't want to tell Anissa no. "What time?"

"You tell me. I'll work around your schedule." Anissa must be desperate.

Gabe glanced at his watch. "It's almost noon. I need an hour at my desk. Can we say two this afternoon?"

"Sure. That would be great. Lane and Stu are the only ones available, but we'll have everything ready."

The Carrington Dive Team kept their boat

docked at the Porter Marina. At two o'clock, Gabe parked his car in the marina lot. To save time, he'd changed into swim trunks and a T-shirt at the sheriff's office. He grabbed his diving gear from the back of his car and made his way to the boat. As he walked down the dock, he could hear Anissa barking orders.

He loved how she took charge and got things moving, but he couldn't deny that he was glad he wasn't the one on the receiving end of her intensity this afternoon. She spotted him and . . . smiled.

Anissa's smiles were rare.

And glorious.

This one held a tinge of the grief they were all operating under, but unless his radar was way off, she was genuinely happy to see him.

"Thank you," she said as he stepped on board. The smile was gone, but the look she gave him — gratitude and something else. Something he couldn't put his finger on. Camaraderie? Maybe.

She was already in her wet suit. Well, halfway in it. It was on up to her waist, but the top half was hanging down, the sleeves falling below her knees. She wouldn't put her arms in and zip it until they were ready to dive. The July afternoon made it way too hot for that.

He settled his gear in front of a nitrox tank. The mixture of oxygen and nitrogen would allow them to stay under longer than the standard air tanks. And that was always a good thing. Although he hoped they would find something of value to the case without a lengthy search.

He'd just gotten on his own wet suit when Anissa fired up the engine and the boat rumbled beneath him. "You good to go?" Anissa called out over the motor.

He gave her the okay sign. She returned it and eased the boat away from the dock. He wasn't surprised she was the one driving. Anissa was picky about who drove the dive team boat. But once she got it out in open water, she waved Lane over and turned the wheel over to him. Then she joined Gabe.

Her buoyancy compensator device, or BCD, was already strapped to her own nitrox tank. She perched on the edge of the bench nearby. "We'll run the side sonar first. See if we get any hits."

"Sounds good." Gabe finished setting up his gear and sat beside Anissa.

They didn't speak as they approached the scene, but he could feel the tension rolling off Anissa. As soon as they reached the scene, she went into full instructor mode.

She explained what they were doing to Stu, gave Lane plenty of opportunities to show off his skills with the sonar — the kid was quite good at it — and began the process of checking the lake floor for anything that warranted further inspection.

They kept their focus on the area near the dock. If the shooter had tossed the gun as the neighbor thought, it couldn't have gone that far. Unfortunately, there were more than a few suspicious-looking objects in the water. After forty-five minutes of searching, they had floated buoys for at least three possible rifles.

They picked their most likely target and Gabe and Anissa prepared to descend. Anissa had shown Stu how to set up a jackstay search and they put the buoys in place. When everything was ready, Gabe stepped off the boat first and swam out of the way. Anissa followed and they began their descent, slow and steady.

The lake wasn't as deep in this area as it was in others. Just twenty-five feet in most places. But the visibility was awful. The heavy rains — and the runoff into the lake — had left the water murky. Gabe could barely make out Anissa and she was only two feet away from him.

Not the best conditions for a search.

When they neared the bottom, they paused a foot from the lake floor. Anissa had the best buoyancy control of anyone he'd ever had the opportunity to dive with. She could hold herself mere inches from the bottom and never touch it.

She made it look easy. It wasn't.

They both took positions on opposite sides of the guide rope.

"You ready?" Anissa asked.

"Always," Gabe said as they laced their pinky fingers together and began the first leg of their search.

Together, they settled into a search pattern a foot off the bottom. If he hadn't been touching Anissa, he would have had no idea where she was. But he knew what she was doing. The same thing he was. A slow, methodical sweep with her right hand while he did the same with his left. They followed the guide rope they'd laid out until they reached the end, then they made the necessary adjustments and repeated the process. Back and forth across the grid they had created. After ten minutes, Gabe's left hand brushed against an object that didn't seem to match the lake environment.

"I've got something," he said.

"Gun?" Anissa held their place on the rope while Gabe investigated further with his hands. When he finally got the object in his hand, he couldn't stop a frustrated groan from escaping.

It was a gun all right.

A toy gun.

"Not quite what we're looking for," Anissa said. "Let's go ahead and take it up. Just to get it out of here, if for no other reason."

They searched the second possible site, only to find a large piece of rebar.

"Third time's the charm." Gabe tried to keep his tone cheerful as they descended a third time. The truth was, he was tired, hungry, and had been down long enough that if they didn't find the weapon soon, Anissa would make him stay out of the water for a while. She had a sixth sense about that kind of stuff. Even without checking his dive computer, she would know that he was due to spend some time in the boat.

"This location makes sense," Gabe said.

"It does," Anissa agreed. "I've been trying to picture it. And the more I think about it, the more I like this location best."

They continued to search and Gabe fought back his frustration every time they made a pass and found nothing. Anissa didn't speak. Not that that was unusual. She didn't tend to talk much on dives, even though their fancy equipment made it possible for them to communicate with each other and with their boat.

"I've got something."

He could hear the edge of excitement in her words.

"Definitely a weapon. I can't see a thing, but this is a gun. Let's bring it up."

It took another thirty minutes before they were able to bring the weapon out of the water. Thirty minutes of Anissa insisting that every single possible bit of protocol be followed to the letter.

And as much as it aggravated him, he'd never been more proud to be a part of the dive team than he was right then.

There were no news cameras. No flashing lights. No one knew what they'd done. How hard they had worked to do it.

And that was okay.

He loved being part of a team that was determined to do the very best possible job. That preserved evidence in every imaginable way, including taking water samples and soil samples from the area where the weapon was located.

A team that got results.

Once the weapon was safely on board, Anissa swam with Gabe to the stairs at the back of the boat.

"Ladies first," he said with a gallant smile.

She didn't argue. They'd been underwater so long, she was chilled through.

It had been worth it though. They had the murder weapon. Not that she had proof.

But it had to be.

When she'd wrapped her hand around the barrel, part of her wanted to throw the infernal object as far away as possible, but the other part of her wanted to cheer.

Instead, she kept herself calm as she watched Lane and Stu follow all the appropriate procedures to retrieve the weapon and preserve it in the lake water.

They would get the weapon to Forensics tonight, but the caliber was right. The location was right. And the sonar didn't show anything else down there.

Of course, there was no guarantee the killer had thrown the weapon into the lake to begin with, but —

She stopped that train of thought. She'd done her job. Her team had performed beautifully.

She wrapped her hand around the ladder at the back of the boat and fought a shiver as she stepped onto the small platform to remove her fins. Once free of them, she pulled herself up the stairs, careful to give her body a chance to adjust to the awkward center of gravity caused from the weight of the BCD and nitrox tank.

She turned back to help Gabe. She took his fins as he handed them to her, one at a time. She waited for him to get out of the water before moving toward the front of the boat to remove her BCD. She and Gabe made a good team. She'd noticed it before. He was a natural at this. And very aware of what was going on around him and what others were doing.

It took only a few minutes for them to get their equipment off and everything strapped down tight.

Gabe stuck out his fist. She bumped it with hers.

"Thank you," she said. It felt like all she'd done lately was thank him. But he just kept showing up and doing things she couldn't help but be grateful for.

"Anytime." He grinned. A tired grin, but a real one.

"Lane," she called. "Get us home."

"Yes, ma'am." Lane gave her a small salute as he fired up the engine.

She leaned closer to Gabe and yelled into his ear so he could hear her as the boat bounced across the water. "As soon as we get back to the dock, you can head out. We'll get your gear and everything for you."

He smiled. "You don't have to do that."

"But we want to."

He looked at Lane and Stu and then back to her. "I'm not sure where you're getting this 'we' stuff from." He laughed. "I think they'd be fine with me taking care of it myself."

"Oh, good grief," Anissa said. "Let me help you."

"Fine," he yelled.

She glared at him for a moment. Oh, he made her so mad sometimes.

But then he smiled.

And that smile . . .

That smile was the thing dreams were made of.

It had taken the rest of the afternoon and into the evening to stow all their gear, get the weapon to Forensics, return to the office, and file all the necessary reports. By nine o'clock, Anissa was wiped out. The homicide office was empty when she called it a night. Gabe was sitting at Adam's desk when she walked by.

He was on the phone. "Yeah. Okay. I did that . . ."

He covered the mouthpiece with his hand. "Adam's trying to talk me through using this program he's got to view the financials." He glared at the computer screen. "I'm not smart enough for this."

He removed his hand from the phone. "Dude. When are you going to be able to come back to work?"

Anissa waved and kept going.

Gabe was plenty smart. Smarter than he let on. He'd figure it out.

But she didn't blame him for wanting Adam to be back at work. Soon. In the meantime, she hoped none of them got whatever bug the others had. It sounded awful.

Her car was parked under a tree in the back corner of the lot. Not the best place to park, but the best she could get when she arrived back at the sheriff's office during shift change.

The parking lot was well lit and she was armed, but something didn't feel right.

Anissa had learned to trust that sense.

She held her pace steady and tried to keep her face impassive as she tuned in to her surroundings. As she neared her car, she slowed. Something was wrong. It looked . . . off-kilter.

She didn't remember that space being sloped.

She slowed her pace and walked on the

other side of the lot so she could get a view of her car without being too close. She pulled her good flashlight out of her bag and pointed the beam toward the car.

What on earth?

It hadn't been her imagination. She had not one but two flat tires. Both passenger-side wheels were sitting on the rims. She was more than capable of changing her own tire, and she had a spare. But she didn't have two of them.

She wanted to get a close look at what had caused the damage. But then she thought better of it. It was darker in this corner and she'd be in a very vulnerable position if she bent over the tires with a flashlight. Not that she thought anyone had done anything on purpose. She'd probably run over some glass or something.

Although it was going to drive her crazy until she found out what had happened.

"Yo, Bell!" Gabe's voice carried across the parking lot.

Great. This was going to be embarrassing. Why did it have to be Gabe always coming to her rescue?

He jogged toward her. "I'm glad I caught you. You left your sunglasses on your desk. I know how much you hate to drive without them. Not that you need them tonight, but for in the morning."

Well, that was . . . sweet. Her annoyance fled. "Thank you. But I don't think I'll be driving anywhere."

"Why not?"

She waved her flashlight over the tires.

Gabe let out a shrill whistle. "Who gets two flats at a time? That stinks. Want me to give you a ride home? We can call the mechanics and get them to fix this first thing tomorrow."

"I didn't think you were heading home yet."

"I'll take this as a sign that it's time to call it a night. Come back in with me. I'll pack my stuff and we'll get out of here."

She looked back at her car. Gabe was right and she was too tired to deal with it now. "Okay. Thanks."

"Need anything out of it?"

"Not for tonight."

Seriously?

A few more steps and she would have been his.

He watched her walk back to the sheriff's office with that other cop. He'd almost risked grabbing her. A quick knock to the head and he could have pulled her back into the shadows before finishing her off the way he'd always dreamed of.

One bullet.

Right between the eyes.

Discarded in the weeds like trash.

His heart rate quickened at the thought. He was so close he could taste it.

But once again, she'd shimmied from his grasp.

Anissa Bell had always been hard to get to.

It was like she had some sort of sixth sense. Whenever he was waiting for her, she always turned and went the other way.

Of course, the last time he'd had an opportunity as good as this one was thirteen years ago.

And she hadn't been a cop then.

What had made him think this time would be any different?

He slunk away into the night.

He'd been waiting four decades to get his revenge.

He could be patient a little while longer.

4

Tuesday afternoon, Gabe parked his car in the overgrown driveway of Mr. Glen Masters.

At least that's who owned the place according to the property records.

Gabe had given up on trying to figure out the maze of ownership last night after he'd gone after Anissa to give her the sunglasses. He hadn't told her yet that he'd asked Forensics to take a look at the tires after the mechanics finished with them. She would flip her lid and tell him she didn't need his help.

She probably didn't, but something about two flat tires in the darkened corner of a parking lot bothered him. A lot.

He'd driven her home and decided that sleep might be the best thing he could do for this case. He hadn't been wrong about that. And when he got to the office this morning, he'd discovered that while Adam was miserable at home, he was still capable of working. He'd gotten through a jumble of convoluted property listings and figured it out sometime during the night.

Well, he'd figured it out to the point that they had a name. Then he'd handed it off to Sabrina this morning. Adam had claimed she'd volunteered. She probably had. Sabrina wasn't the type to flaunt her brain power, but they all knew she was the smartest one of the bunch and it would take her less time than it would the rest of them to make sense of the way this property had changed hands over the years.

Gabe looked around, trying to see what made it special enough for someone to try to hide their ownership of it.

Even after the rain, the weeds were matted down in a few areas, but whether that was evidence that the owner had been home in the past few weeks or that some teenagers had been parking out here recently, he couldn't say.

The area by the shore was still heavily wooded.

The only dwelling on the property was a cabin that rested in a rectangular space that had been cleared at one time. Now it was overgrown with weeds and grasses several feet high, except for a small path from the driveway to the front porch that had been mowed in the past few weeks.

The cabin was in desperate need of some TLC.

Or a bulldozer.

Gabe grabbed the bag of subs he'd picked up, got out, and walked toward the building. The windows were opaque thanks to a thick layer of several years' worth of pollen that even summer storms couldn't wash away. The forensics team had cordoned off the home and he could hear voices carrying from the lake.

Anissa's reverberated above the rest. "Right there. Yes. Thank you very much."

Gabe bit back a chuckle. The forensics team had a love/hate relationship with Anissa. She was unfailingly polite. She was also unbelievably thorough. Forensics had been out here on Sunday afternoon but had returned today — now that the sun had worked hard to dry the land — to check the shoreline again, no doubt at Anissa's request.

He left the house and followed the voices. A rough path wound from the house through the woods, and when he broke through the trees he was thirty feet from the lake. He spotted Anissa fifty feet away studying the ground. She had her hair under a hat. Booties on her shoes. Gloves on her hands. An expression of intense determination.

She caught him staring and straightened. He held up the bag with the subs. She tapped her fist on the top of her head — the diving signal for "okay" — then tapped her watch and held up one gloved finger.

One minute. He could wait.

He pretended to study the crime scene, but mostly he studied her. She was strung so tight he expected her to explode at any moment. Something about this case had messed her up. Worse than the serial killer they'd caught last year. Even worse than the human trafficking ring they'd busted before Christmas.

This recent behavior was on par with the way she was after the shooting.

And he hadn't expected anything to ever rattle her like that had.

She peeled off the gloves and hat as she walked toward him, then pointed to a folding table set up under nearby trees. "Want to eat there?"

"Are you crazy?" Who knew what kinds of stuff Forensics had used that table for. And that clunker Anissa was driving while her tires were being replaced probably wasn't much cleaner. "Come back to the truck.

We'll crank it and have some AC." He didn't wait for her to agree. Her flushed cheeks and sweat-soaked shirt told him she needed to cool off.

They didn't speak as they walked to the truck. He opened the door for her and then jogged to the driver's side, climbed in, and cranked it. He turned the air-conditioning on full blast as she unwrapped the sandwiches.

"We're not helping the environment, idling like this," she said.

"It won't be helping the environment if you pass out from heat exhaustion and wind up in the hospital either. Have you seen the mess EMTs leave behind?"

"Very funny." She held her sandwich but made no move to start eating.

"Want to bless it?" he asked. Anissa always blessed the food.

She shook her head. "You do it."

Gabe bowed his head and kept most of his prayer to himself. *Lord, I don't know what's going on with her, but help me know how to help her, because I just got her to be nice to me and I don't want to blow it.* Then he spoke. "*Dios, por favor,* bless this food. Bless our work. Comfort the families and help us bring justice for Jeremy."

"Amen." She took three bites and a long

77

swig of the lemonade he'd ordered for her before she leaned back against the seat. "Thank you for lunch."

"Welcome."

She stared out the window and didn't look back in his direction. "You okay?"

"Eh. As good as can be expected under the circumstances." Gabe popped a Dorito into his mouth.

"Yeah." Anissa didn't sound convinced. She took another bite.

"You?"

"Same."

"Liar." His comment pulled her attention away from the window.

Her face was pointed in his direction, but her eyes were unfocused. "Not really. I would say I'm doing as well as could be expected under the circumstances. No better. No worse. It's just that my circumstances aren't exactly the same as yours."

A movement in the rearview mirror prevented Gabe from responding. "We have company."

Anissa didn't look. She didn't flinch. She set her sandwich down and reached for her weapon as if nothing was wrong.

A dark sedan pulled past them and rolled to a stop. The driver got out and kept his hands visible. He had the look of a man who knew something was up but didn't know what it was and hadn't yet decided how he was going to play it.

"Cover me," Gabe said as he opened the door of the truck. He kept the front end of the truck between him and the visitor — or more likely the owner — and paused as the man turned in his direction. "Investigator Chavez, Carrington County Sheriff's Office."

The man glared at him. "Name's Ronald Talbot and I live here. You got some sort of warrant?"

"I do." As Gabe stepped out from behind the semiprotection of the truck, the faint click of the passenger-side door opening reached his ears. Anissa was getting out to keep herself in a better position to cover him. If he asked her to get back in the truck, she wouldn't listen. Maybe she'd stay behind the door and give herself a little bit of protection in case this guy went loco.

Gabe kept one hand up and moved his other hand in a deliberate arc to his back pocket to retrieve the warrant. "Mr. Talbot, are you renting this place from Glen Masters?"

"I'm looking after it for him."

"Does he know that?"

"He does."

Ronald Talbot's hair was thinning. His skin, weathered. Teeth . . . he had a few left. This was a man who had lived a hard life. He probably had some substance abuse in his past, but at least for the moment his eyes were clear. He was wary but didn't seem rattled by Gabe's questions. It was entirely possible that the owner of the property knew this guy was staying here and wasn't charging him rent. So, why?

Gabe showed the warrant to Mr. Talbot. "This gives me permission to search the property and anything else I come across that might give us any indication of who was here Saturday night and early Sunday morning."

"Saturday night? Wasn't nobody here." Mr. Talbot spit tobacco juice in a long arc. "I went to Wilmington for a couple of days. Just got back. What happened? Those kids cause some trouble again?"

"What kids?"

He shrugged. "I ain't caught 'em yet. But I know they out here at night partying and hooking up." He ran a tattooed hand through his thinning hair. "I don't sleep good. Doc gave me some of them sleeping pills. They knock me out. But I seen footprints on the dock. Found stuff."

"What kind of stuff?"

Talbot barked a harsh laugh. "Pipes. Needles. Liquor bottles. Beer cans. Other . . . stuff."

"What did you do with it?"

Talbot threw an arm out toward three blackened fifty-five-gallon barrels near the edge of the once-cleared portion of the property. "Burned it."

Great.

"Mr. Talbot, where were you Saturday night around midnight?"

"Told you. Wilmington."

"Where in Wilmington?"

"In my car."

Gabe could believe that, but he had to ask. "Not in a hotel?"

"Do I look like I got cash for a hotel?" Talbot shot another stream of tobacco juice.

"Then why'd you drive all the way to Wilmington? That's a lot of gas money."

"Been in the middle of the country a long time. Hadn't seen the ocean in a lot of years. Looks the same as I remembered, so I came back."

Gabe would have to check out the story. It was a bit too convenient for his tastes. "Do you have somewhere else you can stay for a few days until we're done processing everything?"

"I guess my car will do for another night

or two. You gonna tell me what happened?"

"A boy was killed."

Talbot grunted. "That's too bad."

Wow. Give this guy a medal for sensitivity. Gabe whistled to get the attention of one of the officers at the perimeter of the crime scene and waved him over. "Yates, get this guy's statement and check his hands for gunpowder residue."

Gabe walked back to the truck. "What do you think?"

Anissa's lip curled in distaste. "He's lying."

"What makes you say that?"

"I just know."

"Your sixth sense doesn't make him a murderer."

"Doesn't make him likely to drive to Wilmington to see the ocean either. It's too convenient."

Anissa's sunglasses kept him from seeing her eyes, but he could imagine the glare she was giving him as she spoke. "I agree."

She lowered her sunglasses, and the glare he'd suspected hit him full force. "Then why did you ask?"

"Just wanted to see if you had a different take on it than I did."

Her lips twitched. She settled her sunglasses back on her nose and turned away, but not before he caught the flicker of a smile before she pinched her lips back into a tight line. "You know who you need to talk to?" She climbed back into the truck and closed the door.

He climbed in on the other side. "Who?"

"Mr. Cook."

"Why?" Mr. Cook had lived in Carrington, and on Lake Porter, since before there was a Lake Porter. After the area was flooded to form the lake, his family's property was one-fourth the size it had been previously. But the property that was left was still extensive and now worth no small fortune. Mr. Cook didn't plan to sell any of it. Ever. Much to the chagrin of developers in the area.

"He'll know what's going on over here."

He probably would. And Gabe should have thought of it. Would have thought of it eventually. But Mr. Cook was —

"I know you don't like him." Anissa took another bite of her sandwich. What was she? A mind reader?

"I like him fine."

"Liar."

Gabe took two more bites. Anissa didn't comment further. She pulled a few chips from the bag and went back to staring out the window.

Anissa wasn't one to nag. She didn't need to. Her "wait it out" strategy was far more effective.

After two more bites, he caved. "You're going to laugh. Or say I'm crazy."

Anissa cut her eyes at him.

"It isn't that I don't like him, but he makes me uncomfortable for some reason."

He expected her to roll her eyes. Or mock him.

"He has that effect on people."

He hadn't expected her to understand.

"Mr. Cook is very wise but also very forthright. He calls it like he sees it, and what's scary about it for most of us is that he sees things none of the rest of us see. I think it's because his walk with the Lord is so close that he has insights we miss. And it's disconcerting when he answers a question we didn't ask or asks a question we'd rather not answer."

"But you like him," Gabe said.

Anissa had always seemed comfortable with Mr. Cook, and the tender expression on her face now confirmed it. "I've known him forever."

"How is that possible? You moved to Carrington, what, ten years ago?"

"Yes, but Mr. and Mrs. Cook supported our family on the mission field. He still does. He and my dad are pretty close. He's like an eccentric but lovable uncle. I suspect he keeps tabs on me and reports back to my parents. He and Mrs. Cook sort of adopted me when I decided to stay in the States. They were thrilled that I came to Carrington. They're a big part of the reason I did. Mrs. Cook was an angel. She was even more intuitive than he is. She could see right through me. It was both annoying and wonderful."

Annoying and wonderful. That was a perfect description of his own relationship with Anissa.

"I'll go with you if you want." Anissa took another bite of her sub.

She was offering to spend more time with him than necessary?

"We've been so busy this summer, I haven't seen him in a while. You'd be doing me a favor."

He didn't believe that for a second. Not that she was lying. But he knew she was trying to give him a way to accept her offer without owning up to the fact that he didn't want to go alone. He would take it. "When would you want to go?"

"I'm almost done here. Forensics will be thrilled for me to leave so they can work without me looking over their shoulders."

She glanced at her watch. "I'd say no more than an hour."

"Okay. Thanks."

"Great. I'll give him a call."

This was going to be very interesting.

An hour later, Gabe parked his truck in the circular driveway of Mr. Cook's modest home. Anissa pulled in behind Gabe, letting her gaze rest on the man who sat in the wooden rocker on his porch. He acknowledged them with a slow nod and a smile. Her heart twisted. Goodness, she loved that old man.

Anissa waved to him, and when she did, her phone slid from her lap onto the floorboard. She bent to retrieve it, and when she sat up, Gabe was outside her door. He opened it and reached for her hand.

What was this?

Part of her recoiled from the chivalry. They were on the job. She didn't need help opening her own door.

She understood this part of her. The part that didn't want to be perceived as weak or needy.

But there was another part of her she didn't understand. At all.

That part reached for Gabe's hand — and liked the way it felt when his fingers closed over hers.

That part was acting like a tween with a crush.

But she wasn't a tween mooning over the cutest guy in the class. She was a thirty-three-year-old with a crushing secret, and this guy was not going to be the one who could handle it.

She muttered a thank-you to Gabe as he closed the door behind her. Did she imagine it, or did his hand linger longer than necessary before he stepped back to allow her to go first? And was that his hand that brushed her lower back as they walked toward the house?

She took the porch steps two at a time and bent down to hug Mr. Cook. Under his wrinkles, she could still see the younger version of the man who'd flown to Yap to help build a church building and fallen in love with the people there, just like she had.

He shook Gabe's hand. "Investigator Chavez. Always a pleasure to see you, young man."

"Thank you, sir. Please call me Gabe. You're looking well."

"Ah." Mr. Cook slapped his knee. "I'm one foot in the grave and we all know it. Be fine with me when it happens. I miss Mrs. Cook more today than I did the day she slipped past me on the race to glory. She always was the competitive sort." He pointed to the porch swing. "Sit. Sit."

"Mrs. Cook was an angel." Anissa couldn't help but defend the woman who'd mothered her for years while Anissa's own mom ministered to others half a world away. She sat on the porch swing and Gabe joined her. He pushed them forward and they found a rhythm, swaying slow and steady.

Mr. Cook leaned back in his rocker. "I never said she wasn't. I said she was competitive, as you well know. How many times did she beat you at pinochle and gloat about it? Hmm?"

Anissa laughed at the memory. "More than I can count."

Mr. Cook leaned toward Gabe as if inviting him to a confidential word. "That one" — he pointed at Anissa — "is disturbingly good at pinochle. I always say a woman who can handle both a gun and a bad hand when it's dealt to her is someone you should hang on to. Aren't many of them around."

Gabe gave the barest glance in her direction. "You are right, sir. Even fewer have equal combinations of beauty and brains."

Mr. Cook nodded in agreement. "True. That is a rare gem."

What. Was. Happening? Mr. Cook was the

most perceptive man she had ever known. And Gabe? All chummy and conspiratorial? She had come with him to be nice. To help him chat with Mr. Cook. Not to be . . . to be . . . she didn't even know what this was.

Mr. Cook gave her a warm smile. A wink. Oh no.

"As fascinating as this is" — she tried to keep her tone bored and flat — "we didn't come out here to discuss my skill with guns or games. We have a dead boy in the morgue. A man living — possibly squatting — on the property where we believe the shots were fired from. And absolutely no idea what happened to get us into this mess."

That sobered them both up — and quick.

Mr. Cook nodded. "You're right. I think we should pray on it."

"I assumed you already were," Anissa said.

"Oh, I have been, but I meant right now."

Even though she knew what was coming, Anissa didn't have time to close her eyes before Mr. Cook began. "Father, we're in a mess here."

Gabe set his foot on the porch floor and the swing came to a stop. He leaned forward, head bowed, elbows on his knees, face in his hands. Anissa mirrored his posture as Mr. Cook continued.

"It makes no sense to us, this boy dying at the hands of an evil person who desperately needs you. Right now these young people have the job of finding out what happened, but you haven't given them much to go on. We'd be much obliged if you could point them in the right direction. Help them see what they cannot see and know what they cannot know apart from the power of the Holy Spirit at work within them. Because we know those children weren't alone in the lake Saturday night. You were there. You saw. You know. So we're gonna rest in your goodness and trust that you'll bring the truth to light in your will and your way. Now, what is it you think I might be able to help you with?"

Gabe jerked his head up and looked around, eyes wide. Anissa smothered a chuckle. She both loved and hated the way Mr. Cook prayed. He talked to God like he was in the room and an active member of their conversation. He was, of course, but it was a bit startling when Mr. Cook stopped talking to God and started talking to the humans in the same breath.

Gabe recovered fast. "We're wondering if you might know anything about that property across the cove from Leigh Weston-Parker's place. We think the shooter who killed Jeremy Littlefield was firing from there."

Anissa tried to block the flashes of memory that accompanied Gabe's words. The cracking of thunder and rifle. The smell of ozone and blood.

Gabe shifted on the swing and settled his arm behind her. Not touching her but somehow closer. How did he know when she was agitated? And when had his nearness become comforting rather than aggravating?

"We think it's owned by someone named Glen Masters. But what's the story over there? There's not much information about this guy. Adam Campbell's the one who figured out who owns the place, but he's sick and hasn't been able to dig up anything else."

Anissa could hear the recrimination in Gabe's voice.

"It's early yet. And Adam Campbell's a good man. I bet he's got that girlfriend of his working on it," Mr. Cook said.

"Fiancée." Anissa and Gabe both said the word at the same time.

Mr. Cook's wrinkles curved upward. "That's right. Charles did mention that. He sure does love that girl." Charles Campbell was Adam's grandfather and a longtime friend of Mr. Cook's. "I'm sure she'll find what you need, but I may be able to save you a bit of trouble."

Anissa sat back and Gabe followed her lead, resuming a steady swing. He didn't move his arm, though, and every now and then his fingers would brush against her shoulder. She tried to block out the way her heart sped up with each instance of incidental contact.

She needed to pay attention. Mr. Cook was a wealth of information, but he tended to share it on his own terms and with the occasional detour. She'd learned over the years that sometimes his detours weren't as random as they appeared to be.

"I would appreciate it if you two would keep what I'm about to tell you confidential. I know Charles is talking to Adam this afternoon as well." Mr. Cook laughed. "I'm sure Sabrina will figure it all out by the end of the day without me or Charles saying anything, but this way you won't have to come pay me a visit when she does."

"Charles Campbell?" Gabe raised one eyebrow.

"The same. You see, Glen Masters isn't a real person. Glen Masters is someone Charles and I made up. If you, or I guess I should say if Sabrina looks hard enough, she'll discover that Glen Masters owns quite a few of the undeveloped and underdeveloped lots on the lake."

"If you don't mind my asking, sir, why? I don't mean to be indelicate, but —"

"You think we own quite enough of the lakefront?" Mr. Cook laughed so hard he started coughing. It took him a few moments to compose himself. "Indeed, we do, young man. More than anyone knows. But we're not interested in putting fancy houses on it. We've always dreamed of preserving a big chunk of it. Maybe making a park or something where no one can ever build anything."

"That would be wonderful," Anissa said.

Mr. Cook had a faraway look in his eyes. "It would. But our interest in that particular property is more practical than altruistic. That land directly connects to the back side of Camp Blackstone. The kids who go there seem happy enough. But the guy who owns the camp is no good and has made no secret of the fact that he'd love to get access to Lake Porter rather than just the lake they have on their property."

"Why would that be such a bad idea?" Anissa asked.

"The camp owner, Dennis Vick, is a real piece of work. He's more interested in making money than he is in doing what's best — for the kids or the environment. There've been issues at that camp — issues with sewage, with cleanliness. Always covered up quick. But if he had direct access to the shoreline? He could put cabins in right on the lake and have camp activities. Don't get me wrong. I love kids. Love the idea of camps. But the residential owners of the lake don't want or need that kind of stuff going on. The end of the lake where Charles has his hotels is set up for the commercial craziness. Down on this end, it's quieter. Needs to stay that way. Plus, with the way Vick handles his own property elsewhere in the county, I fear for Lake Porter as a whole if he ever got access to the big water."

"You wanted to buy the land to keep him from getting access to it?"

"In part, yes." Mr. Cook took a sip of iced tea from a mason jar. "I've watched this lake become what it is. Some people want what's best for the people here and the lake. And some people don't."

Mr. Cook pulled a handkerchief from his pocket and wiped his face. "I asked Vick if he would promise not to build on the shoreline. He promised, but I knew he was lying. I usually do." He smiled at Anissa and Gabe. "I always pray over what I should do with my business ventures. That piece of land has been a conundrum. I don't know what God's going to do with it. I've thought about selling it, but I've always felt like the Lord was telling me to wait. Right now it feels like our ownership of that land is the only thing keeping Vick from making a serious mess of things. God keeps reminding me that he will fight for me and I need to hold my peace. I've been holding my peace for a while and I've been asking the Lord if he intends to handle this battle while I'm still here to see him win it, but he's been quiet on the subject."

"May I ask why you didn't want anyone to know about the property you own?" Gabe asked the question Anissa was wondering.

Mr. Cook took another sip of tea. "It was Charles's idea. I liked it. You wouldn't believe the kinds of stuff we deal with. People asking for money, help, land. And some people just ask to be asking — the nosy sort, like reporters and investigators." He winked at Anissa when he said that. "We have our reasons and I don't feel inclined to share them all with you. Some are personal. None are illegal. It would be best if you kept what you know to yourself, but Charles and I will trust your discretion. If you need to share this information, you can."

"What about the guy living out there? Ronald Talbot?" Anissa asked.

"Ah, Ronald. He's an interesting case."

Interesting wasn't the word Anissa would have used.

"He's trying to get his act together. He did some time, years ago. But he's been out for ten years. Clean for seven. Can't seem to catch a break. I offered him the cabin out there. It's not much, but it's a sight better than what he had. It doesn't leak, has air-conditioning, heat, running water, and even a little washer and dryer. He was thrilled to get it. I told him he could live there rent-free if he wanted to, but I wanted him to look after the place. Clean it up. I can't tell he's done much, but he hasn't made it any worse."

"He claims there're kids out there at night," Gabe said.

"He told me. I think it's older kids from the camp. Maybe the counselors, not the campers. They sneak across the road and then sneak back across before morning. But Ronald hasn't caught them yet. Sometimes he's there for a few weeks at a time. Sometimes he disappears for a few weeks. I'm trying to let him figure it out for himself. Thanks to the abuse he's put it through over the years, his mind isn't always as sharp as it could be. He knows he can ask me for anything, but he doesn't ask for much."

"We saw him today. He claimed he had been in Wilmington for a few days." Anissa showed him a picture she'd snapped with her phone. "Is this him?"

Mr. Cook confirmed it with a nod. "I can't tell you if he was in Wilmington or not. And while I'm not one to tell you how to do your jobs, I doubt he's your shooter."

Gabe stopped the swing and stood. "Thank you for trusting us with this, sir. It's been very enlightening."

"Yes. Yes, it has." Mr. Cook looked at Anissa as he spoke and she got the distinct impression that he and Gabe were talking about two very different subjects.

Gabe's phone rang. He quickly shook Mr. Cook's hand, said goodbye, and stepped off the porch to take the call. His voice faded as he walked toward the truck.

Anissa stood up, rested her hands on the arms of the rocker, and bent down to kiss Mr. Cook's cheek. "Thank you."

He held on to her forearms, and his gaze peered into her very soul.

"Something you want to talk to me about?" he asked.

"No, sir." Truer words had never been spoken.

"I hear you've been keeping company with that boy quite a bit." Mr. Cook nodded in Gabe's direction.

"He's a friend."

"Thought you couldn't stand him." Mr. and Mrs. Cook had listened to her stress over the decision to kick Gabe off the team, and Mr. Cook had listened as she'd fumed about letting him back on.

"I might've been wrong about him."

"You might've been wrong about several things." He chuckled. "I do love you, child. I'll be praying on it."

Anissa had no idea what other things she'd been wrong about, but if Mr. Cook was praying on it, she had no doubt she would soon figure them out.

"Looks like he's finished that call. You'd best go." He winked.

Why did she feel like she'd just been handed off at the altar?

She pushed that thought aside as she jogged to her car, where Gabe stood, holding her door open.

Waiting for her.

5

Anissa attended the early service the next Sunday.

She saw Ryan and Leigh sitting on the other side of the sanctuary. Adam and Sabrina were only three rows ahead of her. But she didn't speak to any of them. She was glad they were all feeling better, but she was in no mood to chat.

She wasn't surprised not to see Gabe. He'd been working eighteen-hour days. Typical Gabe on a case. Focused. Determined. Single-minded.

She slipped out during the final prayer and avoided making eye contact with anyone. She took her time walking to her car, pretending she wasn't sure where she'd parked. Her nerves pinged as she approached, then walked around it. Everything appeared to be fine. The mechanics had replaced her tire and returned her car by the end of the day on Wednesday, but when forensics finished examining the old tires, there wasn't anything wrong with them. The assumption was that someone had let the air out. A stupid prank. Probably.

She opened the driver's-side door, then slid into the seat and dropped her head to the steering wheel. All she wanted was to get home, go for a run, and then curl up in a chair and read a book.

This week had had all the reality she could handle.

Forensics had called on Thursday. Their murder weapon, as it turned out, wasn't their murder weapon after all. Same type of gun, a .270 hunting rifle that a homeowner in Chatham County had reported stolen three months earlier, but not a match. No fingerprints. Nothing.

Ron Talbot had disappeared and was nowhere to be found.

Anissa didn't make a habit out of being so invested in cases that weren't her own. And this one was not hers. Not technically. It was Gabe's and he was doing a fine job. But the entire dive team felt some ownership of it.

She most of all.

She ignored the buzzing of her phone as she drove home. Probably Sabrina or Leigh, or both, wondering if she wanted to go to brunch.

She didn't.

It took ten minutes to get to her home in an older part of town. She loved her little house. Her postage stamp of a front yard. The red begonias that spilled over hanging baskets on her front porch. Everything about it — the paint, the decorations, even the mailbox — she'd picked out.

All by herself.

She parked in her one-car garage and disarmed the alarm as she dropped her keys and phone into the seashell sitting on the table by the door. She pulled her Bible and journal from her purse and put them back in their usual spot beside her chair before she went to her room to change into shorts and a tank top. Her phone buzzed again.

It could be her parents. Or her sister. Or her brother. Or her cousin. Or her grand-parents. All of them were missionaries on the island of Yap. It was important work that changed lives for all eternity. The kind of work she'd intended to do. She'd planned to go back after college to help her parents and work to improve the criminal justice system there.

But then she messed up.

And Carly died.

And the murderer was never found.

He — or she — was still out there, and until they were caught, she couldn't leave. No one in the world wanted the killer behind bars more than Anissa did. If she went back to Yap, she'd be conceding defeat. The murderer would never pay for their crimes.

Anissa couldn't live with that.

But she'd never been able to shake the feeling that she'd missed out on God's best plan for her life. That she was no longer good enough for a starting position and had been given a spot on the third string. Every now and then she got in the game, but most of the time she watched from the sidelines while the star players did the real work for the kingdom of God.

She walked back to the door to retrieve her running shoes.

The seashell on the side table rattled. Again with the phone?

She grabbed it, expecting to see "Mom" or "Dad," but instead "Gabe Chavez" lit the screen.

Gabe?

Pounding on her front door startled her and she pulled her weapon from her purse.

"Anissa? Are you in there?"

Gabe?

She yanked open the front door. "What are you doing here?" The "you scared me half to death" was implied.

"Whoa!" Gabe raised his arms. "Put that thing away. What's wrong with you?"

"What's wrong with me? Are you serious? Do you not know how to knock like a normal person?"

"Do you not know how to answer your phone? I've called you six times since church ended."

Oh. She blew out a long breath. "I left it on silent after church." And then ignored it. "Sorry. Come in." She put the gun on the table.

Gabe entered with a wary expression. He had at least a four-day-old beard. Which somehow suited him. With his squared jaw and dark brown skin, he could pull off the look. But his brown eyes were bleary. His face drawn. Lips in a tight line.

He looked exactly like a man with a one-week-old murder on his hands.

And no leads.

"You look rough."

A smile cracked across his face. "I never have to worry about you stroking my ego, Bell."

"I wasn't trying to be mean."

"I know you weren't. I meant it as a

103

compliment."

They stared at each other for a moment. Anissa couldn't decide if she should say "thank you" or "you're an idiot." "So, I'm guessing there's something important going on?"

Gabe pointed to the sofa. "Can we sit down for a minute?"

Uh-oh. "I don't think I want to sit."

"Nis. Please."

Now he was scaring her. Gabe almost never called her anything other than Anissa or Bell. Usually Bell when he was messing with her. He'd asked her once if she had a nickname and she told him what her family called her. "Nis. Like nieces and nephews." He'd laughed and gone back to calling her "Bell."

She stepped into her small den and sat on the sofa. She expected him to sit in the chair across from her, but he sat beside her.

A bit closer than she was comfortable with.

"I need to tell you something." Gabe radiated worry.

She braced herself.

"Leigh's friend Keri called her this morning from the emergency department. Brooke Ashcroft is in the hospital."

"Why?"

He stared at his hands. "She tried to kill herself."

The guarded expression on Anissa's face was replaced with shock.

And horror.

"No." She shook her head back and forth as she repeated the word. "No. No. No."

Gabe reached for her hands. He couldn't believe it when she took his and held on for dear life.

"How did she . . . ?"

"Paisley said Brooke has been a mess this week. Understandably. The doctor had prescribed anxiety medication and sleeping pills. Brooke took the entire bottle of both of them. Paisley found her this morning. They pumped her stomach. She's in the pediatric ICU on a suicide watch. She hasn't come around. No one's sure what the damage is yet."

Anissa didn't look up. She didn't pull away from him either.

"I didn't want you to hear it anywhere else." And based on her reaction, he was glad he'd made that decision.

"Thank you."

He saw more than heard the words. Her lips moved, but almost no sound came out. "I'm going to the hospital to check on them.

Not like I can do anything. Not like Paisley will appreciate it. But it seems like the right thing to do. If you'll turn your phone on, I'll call you with an update."

"No."

She didn't want an update?

"I'll come with you. Let me change."

"Okay. Sure." He stood when she did.

"Give me five minutes."

He'd give her five hours if she needed it.

She didn't. Four minutes and thirty-three seconds later, Anissa emerged from her bedroom. She had on slacks, a flowy top he'd learned she preferred during the summer because it made it easy for her to hide her weapon and the knife she always kept in her belt when it was too hot to wear a jacket, and a calm façade he knew didn't match the emotions she was fighting to hide.

Her brown hair had been in a ponytail when he arrived but was now in one long braid down her back. A few wisps curled around her tanned face. Her hazel eyes studied him. "Sorry it took me so long."

"I'm not in a hurry."

She tucked her weapon at her back and settled her shirt over it.

Wow. She was gorgeous.

"Okay. I'm ready."

What did she say?

"Earth to Gabe."

"Sorry. I guess I zoned out a little."

"Yeah. Maybe I should drive. I bet you haven't had more than three consecutive hours of sleep in a week. You're probably running on coffee and Leigh's cookies."

"Just the coffee. I finished off Leigh's cookies on Saturday."

"I'm definitely driving." She grabbed her keys. "You can doze on the way to the hospital."

He'd laughed when she said that, but twenty minutes later she was saying, "Gabe. Sorry to wake you, but we're here."

He forced his eyes open and found Anissa's face way closer than he'd been expecting it to be. Her forehead and eyes were scrunched as she studied him. "Maybe you should let me go in alone. You could sleep a little longer."

"No." He forced a laugh but cut it short. When was the last time he'd brushed his teeth? He tried not to breathe in Anissa's direction. "If I fall asleep, I may not wake up until tomorrow."

"That sounds like a good plan if you ask me. You're pushing too hard."

Gabe didn't respond. She wasn't wrong. He knew she wasn't. But even with everything he'd done, it hadn't been enough. He opened the car door into a wall of July humidity and climbed out.

Anissa did the same and they walked into the hospital in silence. They nodded at the security guards, said good morning to the volunteers at the front desk, and waited for the elevator.

They got on with several others, but after leaving them on the second floor, they were alone for the trip to the fourth. Anissa turned to him, the pinched look on her face the same one she'd had in the car. "Gabe, what I said, I didn't mean it as a criticism. I wasn't trying to tell you how to do your job. I just think you may be putting too much pressure on yourself. That's all."

What was she even talking about? Did she think he was mad at her? And if so, since when did she care?

The doors opened and Anissa darted into the hallway.

"Wait." He rushed after her and grabbed her elbow. She froze but didn't turn toward him. "I didn't think you meant it as anything other than an expression of concern, Nis. I wasn't giving you the silent treatment. You're right, but I can't stop. I'm making no progress on this case. I don't have a lead, a suspect, a murder weapon. I have nothing."

"You have a random shooting. You're doing everything you can."

"Well, it's not enough."

"Gabe." Anissa put a hand on his arm. "I understand where you're coming from. But not sleeping and not eating real food isn't going to help you solve the case. When we leave here, you need to sleep. And eat something that isn't a pastry." She squeezed his arm. "Promise me."

She wouldn't break eye contact until he responded. He'd been in a staring contest with her more than once. She always won. And he wanted to say yes to her. "I promise I'll try." He pulled a mint from his pocket and popped it in his mouth. "How's that?"

"Not good enough, Chavez. But I'll allow it for now."

They made their way to the pediatric ICU waiting room. Paisley Wilson sat alone in a corner of the room, knees drawn to her chin, arms wrapped around them. She didn't look up when the door opened. Didn't look up when they approached. Didn't look up when they stood right in front of her.

Anissa knelt beside her. "Paisley?"

Paisley jerked like she'd been shocked. Startled, bloodshot eyes flicked from Gabe to Anissa. Mascara ran in black streaks and

109

dripped to her shirt. "You heard."

Gabe pulled over a chair for Anissa, then one for himself. "You told the nurse this morning, Keri, from the emergency department. Do you remember? You told her she could call and let us know." *Please let her remember.* He didn't want to get Keri in trouble for violating privacy laws.

"She said she was a friend of yours. That she could let you know. I wasn't sure if you would want to know or not, but she was sure you would." Paisley spoke in a monotone. "I . . . um . . ." Her words trailed off and she went back to studying her knees.

"Paisley." Anissa's voice was so tender. No one listening would believe she could bark orders like a drill sergeant. Or suspect she was speaking to someone she considered an enemy. "Is there someone we could call? Family? Boyfriend?"

A harsh, scoffing sound was Paisley's only response.

Anissa met Gabe's eyes with a questioning look.

He knew more about Paisley Wilson than was probably healthy. In the weeks and months after the fiasco when she ruined everything, he'd done his best to dig up any dirt he could find on her. He knew her habits, her favorite food, and he knew why she was here with Brooke instead of their parents. "Paisley, do you still live with your grandmother?"

A faint spark lit her eyes, but it didn't catch into flame. "I guess you would know all about me, huh? Makes sense. I know all about you." In that flat monotone, she didn't sound aggressive. More like resigned.

Anissa's gaze flicked from Paisley to him and back again, but she didn't speak.

"This could kill Grandma." Fresh tears poured from Paisley's eyes. "I could lose everyone I love."

Gabe's mind swirled. Part of his brain, a small but vocal part, couldn't help but observe that Paisley was getting what she deserved. That she was feeling the kinds of feelings — despair, agony, helplessness, hopelessness, and sheer terror — that her own recklessness had caused him to feel.

And if he was completely honest with himself, he'd imagined this moment. More than once. When he would get to see her suffer the way she'd made him suffer.

But another part of his brain, a part growing in intensity by the second, screamed at the injustice. Raged against the pain she was in. Reminded him that he was not judge and juror. And forced him to consider the very real possibility that it might be time to forgive her for what she'd done. Maybe.

"Paisley," Anissa whispered. "I know it seems hopeless. But I also know God can restore."

"Really, Investigator Bell? Really?" Paisley snarled the words at Anissa. "I know about Carly Nichols."

Anissa's hand fell to her lap, her tanned face paled, her eyes narrowed, but she didn't respond.

"And I know about the little girl."

Who was Carly? What little girl?

Anissa's response was not what he was expecting. "Then you know I know what I'm talking about. I'm not spouting platitudes at you. I've been here. I've been Brooke. I've wanted to die because of what I did. And I'm telling you that you cannot give up on her or yourself. And you should give your grandma more credit, because she's probably more aware than you realize."

"Indeed, she is." A frail voice spoke from behind them.

Paisley jumped to her feet. "Grandma! What are you doing here?"

The elderly woman pulled Paisley into an embrace. "I'm here to help you, child. You don't have to carry it alone."

Gabe caught Anissa's eye and they slipped

out the door and into the hallway. "Should we stay or go?"

"Go," Anissa said. "The only thing that will help them right now is time. And maybe answers. But the only thing I can guarantee is time."

6

Anissa drove them back to her house, braced for the moment when Gabe would ask about Carly. And sweet Jillian.

But he didn't ask.

He stared out the window, and no matter how hard she tried, she couldn't get a read on his mood. Was he angry? Upset? Annoyed?

She should tell him everything.

But she dreaded the look he would give her. The subtle way their relationship would shift after she'd laid her heart bare.

It had happened before. Years ago. The guy had been everything she thought she could ever want, and early in their relationship — too soon or not soon enough, she'd never been sure — she'd told him. And he'd looked at her like the piece of garbage she knew herself to be.

The relationship ended within the week and left her feeling not only heartbroken but also exposed and taken advantage of. Two feelings she'd spent the past decade trying to avoid.

But she'd avoided this long enough.

She pulled into her driveway and put the car in park. "Do you want to come in?"

Gabe rolled his head from one side to the other. "Sure."

He followed her inside and stood by the door as she tossed her keys in the shell and removed her weapon. "Would you like something to drink?"

"Nah, I'm good. Thanks." He shifted from one foot to the other. Very uncharacteristic of him.

"Look —" Anissa began.

"Listen —" Gabe said at the same time.

They stared at each other. "You first," Gabe said.

Here goes nothing. "I know you want to know about Carly."

"You don't owe me an explanation, but if you're in some kind of trouble or there's something you want to talk about, you know I'll listen."

"I know. Please, have a seat."

He sat on the sofa. She paced the room. "My freshman and sophomore years of college, I mostly stuck to a small group of friends. I hadn't lived in the States since I was fourteen. I was still trying to figure out a lot of cultural stuff and I desperately wanted to be one of the cool kids. But I was the weird little missionary kid who liked to work out and dive."

She didn't dare look at Gabe. "My junior year, there was a guy in my public speaking class. Theo Kavanaugh. He was . . ." She could picture him. Tall, thin, blond, blue-gray eyes, perpetual tan, quick smile. "He was one of the cool kids. It was like a party erupted wherever he was. And I was . . ."

This was turning out to be more embarrassing than she'd expected it to be. She plunged ahead. "I was completely infatuated with him. I knew everything about him, or at least I thought I did. But I didn't think he had any idea who I was. And I never imagined he would want to spend any time with me."

"Oh, I'm sure he did," Gabe said with a grim tone.

"You have nothing to base that on," she said.

"Don't I? I'm not blind. You're beautiful now. My guess is you were one of the cutest girls on campus."

Beautiful? Gabe — admittedly the best-looking guy she'd ever had an opportunity to spend time with — thought she was beautiful? "I think your sleep deprivation is making you delusional."

"I call it like I see it."

"Whatever. Do you want to hear this or not?"

"Sorry." He didn't sound sorry at all. "I won't interrupt again."

She resumed her pacing. "One day Theo started talking to me. He made me feel special. I know how stupid that sounds, but I was used to people ignoring me or teasing me. I wasn't sure what to do with a guy who seemed to really like me. He claimed that he thought my family was cool. He asked me about Yap and the culture there. We talked about diving. I thought we had a lot in common. And then he invited me to a party."

The muscles in Gabe's jaw tightened, but he didn't speak.

"My best friend's name was Carly Nichols. She was the real version of everything I pretended to be. Her faith was genuine. Her joy found in loving Jesus. She didn't care about popularity or status. And she didn't like Theo."

When Anissa closed her eyes, she could see Carly standing in their dorm room asking her why she cared about this guy in the first place.

"I know now that Carly was picking up on things that should have been obvious. But I was so infatuated with Theo I didn't notice. Or maybe I noticed but ignored them. I was twenty years old. It's hard to know. Regardless, she was furious with me for wanting to go to the party."

"But you went anyway."

"Yeah. I went. And when I got there, someone shoved a red cup in my hand."

Gabe closed his eyes and pulled in a shuddering breath.

"This isn't going the way you think it's going, Gabe. He never laid a hand on me."

Gabe's relief was palpable. "What was in the cup?"

"I don't know. It was fruity and didn't taste of alcohol. Not that I would have known the difference. I'd never had any alcohol before." Or since. "I knew I should say no, thank you, but I justified it to myself. I figured I would hold the cup and take a few sips and no one would realize I wasn't getting as drunk as everyone else."

"I'm guessing that plan didn't work out?"

"No. It didn't. We mingled around the room and he introduced me to people I had only seen on campus or had a few classes with but had never spoken to. It was . . . nice." How it burned to admit it. "I was with one of the most popular guys on campus and he thought I was interesting. I realize how incredibly shallow it was of me. I knew it was even in the moment, but it was nice to be wanted. Maybe even to be envied a little. There were some girls there who were obviously jealous. And I was glad."

"Those are normal responses, Anissa." Gabe spoke in a soft murmur. "Most twenty-year-olds would have done the same. Most thirty-year-olds would."

"Well, I wasn't most twenty-year-olds. I knew better. I was raised better. I didn't know exactly what was going on around me, but I was pretty sure some of it was illegal and most of it was immoral. I should have left. I should have realized that there was no way this guy was someone I needed to be spending time with."

"But you stayed."

"I did. I had opportunities to leave, but I ignored them. I kept telling myself that one party wouldn't be the end of the world."

How wrong she had been on that score.

"He introduced me to a guy from Japan, who introduced me to a group of international students. I was enjoying our conversation — I often get along well with people who grew up outside the States the way I did. It was almost two in the morning before I realized that the cup I was holding wasn't the same one I'd started out with. And that my date was nowhere to be found."

"He left you?" Gabe's protective response might have warmed her heart if she hadn't known where this story was headed.

"In a manner of speaking. I excused myself from the group I'd been talking to and went to look for him. I was embarrassed that I hadn't realized he was gone. I thought I'd been rude. Until I found him."

Gabe looked toward the ceiling. "I'm going to guess he wasn't alone."

"Nope."

"I'm sorry."

"The crazy thing is, I wasn't. I was embarrassed, but in a weird way I was relieved. I didn't feel any obligation to stay, so I walked back to my dorm. I got home around three in the morning and crashed."

She walked to the window and stared out into her yard. "Carly woke me up at six. I was supposed to babysit for the youth pastor in our church, but I was so hungover I couldn't do it. I tried to get ready, but I couldn't get out of the bathroom. Carly came to my rescue. She was angry and hurt and disappointed, but she volunteered to babysit for me. She said she would tell them

I was throwing up, which was a hundred percent true, and that she was coming instead. Her car was in the shop, so she took mine —"

Anissa could still picture it. While she had her arms wrapped around the toilet, Carly had pulled her hair back from her face, told her they would talk when she got home. Then she'd closed the bathroom door gently, even though she was furious.

"Anissa?" Gabe was standing right behind her. "What happened to Carly?"

She couldn't stop the tear that broke free and trailed down her cheek. "I don't know. They found her body in a Dumpster four days later. And the little girl — Jillian — was never found."

Gabe put his arms around her. With her back against his chest, his lips tickled her ear as he spoke. "You didn't kill Carly, Anissa. It wasn't your fault. You must know that."

"It should have been me," she whispered. "I should have been with Jillian. I should have died in a Dumpster. I deserved it. Carly didn't. She died for me." The lone tear couldn't contain her agony, and a torrent of sobs shook her body.

Gabe held her and wished he could take

away the pain.

He'd had no idea she carried this kind of guilt around. And her despair about Brooke and Jeremy made so much sense now. She'd seen herself in Brooke — a girl who had made a stupid decision and gotten her best friend killed because of it.

Had Anissa also tried to kill herself in the aftermath of Carly's death?

Was Carly the reason she'd become a cop?

He put his hands on Anissa's shoulders and turned her around so he could see her face. For a brief moment she looked at him and her eyes held an ocean of pain. He pulled her against him. This time her arms slid around his waist and she rested her head against his chest until her sobbing calmed to the occasional tremor.

When had he started stroking her hair? And when had he rested his cheek on her head? He'd like to believe he would do the same thing for any friend who needed comforting, but . . .

Anissa shifted in his arms. Was it his imagination, or had she snuggled closer? *Head in the game, Chavez.* "I'm so very sorry about Carly. And Jillian."

"I had to identify her body."

A fresh wave of horror washed over him.

"Her family was in Ukraine. She was an

MK, a missionary kid too."

Gabe had seen his share of dead bodies. A four-day-old dead body in a Dumpster would be nightmare inducing even if you didn't know the victim.

"The cops questioned me for hours, but I didn't know anything. Carly didn't have any enemies. She was a saint. And she wasn't supposed to be there. It was random. It had been raining all week and Jillian had been cooped up in the house, so her parents, the Davidsons, had told Carly she might want to take Jillian to the park to swing. My car was found at the park, but Jillian and Carly were gone."

He could hear the confusion and frustration in Anissa's voice. "I'm assuming your parents were in Yap when this happened."

"Yes. My mom flew home to be with me, but it took her three days to get here. By the time she arrived, the police had determined that it was a random abduction. There were two main theories. Either the killer was after Carly and Jillian got in the way, or they were after Jillian and Carly got in the way."

"Which one had the most traction?"

"It depended on who you talked to. The local police had been leaning toward the idea that Jillian had gotten in the way. The

FBI got involved because of the suspicion of kidnapping. Once the medical examiner was finished and all the toxicology results and tests had come back, it was determined that Carly —"

Anissa paused so long, Gabe wasn't sure if she was going to finish her thought.

"Carly's neck was broken. Her hands, knees, and elbows were scraped, like she'd either fallen or been thrown to the ground. But there was no evidence of sexual assault or any form of drugs in her system. Once that information came in, the consensus was that Jillian most likely had been the intended target."

Gabe was afraid to ask, but he had to. "Did they find out who did it?"

"No. Carly's killer is still out there."

Gabe now saw all the times Anissa had worried over the way a family member was being questioned, or commented on how fast a case could go cold, or hassled the forensics team to find every possible scrap of evidence in a whole new light.

Anissa wasn't being a pain. She was trying to prevent pain. To keep anyone else from going through what she'd been through.

"I've studied all the case files." Her words were muffled against his shirt. "But there's nothing. Carly had been stripped before she was put in the Dumpster. There was no DNA evidence on her anywhere. Nothing under her fingernails or on her skin. And she'd been dead for four days when she was found. The medical examiner concluded Carly's time of death was between eleven a.m. and three p.m. on Saturday. A traffic cam showed that Carly had gone to the park around twelve thirty. Probably right after she'd fed Jillian lunch."

A quick tremor shook Anissa and Gabe tightened his hold. This time he was sure he hadn't imagined it. She didn't stiffen or pull back.

She leaned in.

He was not complaining. But this was not the time or place to make a move. Anissa was marriage material, but he was not. And whatever this was that had been going on between them couldn't be allowed to go any further.

But for the first time in a very long while, he wished it could.

As if she sensed his thoughts, Anissa stiffened and pulled away. He let her go but immediately regretted the decision. Her eyes, which had been open to him, were now flat, shuttered. She had laid herself bare to him and was now in a full-on retreat.

He reached for her arm, but she pulled it

away. "I'm sorry for the drama." She cleared her throat and wiped her cheeks, never making eye contact. "Now you know. And you can hate me for it. I understand. But I would appreciate it if you'd keep this between us."

Hate her? What was she going on about?

"First off, there's no way I would ever share this with anyone. You know that." A quick bob of her head confirmed that she did. "But what in our entire history would make you think I would hate you for something that happened to you in college?"

"It didn't happen to me, Gabe. I caused it. I was so worried about being accepted and liked that I got my best friend killed and a three-year-old kidnapped. And who knows what happened to Jillian after that."

"I'm sorry, but did you leave out a major portion of this story? Because you just told me the target was Jillian, not Carly, and you had nothing to do with her kidnapping. If you'd been there, you'd be dead. But you aren't responsible for this."

Anissa's mouth twisted. "Semantics."

Gabe sat on the edge of the sofa. "Not to make this all about me, but why would you think I would hate you for this?"

"I made a mistake. Someone died because of my mistake. I know how you feel about that kind of stuff. You despise Paisley Wilson for doing the same thing I did."

How could she think that? "Paisley was an adult —"

"So was I."

"Doing something she'd already been warned could result in unintended consequences."

Anissa pointed to her chest. "Same."

"Which she proceeded to do without regard for how her actions would impact others."

"Again, I did the same thing."

"No!" Was she crazy? "It's not the same at all. There was no way you could have predicted that outcome. When you got home that night, the worst thing you could possibly have been expecting was a hangover. Which you got. But you could not have known what would happen when you agreed to babysit that child, or when you allowed your friend to take your place."

Anissa didn't look convinced.

"Paisley . . ." Words failed him as he recalled the frantic message he'd sent to his boss to warn her off. The horror of the moment he saw her in that stupid helicopter, cameras rolling. The realization that his cover was blown forever. The despair when the seventeen-year-old boy who'd been with him at the time was found two days later. Beaten to a pulp, then shot. A life brimming with potential over far too soon. "She had visions of big awards dancing in her head. She thought she'd uncovered corruption in the sheriff's office when what she'd really done was stumble into an undercover op. She was asked to wait. She was told that moving forward could result in loss of life. But she didn't believe them, and she flew in knowing full well what might happen."

Anissa bit her lip.

"So, unless someone called you and told you that if you went to that party your best friend would die the next day, then you cannot — and, frankly, you never, ever should — compare yourself to Paisley."

Anissa shook her head. "How would you feel if your decisions got someone killed and a little girl kidnapped? You can't blame me for taking responsibility."

"I know exactly how it feels. I befriended that boy. He had no idea I was a cop, but I knew there was a chance he would be in danger if my cover was blown. And then it was and he paid for it. So, I know. And I still say you can't take on this responsibility. You didn't kill Carly. You didn't kidnap Jillian. And for what it's worth, I don't hate Paisley. I think she's an idiot. But I don't

hate her. And I certainly don't hate you. I
—"

He what? How could he describe his feelings about Anissa? They were complex and confusing. "I think you are the most extraordinary person I've ever met."

Anissa turned away from him. She seemed relieved but also upset again. This was making no sense.

She laughed a little. "You certainly haven't always felt that way. About Paisley or me."

She might have him on that one. "True. My overall thoughts about Paisley have mellowed with time." His feelings about Anissa had done the exact opposite. Not that he could tell her that. "As for you . . ."

She looked at him, eyes shimmering with unshed tears, and he swallowed back the joke he'd been about to make. "I've always admired you. Even when you kicked me off the dive team." He almost mentioned the night they never spoke of, but he jumped forward in time. "And even when you made me earn back my place on the team. And even when you gave me the worst assignments."

"I did not." There was no heat behind her defense.

"Sure you did. But the more I get to know you, the more amazing you are to me. You're kind and compassionate and tough and smart, and I've never met anyone quite like you. And what you just told me, what just happened, only confirms what I already knew to be true about you."

Her eyes widened. He'd been more honest than he'd intended, but at least he'd stopped himself from saying the stuff he rarely gave himself permission to think. If he told her that he could stare at her for hours and never get bored, she'd probably slap him.

"I'm not sure what to say to that," she said.

The space between them crinkled with a new kind of energy. Somehow he thought the tentative friendship they'd been building for months now had solidified and also maybe had taken a dive to a deeper place than he'd ever thought they'd reach. Time to swim them back up to a safer spot.

"No need to say anything." He pasted his usual grin on his face. "Just remember this next time someone needs to clean the boat."

Something that looked like disappointment, or maybe even hurt, flashed through her eyes but disappeared almost before he caught it. She gave him a smile, but it was a bit forced. "I'll do that."

Anissa's phone buzzed and she grabbed it

like it was a lifeline. She looked at it and smiled. "It's Leigh. Do you mind?"

"Not at all. Go ahead."

Anissa answered, listened for a moment, and then said, "Sure. I have it. Hang on a second." She held up one finger to Gabe and walked toward her bedroom.

When she disappeared from view, Gabe slid onto the sofa. His eyes closed without his permission, but there was nothing he could do about it. As soon as Anissa got off the phone with Leigh, he would say goodbye and go home. Or maybe he would ask Anissa to drive him home. He probably shouldn't get behind the wheel.

7

Anissa found the swatch of fabric on her dresser. "I have it right here. Do you need it today?"

"No," Leigh said. "Can you send it home with Ryan tomorrow? Keri is an amazing artist and she's going to paint something for me with Sabrina and Adam's wedding colors. I told her I'd get her the swatch for the bridesmaid dresses because she didn't appreciate my attempts to describe that shade of blue."

Anissa could imagine. "That's a great gift idea," she said.

"I hope it will be."

Leigh paused and the lull in the conversation set off some warning bells in Anissa's mind. "Is everything okay?"

"Yes," Leigh said. "I'm just wondering if it would be wildly inappropriate of me to ask if you went to the hospital?"

Anissa should have expected Leigh to be

curious. "We did, but Brooke is unrespon-
sive. We told Paisley to call us if anything
changes. Her grandmother is there, so she's
not alone."

"Oh, good. I'm on tonight, so I'll check in
on them if you want."

"That would be great," Anissa said.
"Thanks."

"Anissa?"

Oh boy. Leigh's tone spoke volumes.

"Hmm?"

"Are you okay?"

It was impossible to hide stuff from Leigh.
She had a sixth sense about people that
would have made her a great cop if she
hadn't gone into nursing. And Leigh knew
all about Carly. Over the past year, Anissa
had told Leigh almost all her secrets. Except
the one about that night and Gabe. "I'm
hanging in there."

"Are you sure? I can come over if you
want some company."

"I'm good. Gabe's here at the moment."
She regretted that last sentence as soon as
it left her mouth.

"Excuse me?" Leigh's tone had gone from
concerned to curious in a microsecond.
"Did you say Gabe is at your house? On a
Sunday afternoon?"

Anissa closed her bedroom door. "It's not

133

like . . . that." The memory of the way Gabe had stroked her hair as she cried caused her to stumble over the words.

"Really? Because you sound a little guilty. I have no idea why, given that Gabe is single, gorgeous, and most definitely available."

A voice in the background said something that Anissa couldn't catch. "Of course he isn't as good-looking as you, babe."

Great. So Ryan was hearing Leigh's side of the conversation. He said something else and Leigh responded, "Here, you talk to her, then."

"Hey." Ryan's voice came on the line.

"Hey." She braced herself for whatever Ryan would want to know.

"Is Gabe okay?"

She should have realized Ryan wouldn't be interested in playing matchmaker, but he would be worried about his friend. "He's exhausted. I don't know when he slept last. I'm thinking about taking his keys and driving him home."

"Good luck with that."

She could hear the frustration in Ryan's voice, but there was no malice behind it. They knew, the three of them, how hard it was to have a case like this.

"How about you? You holding up okay?"

"Eh." She wouldn't lie to him, but she didn't want to get into it. There was no way she was going to tell him she'd broken down in Gabe's arms. Or that somehow having Gabe know about her failures, and not hating her for them, had lifted a weight she hadn't realized she'd been burdened with. Or that now she was confused about her relationship with Gabe in a completely different way.

"Yeah. Okay." Ryan didn't push. Thank goodness. "Let me know if he goes back to work instead of going home, okay? I may grab Adam and the two of us will forcibly remove Gabe from his desk, but I'm hoping it won't come to that."

She knew he was joking. Sort of. "I will."

"Okay. I'm going to go ahead and hang up so Leigh doesn't grill you about why Gabe's at your house. But that is, um, interesting." He chuckled. "See you in the morning."

The phone disconnected and Anissa stared at it for a moment. At least Ryan didn't push the subject. Because right now she'd break under the slightest bit of interrogation. *Investigator Bell, can you explain to me what exactly you were doing snuggled up with Investigator Chavez on Sunday afternoon when you claim to be friends . . . and barely that?*

She shook off the image, returned to the living room, and found Gabe sound asleep on the sofa.

She stared at him for a moment, rather enjoying the opportunity to do so without having to worry about him catching her eye. His face was relaxed, his breathing deep and even.

She could wake him up and drive him home. Or she could let him sleep right where he was.

As she stood there debating, he shifted in his sleep and slid farther down on the sofa. That decided it for her. She propped a throw pillow against the arm of the sofa, then put her hands on his shoulders. He didn't flinch. She eased him to the side until his head was on the pillow. She then moved to his feet. He'd left his shoes by her door, so it was just a matter of lifting his legs up to the sofa. As soon as she got him completely horizontal, he stretched out.

She half expected him to open his eyes and grumble about her handling of him. But rather than waking him, the move seemed to have helped him settle even deeper into sleep. She pulled a throw blanket from the basket in the corner and draped it over him. "Sleep tight, Gabe."

She wandered into her room and caught a glimpse of herself in the mirror. That drove her to the bathroom, where she grabbed a washcloth, ran it under the water, and attempted to fix her face. Her eyes were red, eyelids puffy, makeup completely gone.

Her skin flushed at the thought of the breakdown she'd had. It then flushed deeper at the way she hadn't been able to stop herself from snuggling into Gabe's arms. He was just being nice. She knew that. There was nothing between them but air.

It would be great if she could convince her heart of that.

Even better if she could somehow forget that one kiss. It hadn't meant anything to Gabe. She was sure of that. And she had been prepared for it. She'd been prepared for more kissing than there had been. He'd been far more gentlemanly than she'd expected him to be. When they sent her in that night, his handlers had told her to be prepared for almost anything.

She hadn't been prepared for Gabe to apologize right before kissing her in a way that left her dazed. She tried to tell herself that they had been two people doing their jobs and nothing more. But if that was Gabe faking it, she had to admit she wondered what it would be like to experience a real kiss.

Not that that would ever happen.

Gabe had made it clear, more than once and to anyone who would listen, that he would never marry. Which used to make her happy. She didn't have to worry about things getting weird — well, weirder — with Gabe.

But things had just gotten weirder.

She tried to shake off the memory as she pressed the cool cloth to her eyes. All she could do was make the best of the situation — and pretend it hadn't happened. She had plenty of practice with that.

She would be able to pretend more easily if he wasn't sleeping on her sofa.

She skirted past him and grabbed her water bottle and a protein bar from the kitchen before curling up in her recliner with her laptop. She checked email, responded to some messages from family in Yap, and set the laptop to the side. Gabe continued to sleep, so she pulled her book off the end table and tried to lose herself in pre–Revolutionary War America.

She woke up three hours later.

The book was in her lap and her phone was buzzing on the arm of the chair. "Hello?"

"Investigator Bell?"

"Speaking."

"This is Jocelyn Martinez. I'm a nurse in the PICU at Carrington."

Anissa's heart sank. "Yes."

"Brooke Ashcroft's family asked me to contact you and an Investigator Chavez. Brooke is awake and is frantically asking for the two of you. I told her I would call you."

"We're about twenty minutes away. Tell her we're coming."

"Thank you." Her relief came through the line. "I will."

"What is it?" Gabe's words were slurred with sleep.

"Brooke's awake and she's asking for us."

Gabe's eyes closed again. Was he falling back asleep?

But his lips were moving. Oh. He was praying.

He sat up with a huge yawn. "What time is it?"

"Almost six."

Another yawn accompanied his rise to his feet. "You should have woken me up."

"Not a chance."

"Thanks." He blinked a few times, sleep still heavy on him.

"The bathroom's that way." She pointed down the hall. "And I'm driving."

"Good plan, boss."

Five minutes later they were on the road. They didn't talk. Not because of any tension, but because two minutes after they got on the road Gabe was snoring.

He woke with a start when she put the car in park, and for the second time that day they entered the hospital. The pediatric ICU had strict rules about visitors, but Paisley must have spoken to the nurses, because after washing their hands, Anissa and Gabe were taken directly to Brooke's small room.

Brooke looked so tiny. So frail. The strong girl who'd kept her friend from sinking in the lake was gone. Even through the hospital sheets, Anissa could tell she'd lost weight. Too much weight in a week. Her cheeks were sunken. Dark circles rimmed her closed eyes. Her hand twitched on the blanket.

Paisley jumped to her feet when they entered the room. "Thank you for coming." Her voice was low, rough. "She woke up and kept saying, 'Get them. Get Gabe and Anissa.' "

Paisley looked down at the floor. "I'm sorry to bother you again on a Sunday, but I couldn't deny her request. And she wouldn't settle down until we promised her you were on the way. She fell asleep a few minutes ago. I'm sorry. I don't know what she needs to ask you, but —"

"You did the right thing." Anissa studied Brooke's sleeping form. What could she need to talk to them about?

"Why don't we wait outside?" Gabe's suggestion made sense. The three of them barely had room to stand around Brooke's bed. "Better yet, we'll go grab something to eat in the cafeteria and you can get us as soon as she wakes up."

Gabe rested a hand on Anissa's elbow and steered her out of the room, out of the PICU, and toward the elevator. "I wasn't trying to speak for you," he said with an apologetic tone. "But I'm starving. Do you mind?"

"I'm with you all the way."

The look he gave her had her rethinking her words.

Anissa hadn't meant it the way it sounded.

He knew that.

But he still liked the sound of it. *I'm with you.*

The cafeteria offerings were limited on a Sunday evening, but the sub sandwich shop was open. She ordered a Coke and some chips. She ate like a bird when she was stressed. He, however, ate everything in

141

sight when he was stressed. He ordered a foot-long sub with extra meat and they took a seat. He inhaled the sandwich and was thinking about ordering another when Anissa's phone rang. Brooke was awake.

When they crammed into her small PICU room, Gabe was struck by how frail she looked. Trying to kill yourself and having your stomach pumped would do that to anyone, but the contrast between the girl he'd helped at the lake and the one lying in the bed put his heart in a vise.

He had to find out who had done this.

Who had taken what should have been a stupid teenage decision and turned it into a nightmare that this poor child could never wake up from? Would she, like Anissa, carry it into her thirties and beyond?

He couldn't fix Anissa's case, although he would if he could. But he could do everything in his power to be sure Brooke didn't go through life with this hanging over her head. *God, help me find this monster. Please.*

"Hi." Brooke's scratchy whisper tightened the grip on his heart, but he forced himself to respond in a far more upbeat way.

"Hey yourself." He took her hand in his. "You scared us, girl."

"Sorry." Her eyes looked so big in her thin face. "Swimming is the only thing I'm good at. But when I tried to practice, I couldn't even get my toe in the pool. I panicked."

"It happens," he said.

"Not to you." She looked at him and Anissa. "You didn't panic. You were brave and calm. I don't think I can be that way."

He glanced at Anissa and Paisley. They both looked back at him expectantly. Since when did he get nominated to be the teenage girl whisperer? He didn't know anything about teenagers. Or girls.

"Oh, that's not true." He winked and nodded in Anissa's direction. "She panics all the time."

"Does not." Brooke shook her head, but he sensed her curiosity.

"Not about the stuff you might think, of course. She doesn't panic in water because she can hold her breath for like an hour. Not many people know this, but she's part fish. You can't see the gills she's hiding."

Brooke didn't quite laugh, but a smile flirted on the edge of her lips.

Anissa rolled her eyes in spectacular fashion. She made a great straight man.

"And she doesn't panic on the job because she's the best. But she wasn't always the best. She had to learn. To practice. Same as all of us. None of us are any good at things the first time we have to deal with them.

Take me, for example."

Brooke's eyes flashed with curiosity.

He leaned in. "I don't share this with many people, but the first time I went diving, I panicked."

Her brow furrowed.

"It's true. Water flooded my mask, I forgot how to get it out, couldn't remember how to inflate my BCD — that's the buoyancy compensator device that divers wear to help them descend and ascend — and completely lost it. My diving instructor had to drag me to the surface like a sack of potatoes."

Brooke looked to Anissa for confirmation.

Anissa shrugged. "This is the first I've heard of it, but I can tell you that Gabe doesn't lie."

Brooke looked back at him, so he continued. "It was humiliating. I was fifteen and thought I was tough and awesome. I was pretty good at most of the stuff I tried, and I'd never had something I felt like I stank at."

"What did you do?"

"My instructor let me float on the surface for a few minutes. He held on to my BCD, and he told me to breathe and reminded me about what I'd learned. And then we went back down again. Not quite as deep. Real slow. And when my mask started to

144

fill, he held on to me while I cleared the water out of it and got it settled back on my face. He stayed with me until I could handle it by myself. And now I teach other people how to dive. But it wasn't always that way. I was scared every time I got in the water for months."

"When did you stop being scared?" Ah. There was the real question.

"There wasn't a single moment. But one day, I went for a dive and realized it was all easy and that I loved it. Now I dive every chance I get. Of course, it wouldn't have been that way if I'd refused to get back in the water even though I was scared."

Her eyes filled with tears. "Every time I get wet, even to take a shower, I picture Jeremy. And swimming is all I do. It's how I'm going to get to go to college. It's the only thing I'm good at. And I can't. I'm such a weakling."

Gabe grabbed her hand again. "There's nothing weak about this, Brooke. Nothing. You've been through something way more horrible than my mask filling up with water. It's too soon to worry about getting in the water. Or about being weak. Even if you never get back in the water, that would be understandable. And your sister and grandmother would be okay with it."

In his peripheral vision, he could see Paisley nodding in agreement.

"But I don't think that's going to happen. I think when you're ready, you're going to get back in the pool. And when you're ready to get back in the lake, Anissa and I would be honored to swim with you. Well, Anissa will. Like I said, she's part fish. I'll probably have to get in a boat and float alongside you while you swim."

She snickered at that before her expression turned serious. "I'll think about it."

"You do that. But keep in mind that if you want me to get in the lake in the winter, I'm going to need a wet suit and the promise of hot chocolate."

She nodded and bit her lip. "I want to ask you something, but I'm afraid you'll either think I'm crazy or be mad at me. Although I guess both of those are already true."

He squeezed her hand. "Not possible, *chica.*"

"I dared Jeremy. We were jumping off the dock and goofing off. Laughing." A dry sob followed the words and she closed her eyes.

Gabe took the opportunity to steal a look at Anissa. Her movement was so slight and subtle that even if Brooke had been watching, she wouldn't have noticed the way Anissa made an "okay" sign with her hand.

Normally that meant "I'm okay," but he took it to mean that he hadn't botched anything so far.

Brooke's grip on his hand tightened. "I need to know if there's anything I could have done to save him. Other than never daring him in the first place."

Paisley brushed a stray hair from Brooke's face and gave the kind of shushing sounds women were so good at making when someone was upset.

"I keep dreaming that I knew it was all going to happen and I just let it. That I saw it all and did nothing to stop it. But when I'm awake, I know that's not true."

Anissa didn't move, but he could feel the energy radiating from her.

"But I need to know the truth!" Brooke's wail cut through the quiet room. "I can't stand anyone else telling me that it wasn't my fault and that there was nothing I could have done. I don't want people who will be nice to me. I need someone who will be honest, and I think the two of you will. You're investigating. Tell me what I could have done!"

Her eyes were frantic as they bounced from him to Anissa to Paisley and made the circuit again.

How was he supposed to answer? He

147

didn't know who had done it. He didn't know why they had done it. He couldn't even be sure that she wasn't a target. Or that Jeremy wasn't the target.

"Brooke." Anissa stepped forward. "To the very best of our current knowledge, we don't believe there was anything you could have done to prevent Jeremy's murder."

Brooke froze at Anissa's word choice. She didn't say anything, but the wild fear in her eyes dampened. "Will you tell me if it's my fault?" Brooke whispered. "I think I could handle it better, knowing one way or the other, than all this questioning and wondering."

Paisley's eyes widened. Gabe could tell she would have been perfectly happy to never tell Brooke anything more about the case. But Anissa was nodding. A slow, barely there nod. "You deserve nothing less. You'll get the whole truth from us when we have it, but you have to give us time to find it. Without doing yourself harm while you're waiting."

"You promise you'll look at everything? You won't try to be nice?" Brooke wouldn't let it go.

Anissa patted her hand. "Do you think I'm that nice?"

Brooke's lips curved into a hint of a smile.

Anissa pointed to Gabe. "We look at all the clues during a murder investigation. Niceness has nothing to do with it. I promise you we will look at everything and everyone until we find out what happened."

Brooke relaxed back on the pillows. "Thank you."

8

Gabe and Anissa left the PICU a few minutes later. As they approached the main nurses station, a young girl walked to the desk and leaned against it. She was in pajamas and a robe. One hand gripped an IV pole. A nurse joined her at the desk.

"Someone wanted to come say hello," the nurse said.

"It's Liz!"

"Hey, Liz!"

"Look at you!"

Everyone behind the desk stood and gathered around the young woman.

"How're you feeling?" A young doctor who didn't look much older than the patient asked the question.

"Great," Liz said. "I'm back on solid food. One more night and I may be able to talk them into removing the IV."

"So, I guess they're taking good care of you on the third floor, then?" This came from an older nurse.

"They are, Ms. Lydia. You were right."

"Bet you don't even miss us at all, huh?"

"Of course I do. Y'all were the best! That's why I came to say hi!"

The laughter and teasing continued as Gabe moved around the cheerful group. Such a contrast to the usual somber mood. He could only imagine how much the nurses and doctors appreciated having a patient — clearly on the road to recovery — come back to say hi.

"That was fun." He turned back toward Anissa, but she wasn't there. She was ten feet behind, staring at the crowd around Liz.

Anissa had paled under her tanned skin. Her expression was one of shock, confusion, and fear.

He walked to her side and pulled on her arm. She followed him, but she looked back over her shoulder.

Twice.

This was beyond weird.

He kept a grip on her elbow until they were out of the unit and in a deserted hallway, and then he stopped along the wall. "What is going on with you?"

Anissa's eyes were still focused elsewhere. "Anissa!"

She jerked. "Sorry. I just . . . Did you see her?"

"Who?"

"The girl."

"You mean Liz?"

"Yeah." Anissa turned back toward the PICU.

"Of course I saw her. How could I not see her? It was like a fiesta in there. But what's your deal? You look like you've seen a ghost."

She ran her hands over her face. When she removed them, tears shimmered on her eyelashes. "She . . . she's the right age."

What on earth was she talking . . . "Oh. She's the same age Jillian would be."

"Yes, but . . ."

"But what?"

Anissa swallowed hard. "She looks exactly like her."

"What are you talking about? *Querida,* you said Jillian was only three when she was taken. You don't know what she would look like at sixteen."

"Yes, I do."

Twenty minutes later they had called in a pizza order for delivery and were back at Anissa's house.

Once inside, she flipped on the lights and pointed to the kitchen. "Make yourself at home. I'll be right back."

When she disappeared into her bedroom, Gabe started opening cabinet doors until he found the glasses. He filled two with ice, then opened the fridge and grabbed a sparkling water for her and a Coke for himself.

"You should try something without caffeine," Anissa said from behind him.

"Why?"

"Oh, I don't know. Maybe because it's already late and you need to sleep."

"One Coke isn't going to keep me awake." A million other things might, but not the Coke. He picked up the glasses and turned around. "Wow. This is . . . wow."

Anissa had set up two trifold boards covered in pictures.

On one a young woman smiled out from the middle panel. This was Carly. No doubt about it. From the other, an adorable little girl took center stage. Jillian. A photo of her with her family was in one corner. But around the main picture were a series of photos, much like those frames that have a place for each year's school picture leading up to high school graduation. The pictures weren't real. But . . . there was one . . . third from the last. It had a label. Sixteen. Which was how old Jillian would be today.

Now he understood Anissa's reaction.

He'd just seen that girl — in the flesh — in the Carrington Hospital PICU. And her name was not Jillian. It was Liz.

"Wow."

"That's three wows in twenty seconds." Anissa took the glass of water from him.

"How did you get these?"

Anissa gave him the same look she gave the divers on her team when they asked a stupid question.

"Oh. Sabrina." Had to be.

Sabrina's day job was professor of cyber-security and computer forensics at the local university. But her passion was seeing men, women, and children freed from modern-day slavery. As part of her efforts, she and a group of scary-smart computer nerds got together once a month and worked their magic. They cleaned up security footage, ran facial recognition software, and scoured the internet looking for victims of human trafficking — and their abductors. Their work had resulted in hundreds of found and free people.

"Yes, Sabrina." Anissa took a sip of her water. "I broke down and told them — her and Leigh — one night. All about Carly and Jillian. And you know how Sabrina is. She ran with it. Brought me these photos a few days later. She has her picture set up in one of the database things she uses. If she ever gets a hit on it, she'll let me know."

The doorbell rang.

"I'll get it."

"No." Gabe jumped to Anissa's side. "You've babysat me all day. The least I can do is get the pizza. You weren't even hungry."

She laughed. "Fine."

He went to the door.

"Hey, do you have any cash?" Anissa called after Gabe.

"I got it, Bell." Gabe's voice carried back to her. She set her glass on the table and studied the photos. Sabrina had run the software program with multiple photographs of Jillian. She'd generated three different options. Based on what they knew Jillian looked like at three years old and having images of her parents, Sabrina had been sure one of them would be right.

Anissa ran her finger over the middle photograph. She knew she hadn't imagined it. The young girl who everyone at the nurses station had called Liz could be the identical twin of the girl in this picture.

Or maybe, just maybe, she *was* the girl in this picture.

A thud in the living room forced her attention away from the pictures. "Gabe?"

No answer.

Anissa grabbed the gun she kept in the drawer by her stove and eased into the living room.

Blood. So much blood.

"Gabe!"

"Stay where you are." Gabe gasped out the words.

It took every bit of her training not to run to him. But the front door was open between them and she had no idea what was on the other side of it. She slid her phone from her pocket and called it in. "Officer requesting backup. One seventeen Blossom Street, Carrington. Officer down."

There was no way she was going to let him bleed to death while they waited for the cavalry to arrive. Anissa darted across the room until she was behind the door. She kicked it closed. Nothing happened. No shots rang out. There was a trail of blood from the door to where he lay on the floor. He must have dragged himself out of the direct line of sight. Anissa lay on her stomach and crawled to him.

"Told you. Stay." Gabe spit the words through gritted teeth.

"When have I ever listened to you?"

She rolled him from his side to his back. His shirt was soaked in blood. Above his heart. No. Not again.

"What happened?"

She didn't realize she'd spoken aloud until Gabe gasped out, "Knife."

Someone had been close enough to stab him? Right outside her door? She unbuttoned his shirt and pulled it to the side. There it was. A puncture wound. Pouring blood.

"Ouch."

"Stop whining." Not that he was, but she needed to keep him fighting and he never passed up a chance to get into a verbal sparring match with her.

She put her phone on speaker and continued talking to the dispatcher. "I need an ambulance. Now!"

"ETA is two minutes." The dispatcher's voice was ridiculously calm. Didn't that woman realize Gabe was bleeding out on the living room floor?

She pulled his shirt back over the wound and pressed down.

Gabe moaned a little. Blood oozed through her fingers. This wasn't working.

She looked around. She needed something . . . a silk scarf draped over the arm of a chair caught her eye. Yes! "Be right back.

157

Don't go anywhere."

"Not going anywhere without you." Gabe's words were slurred. Even though he had been stabbed, not shot, she didn't want to make herself an easy target. She stayed low and scrambled to the chair, grabbed the scarf, then crawled back to him. She folded the scarf into a small square. "This is going to hurt."

"Thanks for the warn— ow!"

She hated to hurt him. But even with her scant medical knowledge, she knew that the more blood that stayed on the inside, the better. This wasn't the first time she wished her own skill set included more than the basic first aid and life-preserving measures she'd learned on the job.

The scarf soaked through. Too fast.

She grabbed a throw pillow and pulled off the cover and pressed the fabric to Gabe's chest. "Stay with me, Gabe."

A sheen of sweat covered his face. She wanted to wipe it away, but she was afraid to stop applying pressure. Sweat he could survive. Blood loss? Not so much.

"Lord, we're in a mess here." She didn't mean to pray out loud, but once she started, she saw no reason to stop. "We need your help. We need the ambulance to arrive safely so we can get Gabe's bleeding stopped.

Either that, or we need you to stop the bleeding now. We know you can."

"Backup is on the scene. Ambulance is one minute out."

"One minute," she whispered. Her arms shook from exertion as she pressed down on his chest.

"Never saw him. I think it was a man. Or a tall woman. And it was fast. I'm not sure if he even saw me until he'd already swung the knife."

"Okay. We'll figure it out."

"Nis?" Gabe lifted his head.

"Yeah."

"Thanks."

"For what?"

Gabe's head sank back to the floor.

"No. No! Gabe! Stay with me. Gabe!"

A knock at the door interrupted her. "Investigator Bell? We have the perimeter secure. Can the ambulance —"

"Get them in here now!" She continued to hold pressure as if every drop of blood she could keep inside strengthened his chances of survival.

Which it probably did.

"Investigator Bell?" The door eased open. "I'm Clark. We've met before. Can we come in?"

"Yes," she said, the word more of a sob

than a statement.

Clark rushed to her side. "Okay. I've got this, ma'am."

He was joined by a young woman. "I'm Dorothy. Not sure if you remember me or not."

She did. Clark and Dorothy were a great team. They'd been there when Adam and Sabrina were blown up. And Sabrina's mom —

"Anissa!" This voice was more familiar. "Gabe!" Ryan knelt beside her. How had he gotten here so quickly? "What happened?"

"We have a stabbing to the upper chest," Clark said.

"Heart?" Ryan voiced the question she couldn't.

"No," Clark said. "Too high. But lots of bleeding. May have damage to some important arteries."

He and Dorothy murmured about low blood pressure and shock. They kept it all professional, but Anissa sensed their urgency as they worked. And after they got Gabe on the stretcher, they ran to the ambulance. "Wait!" Anissa tried to follow them, but Ryan grabbed her arm. She spun around to face him. "Let go of me." The words came out sharp and fast.

Ryan loosened his hold but didn't drop

160

his hand completely. She could have easily wrenched away, but he got right in front of her and leaned forward, his face level with hers. "We can't help him anymore, Anissa. You did everything you could for him. The EMTs can handle it from here, and Leigh's at work. She's waiting for him. She'll keep us informed. The best thing we can do to help him now is to figure out what happened." His words came slow. Steady. She'd heard Ryan use this voice before. Leigh called it his "calm the tiger" voice.

And it worked. He was right.

But why did it feel like her heart was racing away as the blaring sirens faded into the distance?

"Sorry. That was unprofessional of me."

Ryan gave her a look she didn't understand. She couldn't tell if he was exasperated or amused. "You don't always have to be professional when it comes to the people you care about."

"I . . ." She couldn't bring herself to say that he was wrong. She cared about Gabe. More than she should.

When had that happened?

He patted her on the shoulder. "It's going to be okay. I have a good feeling about it."

She didn't want to have this conversation now. Come to think of it, she didn't want to have this conversation with Ryan ever.

"But for now" — Ryan grimaced as he looked her over — "I'm going to need you to put on some gloves and go change clothes. I'm the investigator on call, so this whole bizarre situation is my problem. And everything you're wearing is evidence."

Anissa didn't think she would ever feel clean again. She stuffed her blood-stained clothes into an evidence bag and then grabbed a washcloth and attempted to scrub the blood — Gabe's blood — from her arms, face, and hands.

When she returned five minutes later, she found Ryan in her dining room staring at the pictures.

Great.

He looked up when she came in, one eyebrow raised. "You know I'm going to need an explanation for this."

So Leigh hadn't told him. She'd have to be sure to thank her for that. "It's a separate case."

"Not anymore."

If she'd been investigating this case, she would want to know too. You gather all the information possible and worry about the relevance later. "Do we need to talk about it now?"

"Later." Ryan tapped a pen on a legal pad. "I'd just like to know how Gabe got stabbed in your living room. And I think you should start from the beginning. As in, tell me everything you've done today."

She started with church, the phone call, the trip to the hospital, the nap, the second trip to the hospital, and the pizza order. "I thought the pizza was here. We were arguing about who was going to pay for it . . ."

Wait a minute.

"What is it?" Ryan looked up from his notes.

"Where's the pizza?"

"What? You can't be hungry."

She ignored the snide remark. "We ordered a pizza. We were in my car on the way home from the hospital and Gabe was still hungry even though he'd had a ginormous sub at the hospital. We were joking about it, but I went ahead and ordered a pizza. When the doorbell rang, we both assumed it was the delivery person. The timing was right. That's why he answered the door. But there's no pizza out there."

"They may have tried to deliver it after we got here. They would have been stopped at the perimeter." Ryan grabbed his radio. "Any of you guys stop a pizza delivery?"

No one had.

"Let me see your phone."

She handed it over. He tapped the screen a few times, then held the phone to his ear. "Hi. This is Investigator Ryan Parker with the Carrington County Sheriff's Office. Did you receive a pizza order to be delivered to 117 Blossom Street?" There was a pause. "Uh-huh. And when was that?" He listened again. "Was this a man or a woman?" Ryan made a note. "Okay. Thank you very much."

He handed the phone back to her. "Your pizza order was canceled."

"What? When?"

"Immediately after you called it in. They say they got a call about a minute after you ordered. The person, a male, said that you had asked him to call and cancel it."

He stopped, but Anissa had a feeling there was more. "What else did they say?"

Ryan tapped his pen on the notepad. "The caller told them that you'd been called to a murder investigation."

She sagged against the table. This had been premeditated? And someone was listening to her conversations? "What is going on?"

No!

How was this even possible? He'd lined it up just right. He'd been watching her for days. He knew exactly how to thrust the knife so it would pierce her neck. Cut the carotid.

She would have bled out before the ambulance arrived. It was a perfect plan. He hadn't even looked. When the door opened, he lunged.

And stabbed that other cop in the chest. Probably wouldn't even kill the guy.

Why did this always happen?

Anissa Bell was like a cat with nine lives. Although, by his count, she'd already used up four of them.

Sooner or later, she'd run out. But for now, he had to get out of there.

Not that anyone would suspect him.

He'd covered his tracks well.

9

Ryan had insisted on giving Anissa a ride to the hospital, which was gallant of him considering that he'd taken her car as evidence and handed it over to Forensics. If there was anything weird going on, Dante would find it.

Ryan eased to a stop in front of the emergency department entrance. "Go on in," he said. "I'll catch up."

Anissa didn't argue. She hopped out, almost forgetting to close the door behind her before running inside. She didn't have time to show her badge before the security guard waved her through. "Right this way, Investigator Bell. Leigh's waiting on you."

She kept it to a slow jog as she approached the nurses station. Before she got there, Leigh stepped out of a room to her left.

"Anissa." Leigh wrapped her arms around her and Anissa didn't even mind.

"Did you see him?" Anissa asked.

Leigh bit down on her lip. "I did. He was in shock from the blood loss. Low blood pressure. They took him straight to surgery. Dr. Price is the best. He's the vascular surgeon who worked on me. I'm sure he'll get the bleeding stopped and get him patched up."

"Okay."

"I was a little surprised you weren't in the ambulance," Leigh said.

"You can blame your husband for that." Anissa glared at Ryan as he approached.

"I won't apologize." Ryan put an arm around Leigh. "It was safer. If the attacker had been watching, he could have tried to wreck the ambulance. And you were safer at the house surrounded by cops."

Anissa stepped away from Leigh and Ryan. "Me? Why are you so worried about my safety? I'm not the one squirting blood everywhere."

"You can't be serious." Ryan shook his head in disbelief. "Think about it."

What was he seeing that she wasn't? Her car did have those flat tires last week. But there'd been no nails or slices.

Of course, there was a big difference between someone letting air out of your tires and someone stabbing you when you open your door for a pizza.

Although, when they — whoever they were — had messed with the tires, they could have also planted some kind of listening device. Which would have allowed them to know she'd ordered a pizza.

But . . .

"It's a flimsy theory," she said.

"What theory is that?" Ryan gave her a grim smile. They did this a lot in their office. Bouncing ideas. Sharing theories. Poking holes in the ridiculous ones before a criminal defense attorney had the chance to.

"You think I was the target." Anissa laced the words with more skepticism than she had intended.

"I do." Ryan spoke with conviction. "Something weird is happening and I think it's more likely that you were the target than Gabe. Until we figure out what's going on, you're going to need to be very careful. Starting with being unpredictable. No similar patterns, nothing routine."

"I already do that."

"Do it better."

"Fine."

"And for tonight" — Ryan looked around them — "I think you should stay here."

"Fine."

Leigh had stayed quiet during their exchange, but now she chimed in. "I'm shocked you agreed to that. I was going to offer our house. I know how much you hate being at the hospital."

"I'm not leaving until Gabe's awake anyway, so I might as well stay here until Ryan decides it's safe for me to go home."

"Excellent." Ryan kissed Leigh on the temple. "Keep me informed."

"Where are you going?" Leigh asked. Anissa already knew the answer.

"Back to Anissa's house. Forensics isn't done yet and we need to check for listening devices in her house."

"Okay. Be careful."

Ryan winked at Leigh. It had never been in question — they were perfect for each other. She fell for him and he fell for her and they made being a couple look easy.

Ryan pulled his keys from his pocket. "He'll be okay. You'll be okay. Be here for him when he wakes up. Then call me and give me an update."

"I will. And I want an update on my house. Anything you find."

He gave her the okay sign and walked down the hall.

Leigh gave Anissa a wobbly grin. "I know Gabe will be okay. He's in the best hands. But it will probably be another hour before he's out of surgery. I could get you set up in the lounge if you want to wait. We have the best coffee."

An idea was forming and Anissa ran with it. "I think I'll go up to the PICU and check on Brooke." It would keep her mind off Gabe. Keep her from sitting alone in a waiting room. And she might get another chance to see Liz.

"That's a great idea." Someone down the hall called Leigh's name and she started moving toward them. "I'll text you as soon as I hear anything. The OR nurses promised to keep me informed."

"Thanks."

When Leigh disappeared into a room, Anissa followed the signs to the elevators, then to the PICU waiting area. Paisley Wilson was there.

With a laptop.

Great.

Paisley looked up, then jumped to her feet. "Investigator Bell. How are you?"

"It's Anissa. I'm —" She'd almost said she was there waiting on Gabe to get out of surgery, but she caught the words before they could escape. "I'm fine. I was here for another reason but thought I'd come up to check on Brooke."

Paisley gave her what might have been a

smile but looked more like a grimace. "I know you don't trust me not to use this information, but I'm assuming since you're here that Investigator Chavez is still alive."

That was the problem with reporters. And this reporter in particular. You never could tell if they wanted to know something because they cared or if they wanted to use it in a story. Paisley might be the world's greatest actress, but right now she looked like a lonely girl who needed someone to cut her some slack. "Off the record, I would say your assumptions are accurate."

Paisley closed her eyes and blew out a breath as she sat back down. "Thank you. I'm not going to ask you for any details, but I'm glad he survived. I get all the breaking news alerts, and the stabbing is news. But no one's talking. I couldn't tell if he'd made it or not, and honestly, I can't take any more dying."

Anissa sat down across from her. "You and me both." They sat in somewhat companionable silence for at least a minute. Paisley didn't seem inclined to say anything further, so Anissa asked what she hoped was a safe question. "How's Brooke?"

Paisley ran her fingers along the edges of her laptop. "I didn't realize she was in such a dark place or that she was considering such a drastic step, so I don't guess I'm qualified to answer that question. I don't know how to help her. One minute she's sorry, begging me to forgive her, promising she won't do it again. The next minute she's sobbing about Jeremy and blaming herself for his death."

Anissa closed her eyes. *Lord? Really? Does it have to be Paisley? Now?* She knew the answer to her question. *Fine.*

She opened her eyes and found Paisley staring at her. "Can I ask you a question? I promise I'm not changing the subject."

Paisley looked a little confused but nodded.

"How do you know about Carly and Jillian?"

Paisley blew out a long breath. "I'm afraid if I tell you, you'll hate me. Well, more than you already do."

Anissa couldn't help the mirthless chuckle that escaped. "Paisley, how about if you and I agree to be completely honest with each other? I'll go ahead and tell you that if it weren't for your little sister, I wouldn't be sitting here talking to you. But I happen to be the kind of person who believes that God sometimes uses the horrible circumstances in our lives to bring us to a place we never imagined we could get to." Maybe even forgiveness, but she wasn't ready to say that out loud.

Paisley nodded. "Okay. While we're being honest, I should tell you that I truly believed I was doing the right thing that night. But I'd gotten some bad information and was being used by some dishonest people. I know that now. And I've spent the past several years trying to figure out what happened and exactly who was behind it all. I may never know. I have to live with that, and I understand if you don't believe me. But I never, ever wanted to be the kind of reporter the sheriff's office hates."

Anissa wasn't sure if she believed her, but she'd take her words at face value for now. "Fair enough."

Paisley glanced around the room, and Anissa followed her gaze. A couple sat in the far corner, both with headphones in their ears. A man rested in a recliner. Eyes closed. Snoring. No one was listening.

"I got a package. It was delivered to me at the news station. It had newspaper clippings and a CD that had video from news reports. All from thirteen years ago."

Anissa had expected Paisley to say she'd gone digging around in the pasts of different investigators until she found something juicy. Not that someone had delivered it to her on a silver platter. She asked the only question her scattered mind could come up with. "Why haven't you done anything with it?"

Paisley huffed. "I learned my lesson. Information like that? Mailed to the station? It's clear someone has a vendetta against you and they want to use me to help them. I'm not interested in being anyone's patsy ever again."

Anissa tried to consider Paisley's words without bias. It wasn't easy. "So, if you aren't interested in being used, why are you showing up at my crime scenes and at the courthouse when I'm in court? I've seen you a lot over the past few months."

"You noticed?" Paisley had the look of a kid who'd gotten caught snagging a cookie from the kitchen counter. But, to be fair, it wasn't the look of a kid who'd stolen a cookie from a bakery. "Yes. Sorry about that. I wanted to see you in action. I knew you'd never agree to an interview. And I understood why. I wanted to get a feel for who you are now. And . . ."

"And?" Anissa prompted.

"Honestly? I'm afraid for you. You're tough and strong and a great investigator. People respect you. Some of them are afraid of you." She hurried to add, "But only because you're really intense. Not because they think you're dangerous or anything."

Anissa didn't try to hold back the sarcasm. "Well, that's good to know."

Paisley didn't seem to notice. "But someone clearly has it out for you. Every report they sent me had a slant that was negative against you. But when I went digging, I found far more reports that were kind to you. They didn't send me those. They have an agenda, and while I have no idea what it is, I'm certain it isn't good for you."

Anissa's phone rang. She glanced at it. Leigh. "Excuse me for a moment."

She stood. "Yes?"

"They're wrapping up," Leigh said. "Surgery went well. He's stable. Should be in recovery in a few minutes. I've talked to Dr. Price and he'll let you be in the recovery room with Gabe as he's waking up."

"I'll be right down. Wait. Where do I need to go?"

Leigh gave her directions and Anissa disconnected the call. "Paisley, I'm sorry, but I need to go. Gabe's out of surgery. Can we talk later? I think I may be able to help you with Brooke. As you already know, I've been in her shoes."

"That would be great. Please give —" Paisley shook her head. "Never mind. I'll

175

see you later."

"What were you going to say?" Anissa had a feeling she knew.

Paisley gave her a rueful smile. "I was going to say to give Investigator Chavez my best wishes for a speedy recovery, but I'm guessing hearing my name isn't going to help with that, so you should probably skip it."

Anissa patted Paisley's arm. "You might be surprised. I'll be in touch."

Gabe had expected heaven to be more harmonious. All he heard were beeping noises, and it was not going to be cool if he had to listen to them for eternity.

He'd also expected there to be no pain in heaven.

But he hurt. So . . . this was not heaven.

He tried to force his eyes open, but they refused to cooperate.

The beeping got faster.

He pulled in a deep breath and with it came two competing scents. The first, the stronger, was antiseptic. A hospital or medical facility of some kind. The second was sweet with a hint of coconut.

Anissa.

He tried his eyes again, but they refused to move. He forced himself to replay the events of the day. Where had he been? How had he gotten here?

Was it still Sunday?

He was at Anissa's. They'd been talking about the child. Jillian. Pizza. He went to the door . . .

Knife!

The beeping got faster again.

Warm pressure on his arm. Then his hand. Fingers laced through his. The sweet scent overpowered the antiseptic. "Gabe. Relax. You're okay. But your heart rate is making the nurse nervous." Anissa's voice, soft, at his right ear.

Anissa was here. She was okay. Or at least more okay than he was. If he could get his blasted eyes open, then he could see for himself.

"Keep talking to him," a deep male voice said. "His heart rate and respirations settled when you were speaking. He can probably hear us, but the anesthesia has his muscles locked down."

"Gabe? You're okay."

First, that was clearly a lie, given that he was lying in a hospital and couldn't get his body to cooperate with simple commands. Second, who cared if he was okay or not? How was Anissa?

The beeping accelerated.

"Investigator Bell?" Deep Voice again. "Maybe you should tell him that *you're* okay?"

Yes. Listen to Deep Voice.

"Oh?" Anissa sounded surprised.

"He can't see you. And if you were with him at the time of the stabbing, he's probably worried about you."

He was going to owe Deep Voice a coffee.

"Gabe, I'm fine. The only blood on me was yours. Although you scared me half to death when you passed out." Now that she'd started talking, she was rambling and Anissa wasn't the rambling type. "Ryan got there fast. He came in right as the EMTs arrived. He heard it on the scanner and recognized my address. I think you scared him half to death too. Dorothy and Clark were the EMTs. They were awesome. We should probably send them chocolates or something. Anyway, I was going to ride with you to the hospital, but Ryan wouldn't let me. I was ticked. But he was all" — her voice lowered — " 'we can help Gabe better by staying here.' "

If that was her impression of Ryan's voice, it was truly awful. He would tell her that if he could get his mouth to work.

She kept going. "He brought me here and told me to stay in the hospital. He's back at

178

my house with Forensics."

She stopped talking. He wanted to tell her to keep going. Wanted to tell her Ryan had been right. He'd have to thank him later. He wanted to tell her she was in danger. But he couldn't. He couldn't even squeeze her hand. All he managed was to twitch his fingers. But that was enough to get her attention. She squeezed back. "Don't fight it, Gabe."

But he had to fight. The knife . . . yes. There had been a knife. A flash of silver. Searing pain. He couldn't move his arm. More pieces fell into place. But that knife hadn't been meant for him. He was sure of it. The beeping started going faster again.

"Keep talking, Investigator Bell." Deep Voice had a bit of urgency to his tone this time.

"So, while I was waiting on you to get out of surgery, I went upstairs to see if I could check on Brooke. Paisley was in the waiting room. We talked for a bit. I don't think I ever told you that she's been showing up at my crime scenes. Anyway, I asked her why. I kind of figured she had big plans for some big exposé about me or something. But —" Anissa's rambling cut off.

"Ah, how's our patient?" This voice Gabe knew. This was Dr. Sloan. The man had patched him up more than a few times during his undercover days.

"Bit agitated," Deep Voice said. "Calms down when Investigator Bell talks to him. She's doing a great job. Pretty sure he's awake enough to hear us, but the anesthesia has him pinned down."

Dr. Sloan chuckled. The nerve of that man. "Oh, you haven't seen agitated yet. Just wait until he gets his mouth moving. Investigator Chavez is fabulous at what he does. Not so fabulous as a patient."

Anissa laughed. Deep Voice laughed. Dr. Sloan laughed.

Traitors.

"Well, Dr. Price tells me everything went great in surgery. Gabe had lost a lot of blood. His blood pressure was dangerously low and he was in shock from the blood loss, but he's very lucky. I thought the knife had punctured the left subclavian artery when he came in, but it turns out it had caught one of the axillary veins. Dr. Price deployed a stent and the bleeding stopped. He's optimistic that there's no nerve damage. Not that it isn't going to hurt like nobody's business for a while."

"Okay." Anissa sounded like she was choked up about something.

"I understand you did a great job of applying pressure on the scene," Dr. Sloan said.

"I didn't know what else to do," she said. "There was a lot of blood."

"Yes. I imagine that there would have been. But you kept enough inside him."

Someone, Dr. Sloan maybe, patted Gabe's foot. "Gabe, I have to get back to work. It's clear you're being well cared for. If you need anything, let me know."

"I will," Anissa answered. Maybe Dr. Sloan had directed that last sentence to her?

Gabe tried to move again. This time his fingers cooperated enough to catch Anissa's fingers and press down. She responded with gentle pressure. "Hey," she whispered. "Don't stress, Gabe. Just go back to sleep. I'll be here when you wake up."

She was safe. He wasn't dead. There wasn't much else he could do. He relaxed. The beeping slowed.

"Hey, sleepyhead." Anissa's face filled his field of vision.

He blinked a few times. Yay. His eyelids worked. "Hey." His voice sounded strange. He tried to clear his throat, but everything was dry. Had they made him swallow gravel or something?

"Can I give him some ice chips?" Anissa

directed her question to someone behind him.

"Just a couple." Deep Voice. Excellent. Definitely going to get Deep Voice a coffee when this was over.

"Do you want an ice chip?" Anissa's face was scrunched. Tense.

"An ice chip?" Still with the gruff voice. He tried to clear his throat, but that turned out to be a bad idea. "The man said a couple. Don't be stingy."

Anissa smiled. A real smile as she spooned an ice chip — one — into his mouth. "Don't be greedy. I don't have anything to change into if you puke."

"No worries, ma'am," Deep Voice piped up. "If he pukes, I can get you some of these stylish green scrubs to wear."

Anissa acted like she was considering his offer. "Green's not really my color. Do you have anything in blue? Turquoise? Oh, maybe navy?"

"I think you could pull off any color just fine." What? Was Deep Voice flirting with Anissa?

Deep Voice stepped beside him. Gabe looked up. And then farther up. Well, this was great. Deep Voice was the kind of guy that girls liked. Tall. Perfect smile. Good hair. And he'd been hanging out with Anissa for the past how long? "What time is it?"

Anissa didn't even glance at her watch. "It's around three."

"A.m. or p.m.?"

"A.m.," she said. "You came out of surgery around eleven. They let me in here around midnight, but you didn't seem to want to wake up." She offered him another ice chip.

"Dr. Sloan was here," he said. Or mumbled.

"Yes. Did you hear him? We thought you were going to wake up then, but you never opened your eyes."

He nodded. "I heard you." He couldn't stop himself from scanning her face, her arms and hands, every part of her that he could see as she offered another ice chip. "You're okay?"

She bit her lip. "Yes."

"She's refused to leave your side in case you woke up," Deep Voice said. "We were a little worried about how long it was taking until she explained how hard you've been working and how little sleep you've had over the past week. Your surgeon, Dr. Price, figured your body was taking advantage of the situation and we let you sleep."

Anissa shot a quick glare at Deep Voice and then dropped her gaze to the floor.

Gabe reached for her hand. "Thank you."

She laced her fingers through his, but she didn't look up.

"So, what's the plan?"

"Oh, you get to spend a day or two enjoying the sweet comforts of one of Carrington's finest hospital rooms before they'll let you out of here. After that? I imagine you're smart enough to figure it out." Deep Voice looked from Gabe, to Anissa, then back to Gabe with a look that said, "And if you don't, then you're an idiot and I'll be happy to pick up the pieces."

Dr. Price entered before Gabe had a chance to respond. "Well, well, well. Look who decided to rejoin us." His gaze landed on their entwined hands. "Investigator Chavez, I'm assuming you don't mind that we allowed Investigator Bell to stay with you. We generally only allow next of kin, but both Ryan and Leigh Parker assured me you wouldn't mind. And frankly, I'm not sure it would have mattered. She would have been sitting in the hallway if we'd said no."

Gabe tried to catch Anissa's eye, but she was looking at Dr. Price. "This man was stabbed by a knife that was meant for me."

So this was gratitude? Nothing more? A sick feeling that had nothing to do with the anesthesia crept through Gabe's system. He tried to pull away, but she wouldn't let go.

"He was there for me when no one else understood what I was going through. He's my friend and one of the finest men I know. There was no way I was leaving him."

Whoa. Did she really think that?

Dr. Price smiled. "Well, give us a few minutes to make sure he's stable and we'll get him, and you as his self-appointed shadow, into a room. But you should know there's a bit of a crowd in the waiting area."

"What?" Gabe croaked.

"They've been praying since you came in. You may want to think about who you want to allow to visit because the nurses will need to know who to let through and who to turn away."

This was one of the biggest differences between his undercover days and now. Before, when he got hurt — cut, shot, punched — no one knew. No one was there.

The idea that people cared about him enough to be praying for him in a waiting room in the middle of the night, combined with the way Anissa had spoken about him and still had her fingers twisted up with his, left him speechless.

"Want me to run down to the waiting room and give them a quick update and send everyone home?" she asked.

He squeezed her hand. "Not really, but it might be a good idea."

Deep Voice spoke up. "I think that's a great plan. I'll be able to help Investigator Chavez with a few things that you probably don't need to be here for anyway. When you get back, we should be ready to roll to a room."

Anissa stood. "Any specific thing you want me to say?"

Gabe squeezed her hand. "Tell them thank you. Tell them whatever you want. I trust you."

10

"I trust you."

Anissa replayed Gabe's words as she made her way to the waiting area. How much more of a fool could she make out of herself? What was wrong with her? She could be his friend. Just his friend. Besides, someone was out to get her. If she let Gabe get too much closer, he could wind up dead. And it would be her fault. Again.

She opened the door and thirty expectant faces looked at her. She scanned the room. Could one of these faces be the person who'd stabbed Gabe? Her tension eased a fraction when she recognized several ladies from church, a few older gentlemen who were in Mr. Cook's Sunday school class, and a handful of regulars from the Pancake Hut. No one stood out as a threat. She directed her attention to Mr. Cook. "He's awake. Talking. Being a smart aleck. So, you know, back to normal."

Everyone in the room cheered.

Mr. Cook stood and, as was his way, launched straight into prayer. "Father, thank you for taking care of our friend Gabe. Thank you for the doctors and nurses who so skillfully tended to his injuries. We ask for quick healing and a quick nabbing of the fella who stabbed him."

A chorus of "amen" filled the room, but no one made a move to leave. "What's the prognosis, Anissa?"

Anissa couldn't tell who had asked the question, so she answered the entire group. "His prognosis is good. They plan to keep him a day or two, but he is expected to recover fully. They were worried about nerve damage, but they think he'll regain full mobility." She sounded like a hospital spokesperson. "He wants me to thank all of you for the prayers. He really appreciates it."

"What can we do for him?" Another voice she couldn't place. "Can we bring him anything? Maybe some meals?"

"He's not up for visitors and probably won't be while he's here. As for food, right now his diet consists of ice chips." Everyone laughed. "But I'm sure he wouldn't turn down a few meals once he's home."

"How best can we pray going forward?"

This one came from Mr. Cook.

She didn't hesitate. "For protection. For quick healing. For wisdom. Gabe has an open homicide investigation right now. Ryan Parker will be working to find out who stabbed Gabe. Half of our dive team has been sick with that nasty stomach bug that's going around, and now this will take Gabe out of the water for a while."

"We're on it, sweetheart." Mr. Cook gave her a peck on the cheek, then turned to the people gathered. "Folks, this has been a real sweet time of prayer, but I believe it's time we all head home and let these children get back to doing what they need to do."

He turned to her. "I'll get this crew out the door. You go on back to Gabe. When he's home and stable, you come see me. We'll talk."

"Yes, sir."

"I mean it, young lady. Don't you make me call your mama."

"I won't."

With a final squeeze of Mr. Cook's hand, she turned and half walked, half jogged back to the recovery rooms. When she reached Gabe, he was sitting up holding his own cup of ice chips. And if she wasn't mistaken, he'd brushed his hair. She paused in the doorway. Why was she hesitant now?

She knew.

It was easy to hover over him when he was passed out.

But she wasn't his girlfriend. She was barely even in the friend zone.

She glanced around. Gabe was alone. "Where's Ivan?"

"Who's Ivan?" Gabe spooned in another ice chip.

"Your nurse."

"Oh, I didn't catch his name." He spoke around the ice chip. "He'll be back."

Anissa still didn't move from the door.

"Is something wrong?" Gabe shifted in the bed.

"No."

"Then why are you standing over there?"

"I'm not sure." She took one step in, then stopped.

He stared at her. She stared back. There was no way she was wrong about the look he was giving her. It was the kind of look she'd seen on Ryan's face when he looked at Leigh. And Adam's face when he looked at Sabrina. But this wasn't something she was ready for. This wasn't something she would ever be ready for.

She took another step.

Gabe stretched out his hand, palm up, and waved his fingers. "It's not a marriage

190

proposal, Bell. Just a hand."

She took another step. It wasn't a large room. One more step and she'd be —

Gabe grimaced as he leaned toward her, hand still outstretched. He refused to break eye contact. "I promise you, I will climb out of this bed and come get you if you don't get over here."

He said it with a smile, but she knew he wasn't kidding. She took the next step and reached for his hand. As soon as her skin met his, he squeezed and pulled her all the way toward him. Her face was two inches from his. "Why are you afraid of me?" The whispered words hit a fault line in the shell she kept around her heart.

"I'm not afraid of you," she whispered back. "I'm afraid of me."

"Got you a room." Ivan's voice boomed through the small space. She jerked back, but Gabe kept a tight grip on her hand. Ivan had to know he'd interrupted something, but he carried on like he hadn't. "I had to pull some strings, but I got you the finest, police-protected private room on the seventh floor. It's a beaut. Corner room with lots of places for seating. Or sleeping." At this he let his gaze fall on Anissa and gave her a little wink. "I'm guessing you're the type who will be working the case from the hospital room. Am I right?"

"You are," Anissa said.

"Figured as much. Well, if you're ready?" He directed the question to Gabe, and Anissa pulled her fingers from Gabe's grasp. She needed to move out of the way so Ivan could disconnect all the things he needed to disconnect, but she also needed to get away so she could breathe. And think.

Two things she had somehow lost the ability to do when Gabe was touching her.

"We would normally have a transporter take you to your room, but you, sir, are getting the Ivan special. And an escort."

When they stepped into the hallway, they were immediately flanked by a hospital security guard and a Carrington Police officer. He looked familiar. Anissa extended her hand to the police officer. "Anissa Bell. I believe we've met before."

He took her hand. "Yes, ma'am. Although not under great circumstances. George Loftis. We, uh, we met at the mall."

A vise tightened over her heart.

"It was an honor to assist you that evening, ma'am."

She fought to swallow. "Thank you." What else could she say? She hadn't had a choice. She hadn't wanted to kill that man, but it was him or Sabrina.

Thankfully, George let it go at that and Ivan didn't ask for more information. Ivan had been a true gift. A calm spot in the storm that raged in her as she watched Gabe sleep. She would miss Ivan. Gabe would probably get a bunch of cute girly nurses for the rest of his stay, and that was going to be annoying.

She lagged behind the stretcher. What was she doing here? When had this happened — that everyone assumed she would be with Gabe? That she would want to be where he was?

"Bell?" Gabe's question pulled her from her thoughts.

"I'm right behind you. You make a wide load with your protection detail." She tried to keep her voice light.

When they entered the elevator, the only place she could fit was squeezed in the corner at the foot of Gabe's stretcher. She patted his foot and he smiled. It was a sleepy smile. Ivan had told her that even after Gabe woke up, he'd probably sleep most of the next twenty-four hours. The cocktail of fatigue, anesthesia, and pain medicine was a potent one.

"That's better." His eyelids drooped. He blinked several times.

"Don't fight it, Gabe. Just rest."

"When are you going to get some sleep?" His words were a bit slurred and she fought a smile.

"They've already made up a bed for Investigator Bell," Ivan said. "She'll be able to stretch out and close her eyes. Something she very much needs to do."

"And I'll be outside the door to be sure no one enters who isn't supposed to be there." George patted his weapon as he spoke.

"Keep her safe," Gabe said as his eyes closed.

The next time he woke up, it took Gabe a few seconds to figure out where he was. He tried to roll over, but the pain caught him. Maybe he would just look around. Moving his eyeballs didn't hurt. The room was dark but not pitch-black. Random dots of light from IVs and monitors cast their blue and green hues around the space.

He had a vague memory of this place. Of being rolled in. Of a nurse.

They'd made a bed for Anissa so she could stay.

But . . .

She was here. Sitting beside him. Her hand was still in his. Her face was hidden beneath a cascade of hair. He studied her for a long time. Flashes of their conversation, of her fear for him, of her refusal to leave him, of his inability to send her away, of his need to have her in sight — all of it crashed through his thoughts.

Dios, por favor, what am I going to do?

He'd known for years he wasn't the kind of guy who would get married and settle down. He needed to stop this mess and return the two of them back to their dysfunctional normal. The place where she rolled her eyes at him and he annoyed her.

She sat up. Slowly.

"Hey." His voice still wasn't right. What had they done to him?

"Are you okay? Want me to get the nurse?" She whispered the words as she stood.

"No. No nurse."

"Ice chips?"

"Nis."

"What?"

"Go back to sleep."

"I'm fine. If you'll tell me what you need, I'll get it. I'm not good at this nursing stuff. Leigh's so much better at it. It's like she can read people's minds and she knows what they need. I'm not like that. I'm pretty hopeless. I should see if Leigh could sit with you."

He knew how much Anissa hated hospitals, but he'd never realized they could drive her to be so irrational. He reached for her hand and pulled her closer to the bed. "Nis."

"What?"

"Thank you for staying with me. I wouldn't want Leigh to be here."

"You wouldn't?"

"No. Why are you so hard on yourself? You're doing great."

"I have no idea what I'm doing." She waved a hand around the room.

"So what?"

"So, I don't like feeling so —"

"Out of control?"

"Something like that."

That he could understand. Anissa was so terrifyingly good at her job, so confident on a dive, he could see where being in an unfamiliar — and in her case, much-disliked — environment could bring up all kinds of hidden insecurities. "How about this? I promise to tell you if I need something. Or want something. And you promise not to stress about the fact that you can't read my mind and don't have a medical degree. Deal?"

She let out a long sigh. "Deal."

"Great. Now, what I want you to do is go lie down on that little bed they made you and get some sleep."

She dropped her head. "I tried."

"Is it like sleeping on the floor?"

"No. It's fine. It was very kind of them to set it up. But I think I'll wait until I get home to sleep."

His brain was much clearer than it had been earlier in the night and he didn't miss the subtle hesitations, the word choices that told him Anissa was holding something back. "What happened when you tried to sleep?"

She wouldn't look at him. "Just bad dreams. It's fine. Really."

"What did you dream?"

In the dim light, he could see her head shake back and forth. "Tell me."

A little hiccup. Was she crying? She pulled her hand away and wiped her face. She *was* crying. She walked away.

"Hey, come back here."

She shook her head again. "Just give me a minute."

He gave her to the count of twenty. "Nis?"

"I couldn't get the bleeding stopped and —"

"And?"

"You died. Every time I closed my eyes, you died."

There was a soft tap on the door and a nurse bustled in. He was going to have to go home to get some rest. He was going to have to go home to be able to finish a conversation.

"I'll step out." Anissa disappeared before he could stop her.

"How's your pain, Mr. Chavez?" the nurse asked.

"It's fine."

Anissa stuck her head through the door. "He's lying. He was moaning in his sleep, and he's not moving to keep from hurting too much. He needs something, even if it makes him sleep."

Then she disappeared.

Why, that little —

The nurse laughed. "She's got your number, doesn't she?"

Yeah. Apparently she did.

Gabe slept most of Monday. Whenever he woke up, Anissa was there. Sometimes asleep. Usually awake. But they didn't talk about anything other than how he was feeling and his pain levels. There was a little laughter when they brought him a tray with broth and tea and a little bowl of yellow gelatin. As soon as the kind woman who'd delivered the food left the room, he handed the gelatin to Anissa and she tossed it in the trash.

Leigh came by. So did Ryan. Adam and Sabrina stopped in around suppertime with soup and sandwiches from one of their favorite shops.

No one questioned Anissa's presence. Or wondered why Ryan wasn't staying with him instead. At least not in front of him, anyway.

He and Anissa didn't discuss it further. He had no idea what was going on between them. He was pretty sure she didn't either. But until he wasn't addled by pain meds, he couldn't do much about it.

After the evening shift change, the nurse came in. "Time for a walk."

"A what?"

"You heard me, sunshine. Time for those tootsies to hit the floor. We've had a crazy-busy day. I think the entire county has this nasty stomach stuff. And in all the chaos, your sleepy self slid under the radar of your day nurse. But you are a bright blip on mine. If you want to go home, you're going to have to get a move on — and I mean that literally."

Anissa smothered a grin but not before he caught it. Apparently so did Nurse Ratched. "Oh, you can go ahead and laugh, girlie. You're his chauffeur. Let's do this, people."

Anissa closed her laptop and Nurse

Ratched, whose name tag indicated that her real name was Lois, disconnected Gabe from the IV and helped him sit and then stand. She put his arm through Anissa's and pointed them toward the door. "Now, you take it real slow and see if you can get to the end of the hall. Then back here."

"Yes, ma'am." Anissa's arm through his felt warm and strong. He didn't want to lean on her, but a few steps out the door, he did.

"I've got you, Chavez," she said. "Just keep putting one foot in front of the other and tell me if we need to slow down."

Chavez. So she was back to calling him by his last name. Back to normal. Whatever that was. They were going to pretend all those weird conversations and tense moments hadn't happened? Wasn't that what he'd wanted?

They didn't talk as they passed one door and then the next. Gabe would be eternally grateful to Deep Voice for helping him get into a pair of shorts while Anissa was out of the room. At least he didn't have to worry about flashing her and the entire seventh floor as he walked.

"Last night," he said, and the energy between them changed. It was subtle, but she was on edge. "You said something about going to see Paisley and Brooke." And just like that, the tension eased. Interesting.

"When you aren't spaced out on drugs, we need to talk about it," she said.

"Who said I'm spaced out?"

"Oh, believe me."

"What's that supposed to mean?"

"You've been muttering in Spanish. You even sang once. I think you may have proposed to the janitor, but it was in Spanish, and a bit slurred. I didn't catch all of it."

"This is why I hate narcotics." Gabe sensed a rant building and he didn't even care. "I'm done. You hear me? D-O-N-E. Done. I'm going to ibuprofen when we get back."

Anissa snickered.

He stopped walking and turned to face her. "You're messing with me?"

She doubled over in laughter. "Sorry," she said. "I didn't expect you to believe me."

"You're joking about my proposing to the janitor while I'm hopped up on narcotics?"

Anissa was laughing so hard now she was wiping away tears. Her laughter was fascinating. She'd never — not once — messed with him like this. He didn't even know she had it in her. "I can't believe you did that. That's something *I* would do."

"I know!" She laughed even harder. "Sorry."

In his most overdone offended voice, he said, "I don't know what's come over you. It's like I don't even know who you are anymore."

Anissa snorted. She actually snorted.

Then Nurse Ratched appeared. "You two are supposed to be walking."

"Yes, ma'am." Anissa was still laughing as she tucked Gabe's arm back in hers. "You heard the lady. March."

11

They lapped the unit three times before Anissa convinced Gabe to return to his room. And even though he knew she'd been teasing him, it turned out he hadn't been joking about the pain meds.

"I'm done," he told Lois as she helped him settle into the recliner in the room.

"You'll be uncomfortable," she said. "You just had surgery. You were stabbed. It's not a sign of weakness to get some relief."

"I don't care. I'm done."

Lois turned to Anissa. "Can you talk any sense into him?"

Anissa didn't disagree with her, but she didn't see much chance of Gabe changing his mind. "If it gets bad enough, maybe he'll reconsider."

The nurse huffed her way out of the room.

Anissa handed Gabe the remote. "Pretty sure there's a baseball game on if you want to watch it."

He took the remote from her and placed it on his lap. "I want to talk about Paisley."

"Can we wait until tomorrow?"

"Nis. Please. I've been stabbed. Poked by every nurse who walks in the door. Jabbed by needles. Forced to consume wretched food. The least you can do is give me something to think about other than the pain." He ended his rant by batting his eyes at her. "Please."

She couldn't stop herself from laughing.

"See? You feel better already. You'll feel much better after you tell me something about Paisley." He leaned his head back against the chair. "Lay it on me."

Would she feel better? Guess it was time to find out. "First, I need to tell you that Paisley sends her best wishes for your speedy recovery."

Gabe's head popped off the back of the chair. "Really?"

"Yes."

"Wait. When did you talk to her?"

Anissa started at the beginning. She told him about going to see Brooke. Talking to Paisley. And everything Paisley had told her. Gabe didn't interrupt, but his expression grew darker with every new detail.

"Earlier today, I sent her a message and told her I was still here and asked if she'd be willing to let me see the information she'd been given. She emailed all of it to me."

"And?"

"Factually, the reports she was sent are accurate. But all of them are from this one reporter who had grown up in the church and then left the faith and is now an atheist. He was . . . well, it doesn't matter. You can read it later. The point is, whoever gave her this information assumed she would run with it. That she'd do a little checking, discover it was true, and plaster it all over the local news."

"But she didn't."

"No. But . . ."

"What?"

Anissa paced the room. "Why? Why now? I mean, it's all public record. The sheriff and the captain know all about it. Mr. Cook knows. It's obviously not something I'm proud of or share freely, but anyone could get all the details . . . or most of them, anyway . . . if they wanted to. So why do it now?"

Gabe didn't give her a pat answer or common platitudes, and she appreciated that. After a few moments he asked, "What about the girl upstairs and the connection to Jillian? Have you had any luck finding out more about her?"

"No. Not yet." She stared out the window looking out over a lovely view of the next building's roof.

"I'm surprised you didn't go to the pediatric floor and hunt her down."

She knew Gabe was teasing. And it wasn't that she hadn't thought about it. But even when he'd been sound asleep, she hadn't been able to bring herself to leave the room. "Maybe tomorrow."

A soft knock on the door interrupted their conversation. Leigh's head came through the door first. "Mind if we come in?"

"Like we could stop you," Gabe said.

Leigh burst through the door and went straight to Gabe. "Gabe! You're awake. And in a chair. Fabulous. Don't get up," she said in mock seriousness.

"If you insist."

Leigh was followed by Sabrina, then Ryan, and Adam brought up the rear carrying a cooler. "We heard they were starving you, bro," Ryan said as he and Adam opened the cooler and handed out boxes. "Leigh felt it was important to uphold tradition, so we made a run to the Pancake Hut."

"Grits and scrambled eggs for you," Leigh said as she handed Gabe a box. She handed the next one to Anissa. "If you tell me you aren't hungry, I will force these pancakes down your throat. Eat. That is an order."

"Look out, Leigh," Gabe said. "Your mother hen is showing."

Everyone laughed. Even Leigh. After they did a bit of rearranging, the large corner room was big enough for the six of them to sit. Once everyone was settled, all eyes fell on Anissa.

She pulled in a deep breath. "Let's pray." It took her a few seconds before she could find the first word. As she tried to quiet her heart before God, Gabe's hand slid into her left hand. Then Leigh grabbed her right. She glanced up and realized they'd all joined hands and a peace settled over her. "Father, you know our hearts. You know our fears and our desires and our failings. You know our weaknesses and our weariness. Your Word says that your strength is made perfect in our weakness. That when our flesh fails, you will never fail. So we ask that you will give us the strength to trust in your faithfulness to us. Give us the hope that you are working all things for the good and for your glory. Thank you for loving us. For the food and friendship we share. May we glorify you in all things. We love you, Jesus. You're the best. Amen."

Five murmured "amens" were followed

by the sound of take-out boxes opening and plastic utensils being pulled from their wrappings.

Gabe squeezed her hand — one quick pump before he released her.

"Thank you for this, Leigh," he said. "But I need to go on record that I think we should set up a system of some kind. Like one stab wound equals three dozen cookies. Two stab wounds —"

"Two?" Sabrina laughed. "How about if you ask Leigh to bake you cookies without requiring any perforations to get them?"

"Well, your way might be easier," Gabe said.

"Yeah. I should think." Sabrina took a bite of her eggs. "It's not like Leigh needs an excuse anyway."

"True," Leigh said.

They enjoyed the food, chatting and laughing until everyone had finished. When Anissa reached for Gabe's empty plate to throw it in the trash, he grabbed her arm. "Don't you think you should tell the others?"

She had been wondering if she should. But now?

She'd given Leigh and Sabrina permission to tell Ryan and Adam her whole story, so she knew they were up to speed on that.

But she hated to be a Debbie Downer and suck the life out of the party.

But Ryan needed to know as he investigated the shooting.

Before she could start, Leigh brought the festivities to a screeching halt. "I have something I need to share with y'all," she said. "Not like we don't have enough craziness to deal with, but we have a serious public health issue in Carrington."

Sabrina, Ryan, and Adam all nodded, so they must have already known what Leigh was talking about. Anissa looked at Gabe and he raised his shoulders and shook his head. So he was as confused as she was. Anissa turned to Leigh. "What have we missed?"

"Funny you should ask, because I'm curious about that myself." Leigh wagged her eyebrows at the two of them. "But that will have to wait, because what I have to say will affect all of us starting, well, now. The news will break tonight. We've had twenty kids from Camp Blackstone in the ED this weekend. We've finally gotten tests back and they are positive for cryptosporidium."

"Ugh." Sabrina groaned.

"So, I'm guessing that's bad?" Gabe asked.

"Very. That lovely stomach bug everyone's been getting? Not your standard stomach bug. Highly contagious and can take weeks to recover from."

"We were out at the camp a couple of weeks ago doing a diving demo," Adam said.

"Yes, and then we got sick a week later and it was probably crypto." Ryan pointed his fork at Anissa. "You should be glad you had to be in court that day or you would've been in the same boat as the rest of us."

"The state's environmental folks have been out taking samples and trying to find the source of contamination. They think it's something specific to the camp, but they're also testing Lake Porter and the municipal water. Crypto is highly resistant to chlorine, so the standard disinfection methods they have at the camp aren't enough." Leigh threw up her hands in frustration. "These kids are so sick. And if the environmental folks can't find it and contain it, they'll have to shut down the camp. They've already stopped water activities and are boiling all the water."

"Poor kids." Anissa couldn't help but feel sorry for them. Who wanted to be away at summer camp and not be able to go swimming?

"Yeah, and we need to pray there's no contamination in the lake. The water treatment plant has the right kind of setup to

210

remove it before it enters the drinking supply, but they have been asked to double-check to be sure every system is working correctly. But if they find it in Lake Porter, it would be a tourism disaster. They could have to close the lake to swimming and skiing."

Anissa tried to imagine Lake Porter closed for business. It wasn't just inconvenient. It was potentially life-altering. Carrington and Carrington businesses and Carrington jobs all relied on Lake Porter. Without it . . . Anissa didn't even want to think about the consequences.

"We're still waiting on test results for some of the kids, but all the tests that have come back so far have been crypto. No deaths yet, thank goodness. For most people, crypto presents as a bad stomach bug or food poisoning. It's unpleasant" — Ryan, Adam, and Sabrina all confirmed that with vigorous nods — "but not life-threatening. The problem comes when it gets into a water supply and affects our immunocompromised populations. The very young, the very old, anyone who is currently on chemotherapy, is HIV-positive, or has had an organ transplant and is taking antirejection medications. All are at risk. It can and will kill people."

Leigh took a deep breath and kept going. "We have three patients in the hospital now with confirmed crypto who fall under those categories. An elderly grandma, a thirty-three-year-old man with testicular cancer, and a sixteen-year-old girl who had a kidney transplant a few years ago and was at Camp Blackstone for the summer. When all three tested positive for crypto, doctors tried to determine if they had anything in common. All of them had been at the camp. The young girl had been there as a camper. The young man with cancer is an IT specialist. He had been at the camp to fix a computer issue. And the grandma had been there to visit her grandson, who had a stomach bug, which was probably crypto."

"When did they come in?" Gabe asked.

"Last week. I saw the young girl when she came in through the ED. Precious thing. Her mom is in China or something and still hasn't made it back to the States. She seems to be on her way to a full recovery. She got out of the PICU a day or two ago and is on the regular pediatric floor now. The grandma and the young man are both in ICU. Now that we know it's crypto, the number of kids we are seeing in the ED from the camp who are dehydrated makes a lot more sense. We didn't need to admit any of them, but it's clearly getting worse over there, not better."

Anissa's thoughts were on the girl from camp with parents in China. She'd been that girl. She was that girl. If anything happened to her, it would easily take her family days to get to her.

Ryan pointed at her. "By the way, you can't go home either."

His remark yanked her thoughts back to the here and now. "Why not?"

Ryan shrugged. "Crime scene. I haven't released it yet."

"Well, you can just get on with releasing it. I live there, Ryan Parker. And in case you've forgotten, I happen to be a homicide investigator and there's nothing in my house that can be considered evidence besides some bloodstained furniture."

Ryan's only visible reaction to her outburst was a smirk. "Were you planning to go home tonight, Investigator Bell?"

"I . . ." She couldn't finish the thought. The truth was that Gabe was off pain meds and stable and had a police officer at his door. She didn't, technically, need to be here.

But she didn't want to leave. And she didn't want to think that through right now either.

Leigh shoved her shoulder against Ryan's. "Be nice." She turned to Anissa. "Investigator Parker" — she said the name with so much sass the others laughed — "allowed me access to your crime scene of a home today and I brought you a change of clothes and toiletries and everything. You'll have what you need regardless of whether you stay here or come back to our place."

"Thanks." She could feel Gabe's eyes on her and refused to look in his direction.

What was she going to do?

Gabe loved this crazy group, but right now he wanted them all to leave. "Anissa, why don't you fill them in on the Paisley Wilson situation." The sooner she did, the sooner he could make them get out of his room.

Anissa recounted the story, again.

"So someone sent it to her specifically?" Sabrina asked when Anissa finished.

"Yes."

"All digital files?" Sabrina pressed.

"Some newspaper clippings, some digital. Why?"

"Can you get her to give you the originals, not the copies?" Sabrina answered with a question, which wasn't really an answer, but Gabe had a hunch he knew where she was going with this line of inquiry.

Anissa must have understood as well because she answered with a question of her own. "Do you think you might be able to figure out where the information came from?"

"Possibly." From anyone other than Sabrina, that answer wouldn't have been encouraging. But coming from Sabrina, possibly was like saying yes. Though Sabrina didn't like to say yes until her confidence level was at 110 percent.

"I don't know if she'll give it to me or not," Anissa said, "but I don't mind asking. She said they were moving Brooke to the regular pediatric floor today, so she should be easy enough to find tomorrow."

Sabrina had a look on her face that Gabe recognized. She was on the hunt. When she got the scent of something she could track down, it was beautiful to behold.

"What are you thinking, Bri?" Adam asked.

She gave a little shrug. "Sometimes people leave things behind. Fingerprints. DNA. Digital fingerprints are good too. I might be able to figure out the source if I have the original materials."

"Might?" Gabe couldn't help but scoff. "You'll probably have their entire life story for us by breakfast."

Sabrina flushed and leaned against Adam. Everyone else laughed. Even Anissa.

Ryan was the one who got serious first. He gave Gabe a long look. Gabe wasn't quite sure what Ryan was trying to communicate, but he paid close attention as Ryan spoke. "In light of this information, I do think Anissa should stay here tonight."

Ah. Ryan must have been trying to get a feel for whether Gabe wanted Anissa around. Gabe almost said yes, but he caught himself. This was Anissa's decision to make. Not his. Although if she stayed tonight, they might have to have that conversation he'd been putting off.

"Agreed," Anissa said. "As long as I can get a shower and a change of clothes, and as long as you get Forensics out of my house."

"Deal." Ryan stuck out his hand and she shook it.

The party broke up as everyone, except for Gabe, stood. They tossed trash, scooted chairs back to their original positions, and gathered purses and phones.

"Anissa," Leigh said. "If you want to come with me, I can get you into the staff locker room for a shower. I've got your bag down in the ED."

"Oh, um . . ." Anissa had a deer-in-the-

216

headlights look.

"I'll stay with him," Ryan said.

She visibly relaxed with Ryan's offer. "Okay." Anissa followed the crew out.

As soon as the door closed behind them, Ryan turned to him. "So?"

"So what? You just gonna stand there while I attempt to get out of this chair?"

"No. I'm going to stand here until you tell me when you figured out how you feel about Anissa."

"I don't know what you're talking about."

Ryan crossed his arms. "I don't see what your problem is. What the hesitation is. She's a catch. And you somehow have managed to crack that impervious shell she lives in. She even laughs at your jokes now."

"Everyone laughs at my jokes."

"Not everyone has put their life on hold while you've been in here. Not everyone has refused to leave your side."

"I got stabbed. She thinks it was meant for her. She's grateful. That's it."

"I was buying it until that last bit," Ryan said. "I'm sure she's grateful. But Anissa's pragmatic. If she were thinking clearly, she'd have been in the office today. Which she wasn't."

"She was working from here."

"Yeah. And it was fine. But it wasn't like

her. And I want to know why."

"Why do you care?"

Ryan fixed a withering glare on Gabe. "You happen to be one of my best friends. I think you and Anissa could be a great couple and I'd love to see you happy. But I also think you could explode and the fallout would hurt a lot of people whom we both love."

Gabe leaned back against the chair. "I'm trying to figure out how to get out of it without it blowing up. I'm going to talk to her tonight."

"Why would you try to get out of it?"

"I'm not marriage material."

"You've said that before. But why do you think that? You have a real job. You're a responsible person. You love the Lord. If you aren't marriage material, then who is? So your childhood was a mess. That doesn't mean your adulthood is. You need to get over that. It's an excuse. Not a reason."

"Anissa deserves better."

"Is that what she thinks or what you think?"

"It's what I know. She misses her family. She misses Yap. She's only staying here because of Carly's case. When it's solved —"

"Whoa. Hold up." Ryan put one hand in

218

the air like he was stopping traffic. "She may have stayed because of Carly's case, but that's not why she's here now. She has a lot of other reasons to be here. And you're one of them."

"She can barely tolerate me."

A soft knock on the door ended their conversation. A custodian entered and asked if he could clean the room. Ryan and Gabe watched TV while he swept, emptied the trash, and spent a few minutes in the small restroom. When he left, a nurse came in to check vitals. She'd been gone only a minute when an aide stopped in to see if he had a dinner tray that needed to be removed.

When she left, Gabe couldn't stop himself from grumbling. "I don't know how anyone gets better in a hospital. People are constantly coming in and out. Drives me crazy." There was yet another tap on the door. "See what I mean?"

Ryan went to the door and cracked it open. He turned back to Gabe. "I don't think you'll mind this intrusion."

Anissa entered, followed by Leigh. "We brought you a Coke," Anissa said as she put the can on the bedside tray. "This way we won't have to sweet-talk the nurse when you decide you need one at midnight."

She turned to put her bag down and Ryan mouthed, "Can't tolerate you?"

"Shut it," Gabe said under his breath.

Leigh came straight to Gabe's chair. "Let's help Gabe get settled before we go."

By settled, Leigh meant ready for bed. She was in full nurse mode, and he'd brushed his teeth, put on fresh shorts, and been tucked back into bed before he knew it.

Ryan and Anissa had stayed back in the corner while Leigh did her thing. Probably wise on their part. He could hear them murmuring, but he couldn't catch any of their conversation.

"You ready to go, babe?" Ryan said to Leigh. "I'll walk you down."

"If you need anything tonight, text me. I'll be downstairs. I'm not officially on the schedule until eleven tonight, but my guess is they'll need me earlier," Leigh said as she gave Gabe a gentle hug on his uninjured side, then turned to Anissa. "If he gets obnoxious, let me know. You can come hang out with me."

"Thank you." Anissa returned Leigh's hug.

Ryan and Leigh walked to the door.

"Now that he's awake, I may have to take you up on it." Anissa's stage whisper carried to him with no trouble.

"Hey! I heard that." Gabe tried to toss a pillow at her as the door closed behind them, but the motion sent pain radiating through his chest and the pillow barely made it to the side of the bed.

"Watch it, Chavez. I'll get Lois in here if you won't take it easy."

"You don't scare me, Bell. You'd better sleep with one eye open."

She laughed.

He laughed.

And then they were staring at each other again. Anissa was the first one to break the tension. "You must be exhausted."

"I've slept most of the day."

"That probably just got you past the sleep deficit you were in."

He wasn't tired, but she had to be dead on her feet. Maybe if he pretended he was ready for bed, she would go to bed. "You're probably right," he said. "I can crash whenever you're ready."

"I'm not the one with stitches," she said. "You decide."

"Well, let's call it a night, then."

"Sounds good."

Ten minutes later, Anissa's breathing had found a steady rhythm as she settled into a deep sleep. Gabe stared at her slumbering form. She was on her side, with her back to

221

him, and in the darkness all he could see was the outline her body made.

It was the last thing he saw before his own eyes closed.

12

The buzzing woke her.

Where was she?

Anissa blinked a few times. Her phone buzzed again. She'd fallen asleep with it in her hand. The screen glowed and Ryan Parker's name shone in the night.

"What?" It was the best she could manage.

"There's been a bomb threat at the hospital."

"What?" She was fully awake and on her feet.

"What's going on?" Gabe asked from across the room. Anissa didn't answer, but she did put her phone on speaker so he could hear.

"Have they ordered evacuations?"

"Not yet. Still assessing. Leigh called me. I'll keep you informed. Can you hear the codes they call out in the hospital?"

"I can if I'm awake. Which I am now," she said.

"Okay. Code Green is the bomb threat. Someone will probably be in your room soon to look around. If they find something suspicious, they may go to a Code Red and evacuate. Or they may wait until the bomb unit knows what they are dealing with. Here's the thing though. The bomb threat was specific to your floor. And that makes me wonder —"

"If someone's trying to smoke us out." Anissa finished his thought.

"Exactly." Ryan confirmed her suspicion. "It's entirely possible that there's nothing at all dangerous and they just wanted to force you to leave."

"Or there's a bomb about to go off and blow us to bits." Anissa appreciated Ryan's obvious attempt at minimizing the risk, but she didn't feel the need to sugarcoat the situation.

"Yes, there is that. Just don't leave the hospital. If they evacuate, then go down to the ground floor but don't leave the building. Not until we have a better idea of what's going on."

"Got it."

"I'll be in touch." With that, Ryan disconnected the call.

"We have to figure out who you ticked off." Gabe raised the head of the bed so he was sitting up.

Anissa couldn't stop herself from snorting. "In case you haven't noticed, I've ticked off a lot of people. The list is going to be long."

"You're intense. That's not the kind of thing that creates enemies who want to kill you."

Anissa wasn't buying it. "Please."

Anissa's phone buzzed in her hand again. Paisley? At 4:30 a.m.? "Anissa Bell."

"Oh, thank goodness. There's been a bomb threat made to the floor Investigator Chavez is on." Paisley sounded frantic.

"We know." The words were clipped. Not out of frustration at Paisley for calling, but out of general frustration.

"Oh. Sorry for bothering you."

Anissa could almost hear the air deflating out of Paisley's balloon. "Thank you for calling to tell me. That was very kind."

"Oh, you're welcome. Are you in the hospital?"

Anissa considered her answer. She wanted to believe Paisley had changed. But . . . what if she hadn't? What if the story Paisley had told her was a lie? What if it was all a ruse to get into their good graces while she planned to . . . what? Have them killed? That was a drastic move. Even for Paisley Wilson.

"Gabe will probably be released later today. I stayed . . ." She ran out of words. She wasn't about to tell any reporter that there was a possibility someone was out to kill her, and she also wasn't sure why she'd stayed to begin with. "Listen, since I have you on the phone, I need to ask you something. Would you mind letting me have the original files about me that were sent to you?"

"Why?" Paisley drew out the word.

"Are you familiar with Dr. Sabrina Fleming?"

"I don't believe so."

"She's a professor at the university — computer forensics and cybersecurity."

"Oh," Paisley said, "you want to see if she can figure out where they came from by, well, doing whatever it is she does?"

"Pretty much." Anissa appreciated that Paisley didn't try to pretend she had a clue what Sabrina did.

"I'm sure I can get them for you. It's all in my desk at work. I have copies of everything, so I'm happy to share it."

"Great. When will you be back at work?"

"My grandma is coming this morning, so

I can run over to the station for a few hours — assuming they let her in with the bomb threat going on. I'm planning to be back by ten a.m."

"Excellent. Maybe Gabe and I could pay Brooke a short visit around eleven?"

"Perfect."

Anissa almost disconnected the call, but she stopped herself. "Paisley?"

"Yes?"

"If we hear anything further about the bomb, I'll let you know."

"Thank you. Same here."

Anissa disconnected the call and went back to staring at the door.

"Well, aren't you two chummy." Gabe's observation dripped with sarcasm, and maybe a little bit of hurt.

"My instincts are still warning me about her. I'm analyzing every word she says and every word I say to her." Anissa turned so she could see Gabe's face. "But her little sister is here. If my little sister was here . . ."

Gabe ran his right hand through his hair. "You're right. I'm being petty."

"I'd say you're allowed."

"Why? Because I got stabbed?" Gabe pointed to his left shoulder. "That excuse will only go so far."

"Not because you were stabbed. Because

she betrayed you. That's a fact. And not one you can — or should — ignore. It's not easy to trust someone who's let you down. Or thought the worst of you."

Gabe didn't respond.

"I'm still not sure if I want to believe her or smack her. I think it's a bit of both," Anissa went on. "I want to believe her because I want to believe people can change. I want to believe that one mistake doesn't define them forever. I need to believe that."

What had gotten into her? Why was she compelled to drop her deepest fears and ugliest truths right into his lap? Was she trying to push him away? Give him reasons to hate her so he would reject her and she wouldn't have to deal with the roiling emotions she didn't want but couldn't stop?

She'd been pushing him away since . . . well . . . since that first dive. She'd never met anyone like him. She knew his type. So confident. So sure. So . . . dangerous to her heart. He showed up and the training exercise became a party. He had everything she didn't. Charisma. Charm. He took the last dive of the day, waiting until everyone else went, even though he had to have been itching to get in — or under — the water.

She tried to hide it, but she was thrilled to get to dive with him and she wasn't disappointed. He was the best kind of dive partner. Attentive, calm. For all his antics in the boat — the jokes and carefree manner — he was all business on the dive.

She respected that.

She never forgot it.

She should explain. She owed him that much. Especially given the way he'd been there for her. And got stabbed for her. And now he might get blown up because of her. "Gabe, when I kicked you off the team —"

"It doesn't matter."

"You need to know. It wasn't because I didn't trust you. It wasn't because I didn't think you were a great diver. It wasn't even because I thought you were bad for the team. But . . . I couldn't have lived with myself if anything had happened to you. You were diving what? Once, twice a year? It wasn't enough. I couldn't risk being responsible for someone else's death."

"Anissa —"

"I know I should have explained then, but it was just awkward. Not like this isn't awkward." She was rambling again.

"You think too much." His teasing but gentle reproach caught her off guard. He should be angry with her. She deserved it.

Why did he insist on being such a gentleman?

A knock on the door. Not soft. Not gentle. Purposeful. She was relieved to have a reason to turn away from Gabe. "Investigator Bell, these people want to come in and inspect the room for explosives." It was the officer who'd been outside the door. "Can I let them in?"

"One person. And you come too." She waved the officer in. They flipped on the overhead lights as they entered. She stepped back until the bed hit the back of her legs. She didn't try to hide the weapon now in her hand. She angled her body so no one entering had a direct line to Gabe.

The bed shifted behind her. Then a warm hand at her waist. A low chuckle. A quiet breath at her ear. "Slide over so I can see."

Anissa wouldn't budge.

"Scoot." Gabe whispered the word right at Anissa's ear. When she didn't move, he shifted his hand and squeezed her waist. Not hard. More a flex of his fingers.

She jumped but settled back against the bed a mere three inches from where she'd been.

That was interesting. "Are you ticklish, Investigator Bell?"

No response.

"If you don't move, I'll tickle you again."

230

A low sound came from Anissa's throat. "Did you just growl at me?"

Anissa shifted another inch. "It wasn't a growl, it was a . . . um —"

"A growl." Gabe had to bite down on his cheek to keep from laughing.

"I am trying to concentrate." Anissa enunciated each word.

"Sorry." He wasn't though.

The officer and hospital security guard moved through the room efficiently and then with a low "Sorry to bother you," they left the room.

"Well, that was fun," Gabe said.

Anissa whirled around. "Fun? That was not fun. What if one of them had tried something? Did you think about that? You wouldn't hold up well in a fight right now. And I only have one gun." She slid the gun into the waist of her pants. "A gun I was trying to keep between them and you, and you tickling me didn't help." She poked him in the chest, eyes flashing with fury, and maybe fear. He had never seen anything more beautiful in all his life.

He caught her hand in his and raised it to his lips. *"Gracias."* He kissed her fingers once more and released her hand. Her eyes, which had shot bolts of frustration moments earlier, filled with a new, no less terrifying emotion.

Hope.

She blinked, and the window to her heart shuttered. *"De nada."* She stepped away from the bed and flipped off the overhead lights. "You should try to get some sleep."

"That's not going to happen. But you go ahead."

"Not likely." He could almost hear her eyes rolling in her head.

"Then turn the lights back on."

"It's five thirty a.m. What else are we going to do?"

Anything that would keep him from spilling his guts. From begging her to consider throwing her life away and spending it with a guy like him. "If we weren't in our current condition, I would say we could go for a run. That's what I'm usually doing at this time of day. What about you?"

"I go to the gym."

"Well, that's not going to work. We need a Plan B."

"Technically we're on Plan C. Sleep was Plan A. Exercise Plan B."

She was fighting a smile. He could see it flirting with the edges of her lips. "Fine, Plan C. We could talk about the case."

She scowled.

"Fine. Plan D. Tell me about Yap."

"I've told you about Yap before. How about Plan E? You tell me how you wound up in Carrington. I know you were born in Florida. I know you still have some family there. But I don't think I've ever heard what brought you to North Carolina."

"It's a boring story."

She didn't offer a Plan F.

"Fine. Plan E it is. I was running away from something. Looking for possible job openings pretty much anywhere on the East Coast. I thought about Texas and the Gulf Coast states — better diving. But Carrington seemed nice. And the sheriff's office was specifically looking for Spanish-speaking officers. I got a bonus for being bilingual." He winked at her.

She studied the floor. "What were you running from?"

He could blow off the question. Change the subject. Run away. Again.

Or . . .

"Forget it," she said. "It's none of my business." She turned to the window, her back to him.

Another tap on the door. "Investigator Bell? They're dropping the Code Green. Nothing was found."

"Thank you." Her tone was brisk. Formal. Official. She picked up the pillow she'd been using.

The door closed. He could let the whole thing drop . . . "I had to get out of there."

She didn't turn her body, but her head tilted to the side. He knew that look. That was her "I'm listening and thinking about what you're saying" look.

"My dad took off when I was a kid. My mom worked three jobs to keep food on the table and clothes — at least shorts and T-shirts — on three kids. She tried. I know she did her best. But she was always dating. Always trying to find the guy who would solve all our problems. Not that any of them ever did. They'd show up, take her to dinner — sometimes they'd even take us — and then three months or three years later, they were gone. So, I had plenty of male role models. All of them brilliant examples of how to screw up kids and mistreat women."

He had her attention now. She'd turned halfway around and he could see it in the set of her shoulders. The way her hands strangled the pillow. He could even hear her swallow — hard — in the silence of the dimly lit room.

"I was the youngest. The only boy. My sisters doted on me. Tried to protect me from the worst things. But somewhere along the way, I learned the best way to survive was to make a joke out of everything. Keep people laughing and keep things light and you don't have to think about the hard stuff. So that's what I became. The class clown. The crazy kid. The one who could make the meanest guy laugh and leave me alone. Or more importantly, leave my mom or my sisters alone."

Anissa turned and sat on the edge of the little bench seat. She hugged the pillow in front of her.

"Anyway, despite it all, Mom eventually picked the wrongest of wrong guys. He put her in the hospital. And we wound up in foster care. Foster care for teenagers is — tough. My oldest sister got pregnant at seventeen. She had an abortion, aged out of the system fast, and followed in our mom's footsteps. She died at twenty-three."

"And your other sister?"

He could hear the hesitation in Anissa's question.

"Group home. No one wanted us at first. She ran away before I was placed. I've never been able to find her, not that I didn't try. Still try. Sabrina keeps an eye out for me." He barked a mirthless laugh. "I guess Sabrina knows all our dirt, doesn't she? She's amazing at keeping secrets, that's for sure."

"Yeah." Anissa rocked back and forth on the bench.

He could hear her inhale and exhale, slow, like she was trying to keep herself under control. "Anyway, a few weeks after she bolted, this family shows up. Takes me home. I couldn't believe it. Older couple. Their kids were all in college and they even had a few grandchildren at that point. They claimed they didn't like having an empty nest. I didn't really believe them, but I wasn't going to argue. I was a fourteen-year-old boy in the system. Families that wanted kids like me didn't come along often."

He couldn't stop the smile that spread across his face as he thought of them. "They were nice. Their house was clean. I called them Papa and Mama. Papa was Asian. Short, black hair, killer laugh. Mama was Scandinavian. Tall, blonde, the kindest blue eyes I'd ever seen. She looked like a queen to me. They had two biological kids and four adopted kids. All different ethnicities. My brown skin and accented English fit right in to the mix."

He closed his eyes. He could picture the house. His room. The smell of tacos and chocolate chip cookies that Mama had fixed for dinner that first night. That was probably why he loved Leigh's chocolate chip cookies so much. He would forever associate them with home and family.

"I owe them for — everything. I came to Christ while I was living there. They got me tutors to help me get back on grade level. Sent me to community college for a couple of years — and I lived with them during that time. They asked me if I wanted my own place, but I told them I was making up for lost time having a real home. And they were fine with that. They couldn't adopt me. Legal stuff prevented it. But I knew I was one of the family. And I wasn't the only one. They brought in another teenage boy when I was sixteen. Then another when I was nineteen. They had a real heart for the kids who still stood a chance if someone would just give it to them."

"What happened?" Anissa asked.

"I had transferred to the university. It was my senior year. I'd moved out, had a job, was living in an apartment, keeping up my grades, keeping my nose clean. And Papa died. Brain aneurysm. Totally out of the blue. The man was the specimen of health when he died. About six months later, a group of kids broke into the house. Stole everything of value. Beat up Mama. It was awful. The buddies of the last foster kid Mama and Papa had taken into their home were the ones who did it."

"Oh no."

"Yeah. His name was Mikey and he hadn't made a clean break from his old buddies. I tried to tell him to walk away from it all, but he wouldn't listen. Kept hanging out with the old gang from time to time. They got wind of the fact that Papa was gone. That there was some money, a little jewelry, and they decided it was an easy score. It would have been, but Mikey, well, Mikey testified against them. They went to jail, but not before the gang got their vengeance on Mikey. Mama wasn't able to go to his funeral, but the rest of us did."

Gabe tried to adjust his position on the bed. His entire chest and arm ached.

"Are you okay?" Anissa was by his side.

"Yeah. Just achy. No big deal."

"Right." Anissa's sarcasm game was solid, but she softened her tone as she continued. "I still don't understand why you felt like you had to run."

"The gang," he said. "The ones who had avoided prosecution were furious. They put up pictures of all the kids and Mama all over the community. Threatened revenge. After what they'd done to Mama and to Mikey, we were advised by the authorities to take the threat seriously. Two of my brothers already lived elsewhere. I was graduating, so it made sense to move along. The rest of my siblings scattered too. Mama lives with my sister in California now."

"That seems reasonable," Anissa said. "And not like running away so much as doing the smart thing."

"I should have been there," he said. "I should have seen it coming and stopped it. I knew Mikey had been in with a bad gang, but I missed the signs. I failed him. I failed Mama, Papa, and my entire family. They'd given me everything and I couldn't stop it. And now we're scattered all over the world and this amazing thing that these two incredible people did is just gone. We should all get together for cookouts and pool parties and Mother's Day, but we don't. I send her a card." He looked away from Anissa. "A stupid card. And I call her on her birthday. She's in her nineties now, and I haven't seen her in three years. Which is another way I've failed. I've never been able to figure out how to do family. Papa knew. Mama knew. But I don't. I don't know how to make it work."

He struggled to pull in a deep breath. The effort shot arrows of pain through his torso. Why had he decided now was a good time to tell Anissa this stuff? Now, when he was

239

stuck in a blasted bed and couldn't get away from the soft look on her face, the tears glistening on her lashes, the hand that now clung to his.

"That's why I wanted to work with gangs. Why I risked everything going undercover. I don't need a therapist to explain it. I don't have a pathological need to experience danger or anything. I'm just trying, always, to make up for my messes. Trying to do enough to be worth the sacrifice they made. To make a difference that will somehow make it all worthwhile."

13

How had she ever thought he was shallow? Anissa squeezed Gabe's hand. *Lord, what do I say to this? How do I help him?*

"Gabe —"

A knock on the door interrupted her. She wasn't sorry. She still didn't know what to say. She stood and rested her hands behind her back in what she hoped looked like a casual stance.

Gabe flashed a smile at the young woman who entered with a tray of food.

"I have breakfast for you, sir," she said with a bright smile. "I think it's eggs and a biscuit. And coffee."

"Is it fit to eat?" Gabe shot a playful glare at the girl and she giggled.

"Probably not, but it won't kill you."

Gabe snorted. "You'd like to think that, wouldn't you?"

The girl giggled again. "Have a good day, sir. Ma'am." She exited and Gabe shoved the tray away. "I cannot eat that. It's Leigh's fault. I used to be able to eat anything. Food was fuel. Didn't have to taste good. But now? I want fancy omelets and real coffee and fresh fruit for breakfast."

"Or biscuits and sausage gravy," Anissa said.

"Yes. Or cinnamon rolls."

"Mmm." Leigh's homemade cinnamon rolls were what would happen if someone took poetry and turned it into food.

Gabe got a glint in his eye. "Ryan's going to get fat."

Their eyes met and they laughed.

"Want me to go downstairs and get you a real coffee?" Anissa asked.

"No," Gabe said.

Had he meant to say that out loud? He had a look on his face like maybe he hadn't.

Anissa didn't know what to say or where to go or what to do with her hands. She walked over to the window and stared at the top of a nearby building. *Help me out, Lord.* She waited. So often she was guilty of praying and then not giving God a chance to answer her. She watched a bird land on the edge of the roof and then stroll along like it was no big deal to walk around six stories high. What would it be like to be unafraid of falling?

She had no idea. Because she knew one thing for sure. She was falling for Gabe.

And she was terrified.

It had been a long night.

He'd left the backpack. Called in the bomb threat.

Waited. She would come outside in a stream of people, all fleeing the bomb that wasn't there. In the chaos, he would finally have a shot at her. A nice up-close-and-personal shot.

But she never came. No one ever came.

He saw the bomb squad pull up. Saw them leave.

But no mass exodus of patients and scrub-clad nurses and staff.

He waited until the sun came up before he accepted that it wasn't going to happen.

What was it going to take to get to her? Maybe it was time to change his strategy.

If he couldn't get to her, maybe it was time to make her come to him.

There was no chance to revisit the conversation from the early morning hours. Gabe's room had turned into Grand Central as soon as the sun was up. Leigh had taken pity on them and brought them chicken biscuits and sweet tea. Dr. Sloan had come

243

by. Then the captain.

That visit had been a bit awkward at first, but if the captain wondered why two of his homicide investigators were spending so much time together, he didn't mention it. He stayed five minutes, told them both to be careful, and excused himself when a nurse came in.

Between the visitors, the texts, and the phone calls, Anissa didn't have time to worry about bombs or knives or even cryptosporidium outbreaks. When her phone rang, again, she held it out to Gabe. "Do you think anyone would notice if I threw this out the window?"

He frowned at his own phone. "If you find a way to open that window, I'll give you mine and you can chuck them both."

"Deal."

When 11:00 a.m. rolled around, Anissa was ecstatic to have something specific to do. "I need to go see Paisley," she said.

Gabe clasped his hands together. "Take me with you. Please. I will go crazy if one more nurse, or technician, or janitor, or pretty much anyone else comes in here. It wouldn't be wise to leave me alone. I was stabbed. I'm probably unstable. I might snap."

His mock seriousness made her laugh.

"You want to go see Paisley? You really are desperate."

"Exactly. And I am. I cannot stand another second in this room."

Another knock on the door. For real? Anissa's distaste for hospitals was roaring back. How could anyone ever get better in a place like this?

But this time it was Gabe's nurse. They hadn't seen her in almost three hours. Her shoulders were slumped and her eyes had a frustrated glaze. "I'm so sorry. I promise I'm a good nurse, and I'm sorry you're not getting more attention from me. But I know you're here" — she nodded at Anissa — "and I'm trusting you to let me know if there's an emergency. We're covered up with patients. They keep moving all kinds of people to the floor who don't belong here, but we've got to put them somewhere. This stomach bug business is nasty. If you want my advice, as soon as Dr. Price comes to see you this afternoon, beg him to let you out."

"When do you think we'll see Dr. Price?" Anissa asked.

"He usually makes rounds after two."

"Would it be okay for us to take a little excursion as long as we're back by one?" Gabe smiled at the nurse. Anissa recognized that smile. That was his "I'm adorable and you're going to let me do whatever I want" smile.

The nurse glanced at the IV dripping antibiotics into Gabe's veins. "What kind of excursion?"

"We have a young friend on the pediatric floor. We thought we might pay her a visit."

The nurse fixed her gaze on Anissa. "A friend?"

"Yes." Anissa knew the moment the nurse caved.

"Fine. Just to Pediatrics. No wandering around anywhere else. Straight there. Straight back."

Gabe raised three fingers. "Scout's honor."

The nurse laughed as she disconnected all the IV tubing and adjusted the sling around Gabe's left arm. "If you pass out, don't blame me."

"I wouldn't dream of it."

The nurse turned to Anissa. "Let me know when he's safely back."

"I will."

Walk slowly. Anissa imagined she was at a wedding. She took a quick look at Gabe. Wait. No. Wrong image. Not a wedding. A graduation. That was better. She stole another glance. He was hanging in there.

His breathing was even. No sweat beaded on his face. He was fine. Still, she would have preferred him to take this trip in a wheelchair rather than on his own two feet, but that had been a losing battle from the moment she first mentioned it.

They reached the pediatric wing of the hospital, all shiny and new and a bit over-the-top in its attempt at cheeriness. At least in Anissa's mind. But then, she'd been in this hospital for over twenty-four hours now without going outside. She'd survived but not thrived. But she had laughed. More than once. And that was significant progress.

They rounded the corner and she skidded to a stop. It was her. Right there. The girl. Liz? Or Jillian? It couldn't be. But . . . maybe?

She tried to lean against the wall and act like she hadn't stopped for no reason. She was certain she hadn't succeeded, but Gabe pulled it off with ease.

"Anissa." He spoke in a light, conversational, almost playful tone. "Would you care to let me know why you decided to pause here? There's a waiting room thirty feet away."

She didn't answer. Instead, she risked another look at the girl. The girl was leaning against the nurses station, laughing.

Eyes clear. Skin pale, but not as pale as it had been two — had it only been two? — days ago. She was drinking from a bottle of water, and Anissa wanted nothing more in that moment than to get that bottle and send it off for prints and DNA.

Gabe removed his arm from hers, cleared his throat . . . and went straight to the nurses station. What was he doing?

"Hello, ladies, oh, and gentleman." He tipped an imaginary hat. "How is everyone this lovely morning?" Murmured responses floated back to Anissa, where she stood as if stuck to the wall with superglue. She forced herself away from the wall and approached the nurses station.

He turned to Liz/Jillian. "I see you're rocking the same designer threads I am. We really must speak to the management. This is so embarrassing." He tsked in mock horror. "I was assured no one else would be wearing the same dress, and look at you. Although I must say, you'll win the 'who wore it better contest' for sure." Gabe's accent had crept back into his speech, the way it did when he was flirting, or showing off, or . . . well, being Gabe.

Liz/Jillian laughed. So did everyone else within hearing distance.

Gabe extended his hand. "Gabe Chavez."

"Liz Brown."

"Pleasure to meet you." He dipped his head and flashed a smile so radiant Anissa caught her breath from ten feet away. If Gabe wasn't careful, Liz/Jillian would have a crush on him by the time he said goodbye.

"Likewise." Her skin had a decidedly pink glow to it.

Anissa could see it on the girl's face. The way she smiled. She was already smitten.

Get in line, girlfriend.

Paisley stepped out of a door at the end of the hall, a large bag slung over her shoulder. She smiled when she saw Gabe. Or was she smiling at Liz? "Investigator Chavez, I see you've met the ray of sunshine here on the third floor. She's probably well enough to go home, but no one wants to lose their daily dose of Liz."

"Investigator?" Liz asked with eyes wide and intense. If she had any fear of Gabe as an investigator, she hid it well. "What kind of investigator?"

Gabe shrugged off her question. "Oh, all sorts of things. Earlier today I was called on to investigate the disappearance of a dozen chocolate donuts. I knew immediately that they had been absconded with by none other than my friend here." He pointed to Anissa. "But since she's also an investigator, she had covered her tracks well."

Anissa looked from Liz to Paisley and gave them her best "what are you gonna do?" look. "Do I look like a donut thief to you?"

Liz laughed. Paisley smiled.

"It's always the innocent-looking ones." The dramatic sigh that accompanied Gabe's pronouncement had Liz laughing even harder.

Anissa bit back a gasp. When Liz/Jillian laughed . . . she'd heard that laugh before.

But it couldn't be.

Could it?

And if it was possible. If this precious child standing here who looked like a grown-up Jillian, and who laughed like Jillian's mother, if Liz really was Jillian . . . what would that mean for all of them?

"I'm Liz," the girl said, hand outstretched.

Anissa took her hand. "Anissa Bell." She couldn't quite bring herself to say "nice to meet you."

She had a strange feeling that she already had.

Gabe leaned against the nurses station. That walk had probably been a mistake, but there was no way he was going to ride in a wheelchair.

He eyed the water bottle young Liz was

playing with. He wanted that water bottle in the worst way. But how could he get it?

Paisley flashed that TV smile of hers at Liz. "Liz, love. Is there any chance I could presume upon your kindness once more and get you to watch *Parent Trap* with Brooke for a few minutes while I talk to the investigators?"

"Oh, are you working on a news story, Ms. Paisley? How exciting!" Liz oozed energy and joy. Gabe didn't dare look at Anissa in this moment. If she was right, if this child was the missing Jillian from thirteen years ago, what would this do to her? To the family who had raised her to be this delightful young woman? To the parents who, he had no doubt, had never stopped loving and praying for her to be safe and someday returned to them?

No one could win in this situation.

If Liz was Jillian, they were bound to reunite her with her parents and prosecute whoever had taken her from them. But the cost would be high.

For everyone.

Liz, still smiling, moved in the direction of Brooke's room. And took her water bottle with her. *Lord, it would be awesome if she tossed that thing in the trash can in Brooke's room. Just saying.*

"You know, *Parent Trap* is one of my favorites," Liz said. "You're doing me a favor."

Everyone watched Liz as she walked down the short hallway and said, "Hey, Brooke, your sister said you were watching *Parent Trap.* Mind if I join you?"

Paisley exchanged a knowing look with the nursing staff. One that set off all of Gabe's internal warning sensors.

"What's the deal with Liz?" Anissa asked the question. She must have seen the look too.

The nurses shook their heads. "We can't talk about it. Patient confidentiality." An older lady, June, nodded at Paisley. "But she can."

"Yes, I can," Paisley said. "But not here. I don't want to risk her overhearing."

"If y'all need to talk, there's a conference room you can use," June said. "The doctors use it when they need to talk to the parents." She pointed to her left. "Five doors down. It should be unlocked."

"Thank you, June." Paisley smiled at June in a way that was warm and appeared to be authentic. Maybe she wasn't as awful as he'd always assumed she was. Maybe.

The trio made their way to the conference room. Gabe waited until they were in the

252

room to speak. "The nurses look exhausted."

"They are," Paisley said. "Every room is in use. Kids with horrible stomach issues. Several of them from the same camp Liz was at. Several of them don't have parents here yet, which makes it more complicated for everyone." She paused. "I'm glad Brooke is out of the PICU, but I need to get her home and away from this mess. And I don't think Liz should be on this floor either. I heard one of the nurses saying they were asking the doctors if they could get her out of here. Not because they don't want her, but because they're afraid she'll get sick again. And another round of crypto could do serious damage to her."

"What's the story on Liz?" Gabe attempted to ask the question in the most nonchalant way possible. He didn't even make eye contact with Paisley, but instead pulled out a chair for Anissa before walking around the table to sit across from her and Paisley.

When Paisley didn't answer right away, he risked looking straight at her. She was sitting now, staring at the table and taking slow, deep breaths through her nose. Was she trying not to cry?

"I'm sorry," she said as the tears spilled

253

over. "It's just . . . it's awful."

Anissa, typical Anissa, grabbed a tissue and handed it to Paisley with one hand while she put her arm around her. "Tell us what's going on," she said.

Paisley dabbed at her eyes, pinched her lips together, and straightened her shoulders. With a little shake of her head, she pulled herself back together. "Her mother is sick . . . really sick . . . and Liz doesn't know."

Gabe sat down hard, too hard, in his chair. Pain radiated through his chest and a small grunt escaped. That earned him a concerned frown from Anissa, but he waved it off. Who cared about a little residual stabbing discomfort when that radiant young woman down the hall was facing more turmoil than she could possibly imagine?

Anissa was the first one to recover from the shock of Paisley's pronouncement. "How do you know?"

Paisley reached into her bag and pulled out an iPad Pro and a large file folder. She placed the iPad on the table and handed the file folder to Anissa. "First, this is everything that was sent to me about your case. This outer file is mine, but the one inside is the folder it was in when it was sent to me. Obviously, my fingerprints are all over it. Probably the mail clerk's as well. But I haven't shown it to anyone, so anything else you find should be a clue worth following up on."

"Thank you," Anissa murmured. "Somehow this seems unimportant at the moment."

Paisley gave her a wan smile. "I don't think you should ignore it, Investigator Bell. Your life may depend on you finding out what's going on. But I do appreciate the sentiment. Liz's situation is truly heartwrenching."

She tapped a few buttons on her iPad and turned it so first Anissa, then Gabe, could see it. "This is Liz's mom. Her name is Velma Brown." The woman smiling back at him in the photo didn't look like a criminal. But then, not everyone who was guilty of kidnapping did.

Paisley swiped the screen and the image changed. "She was married to a guy named Bernie Brown."

Bernie looked like he was capable of anything. He had a predatory look that Gabe had come to recognize over the years.

Paisley continued. "They divorced ten years ago when Liz was six. This was during the time when Liz had gone into kidney failure and was on the waiting list for a kidney. Dialysis three times a week, in and out of hospitals. It was a bad time."

Anissa pointed to the tablet. "How do you know all this?"

Paisley shrugged. "It's my job. I know you hate what I do, but I investigate people too. Although I'm not constrained by the same legal issues you are, and I don't have to be sure my information can stand up in any court other than the court of public opinion." She took back the tablet and swiped and tapped for a few seconds. When she turned it back around, it was a YouTube video. "I found this. I'll send you the link if you want. It's a video that a church in Columbia made. The church Liz and Velma attend. It was made five years ago, and in it Velma talks about how the church was there for them during that difficult time when Liz was getting her transplant. From this, I was able to do some searching and find the divorce decree, and create a bit of a timeline."

"Why are you doing this?" Gabe couldn't decide if Paisley was brilliant or demented.

"At first I was just trying to help," she said. "Liz told me her mother was on a mission trip in China and that no one had been able to reach her. I thought I might be able to use some of my media contacts to help hunt her down. But then I found her in a rehab hospital in South Carolina. She's recovering from surgery. It's bad. Her adoptive father split years ago and I can't find him, or any other relatives. I told the nurses this morning and asked them what would happen if no one comes to get Liz. They said she'll be put in foster care. Or a group home or something."

"How much time does Velma have?" Anissa grabbed another tissue and handed it to Paisley.

"I don't know. The only way I know any of this is that I took a chance and called the house — they still have a home phone, if you can believe it — and the person who answered told me where she was. I think it was someone from the church who was cleaning or something. It sounded like a bunch of people were there. And obviously I can't ask Liz. I mean, I've been trying. I've learned a lot. I know she was adopted because she mentioned it when she was telling me about her kidney transplant, about how she didn't have any family history so she had no way to know if there was someone out there who would've been a good match."

Gabe hoped Paisley hadn't noticed the way Anissa stiffened when she'd mentioned adoption. So many things about this were falling into place.

He was starting to believe it.

Liz Brown was Jillian Davidson.

14

Anissa's mind was spinning in a million directions. She kept her hands tucked under the table so Paisley wouldn't see how much she was trembling.

"But why isn't Velma letting Liz know what's going on?" Gabe steepled his fingers, which were not shaking at all. "Wouldn't she want Liz to be with her?"

Paisley threw her hands out. "I know, right? That's what I would want. I keep thinking there's some piece of this puzzle that I'm missing that would help me make sense of it."

There was a missing piece all right, but there was a zero percent chance of Anissa sharing it with Paisley.

"I'm sorry." Paisley muttered something to herself that Anissa didn't catch. "I know you have enough on your plates. I'm going to keep digging. I have a friend at a station in Columbia who's agreed to try to find out more about what's going on, but I'm not sure if it will happen soon enough for Liz. They can send her back to camp when she's discharged, but given the issues they are having with the water there, I'm not at all sure that it's a good idea and —"

"Paisley." Gabe held up a hand. "We get it. And we asked. Remember? We're concerned about Liz. And the same friend who is going to take a look at that file on Anissa is an absolute whiz at this kind of stuff. We'll ask her to see what she can uncover about the Browns."

"Thank you." Paisley rubbed circles on her temples. "Between Brooke and Liz . . . I'm not cut out to be the mother of teenagers."

They all stood and slid the chairs back underneath the table. "How is Brooke?" Anissa asked.

As much as she wanted to figure out this situation with Liz/Jillian, she didn't want to lose sight of the hurting soul down the hall.

Paisley twisted the handles of her bag. "Physically? Fine. No permanent damage. Which is great, of course. But emotionally? Mentally? I don't know. I can't tell if she's okay — or moving toward okay — or if she's humoring me and planning something worse when we get home. I can't keep her under lock and key without getting arrested."

Gabe acted like he was considering her comment. "I don't know. We might let you slide under the circumstances."

His remark cut through the tension — he was so good at knowing what to say and when to say it — and they all chuckled.

"Seriously, though, we're praying for her." Gabe held the door open for them. "Is she going back to swim practice soon?"

"She says she wants to go tomorrow. Which, of course, is ridiculous. Her coach says to get her back in the water ASAP. But I'm afraid she'll bolt."

Anissa debated about what to say. She wanted to offer to help. But if someone was targeting her, then having a kid around could be disastrous. She didn't want to risk being responsible for another death.

Paisley lowered her voice. "I've already talked to the doctor. He says no swim practice until next week. She doesn't know that yet, so I'd appreciate it if you wouldn't mention it."

Whew. Maybe by Monday she could offer to swim with Brooke.

She just needed to figure out who had stabbed Gabe, what the deal was with Liz, and who had shot Jeremy . . . so, Monday

261

might be a bit of a stretch. *Lord, we need some help and a lot of it.*

They followed Paisley to Brooke's room. The door was open and the girls were laughing. Brooke's laughter gave her hope. Liz's laughter broke her heart. That sweet girl's world was already disintegrating. She just didn't know it yet. When the dust cleared, would she be able to laugh again? *Jesus, please let it be.*

"Have y'all ever seen this movie?" Brooke pointed to the screen. "It's fabulous. How did I not know these movies existed?"

Gabe stroked his chin and studied the screen. "You mean to tell me you've never seen the original *Parent Trap*? This is a classic."

As Gabe continued to chat with the girls, Anissa scanned the room. The trash can by the door was almost full. Sitting right on top — a water bottle. Was it the same one Liz had been playing with before? She couldn't be sure. Worst-case scenario, she could have the forensics team come to this room and brush for prints. The chair Liz was in probably had a few good sets on the arms. For that matter, they could brush Liz's room.

But —

A nagging worry shot down that idea. If

Liz was Jillian, she had no idea. She hadn't lived a life of fear. It was clear she knew about her adoption and had lived a full life. No one had been keeping her in a cage. Her parents had sent her to school. Even sent her to camp alone. Those weren't the actions of people who had kidnapped a child.

But if her parents had nothing to do with her kidnapping, the person or persons responsible might be keeping tabs on them. It was a long shot. More likely the kidnapper had pocketed whatever money they got for Jillian and never looked back. Still . . . Anissa wasn't in the mood to take any chances — or disrupt this young girl's life — if it wasn't absolutely necessary. If they could get that water bottle, or something with her prints on it, they would be able to know by the end of the day if Liz was Jillian.

Then they could go from there.

The Davidsons would want to see Liz immediately. After thirteen years of waiting, every second of delay would be excruciating for them. They might hate Anissa when they found out she'd suspected Jillian was alive and hadn't told them, but she could live with that far easier than she could live with herself if she brought them hope of a reunion that was never to be.

Or if her investigating resulted in Liz's

death before her birth family had a chance to know her.

One of the nurses paused by the door. "I'm sorry to interrupt," she said. "But these two ladies promised a certain young gentleman down the hall a rematch and he's ready to play."

Liz and Brooke crowed with delight. "Oh, he is, is he?" Liz hopped to her feet. "He's going down."

Brooke slid off the bed, a wide grin on her face. "He'll be sorry. Come on, Pais . . . you can be our objective witness and report the facts of our victory." She tugged on Paisley's hand as she moved out the door. "Do you want to come watch?"

Liz spoke in a conspiratorial whisper. "I'm sure Joey would love to meet a real, live policeman and policewoman. He's eight. His mom and dad have to work, so he's here alone most of the day. We've been trying to keep him company."

Gabe held out his arm to Liz. "Lead the way, my lady."

"Are you coming?" Liz asked Anissa.

"I'll be right behind you. I just need to check on something." Anissa waved her phone at the departing group. As soon as they were out of sight, she grabbed a few gloves from the boxes on the wall. She opened one up, used the other to pick up the water bottle, and slid it into the opening. Then put the other glove over the top. She paused to unwind the string that kept the thick file folder Paisley had given her closed. She lifted the flap and slid the glove-shrouded water bottle onto the top edge of the files. Then she wrapped the cover over it and laced the string again. If anyone had been paying attention, they would notice that the expandable file folder had grown quite a bit. But if she kept it tucked under her arm, maybe it wouldn't be quite so obvious. She studied her reflection in the mirror. The water bottle couldn't be seen.

Now, to get Gabe released, get the bottle to Forensics, and figure out once and for all the truth about Liz Brown.

At 4:00 p.m., Gabe shifted his position in the passenger seat of Ryan's car. Anissa was in the back. Ryan was driving. Leigh had insisted that Gabe come stay with her and Ryan, and she hadn't had to twist his arm to get him to agree.

Gabe closed his eyes as Anissa filled Ryan in on the day's events. Sabrina was already doing everything she could to find out the real story about Velma and Liz Brown. Adam had come by the hospital around one and had taken the water bottle to Forensics, but there'd been no call yet. Dante had promised a quick turnaround even though he had no idea why he was checking the bottle for prints.

Ryan listened, commented, and grunted in all the right places, but something was off. Gabe couldn't get a read on it, but something was wrong. At one point he caught Ryan's eye and gave him a "what's going on?" kind of look, to which Ryan responded with a quick shake of his head and a glance over his shoulder. Gabe interpreted that to mean that it had something to do with Anissa.

Ryan wasn't one to hold back unless he had good reason, so Gabe tried to be patient.

He trusted Ryan. Trusted his friendship and his instincts. But if he didn't offer up some information soon, Gabe was going to get it out of him one way or another. He knew what Ryan had planned for Leigh's birthday. He could threaten to let it slip — by accident, of course.

They arrived at the Weston-Parker home around four thirty and there was no chance to talk for the next thirty minutes. Leigh was back in nurse mode, fussing that Gabe didn't want to wear the sling the hospital had given him and asking him what pharmacy filled his antibiotic and blood thinner prescriptions and then calling Adam to pick them up. All of this from behind the kitchen island where she was dicing and slicing the makings for a ginormous salad bar.

Ryan gave her a quick peck on the temple. "Why don't you have Anissa fill you in about what's going on and I'll get Gabe to rest on the dock for a few minutes?"

"The dock? It's ninety-five degrees. That's not restful."

Anissa slid onto a barstool and snagged a slice of red bell pepper. "I have to agree with Leigh on this one. It's a sauna out there. Now, when you guys get that nice little covered area built . . ."

Ryan groaned. "Not you too."

Anissa winked at Leigh and they both laughed.

Gabe didn't necessarily disagree with Leigh and Anissa, but Ryan must be up to something and he was more than willing to play along. "Leigh, I've been cooped up in a hospital — a hospital" — he infused the word with angst and disgust — "for days." Only a wee bit of exaggeration there. "I need fresh air. I need water. I need —"

"Oh, hush." Leigh waved a chef's knife in his direction. "Go. Look at the water. But don't you dare get in that boat and don't stay out so long you get heatstroke."

"Yes, ma'am." Gabe gave Leigh a small salute and then sent a quick nod in Anissa's direction. Anissa cut her eyes between him and Ryan. She was totally on to them. But she was playing along too.

Interesting.

Gabe followed Ryan outside. Ryan didn't speak until they were all the way on the dock. The lake was smooth. It would be a great afternoon for skiing.

Not that Leigh or Anissa would ever tolerate that.

Gabe fixed his gaze on a point across the lake. "What's going on?"

Ryan walked around the dock to look as though he was inspecting it. "Anissa's car had been bugged. Two bugs, in fact. And there's a good chance whoever planted them knows we have them."

"Why are you telling me this and not her?"

Ryan snorted. "You're kidding, right?"

"I don't know what you mean."

"Dude. We all know."

"Know what?"

"She stayed with you — in a hospital — for two days. Anissa can barely stand to be in a hospital for half an hour, much less two days. I don't know how long this has been

268

going on —"

"It hasn't."

"You mean to tell me that you two aren't a couple? 'Cause you're sure acting like one."

"I . . ." What were they? They were friends. More than friends. Friends who flirted? Friends who were attracted to each other but didn't think they stood a chance of finding happiness together so they avoided it?

Ryan smirked. "Yes?"

"I don't know what we are and that's the truth, the whole truth, and nothing but the truth."

Ryan cocked his head to one side. "Can I give you a little advice?"

"If it's about romance —"

"It is. Well, about love, really."

"Then, no."

Ryan ignored him. "Anissa is tough and strong and smart and different from a lot of women. But she's also just like all the rest of us. She wants to be loved. She wants people she can trust. She wants to laugh. She wants to be respected. And she probably wants you to quit fiddling around and make a move."

"Anissa's not exactly a fast mover."

"I'll concede your point," Ryan said. "But I would also argue that if you keep up this pace, you're going to be giving Campbell a run for his money in the slow-to-action department."

It had taken Adam two years to tell Sabrina how he felt.

"It's worked out okay for him. He got the girl." Gabe laughed at his own remark.

"Can you be serious for two seconds, man?" Ryan raked his hands through his hair. "This is no joke. You need to either make a move or back off. And I mean way off. It's not fair to her, you, or any of the rest of us. And given that someone has it out for her enough to bug her car and then attempt to stab her, you can't mess around. You need to either man up and be there for her or come up with a way to get some distance."

Gabe leaned against one of the poles supporting the upper level of the dock. Ryan wasn't wrong. But distance? From Anissa? When he was already starting to have some anxiety about being away from her now and she was just in the house?

Being around her nonstop for two days hadn't made him want space. It had made him never want to be in any space without her again. He'd never been more willing to give up his own . . . everything. He hadn't taken that knife for her on purpose, but he

270

would have.

And he would do it again.

But this wasn't a conversation he wanted or needed to have with Ryan. "What's the deal with the bug?"

"Bugs," Ryan corrected him.

"Okay. Bugs. What does it matter?"

"It matters because they appear to have been placed at two different times. One was recent. Probably Sunday. The other older. Dante's speculating, but he thinks the first bug was placed around the time the air was let out of her tires last week."

"None of this makes sense. And I'm still not sure why we're having this conversation without Anissa."

Ryan blew out a long breath. "The thing with Anissa was mainly me trying to figure out where your head is with her. The real reason I brought you out here is that the captain's thinking about taking you off the Littlefield case."

"What?"

"I thought you should know."

"Why?"

Ryan pointed at Gabe's shoulder. "You've been out of the office for two days. You aren't at full strength. He's concerned the family will be upset —"

"Does he know you're telling me this?"

Ryan pursed his lips. "No. I'm guessing he has to know it's a possibility given our friendship, but he's planning to make a decision tomorrow."

"How do you know?"

Ryan didn't answer.

Oh. "He's going to give the case to you."

"I don't want it, Gabe. I told him that I don't and that I don't think it's wise to switch investigators midstream. I don't guess you watched much TV while you were in the hospital, but there's a lot of public interest and pressure on this case. There've been no arrests and there are no leads. He's getting tired of having nothing to say to the press."

The press was going to ruin him again. "I need to get back into the office."

"Not tonight you don't, but tomorrow? Probably. Leigh will lose her mind, but I'll back you up."

Gabe's thoughts ricocheted from the Jeremy Littlefield case to the Liz Brown/Jillian Davidson case to the stabbing and the bugs in Anissa's car. He'd been in over his head plenty of times before.

But this time it might finally be too much.

If he dropped a ball, who would pay the price?

15

By unspoken but mutual consent, no one talked about the real reason they were together until after supper. Adam and Sabrina arrived around five fifteen and by five thirty the six of them had gathered around the dining room table with loaded salads and baked potatoes.

An hour later, everyone had eaten, the kitchen was cleaned, and Sabrina, in true professorial form, had her laptop connected to Leigh's television screen and was flipping through what appeared to be a PowerPoint presentation, but it was too fast for Anissa to catch what she'd prepared.

"She made slides." Gabe spoke from behind Anissa, his tone heavy with both amusement and respect. "She probably has all our cases solved by now."

"I do not, Gabe Chavez." Sabrina mock-glared at Gabe over her glasses.

"We'll see, Dr. Fleming soon-to-be Campbell."

Except for when he was telling her about the listening devices Dante had located in her car, Gabe had been his usual jovial self since he and Ryan had returned from their lakeside powwow. But he'd stayed unusually close to her as well.

She didn't mind.

But she minded that she didn't mind.

Man, she was a mess.

When Gabe picked a spot on the left end of the sofa so he could prop his elbow on the arm — and take off the sling — and then patted the spot to his right, she sat without hesitation. Then she caught Sabrina's reaction. The slight lifting of her eyebrows. The way she looked at Leigh, and Leigh gave her a knowing nod.

Anissa had already spent thirty minutes deflecting Leigh's questions. Questions she didn't have answers to.

She had no choice but to admit that there was one big difference between this week and last. Last week, she'd held any rogue emotions about Gabe in a firm chokehold.

Tonight? They held her.

"Are we ready?" Sabrina glanced around the room.

"We're ready, Bri." Adam said the nickname like an endearment. Kind of the way Gabe said "Nis."

Sabrina perched her glasses on her head. "As I understand it, we need to talk through three separate incidents tonight. We'll start with the one that I actually have something to talk about — the situation regarding the young girl at the hospital, Liz Brown, and her possible connection to the thirteen-year-old missing persons case of Jillian Davidson. Then we'll discuss the Jeremy Littlefield case and then the situation with Anissa — the stabbing and the bugs."

Anissa couldn't keep herself from flinching at that last part. Gabe's right arm, which had been behind her on the sofa, landed across her back. His hand squeezed her shoulder, and then it was gone and his arm was back up on the sofa.

Heaven help her, but she missed the weight of his arm, the warmth of his hand. She forced herself to sit straight and not lean against Gabe. She'd never had a problem avoiding him before, but now that her heart had grabbed the reins from her mind, it was running wild.

She didn't like this out-of-control feeling. At all.

"Anissa?" Sabrina's question pulled Anissa's brain back to the situation at hand.

"Yes?"

"I have your permission?" Sabrina didn't elaborate further, but Anissa knew what she meant.

"Yes. I think everyone is familiar with the circumstances, and you're free to share anything we've talked about previously. I'm an open book these days."

Sabrina frowned at her comment. "Anissa, I don't like to operate in a world of opinion. I prefer facts and verifiable data. But from personal experience, I am confident that I can tell you this. Your life will be so much better for having everything out in the open. Living with secrets is exhausting. I, perhaps better than anyone else here, appreciate the difficulty in coming to terms with a new normal. A place where your dirty laundry is exposed for all to see."

Sabrina's family had held a woman as a slave for a decade. Not the kind of thing you want to post on social media.

"I was terrified of exposure. Of the truth being revealed. But it turns out that open books aren't so bad. They let the people who love you most help you read them correctly. Most of the time people who keep everything closed and secret don't have an accurate interpretation of the facts."

Anissa couldn't respond with anything

other than a nod. Thankfully Sabrina wasn't a superemotive person and Anissa's nod was enough for her. Leigh, however, was sniffling across the room and Ryan got up to get her a tissue.

Sabrina turned back to her slides. "So, as we know, three-year-old Jillian Davidson disappeared from a park in Virginia and was never seen again. No body was found. No ransom request made. The case remains open, but there have been no sightings and no new leads for years."

She tapped her laptop and the age-progression images Sabrina had created appeared. "Anissa shared the story with me last year. I asked my friends to run three different photographs of Jillian Davidson through the software we use in our human trafficking work. These are the results we got for what she would look like at ten, thirteen, sixteen, and twenty-one."

Another tap. Another slide. This one with two pictures. Side by side.

"Whoa." Ryan leaned forward in his seat. "The picture on the left is the picture from your software. Where'd you get the picture on the right? Is that the girl from the hospital? Liz Brown?"

"It is." Sabrina pointed to the photograph. "I was able to obtain this from my good friends in the hospital security department. They gave me access to some footage. I told them nothing about the specifics of this case, only that I was working on a possible kidnapping, and they gave me what I needed."

The hospital security team probably shouldn't have done that, but then again, Sabrina and Anissa had worked closely with them last year when Leigh was kidnapped, and it wasn't like any of this would be needed in court.

Neither Ryan nor Adam had seen Liz, and their surprised reactions further confirmed Anissa's suspicions.

"If that isn't the same girl, then she has an identical twin out there somewhere." Adam rubbed his hands over his face. "What's the next step?"

Sabrina tapped her screen. "Dante is running some prints off a water bottle Anissa got from Liz at the hospital — they weren't awesome prints, but he's hopeful. If we get a match, we'll be able to get a warrant to get DNA. But we have to be careful. For one thing, based on Anissa's and Gabe's observations, this sweet child has no clue she was kidnapped as a toddler. She knows she was adopted. That's it. This is going to be potentially earth-shattering. As ecstatic as Mr. and Mrs. Davidson will be to have their daughter returned, this is a complicated and messy situation no matter how you look at it."

"So much pain all the way around." Leigh blew her nose.

"Indeed." Sabrina put a new slide on the screen. "It's further complicated by the fact that Liz Brown's mother, Velma Brown, is currently receiving oncological care in Columbia, South Carolina, for a brain tumor. I was able to do some checking and it appears that the whole story Liz told Paisley about her mom being in China was false. The mom knew she was going to be having chemo and didn't have anyone to help care for Liz, so she sent her off to a two-month summer camp."

"I haven't decided if that was merciful or diabolical." Gabe voiced Anissa's own thoughts.

"I may be able to shed a little light on that," Leigh said. "First, brain tumors can cause erratic and irrational behaviors in their own right."

Leigh would know. She'd once had a patient with a brain tumor who'd become fixated on her and almost killed her.

"But this afternoon I learned that the type of tumor Velma Brown has is one that often responds well to treatment. It's possible — and I am speculating here — that she honestly believed that if she sent Liz to camp, she could give her daughter a fun summer and spare her the angst and fear of watching her mother go through a brutal chemo regimen. And when she came home, it would be either over or almost over and she'd be well on her way to recovery.

"Unfortunately, it seems her tumor, while it has responded to treatment, hasn't shrunk enough for her doctors to attempt surgery and she's facing months of chemo. There's no way she'll be able to hide it from Liz. She may have another five to ten years. Maybe even more. But they will be tough years. At least physically."

A somber hush fell on the room.

Gabe broke it. "What about Liz's dad? She told Paisley that he'd been gone for years."

"Yes. Bernie Brown. Split ten years ago around the time Liz got sick." Sabrina flipped to a new slide. "I found him. Well, to be precise, I found his death certificate."

"What?" Anissa hadn't heard this part.

"I found it this afternoon," Sabrina said. "He died as the result of a hit-and-run in New Jersey in March of this year."

This year. Was that significant? Maybe.

Maybe not.

"Do you think Liz knows? About her dad?" Adam asked.

"Paisley or Brooke might know for sure. All we got was that he'd taken off when she was a kid." Gabe shifted his position, and the sofa cushions tilted Anissa in his direction. She had to lean away to keep from falling against him.

"I always thought if I ever found Jillian that it would be a glorious reunion. That everything would be happy and wonderful. I never once imagined that reuniting her with her biological family could mean ripping apart the only family she's ever really known. I wanted her to be both safe and happy, but also happy to go home. If that makes any sense. There's no winning here."

If she could get her hands on the man who did this . . . what? Would she kill him? Would it change anything if she did?

"We have to do the next right thing." Gabe spoke in a tone both soothing and confident. "Not oblivious to the complexities of the situation, but not fearful of them either. God's big enough to handle this. If he's put you in a position — now — after all these years to restore this family, then we have to trust he has a plan for dealing with the fallout."

"She's so . . ." Anissa's voice cracked.

"I know." Gabe patted her shoulder, and this time his hand rested there as he spoke to the group. "Y'all would love this girl. She's fun. Spunky. Great attitude. I don't want to be responsible for putting her spark out. We have to be very, very careful as we move forward."

"If Dante can't get a usable print off the water bottle, I'm prepared to go back through her trash can and find something. And if that doesn't work, I'm prepared to take all this to the captain and get permission to get a print no matter what." Anissa's stomach roiled. "But I don't want her to have a clue about any of this until we're one hundred and ten percent certain."

"Agreed," multiple voices responded.

"Did you say Velma Brown is in Columbia?" Gabe asked.

"Yes."

"What if I call Brady St. John and see what he can find out about her? He might even be able to talk to her. Go by her place and see what there is to see."

"Who is Brady St. John?" Leigh asked.

"He's Gabe's buddy," Ryan said. "Under-water criminal investigator. You remember. He's the one we helped out last year when that boat was at the bottom of Lake Porter."

"Oh yeah. The one where lots of bullets went flying? He sounds perfect for a job like this." Leigh's tone and smile were a master class in sweet sarcasm.

Gabe ignored Leigh. He moved his right arm away from Anissa and tugged his phone out of his back pocket. "I'll text Brady now. Sabrina, please proceed."

"Thank you," she said.

He rested the phone in his left hand and bit back a hiss of pain when he moved too fast. It was annoying to have his entire left side so stiff and achy. Getting stabbed stank. He finished the text and left the phone on his leg. It was easier than trying to squirm around and put it back in his pocket.

He settled back into the corner of the couch and caught Anissa watching him. Not in an obvious way. More of a side glance. He would have taken another stabbing to have a clue what she was thinking.

"So, we have a loose plan going forward regarding Liz Brown, who may or may not be Jillian Davidson." Sabrina tapped a screen. "On to Jeremy Littlefield."

Sabrina wasn't one for lengthy transitions.

"I have been digging into both of the families — both Jeremy's and Brooke's. The Littlefields are well-off. Finances are good.

Marriage seems to be good. Work situations stable. Mr. Littlefield is well liked. I've run through numerous scenarios and can't find any reason for anyone to target the family."

A picture of Paisley Wilson filled the screen.

Leigh let a little hiss escape. "I don't like that girl."

"Join the club," Sabrina said. "Paisley Wilson has ticked off more than just the Carrington law enforcement community. Since becoming a reporter, she's exposed a representative's illicit affair, blown the lid off another county's bribery scheme involving a sheriff, and been ferocious in her reporting on everyone associated with the human trafficking ring we busted last year."

Sabrina shrugged. "Any one of these people, plus about twenty others, could have been angry enough to go after her in some way. But targeting Brooke instead of Paisley herself? That's pretty cold. And it doesn't fit the facts. From what I was able to gather, their dip in the lake was spontaneous. They'd spent the day on the lake and were sitting on the dock at Jeremy's aunt's house. Brooke dared Jeremy. They dove in. No one could have known they would be in that lake at that time. I'm not saying it's impossible, but the facts we have available to us don't support that this was anything other than a random shooting."

She looked at Gabe. "I'm sorry. I was hoping for a smoking gun — literally or digitally — but I don't have one right now."

"It's okay. This is all important too. We have to rule it out so we know we're looking in the right direction. Thank you."

She blew out a breath and a new slide appeared. Two electronic listening devices. "Moving on. These are the bugs found in Anissa's car. Dante is trying to find out where they came from, but it's a long shot and we both know it. The bottom line is that given the timing of the placement of these devices — one a week ago and one within the last seventy-two hours — the air out of your tires takes on a whole new dimension. It's an educated guess, but it seems likely this one was placed whenever the culprit let the air out of your tires. This one? I don't know for sure, but I've checked surveillance footage from the sheriff's office and it didn't happen there. It could have happened at the gym — you go early in the morning and it's dark and they don't have cameras. It could even have happened at church Sunday. Big, open parking lot. Lots of people. There's no way to know, but the one thing we do know is that someone who does not like you has gotten very close to you. And, of course, the stabbing — I analyzed the placement, how Gabe would have been standing, et cetera. If you had opened the door and the knife had taken the same trajectory . . ." Sabrina ran out of words. Not normal for Sabrina when giving a presentation.

"Go on," Anissa said.

"The knife would have been at your neck." Sabrina didn't stop there. "You need to get it in your head that someone is trying to kill you and they don't seem likely to stop trying anytime soon."

Anissa didn't flinch. "My list of people with motive is longer than Paisley's. Where do we even start?"

"I think you need to go through all your old case files. See who's still in jail, who got out recently, that kind of thing. Because I think we need to consider the timing."

Another click and the screen changed. This slide had a timeline on it.

"Paisley was sent the file on the murder of Carly and kidnapping of Jillian back in March. Liz Brown may be Jillian. Her adoptive father was killed by a hit-and-run in March. Both Velma and Liz have been very vulnerable for weeks and nothing has happened to them, which leads me to think they aren't targets. Possibly because they don't know enough to be a danger. I'll admit that this is a bit of a leap, but based on everything in front of me, it's entirely possible that whoever killed Carly and kidnapped Jillian is coming after you."

Gabe didn't like it when Sabrina made leaps in her logic.

Well, that wasn't true. Normally he liked it a lot. She was disciplined, methodical, and didn't like to guess at anything. When she did, her guesses were almost always accurate.

Sabrina's willingness to throw out a suggestion like this, with so little to go on, meant she was truly worried about Anissa's safety.

His hand twitched on the back of the sofa. He had to squeeze the cushion to keep himself from squeezing Anissa. That would go over about as well as Sabrina's pronouncement.

A grim mood settled over the room. It didn't fit this space where laughter and warmth and joy were the standard. No one spoke for several seconds. Then everyone was talking at once.

Adam and Ryan launched into a conversation that had Adam pulling out his phone and going outside on the massive wraparound porch. Leigh joined Sabrina as she closed her computer.

Anissa didn't move. She swallowed. She took breaths. But other than that, she sat ramrod straight beside Gabe.

He shifted his weight and leaned toward her just enough that he could keep his voice low but she would be able to hear him. "I'd offer you a couple grand for your thoughts if I had that much."

"Why now?"

Why now? Why would he pay big money to know what she was thinking when someone might be coming after her for something that happened thirteen years ago? Or why did he care now when he hadn't cared before? How could he answer that? *"Oh, I don't know, Anissa. I guess I've realized I can't live without you and I want to try to make you happy and it would really put a crimp in my plans if someone decided to kill you before I figure out how to broach the subject . . ."* Yeah, that wouldn't be great.

"Why come after me now?" Her slight clarification changed his entire thought process.

It's not all about you, Chavez. He focused on her question. "I don't know. But we'll figure it out."

She turned to face him then. "We?"

There were a million questions in that one word and he was tired of not answering them. "You and me. Together."

Her skin took on a rosy hue, but she didn't break eye contact. "Together."

16

Sabrina and Adam left thirty minutes later.

Leigh was fussing at Gabe about not wearing the sling on his arm and Ryan took the opportunity to corner Anissa in the kitchen. Literally. She turned around from putting a cup in the cabinet and he had her blocked.

"I think you should stay here tonight."

"I can't." She'd already thought it through. If someone was targeting her, she needed to get as far away from her friends as possible.

"Well, you can't go home. That would be like saying, 'Hey, here I am. Come blow me up,' and I know you're smarter than that."

"I won't go home. Or be predictable. I'll Uber downtown. Then walk. Then Uber. I'll get a hotel somewhere and I'll see you guys in the morning."

Ryan stood in front of her. Arms crossed.

"I know you're not trying to bully me, Ryan Parker. We both know I can get around you if I want to." Theoretically.

He grinned but didn't move. "You aren't going anywhere."

"You cannot tell me what to do."

"I'm not telling you what to do. I'm stating a fact. You aren't going anywhere because if you do, Gabe will go with you. And you won't want Gabe to do that, so you'll stay here even though you're afraid we'll all die a horrific death because of it."

"He doesn't have to know I'm leaving."

Ryan had the nerve to laugh. "He'll follow you. Or try to. Go ahead. I'll give you all of the five seconds you're going to need to know that I'm right."

With a certainty that made her limbs feel like deadweight, she saw the truth in Ryan's words. "I don't want to put anyone at risk. I can't survive adding any more friends to my own personal body count."

"You aren't adding anyone to your body count, Anissa."

"What are we going to do? Stay up all night while Gabe and Leigh sleep? Take turns patrolling the place?"

"No. We are all going to sleep. First, this place has an awesome security system. Second, Adam's been on the phone. He called the captain. Some uniformed patrol officers will be adding the house to their route tonight."

"Great. I'm sure the captain was thrilled."

"He didn't mind. Adam's second call —"

"There's more?"

Ryan nodded. "Oh, there's more. Adam called his grandfather."

"He. Did. What?" Anissa didn't think she could breathe. "Why?"

"Grandfather Campbell adores you."

It was true, although she had no idea why. "I'll concede the point, but what does it have to do with our current situation?"

"The Campbells have a private security division that works all their properties. It's not a huge division, but over the past couple of years they've been hiring some of our officers who need extra hours. It's a win for everyone. They get highly qualified security and they get to help the men and women in blue with a second job that pays well and usually only involves making sure no punk kids are tossing pool furniture into the lake."

"Okay. Still not seeing what this has to do with me."

"Adam thought it would be best to get permission before he called in a favor. After he finished talking to his grandfather, his third call was to the private security division. They're sending us some extra help for the evening. We'll figure out the rest later, but I suspect you're about to have a personal bodyguard anytime you aren't in the sheriff's office."

Anissa opened her mouth to protest, but before she could get a word out Ryan continued. "Don't be mad. And please don't kick me off the dive team for saying this, but don't get all huffy with Adam about the security. He cares about you. He cares about all of us. This is a small way he can help, and he would be hurt if you didn't accept it. This would be a good time for you to just thank the Lord for the friends he's given you and thank your friends for looking out for you."

Sometimes Ryan nailed the role of older brother that he had taken on for himself.

This was one of those times.

"Fine." She knew when to give in, and this was one of those times. But she was not happy about it.

"Everything okay?" Gabe's voice came from behind Ryan. Anissa couldn't see Gabe, but she could hear the concern in his question. "Parker? Is there a reason you have Anissa pinned in a corner?"

"Just having a little heart-to-heart," Ryan said.

"Okay." Gabe's tone said that it was anything but okay.

"I'll let you handle it from here." Ryan turned and walked out of the kitchen. He tapped Gabe, with far more gentleness than usual, on his right shoulder. "I need to see if Leigh needs any help getting the rooms ready for y'all. Gabe, you're downstairs. Anissa, upstairs."

Gabe didn't move from his spot at the edge of the kitchen. When Ryan was out of sight, he spoke in a low voice. "What's going on? Was he being a jerk to you? Because he has no business —"

"No." Anissa had to stop that line of thinking. Ryan was Gabe's best friend. She couldn't have him thinking Ryan was being a jerk.

Although this might be the first time in, well, ever, that Gabe had assumed Ryan was in the wrong instead of her.

Interesting.

"We were discussing my safety and the safety of those around me."

"You were not thinking about leaving here alone." He stalked toward her.

"I was considering it."

Gabe started to speak. Twice. She wasn't sure if he didn't know what he wanted to say, or if he was trying to stop himself from saying what he wanted to say. He finally sputtered, "You can't."

"I know."

"Promise me."

"Promise what?"

Gabe took another step toward her. Only a few inches separated them. "Promise you will not take any unnecessary risks. That you will stay safe."

"I will. I don't think you have to worry. Apparently Adam's lining up private security. Which is —"

"Brilliant."

"No, it isn't. It's ridiculous."

Gabe's right hand stretched toward her. Was he reaching for her hair? Her face? She held her breath. If he did — ?

"Bedrooms are ready." Leigh's voice crashed into their moment of . . . whatever this was.

Gabe blew out a breath and took a step back. "Ridiculous would be if I locked you in a safe room until this was all over. Which, for the record, is still my first choice."

Leigh breezed into the kitchen and went straight to the fridge. "Am I interrupting something? I certainly hope I am. Don't mind me. I'm grabbing some water bottles to put in your rooms and then I'll be gone."

"Not funny, Leigh."

If it wasn't funny, why was Gabe grinning?

"It's hysterical and you know it." Leigh

winked at Anissa, blew them a kiss, and skipped out of the room, hitting the light switch as she went, which left them in the dim glow of the over-cabinet lighting.

"What was that about?"

Gabe traced a pattern on the counter. "I interrupted her and Ryan once before they were officially a couple. May have used a similar line. That was payback."

"Oh." She'd have to remember to ask Leigh about it.

Gabe's phone rang. A range of emotions flashed across his face. The predominant one was aggravation and it was clear in his tone as he answered. "Chavez."

She wasn't trying to eavesdrop, but as she was still somewhat stuck in a corner of the kitchen and Gabe didn't seem inclined to move, she couldn't help but see the way his brow wrinkled in surprise. Then concern.

"Are you sure?" Gabe closed his eyes. "I'll be right there."

He put the phone on the counter. "The cabin on the Masters property is on fire."

Thirty minutes later, Gabe stood on the edge of the Masters property. The cabin, such as it was, steamed under the spray of the fire hoses.

There had been several ways this evening

could have ended. Some of them might have been wonderful.

Spending the evening watching a cabin burn down hadn't been anywhere on Gabe's list of possibilities.

"We didn't have a chance of putting it out," the fire chief said. "This thing was burning hot and fast. The fire marshal will have to confirm it, but I'd bet my next paycheck that you have an arson on your hands."

"Was anyone inside?"

"Don't know yet. By the time we got here, there was nothing we could do but focus on putting out the fire and keeping it from spreading to the rest of the property. Sorry you came out, but I don't think there's anything you'll be able to do or see until the morning."

"It was no problem," Gabe said. "I wasn't too far away."

He would have been here sooner if he hadn't had to argue with Anissa about her staying at Ryan and Leigh's. She'd wanted to come. He'd pointed out that whoever was trying to get to her could have set the fire. She argued that he shouldn't drive. He noted that he hadn't had anything stronger than ibuprofen in almost twenty-four hours and his right arm worked just fine.

She was furious when he left. Boiling mad. And she hadn't been completely wrong. He was hurting. But he couldn't shake the feeling that standing out here, silhouetted by the flames, she would have been an awfully easy target.

He spotted a familiar figure across the yard and walked over to join him. "Mr. Cook. How are you, sir?"

"Better than most, I expect." Mr. Cook nodded at the cabin.

Gabe couldn't argue with that.

"How's our girl?" There was the hint of a challenge in Mr. Cook's question. A reminder. Messing with Anissa would not go over well with Mr. Cook. Best to be honest.

"She's mad at me."

"What did you do?"

"Wow. Not even a chance that I'm innocent, huh?"

Mr. Cook laughed. "This is no court of law. That child has my heart. As far as I'm concerned, you're guilty until proven innocent."

"That's what I thought." Gabe stared into the smoking remains of the cabin. "She wanted to come, but I, well, we — Ryan and I, and even Anissa for that matter — have some concerns that make her coming out here a bit of a dangerous proposition."

"Someone's after her." Mr. Cook didn't ask it. He stated it.

How could he know? Gabe didn't have the mental energy to try to understand where Mr. Cook's insights came from. "I think so."

"So why's she mad at you? She's not one to get sideways about the truth."

Keen observation. Why was she mad? "I'm not sure. If she disagreed with me, she would be here by now. It's not like I can keep her from doing something she wants to do."

"It's good you've already figured that out." Mr. Cook gave Gabe an approving nod. "Save you a lot of trouble down the road."

Gabe didn't see any point in trying to set Mr. Cook straight about the nature of his relationship with Anissa. Especially since the older gentleman had a better handle on it than he did. Agreement was the only option. "Yes, sir."

Mr. Cook looked him up and down. "Didn't they let you out of the hospital today? Are you supposed to be driving?"

"I'm fine. Really. It was a very short drive. My right arm is fine." He waved it to prove his point. "No problems."

"Huh."

The fire chief came over to speak to Mr. Cook. They chatted for ten minutes and covered the weather, the lake levels, the tourism season, the cryptosporidium outbreak at the camp, and what might have caused the fire. Gabe didn't try to interject. He'd learned a long time ago that sometimes the best way to gather information was to shut his mouth and open his ears.

A sweat-soaked, soot-covered firefighter approached, pausing several respectful feet away.

"What is it, Jensen?" the fire chief asked.

"We're ready to shut things down, sir."

"Okay. I'll be there in two minutes." The chief turned to Mr. Cook. "You'd better head on home." He nodded in Gabe's direction. "The both of you. There's nothing you can do here tonight. It's too hot to touch until morning. The marshal will be out first thing." He nodded at Gabe. "I'll call you as soon as I have anything to say other than what you already know."

"Thank you."

Mr. Cook shook the chief's hand, then turned to Gabe as soon as the chief walked away. "Is she staying with Ryan and Leigh tonight?" No preamble. No warning. No "hey, I'm about to get all up in your business again."

"Yes, sir."

"You staying there too?"

"Yes, sir. Leigh doesn't think I should be alone, which is ridiculous. And none of us think Anissa should be alone."

"Want some advice?"

Somehow Gabe thought Mr. Cook really meant that as a question. Like he could turn it down if he wanted to, but if he asked for it, he'd better be prepared to heed it. "Yes, sir."

"Apologize."

"For what? No offense, sir, but I didn't do anything wrong. I'm willing to grovel if need be, but it would help if I knew what to grovel for."

Mr. Cook chuckled. "You apologize for upsetting her."

"But I don't know why she's upset."

"Doesn't matter."

Mr. Cook's words rang in Gabe's ears as he pulled into Ryan and Leigh's driveway twenty minutes later. He spoke to the officer patrolling the property, then let himself into the house and stopped in the kitchen for a cupcake. He took some pain relievers, guzzled a bottle of water, and made his way to the stairs.

Anissa was sitting on the sofa reading a book.

"Hey." How unoriginal could he get?

She didn't speak. Just looked at him for a few seconds and then went back to her book.

He'd messed up with her tonight. Hurt her feelings. Made her angry. He was a long way from perfect, but he wasn't the kind of guy who refused to admit when he messed up.

He walked over to where she sat, pulled the book from her hands, and tugged her to her feet. Confusion and frustration danced across her face, but she stood and didn't back away when he pressed his forehead to hers. "I'm sorry."

"You didn't have to go tonight." Was she trembling?

"But I did. I needed to see it. I learned a lot. Now I can sleep. I know you understand that." She had to. She did the same thing all the time.

"He could have come after you. You're not anywhere near one hundred percent. He could have done anything. Taken a shot at you. Run you off the road. Kidnapped you and tortured —" Her words cut off in a strangled gasp.

302

"Whoa." He squeezed the hand he still held.

"Sorry." She stepped back. "I'm glad you're okay. Good night."

"Come back here." He pulled her toward him with his right arm.

She took one step in his direction but then put her other hand gently on his chest and stopped him from pulling her any closer. "I can't. I'm sorry, Gabe. I just can't."

He released her hand but couldn't stop himself from asking, "Why not?"

Idiot. He should have let her go. Let it all end. But he couldn't. He didn't want to let it end. He wanted to see what would happen if they let it begin.

Her face was turned to the floor so all he could see was the top of her head as she shook it back and forth. She didn't move away from him. Her hand still rested flat on his chest.

The wait was torture.

"I . . . I don't know." A faster shake of her head accompanied her whispered confession.

The memory of a conversation he'd had with Adam last winter flickered through his mind. One where he'd given Adam grief for expecting Sabrina to be able to read his mind.

In this moment, he had a choice. He could keep pretending this was all a game and it didn't matter to him. Or he could man up. Tell her how he felt. And deal with the fallout, for better or worse.

He pulled in a deep breath. Pain sliced through his chest. Was he ready for her to do the same to his heart?

"Anissa?" He didn't like talking to the top of her head, but that was all she was willing to give him at the moment, so he'd have to work with it. "There's something I need to tell you. I'm not sure if now's the best time. Or if there will ever be a good time. And maybe I should keep my mouth shut, but I can't. Not anymore. Because I can't stop thinking about you. Ever. I want to be with you all the time, and even when we aren't in the same physical space, I want to know that you're *with* me."

She looked up. She took quick breaths through her nose and looked for all the world like a cornered animal.

He was doing this all wrong. "Is it so awful to think about being with me?"

Her face registered confusion. "No. It isn't awful at all."

It was his turn to be surprised. "Then what's the problem?"

She looked away, blinked a few times,

swallowed. The fingers on his chest curled into a fist. "I'm the problem, Gabe. Assuming you don't wind up dead, which, if you haven't noticed, is what tends to happen to people I care about, I'll end up hurting you. I think we both know that."

He wrapped his right hand around her fist. "What if we decided to take it a day at a time?" He lifted her fist off his chest. "What if we agreed not to project our fears about something that might happen onto what's happening right now?" He laced his fingers through hers. "What if we took a chance?"

She stared at their hands. "I didn't think you were the type to ever take that kind of chance. What is it you always say? Relationships are too important to take risks with?"

"You're the only one I've ever been willing to risk everything for, Anissa."

17

Anissa soaked in Gabe's words.

He'd never been so blunt. So bold. Until now, everything she'd suspected about his feelings for her had been just that — suspicion. And sometimes suspicions were way off. But this was fact. Laid out there with no pretense. No holding back.

His words were warm sunlight on dive-chilled skin, cool water after a tough workout, hope in a dark universe.

He slid his left arm out of the sling, and his hand found her waist. She stepped closer and he dropped the hand he'd been holding. Now both of his arms were around her.

She rested her forehead against his chest, careful to avoid the stab wound, her arms pinned between them. Her last little piece of resistance. If she moved . . . there'd be no turning back.

Oh, who was she kidding? He already had her heart. He just didn't know it. What was wrong with her? She looked up and lost herself in his eyes. There was no judgment, no hurry, no frustration in them. She saw understanding, and a little bit of a challenge.

He had put himself out there and was waiting to see what she would do. How she would respond. She slid her arms around his sides, taking extra care on his left side, and rested her face against his chest. He pulled her closer and settled his head on top of hers. She could feel him inhale, deep and slow.

"Would this be a good time for me to ask you out on a date?"

"Hmm . . . maybe," she said.

"Maybe?" He pulled back until he could look at her, his brow furrowed in mock concern. "If this is a maybe, we need to discuss your communication skills."

She pretended to think about it for another second, then shrugged. "What did you have in mind?"

"Oh, so that's how it's going to be? You're going to wait to say yes until I come up with some big plan, huh? Talk about pressure."

He was laughing, joking. She knew it. But . . . she tucked her face against his chest. "I'll go anywhere, Gabe. Or nowhere. It doesn't matter."

She could feel his surprise at her words. The way his chest froze in mid-inhale, then deflated rapidly. "So a sunset boat ride would work?"

"Mm-hmm."

"Then it's a date."

"It's a date." She had a date with Gabe Chavez. That was . . . great, and terrifying.

As if he could read her thoughts, he whispered, "One day at a time. We'll take it slow so neither of us panics. Deal?"

"Deal."

As much as she hated to, she pulled away. "Leigh will strangle us both if you don't get some sleep."

"Yeah."

The way he was looking at her . . . was he going to kiss her? She wanted him to. But then, she didn't. She'd never forgotten their kiss. It had rocked her world and he hadn't even meant it.

He took a step toward her, his lips landing on her forehead. "Good night, Anissa." He ran his thumb across her cheek. The gesture was so tender, so careful, like he was stroking a fragile piece of art. He winked at her, then turned to the stairs.

"Good night."

The next morning, Anissa sat at the kitchen

counter nursing her coffee.

"Everything okay?" Leigh asked as she set a scone in front of her.

Anissa pasted on a quick smile. "Yes."

"You sure? You were pretty ticked at Gabe last night."

"Oh yeah, that. I'm fine."

Gabe chose that moment to enter. "Morning, ladies." He went straight to the coffeepot. Anissa wasn't sure what she'd expected. It wasn't like they were to the point where he was going to start the day with a good-morning kiss. But maybe he could have winked? Smiled? Stopped by her side first?

"Where's your sling?" Leigh glared at Gabe.

"I'll get it after breakfast. Promise."

"It's to help you not pull —"

"I know. I know. I promised, didn't I?"

Ryan entered and went straight to Leigh. After planting a very nonpecky kiss on his bride, he turned to Anissa. "We diving today, boss?"

"Yes. After lunch though. I've got some stuff I need to do in the office, and neither Lane nor Stu can get loose before then either."

Gabe took the scone Leigh offered him and sat beside Anissa. "I notice you haven't invited me on this dive."

"You can't dive!" Leigh turned to Anissa. "You can't let him dive."

Her horrified expression wasn't meant to be funny, but Anissa couldn't stop herself from laughing. "He isn't diving." For emphasis, she turned to Gabe. "You aren't diving."

He gave her his most annoyed look. "I don't think I like you right now, Bell."

She had a flicker of panic. Was he already wishing last night had never happened? Because no one watching would be able to tell that anything had changed. Or maybe that was the idea?

Then he shifted in his chair and his left knee pressed against hers. And stayed there. His annoyed expression remained, but she now had a different take. She could play this game.

In fact, she liked playing this game.

"Get used to it, Chavez. You're out of the water. One month."

Gabe threw his hands in the air and turned to Ryan. "Help me out, man. Can't you overrule her or something?"

"No, he can't. I rule with an iron fist." Anissa took a bite of her scone as Leigh and Ryan laughed.

Gabe glared at all of them. "I don't like

any of you people right now."

They only laughed harder.

"I bet Anissa will let you drive the boat," Ryan said. "If you're very, very nice to her."

"What do you think, Leigh? Should he be allowed to drive the boat?" Anissa asked.

Leigh shook her head. "I don't like it. But if you're in a bind, I guess it would be okay. Maybe. But, Gabe, really, you can't get in that water. Not with a stab wound. Lake water is —"

"He won't," Anissa said.

Gabe gave her a look she couldn't quite decipher. At first she thought he might be ticked, but the longer he looked at her the more she suspected he was pleased.

"Do you two need us to give you the room?" Ryan asked.

Leigh didn't wait for them to respond. "Babe, they're going to start either yelling or kissing. I can't tell which. We should clear out either way."

Ryan threw back his head and laughed.

Leigh leaned toward Anissa and didn't even try to keep her voice down. "You have some explaining to do, young lady. 'Oh yeah, that. I'm fine.' " Leigh mimicked Anissa's earlier statement. "Liar."

"I wasn't lying."

Leigh glanced at Gabe, then back to

311

Anissa. "Lies by omission are still lies."

A knock on the door brought the moment to an abrupt end. Three hands rested on three weapons. Leigh stood behind Ryan.

"Open up, Parker."

Adam.

Ryan went to the door. Adam entered.

"Coffee, Adam? Scone?"

"Oh, Leigh, that would be wonderful. But would it be horribly rude of me to get them to go?" No matter what else was going on, Adam's manners were always on point.

"Of course not. Will you see Sabrina before I do?" Leigh was already putting scones in a tiny paper box.

"Yes, I'm headed to the university."

Leigh added another scone as Ryan handed Adam a paper cup. "Talk while you fix your coffee. What's going on? Did they find a body in the house or something?"

"There's no body to my knowledge. But Sabrina called me at five thirty this morning and she's had an idea that she's running with. She's doing some kind of cross-check of people associated with Anissa's cases who were let out of prison in March or earlier."

"That's a good idea," Anissa said. "Please tell her thank you."

"I will."

"And I hate to ask, but can you dive this

afternoon? The firefighters found some evidence near the dock that makes them think the arsonist might have tossed some accelerant into the lake. They want us to check it out. And get it out of the lake, if possible."

"What time?" Adam took a sip of coffee.

"One thirty at the house. We need to run the sonar first. There might not be anything down there at all. But the property is a lot closer than driving all the way to the marina, so we can pick you up off the dock." She turned to Gabe. "No diving for you."

He clutched his chest. "You're wounding me, Bell."

Adam put a lid on his cup. "Perfect. Sabrina's already got some results for me. I'm also checking on something for the captain on the camp's property. So as soon as I finish up with Sabrina, I'll be in the office until we dive."

He grinned at Anissa. "I know you're ticked, but Grandfather says if you try to dodge the security guards he's assigned to you, he'll never get you that boat he promised."

"He promised you a boat?" Ryan and Gabe asked together.

"He never promised me a boat." Adam winked.

Was his grandfather seriously thinking about getting them a new boat? "This is coercion, Adam Campbell."

"Take it up with him, Anissa. I gotta run."

Adam took his scones and coffee and blew out the door as quickly as he'd blown in.

The reality of security guards had popped the pleasant morning balloon she'd been enjoying. That and the realization that she didn't have a car. "When can I get my house and my car back?" she asked Ryan.

Gabe stiffened.

Ryan cut his eyes between them. No way he'd missed Gabe's reaction. "The car? Today. Dante said he'll have it at the office. The house is ready. It was ready yesterday. But I don't recommend going in alone. Or staying alone."

"I won't." She responded to Ryan's words and Gabe's tension. "I won't. I just . . . I don't like this."

"None of us do." Ryan poured himself another cup of coffee. "I have to go to the courthouse first thing. Will you two be okay to ride in together? Or should we make other arrangements?" He smirked at Anissa and Gabe.

"We'll manage." Gabe gave Ryan the fakest of fake grins. "Don't you give us a second thought."

"We? Us?" Leigh laced her arm through Ryan's. "Come on. We definitely need to give them the room."

When Ryan and Leigh were almost out of the kitchen, Gabe winked at Anissa and made no effort to speak quietly. "I didn't think they would ever leave."

"I heard that, Gabe Chavez," Leigh yelled back.

Gabe couldn't resist messing with Leigh. "Is that your mad voice, Leigh Weston Parker? Because it's pathetic."

Leigh's laughter faded away. The sound of a door closing cut it off completely.

Anissa's expression morphed from amused to . . . tentative. He reached for her hand. "Good morning."

She squeezed his fingers. "Morning. How did you sleep?"

"Eh. I sleep on my left side, so . . ."

She grimaced. "Sorry."

He raised her fingers to his lips. "Any second thoughts?"

"About letting you dive?" She smiled at him. A devious smile. A flirty smile. "Nope. There's absolutely nothing you could do to make me change my mind."

Gabe almost dropped her hand. Anissa Bell was flirting with him. His heart thudded against his rib cage as he kissed one knuckle, then the next, then the next. "That sounds like a dare to me."

Her teasing smile softened. "I think we'll have to table this discussion for later. I have a lot to do before we dive. Well, before I dive."

He released her hand. "Fine, but don't think for a second that I won't bring it up again."

"I'm counting on it."

Forty-five minutes later they were the only two investigators in the homicide office. She was working. A study in intense concentration.

He was intensely concentrating on her.

"Gabe," she said without looking away from her computer.

"Hmm?"

"If you don't quit staring at me like that, our first real kiss is going to be in this office, and for what it's worth, I'd really rather we save it for somewhere — anywhere — else."

He almost fell out of his chair. "What do you mean our first real kiss?"

She cut her eyes at him for a second and then trained them back on her monitor. "You know exactly what I mean. I know you remember. You weren't drunk that night. At all."

Oh, he knew. He'd never forgotten anything about that night. Not one moment. Especially not the kiss.

She didn't think that kiss was real? Did she think he went around kissing everybody like that?

The phone rang. "Chavez." It was the captain requesting his presence. "I'll be right there, sir." Great. Time to find out if he'd lost the case.

Even with his stress levels reaching the stratosphere, he couldn't resist leaning over Anissa's back as she sat in her chair. He put his right hand on her shoulder. His lips brushed the tip of her ear. "Whoever said that wasn't a real kiss?"

He squeezed her shoulder and left the room before she could respond. But as the door closed behind him, he looked back. She was staring after him, eyes wide, face red . . . smiling.

Gabe wasn't smiling when he got back to the office fifteen minutes later. Anissa wasn't at her desk, but Ryan was at his.

"What's the matter with you, man?" Ryan asked as he slid into his chair. "Honestly, I would have expected you to look a little happier. Did she break up with you already?"

"No, she didn't," Anissa said as she returned to the office and sat at her desk. "Don't we have work to discuss?"

"Yes," Gabe said.

"Not really," Ryan said.

Anissa shook her head at the two of them. "I'm with Gabe."

"She's with me." Gabe pointed to his chest. Ryan made a disgusted face, but Gabe could tell he wasn't displeased. Maybe cautiously optimistic.

"Work?" Anissa prompted. She didn't look up. She started typing something, her gaze locked on her screen.

"Right. Work. The captain is sure Anissa's in danger and not thrilled the Campbells are providing security but rolling with it for the moment. And if I ever want to see a promotion, I need to solve the Jeremy Littlefield case. Yesterday."

Gabe needed a break in this case. How could he ever be what Anissa needed if he couldn't even keep his job? There were so many reasons — reasons he'd barely allowed himself to consider — why Anissa was the perfect person for him. But this work drama was one reason why dating Anissa was a bad idea. How could he keep her fooled into thinking he had a clue about what he was doing in life if she was sitting across from him, a witness to every failure — big and small?

Anissa never stopped typing. "Number one, the danger to me has nothing to do with the Jeremy Littlefield case. Number two, the captain can't hold you personally responsible for what Charles Campbell is doing. If anyone should be worried about the captain's annoyance with the Campbells, it should be Adam. Third" — she looked at Gabe this time — "the captain is the one worried about his promotions, so he's taking it out on you."

Ryan pointed his pen in Anissa's direction. "I agree with everything she said."

"You weren't in there." The captain had been . . . ticked.

"I've been in there before," Ryan said.

"Same here," Anissa said. "Your success rate is so high that you haven't gotten the 'this case is two weeks old and I'm looking bad' lecture before. Welcome to the club."

"We should get jackets," Ryan said.

"Yes," Anissa agreed. "With patches or something for repeat lectures."

"I like it," Ryan said.

Gabe couldn't decide if they were being helpful or truthful. Or both.

"Did he say anything else about taking you off the case?" Ryan asked.

Anissa stopped typing. "What? No. He can't."

"No. He said as long as I could work this week, he'd rather me stay on the case."

"That was big of him." Ryan tossed a wadded-up piece of paper into the recycling bin. "I'd like to see how quickly he'd come back to work after getting stabbed."

"Exactly." Anissa took a sip of coffee, but instead of staring at her monitor she was looking at him. When they made eye contact, she smiled. That same tentative smile from this morning. The one that said, "Hey, I like you and I'm excited to see where this goes." Or at least that's how he'd chosen to interpret it.

If he could get smiles like that from time to time, maybe working every day with Anissa wouldn't be so bad after all.

Not diving with Anissa was torture.

At one that afternoon he stood on the dock and watched as she ran the side sonar from the boat. Lane was with her. And Stu. And two other guys dressed in casual clothes who would have looked dangerous even if they hadn't been armed to the teeth. Where had Charles Campbell found these two?

320

They weren't from around here, that was for sure.

Adam, in a wet suit and carrying his BCD, joined Gabe on the dock. "Have they found anything?"

"No."

"Ryan coming?" Adam called out to Anissa on the boat.

"Right behind you." Ryan joined them. "Someone tell me again why we think the arsonist tossed accelerant into the lake? This dock is a long hike from the cabin. Or what's left of the cabin."

"Your nosy neighbors." Gabe pointed to the docks across the lake.

"My nosy neighbors?"

How could Ryan not figure this out? "Apparently after that situation we had last year. You may remember it? We were on a training dive and found a —"

Ryan held up a hand. "What's your point, Chavez?"

"My point is that most of the folks in the cove upgraded their security systems. Bigtime. Cameras on their property and cameras pointing out into the lake." He pointed to a house in the dead center of the cove. "That guy went all out. He heard about the case after he moved in here this winter and now he's got cameras everywhere. Well-hidden cameras. Good cameras. He's the one who called the cops before we even got off the water last week. And he has a blurry but convincing image of someone dumping something last night before the cabin went up in flames.

Anissa had turned the boat back toward the dock and made another pass near the left side of the dock.

"I don't like this at all," Gabe muttered, still staring at Anissa in the boat.

"What's his problem?" Ryan directed the question to Adam.

"Pouting." Adam had the nerve to laugh.

Gabe ignored him.

"Ah. Jealous."

"Agreed. But I can't decide if he's jealous of us getting to dive or of the security guards."

Ryan made a show of studying the boat, and the people in it, before he responded, "Both. Definitely both."

"You two can shut —" A piercing whistle stopped Gabe's retort.

Anissa had idled the boat five feet from the dock and was now hovering beside Lane.

"Is that what I think it is?" Did Lane's hand tremble as he pointed to the screen?

18

Another body?

Really?

She studied the sonar image. Unlike the last body they'd found, this one hadn't been wrapped in plastic. Arms and legs were clearly visible.

Anissa patted Lane on the back. "It's okay. Let's mark this location and finish our scan."

She leaned over the side of the boat. Gabe, Ryan, and Adam all stood at the edge of the dock, as close to the boat as they could get. She focused on Gabe. "This was not here last week."

Gabe's frustration was evident. He wanted to be on the boat. Diving with her. Taking care of business.

Ryan's expression was resigned. They all knew he would be going down to get the body.

Adam's skin had a definite green tinge to

it. She'd spare him the body work if she could because this one was going to be gory. Adam had driven the dive van to the scene from the sheriff's office. "Adam, I may be wrong. I hope I'm wrong." She wasn't wrong, but maybe some kids had dropped a dummy or something that looked exactly like a human in the water. "But I think we'll need a body bag. Would you be willing to get everything we need from the van? I don't want Gabe trying to carry stuff with that arm."

Adam nodded. Relief and gratitude in his eyes. "On it."

She turned back to Lane and Stu. "You don't have to do this. Ryan and I can handle the actual recovery. But I think you both need to be prepared to assist."

"Yes, ma'am." Lane swallowed hard.

Kelly Stuart blinked three times in rapid succession before she managed a nod.

Lane dropped the buoy and they spent the next thirty minutes finishing their search pattern. Two other large objects rested on the lake bottom, to the left of the dock. Anissa sent Lane and Stu down to get them first. Two gasoline tanks that had probably — hopefully — been empty before they'd been tossed in the lake, where they'd filled with water and sunk.

She left Adam on the boat and Gabe supervising from the dock as she, Ryan, Lane, and Stu descended the buoy line at the body.

Visibility wasn't awful, which in this case was both a blessing and a curse. The visibility would make it easier for them to work together and get the body in the bag. But it also meant they could see the bloating and putrefaction. And the fact that there wasn't much of a face on this body. Stu got one good look and swam away. They could all hear her retching. But to her credit, she returned.

There was a gun — a pistol — a few feet away. And weights — not enough to keep him down for long but enough to have pulled him to the bottom.

A suicide? A murder? She didn't know. And in this moment, she didn't care. She would care about that later, but not until they had recovered all the evidence.

Anissa focused all her attention on whether her team was doing what they'd trained to do. She and Ryan gave them pointers and advice, but for the most part the two relative newbies handled the recovery on their own. Anissa was so proud that she wanted to hug both of them. Instead, she fist-bumped them and told them they were awesome as they brought the body to the surface.

Gabe had called Dr. Oliver and she was waiting for them at the dock. So was the forensics team.

And Mr. Cook.

As soon as they had the body on the dock, he identified him. "That's Ronald Talbot." There was so much sadness in his voice that Anissa longed to put her arm around him, but she didn't want to leave him a dripping mess.

"Are you sure?" Gabe didn't ask the question in a mean way. But the truth was, there wasn't much face to go on.

"Tattoo. Left arm."

It was a distinctive tattoo, and while neither Anissa nor Gabe recalled seeing it during their brief encounter with Ronald Talbot, Anissa had no doubt Mr. Cook would be proven right.

The sun was low over the lake by the time Anissa was ready to call it a day.

Dr. Oliver had taken the body to the morgue and Forensics had taken charge of all the underwater evidence they'd recovered.

Stu and Lane were draped across seats on the boat. Both of them wearing the look of people who were proud of what they'd done but wished they hadn't had to do it. Anissa's two bodyguards were on the dock, looking like they wanted to be anywhere other than where they were. She understood the feeling.

Anissa stood on the dock with Adam, Ryan, and Gabe. "Adam, if you'll take the van back to the office, I'll go with Lane and Stu. We'll take the boat to the marina. All our cars are there."

"Anissa, you can go home tonight if you want to as long as you take your security detail with you," Ryan said. "The house has been checked for explosives, listening devices, everything. Gabe, Leigh says she'd rather you stay at our place tonight, but she understands if you're ready to go home too."

All Anissa wanted right now was to sleep. In her own bed.

"I'm coming with you," Gabe said.

She didn't have the energy to argue. They both climbed onto the boat. "Take us home, Lane."

Lane grinned and fired up the engine.

An hour later, after a quick stop for takeout, she stood outside her house with Gabe as her two security guards entered first. When they had cleared the house, they opened the door. "We'll stay out here for now, ma'am.

When you're ready to call it a night, let us know."

"Thank you."

Gabe was talking to the security guards as she walked into her house. Her space. Her little corner of the great big world.

And nothing felt right.

The crime scene cleanup crew had done a great job, but the chairs were in the wrong place. The bare pillow taunted her. The last time she'd been here, Gabe had nearly died.

The door closed behind her — a soft click that startled her just the same.

"Nis?"

Gabe stood a foot away, his right hand outstretched toward her. She wasn't used to this. She usually came home from a dive or a crime scene and dealt with it.

Alone.

She took a step in Gabe's direction and he closed the distance. His right hand slid around her waist and pulled her against him. He didn't speak. She didn't either. She soaked in the strength of his presence.

"Would you rather I leave you alone? Give you some space?" Gabe whispered in her ear.

Would she?

No. No, she definitely would not.

■ ■ ■ ■

Gabe's phone buzzed in his back pocket. "You have got to be kidding me." He spoke the words into Anissa's hair. He would never, ever get tired of having her head an inch below his chin. Or of the thrill he got every time she stepped toward him rather than away from him.

Her laughter shook against his chest. "Better get that, Investigator Chavez."

He had to let go of her to get the phone. Stupid sling.

"Don't go away," he said as he pulled the phone from his pocket. "Yes?"

"Gabe, yo, man. This is Dante."

"Dante? What's up?" Anissa had stepped back, her brows drawn. He held the phone out and whispered, "Put it on speaker."

She did.

"I tried to call Investigator Bell, but her phone went to voice mail."

"Sorry about that, Dante," Anissa said. "I was on a dive. I think my phone may still be in my bag."

"Yeah. I saw all that stuff you sent us from your dive." Dante didn't sound enthused. "You're keeping me crazy busy."

"Call it job security." Anissa laughed. "You

got something for us?"

"I do. Those prints you asked me to get off the water bottle."

"Yes?" Anissa prompted him.

"I finally found a good one and they are definitely a match."

Anissa dropped to her knees.

"But I got to tell you," Dante continued, "the method I used destroyed the print, so unless you can get me another one, I've got nothing to go to court with. You said you didn't care about that, so I risked it."

Anissa put her face in her hands and rocked back and forth.

"Yo. Did you hear what I said? The prints match. That's what we wanted, right?"

"Dude," Gabe chimed in. "You have no idea. We owe you big-time."

Gabe was almost sure Anissa was praying. And maybe crying. She cleared her throat. "Thank you, Dante. You have no idea how important this is."

Gabe would have to explain everything to Dante later. For now, he needed to get off the phone. "Listen, Dante. In the morning, do you think you could focus on anything you get from Dr. Oliver? I know you guys are swamped, but the guy we pulled out of the lake may be our shooter in the Jeremy Littlefield case."

"Oh man." Dante's tone changed. "Seriously?"

"Seriously."

"We'll take care of it."

"*Gracias*, Dante. I'll check in with you tomorrow."

Gabe disconnected the call and laid the phone on the floor. He knelt in front of Anissa.

Lord, I'm going to need some help. I have no idea what to do here.

"Jillian is alive," Anissa whispered.

"Yes."

"I need to get a warrant for her DNA. I need to talk to Velma Brown. I need to call Mr. and Mrs. Davidson." She looked at Gabe then, full-on panic in her eyes. "Oh my word, I need to talk to Liz."

"Not tonight."

"Gabe."

"Not tonight. We still don't know what Velma Brown knows or doesn't know. We go in asking a bunch of questions in the wrong order and we could make a mess."

Anissa nodded in slow motion. "Sorry. I don't know what's wrong with me. I'm not usually this —"

"What? You're telling me you have a lot of experience with finding a lost child thirteen years after her abduction?"

331

"Of course not."

"Okay, then I think you're allowed not to know how to react." He lifted a strand of hair that had stuck to her cheek and tucked it behind her ear. She didn't flinch or pull away. "I have no idea how it's going to work out. And I'm not going to give you any false promises. It may get harder before it gets easier. But I can promise you one thing."

"What?"

"I'll be here. No matter what."

"I don't think you're going to want to hang around for this."

"Just try to get rid of me." He traced her cheek with his thumb. Her cheek warmed under his touch.

He got to his feet, then helped her up. "What do you want to do?"

"Eat."

"Oh, thank goodness. I'm starving."

Anissa laughed, then closed her eyes. "I don't know how to do any of this, Gabe. I don't want to hurt you and I'm afraid —"

He put one finger on her lips, then traced her jaw. "One day at a time, Nis. Remember? We aren't going to figure out our whole lives. We're going to eat. Then sleep. And see what tomorrow holds."

"You just promised me you weren't going anywhere."

He walked over to the table and pulled out the aluminum foil trays of tacos, the paper bag of tortilla chips, and the foam container of salsa. Doing everything without the use of his left arm was annoying. "Oh, I'm not."

"Do you not see the flaw in your argument?" She grabbed a chip.

"There's no flaw. *I'm* not going anywhere. But if I start professing my eternal devotion, you're going to kick me out because you'll think I'm moving too fast. And I really don't want to have to sleep on your porch."

She rolled her eyes and shoved a plastic fork into his hand. "Eat."

It turned out that Anissa's couch slept great. But the sun shining through the transom windows woke Gabe bright and early. He found Anissa's coffee and started a full pot. He opened the front door and spoke to the guard right outside. The guard assured him everything had been quiet and handed him a container. "A friend of yours stopped by. She said you would need this."

Gabe recognized it immediately. It was one of Leigh's cupcake holders with little spaces for each cupcake. Gabe opened the lid. Six ginormous blueberry muffins were interspersed between six cupcakes. Clementines took up six more of the spots, while silicone cupcake liners holding a mixture of blueberries and strawberries filled the remaining spaces.

"She also said to tell you to share." The guard was all but drooling.

"Help yourself."

The guard grabbed a muffin and some berries.

Gabe left an assortment of the goodies on the little table on Anissa's porch and carried the remaining items inside. He selected a muffin and a clementine and took a huge bite of the muffin before pouring himself a cup of coffee.

He thought about waiting for Anissa, but he was starving. And he had no idea how long she would be.

She probably wouldn't mind if he nibbled on a muffin while drinking his coffee.

He settled himself at Anissa's kitchen table and picked up his phone. The first order of business for today — after coffee — was to check in with Brady St. John. Brady had texted him last night, but with the busyness of bringing up the body Gabe hadn't had a chance to call him back.

"What did you find out about Velma Brown?"

"She's sick but not dying. At least not yet. It's dicey. She won't be able to return to work anytime soon. She's a wreck about what this is going to mean for her daughter. She's disappointed that it isn't as simple as a few months of chemo and then straight to the land of recovery. But she's thankful to be alive."

"How'd you get all this?"

"I asked her."

"You did what?"

"It seemed like the easiest approach. And I agree with your hunch. No way that woman knows there was anything hinky about the adoption. She adores that girl. And she wasn't nervous to be talking to me. She was embarrassed that her plan hadn't worked. Said she was afraid everyone would think she was a bad mother but that she'd been trying to give Liz a fabulous summer. I asked her if she was well enough to come up to Carrington if we could get her there. She said she was. I told her I'd be back in touch today."

Gabe considered the possibilities. "It would be best if she could come here. I might know of a place she could stay." He knew without asking that Leigh would fall all over herself to welcome Velma and Liz into their home. Ryan would roll with it.

"So, the girl in the hospital, she's definitely your missing person?"

"Prints confirmed it last night. And the pictures. The resemblance is uncanny. The timing. Everything. And Anissa says she has mannerisms of her birth mother. We need DNA to be one hundred percent sure, of course, and we'll get that ball rolling today. But there's no doubt in my mind that Liz Brown is Jillian Davidson."

Brady let out a low whistle.

"Tell me about it."

"Well, I owe the Carrington folks for eternity anyway, so I'm good for whatever you need. Especially in a case like this. If you give me the go-ahead, I can get Velma Brown up there today. She seemed anxious to see her daughter. To tell her the truth about her illness."

"Okay. Let me do some work on this end and I'll get back to you."

Anissa stumbled into the kitchen as he disconnected the call. He hopped up from his chair and poured her a cup of coffee. He set it in front of her, along with a muffin and a cupcake liner of strawberries and blueberries, but he didn't speak.

Anissa had many wonderful attributes. Waking up cheerful was not one of them. She operated best after nine hours of sleep.

And if she'd been shorted, then it was the better part of wisdom to wait to speak until she had consumed at least one cup of coffee.

"Thank you," Anissa said after she finished the muffin.

"Welcome."

She stood to refill her cup and trailed her hand across his shoulder as she passed.

If he hadn't been awake before, he was wide-awake now.

She returned with a cupcake and a full cup. She broke off the bottom of her cupcake and crammed it on the top, sandwiching the icing in between. She caught him watching her. "I know. I know. I'm weird."

"I like weird."

She smiled. "Who were you on the phone with?"

He filled her in on his conversation with Brady.

"I've been thinking about it. I want to go talk to Mr. Cook this morning. Find out as much as I can about Ronald Talbot. We already know the guy's house is gone. Forensics has been all over that property for days. All that's left for me to do is run financials and try to find out if he owned anything anywhere else, and Mr. Cook may be able to help me with that. Then I need to be at the morgue by eleven. Dr. Oliver said she would start the autopsy around then."

"Are you going to tell him about Liz? Or should we call her Jillian?"

"I think I will tell him. He's prayed about that situation since it happened. I think he would be able to give me some solid advice. As for her name . . . I think we'll have to let her decide when the time comes. She's about to have her whole world upended. The least we can do is let her decide on her own name."

19

Anissa pulled into Mr. Cook's driveway thirty minutes later. Her security detail parked behind her.

Gabe hadn't been thrilled about going their separate ways, but she'd promised to call him and give him regular updates. He'd promised the same.

She was trying not to think about how weird it all was, but she did like it.

Mr. Cook didn't give her a chance to close the car door before he called out to her. "Where's Gabe? Surprised to see you without him."

"He's working. Same as me."

Mr. Cook chuckled as he held the screen door to the porch open for her. "Come here, child."

He put his arm around her shoulders and led her to the rocking chairs. "Hungry?"

"No." She rubbed her stomach. "Leigh sent over muffins, cupcakes, and fruit this morning. She sent enough for a dozen people."

"How many people were there?"

"Four."

Mr. Cook slapped his knee and howled with laughter. "That girl. She has her mother's way. Hospitality oozing out of every pore."

"I didn't get that gift." Anissa tried not to sound bitter.

"You got plenty of your own. You've found your own band of travelers to go through this life with and all of you have your own strengths. If you and Leigh both cooked, the whole lot of you would be miserable. You only need one Leigh. God knew."

"Yeah. God knew I would need friends to pick up all my slack. It's not like I bring anything to the table."

"Balderdash. You're organized. Smart. You think things through and don't run off half-cocked. You're a teacher. A leader. They all count on you and you always come through."

She'd never thought about herself that way.

He bequeathed an indulgent smile on her. "I love seeing you find your place in this world."

Had she? "I always figured I was a big

disappointment. To you. To my family."

"What have any of us ever done that would make you think that?" Mr. Cook leaned toward her, intensity sparking in his wise eyes. The question wasn't rhetorical. He wanted an answer.

"I mean, because I stayed here. Became a cop. Didn't go to the mission field. It's not like what I'm doing has the same kind of importance as —"

"Whoa. You stop that nonsense this moment."

"It isn't nonsense. I'm not leading people to Christ. I'm not changing their eternal destination. By the time I get the case, they're already wherever they're going to be."

Mr. Cook leaned back in his rocker. "So you're saying that since you aren't on the mission field, your work isn't important?"

"I'm saying it isn't *as* important. It's not like I got called back to Yap. I had to stay."

"Why is that?"

The why wasn't that complicated from her perspective. "I never felt any peace about leaving. Always felt like this was where I was supposed to be. I couldn't leave with Carly's death unsolved."

"So you were called to stay here?"

"No. I wouldn't say it was a calling. Just

that —"

"Why wouldn't you say it was a calling?"

"Because I was already here. I just stayed. I messed up and I had to stay."

Mr. Cook looked out over the porch railing toward the lake. "Funny. I've never thought of it that way. From where I sit, I see a young woman who stayed to do something she felt like she should do. That sounds a lot like a calling to me."

"But —"

"Let me ask you a question." Mr. Cook waved a hand toward his yard. "Do you think my life has mattered?"

Anissa had no idea where he was going with this, but she would play along. "Of course."

"Why? I haven't lived anywhere else. I was born on this land. Well, technically I was born on land that's about two hundred feet below the surface of Lake Porter now, but on this same land my daddy and granddaddy owned. I've been to Yap a few times. Sent some money. But I've never spent more than a few weeks on a mission field. I don't preach. What's been so special about my life?"

How could he even say that? "You're kidding, right? You've changed lives all over the world. You've supported my family and lots of others. You're a pillar in this community. You've protected and preserved land around the lake, you've supported everything from churches to Little League teams. I bet there's not a single person in Carrington who hasn't somehow benefited from your presence in this community."

"But I was never called to the mission field. Never called to preach. By your standards, that means I'm not as important as others."

"I wasn't talking about you." Anissa could see where his argument was heading now.

"You could have been. When I was young, I told God I would do anything he wanted me to do. Go anywhere he wanted me to go."

"So did I."

Mr. Cook patted her hand. "Do you think God looked at me and thought, *Eh, he's not that great. Let's leave him in Carrington, a Podunk town where he won't be able to cause much trouble?*"

She couldn't answer.

"I know you think you messed up and missed God's best for you. But I wish you would consider the possibility that God called you to police work. That he gave you the skills needed to be a fabulous investigator. That his plan — his good works planned for you before the foundation of the world — was always for you to change lives right here."

He leaned back in his chair. "When I told God I would do whatever he wanted, I thought it would be big and flashy. I never dreamed it would mean staying here. Working this land. Doing his work but doing it from the sidelines, wearing a pair of overalls.

"Sometimes God calls his children to sacrifice everything and serve him in far-flung places. Sometimes God calls his children to sacrifice everything and serve him in the up-close spaces. In the hospital, the courtroom, the classroom, the sheriff's office. Staying put and doing the hard work right where you are takes the same obedience, the same passion for the Lord, as any other calling."

Anissa tried to see things from his perspective.

"And don't tell me you don't make an eternal impact because it's too late for the people you come across. Yes, you pull bodies from the lake and the ground, and for them it's too late to change anything eternal. But then you work with their families. Their friends. You change things for them. Those things are huge. In the world we live in, God needs his children, men and women who love him first, to sacrifice themselves and protect our communities. Don't you think for a second that what you do doesn't matter to him."

He paused and pointed toward the lake. "You pulled a child from the lake who would have drowned without you. That child, her sister, her grandmother, they need Jesus every bit as much as the children in Yap."

Anissa considered his words.

"God's callings are as varied as his children, Anissa. All are necessary. None are reserved for the weak and unimportant to handle. You've spent your entire career looking toward a future that God never intended for you instead of resting in the amazing life he's called you to right here."

Anissa brushed away a tear. She hadn't come over here to get her entire philosophy of career and calling turned on its head.

Mr. Cook pulled in a deep breath and blew it out. "I do love you, child. Not sure why God decided this morning was the time for me to unload all that, but it's been building for a while. His timing is always perfect. I know that for sure. Now, what did you come over here to talk to me about?"

God's timing was interesting. She knew that for sure. "I need to talk to you about

Ronald Talbot. And I need some advice, because I've found Jillian Davidson. She's alive and reasonably well in the Carrington Hospital."

Gabe checked his watch.

Again.

Anissa had been gone . . . well, she'd been gone only two hours, which wasn't that big of a deal. She was probably still talking to Mr. Cook. They were probably having a prayer meeting for all he knew.

She wasn't even supposed to be in the office until afternoon. Staring at the clock wouldn't speed things up.

He buried himself in the paperwork and details of the Jeremy Littlefield case. The reports on the gun — a .270 hunting rifle — didn't exactly narrow down the suspect pool. Deer hunting was a popular pastime in central North Carolina and lots of hunters owned .270s.

Most people with .270 hunting rifles kept a scope on them. They were powerful rifles designed to take out game from a significant distance. With the right scope and a bit of luck, a good shooter could hit something a quarter of a mile away. A marksman could hit something a lot farther away, which was interesting enough, but Ronald Talbot hadn't struck him as a hunter. Or a marksman. And that left Gabe with a suspect list that now included every hunter in the state.

The phone on Anissa's desk rang. Gabe hopped up and answered it. "Chavez."

"Oh, hey, Gabe. It's Dante again. I was trying Anissa. Is she there? If not, I'll call her cell."

"She isn't in the office yet. She was running down some leads on Ronald Talbot and then going straight to the autopsy."

"Okay, thanks."

"Wait, Dante. Come on, man. You're killing me. Whatcha got?"

"You'll have to talk to Anissa. Sorry, man, but it's her case. And I don't know what's going on with you two, but I don't think you're quite to the 'what's mine is yours and what's yours is mine' stage."

Dante's laughter ended abruptly as he disconnected the call.

Gabe stared at the phone. *That little . . .*

He sat in his chair. Dante wasn't wrong to shut him down. But now he was dying to know what Dante had found. And how did he know about him and Anissa?

His phone rang. "Chavez."

"This is Paisley. I, um, I was wondering if we could talk."

Gabe pulled in a deep breath. *Help me be*

wary of any tricks she might be pulling, Lord. "Sure."

"First, how are you feeling?"

"Fine."

One-word answers weren't exactly conducive to true conversation, but he was still suspicious of her motives.

"That's . . . good." Paisley sounded unsure and hesitant. "Listen, the hospital is releasing Brooke this morning. We're heading home, and I'm worried about Liz. I've gathered that the doctors are ready for her to go home, too, but they keep coming up with stuff to test or check because they are trying not to release her."

"Right. Look. This is off the record, and if it winds up on the news —"

"It won't."

"Fine. A buddy of mine in Columbia talked to Liz's mom yesterday. She's sick, but there's hope. She wants to talk to Liz face-to-face to explain what she did and why, but she's not healthy enough to have Liz come home yet. I mean, Liz isn't a three-year-old, but she's recovering herself and doesn't need to have to take care of her mom. We're working on getting Liz's mom up here. I still have some phone calls to make, but we haven't forgotten Liz and we're working on it."

"That's wonderful! What a relief! I feel so responsible for her. Like leaving her here is deserting her. She's been the best thing that could have happened to Brooke."

Gabe could imagine. "I give you my word that we won't leave her there. And she can't go back to camp anyway. Did you hear the health department shut them down yesterday and sent the kids home?"

"I did. I'm supposed to be interviewing the owner of the camp tomorrow. He's furious."

"Well, he should have taken better care of the place and not let all those kids get sick. From what I've heard, it was completely preventable. I'd be willing to cut him some slack for an honest mistake or a situation where he didn't know about something in some old pipes or whatever. But by all accounts, he'd been warned."

"I promise I won't quote you on that." Paisley laughed and Gabe believed her. "But I couldn't agree more. I've got reports, sources, and —"

"And?"

"Maybe we should leave it at that." Paisley didn't sound hostile. But she was up to something.

"Paisley?"

"Yes?"

"Be careful. That owner out there? I don't get a good feeling about him. You aren't going to be interviewing him alone, are you?"

"My cameraman will be out with me."

"That's it?" Gabe pictured a guy. Six feet tall. One hundred forty pounds. Barely able to hold the camera.

"Have you ever met my cameraman?"

"Based on your response, I'm going to assume he's large and terrifying?"

Paisley laughed. "He played linebacker for NC State."

"Okay, so that's impressive, but how many years ago? Thirty?"

"Three. And he's still in great shape. I'll be in good hands. But thank you for the concern."

Gabe had to admit that Paisley Wilson — at least the version he'd met in the past week — wasn't as bad as he'd made her out to be. Maybe her mistakes were worth forgiving. "You're welcome. Just make sure they know at the station when you leave and when you're expected to return. I'm serious."

"I will."

He hung up and called Anissa.

"Bell," she answered in a soft voice.

"Are you in autopsy?"

"Yes."

"How would you feel about Brady bringing Velma Brown up here today if we can get Ryan and Leigh to let her stay at their house with Liz? Well, once Liz is out of the hospital."

"I think it would be great. Although I do worry that she will feel like we've ganged up on her."

Leave it to Anissa to worry about that.

"I don't think there's ever going to be an easy way to say, 'Hey, your daughter who you think you legally adopted was kidnapped and sold.' "

"True. And it would be easier to tell her here than there. If Brady would bring her up here, we could tell her tonight."

"Fine." Gabe was not looking forward to that at all. "I need to talk to Ryan and Leigh. Paisley Wilson called. They're releasing Brooke today."

"Good."

"And she says the nurses are finding every little thing they can think of to check on Liz in order to keep her a little longer, so my guess is if we show up with her mom, they'll let her out."

"Sounds good. I'm sure Leigh will say yes," Anissa whispered.

"Me too. Ryan may be less enthused, but he'll go with it."

"Agreed."

"Any news there?"

"Possible suicide. Possible homicide. Dante called. The keys we found on the body go to his car, the house, and a storage facility. I'm going to meet Forensics over there tomorrow morning at eight."

"Not today?"

"No." Anissa's frustration was evident. "Dante says they're swamped and the storage building is a low priority compared to some of the other stuff they're working on. Apparently there are other issues in Carrington besides the cases we have."

"Imagine that."

"But it may be for the best. I'm still not sure how to handle the whole situation with Velma Brown. I'll focus on that for tonight and then I'll be at the storage unit in the morning and drive Dante crazy."

"Want company?" *Please say yes. Please say yes.*

"Sure."

Sure? That was hardly the warm, flirty "yes, Gabe, I'd love to spend every second with you" kind of response he'd kind of been angling for, but at least it wasn't a no. "Okay. It's a date."

"Oh no, it isn't." Anissa was laughing but serious. "You cannot call a visit to a crime scene a date. It's business."

"Oh, come on. If we count crime scenes and dives, we could be up to a hundred dates in no time."

"Is there a rush to get to a hundred dates?" Anissa was laughing now.

"No. Just seems like a nice round number. Like after you've been on that many dates people kind of expect you to keep going on them and they aren't surprised by them."

"You're weird." Was it his imagination or did she say that in a very affectionate way? He was going with that.

"What's next for you today?" he asked.

"I'll be back in the office by three. I hope. And then I have to figure out how to find out what Velma Brown knew about Liz's adoption."

"Okay. See you in a bit. Be careful. Don't ditch your security guards."

He disconnected the call and punched in Ryan's number. He wasn't surprised at all when Ryan's response to the request was to call Leigh. Five minutes later, Ryan called him back. "We're in. Leigh's going to call Anissa, but she said our place might be a nice, safe space for Mr. and Mrs. Davidson to come see Liz as well."

Leave it to Leigh to think about that. "It would definitely be less hostile than a police station."

"Indeed. Although we have to see what Velma Brown's statement is, first. I think that will probably need to happen here."

"Yes. I agree," said Gabe.

"I guess Anissa's going to handle that?" asked Ryan.

"I guess. She's being pulled in so many directions and everything is happening at once. She's just trying to stay one step ahead of it. For today, I'm asking Brady to ask Velma Brown to come to Carrington. He's going to tell her we've been doing some investigating into her late husband's death and would like to speak with her about that if possible. Hopefully she'll come willingly and before we take her to get Liz. We can't let her go back to Liz if she was somehow involved in kidnapping her."

"True. Poor kid. I'm praying for the best outcome for everyone, but I sure can't see what it will be." Ryan summed up Gabe's own worries in that one line. "I'll be in the office later. Let me know what you need. The house will be ready for them tonight."

Gabe spent the next hour on the phone with Brady. Then on the phone with Velma Brown. Then on the phone with one of the pediatric nurses at the hospital. A quick call to Anissa, then to Brady, and the wheels were in motion. Velma Brown would arrive at the sheriff's office around four.

Father, please let us be doing this right.

20

Nothing went as planned.

Brady called Gabe at three that afternoon. He had Velma packed and headed toward Carrington, but there was no way she would be able to come to the sheriff's office. She was weak and fragile. She'd almost fallen twice on the walk to the car.

Instead of taking her to the sheriff's office, Brady went straight to Leigh and Ryan's house.

Leigh had explained the situation to the hospitalists working with Liz, and it took a few hours to figure out how to legally get Liz out of the hospital and to the Weston-Parker home without violating any laws. Not that anyone involved would press charges, but they needed to be sure they had all their paperwork correct in the case of an audit.

Someone figured something out. They explained it to Gabe, but after a few seconds, all he heard was "blah, paperwork, blah."

The result was that Velma Brown was welcomed into the care of Leigh at four thirty that afternoon. Leigh got Velma's signature on the forms they needed for Liz and handed them to Ryan, who took them back to the hospital. While Ryan handled the paperwork, Leigh tucked Velma into a cozy spot, fed her some homemade chicken soup, and insisted she sleep.

Liz was released from the hospital around seven that night and taken straight to the Parkers'.

Anissa and Gabe watched the reunion between mother and daughter from the deck. Liz was so forgiving and so worried about her mom. That girl was a gem.

But she'd been sick. And Velma still was.

They called it an early night and no one could blame them. The truth was that everyone involved was relieved to have this part of the process over.

Tonight had been easy enough.

Tomorrow night would be very different.

After another night on Anissa's sofa, Gabe volunteered to swing through the Chick-fil-A drive-through and grab biscuits for everyone, the security guards included. "I'll meet you at the storage unit at eight."

He wasn't sure if Anissa had given up

arguing with him about driving or if she just really wanted that chicken biscuit.

"What girl could resist a guy who brings Chick-fil-A?" Anissa called to him through her open window as she pulled out of her driveway, the security guards close on her tail.

But eight turned into eight thirty when someone who was allergic to bee stings was stung in the middle of the drive-through line. Everything stopped for fifteen minutes while the EpiPen was administered, the ambulance was called, and the minivan was moved out of the line and into a parking space.

With bags full of biscuits and minis, Gabe pulled into the storage facility parking lot and chose a spot between Anissa's car and the forensics van.

Two deputies were flanked by two Campbell guards. They stood on either side of an open roll-up door at the end of a long row of storage units. "Yo!" he called down the hall. No response.

"Yo!" he hollered again as he got closer. "I come bearing gifts."

This time Dante met him ten feet from the door and held up a hand. "Hold up, bro."

What was going on? "Where's Anissa?"

"She's inside. She's fine. Well, she isn't

fine. But . . . prepare yourself. Okay?"

Gabe handed Dante the bags and ran to the door.

Nothing could have prepared him.

Pictures of Anissa covered every square inch of the unit, including the ceiling. Newspaper articles highlighting her cases. Pictures of Carly. Pictures of a three-year-old Jillian. Pictures of Anissa's family in Yap.

Most of the pictures were a few years old.

But not all of them.

He spotted pictures of him and Anissa on a run. When had that been taken? Maybe April?

Pictures of him eating tacos with Anissa outside a food truck. That had been in May. Cinco de Mayo.

His gaze finally landed on the real, very much alive Anissa. She was in gloves, booties, and a hairnet, walking around the ten-by-ten space. She made the circuit and stopped when she saw him at the door. Confusion. Fear. Misery. All raced across her features. "Why would Ronald Talbot have these pictures of me? I don't understand any of this."

He didn't either.

Three hours later, Anissa still had no idea what was going on.

The cursory evidence in the storage unit indicated that Ronald Talbot had known Carly and held a grudge against Anissa for what happened to her.

There were copies of the documents that had been sent to Paisley Wilson. Exact duplicates. No way a different person was responsible.

Journal entries documented Anissa's friends, her favorite restaurants, her work schedule, her church, her gym, even her preferred grocery store.

At first blush, it appeared that Ronald Talbot had been a stalker — the photographs and obsession with Anissa's activities — but he didn't seem to have had any desire to obtain any truly personal information. No favorite books or movies or music. No favorite foods or brand of tennis shoe.

No. This data collection only made sense if his purpose had been to try to figure out the best way to kill her.

Anissa slid down the wall in the hallway outside the storage unit. She pulled her ponytail out from the hairnet and peeled the latex gloves from her hands.

The entire facility was shut down for the rest of the day. The sheriff personally stopped in — a very abnormal event. The captain spent an hour generally annoying everyone but then gave them free rein to do whatever they needed to do to figure out who had created this bizarre shrine to Anissa. If Ronald Talbot was the guilty party, then he was no longer a threat, but no stone was to be left unturned. No witness left unquestioned. No possibility left unexplored.

Forensics determined that prints were nonexistent. Nary a hair or a fiber was uncovered.

The management of the facility fell all over themselves to help, but they didn't have a clue. The security tapes — such as they were — were placed in Sabrina's hands when she stopped by to see the unit for herself.

Sabrina spent the vast majority of her time working in her lab with her computer as her weapon of choice, but once in a while she liked to see the scene of the crime for herself. She said it gave her a different perspective on the person she was trying to make sense of through their computer files. She arrived an hour after Gabe did, Adam at her side. Sabrina studied the room for fifteen minutes without saying anything. No one interrupted her. When she came back into the hallway, she wore a frustrated expression and needed only three words to explain what she'd seen. "This is — bizarre." Sabrina's nontechy pronouncement somehow made Anissa feel better.

Bizarre was the only word for it.

The autopsy of Ronald Talbot was bizarre too. He'd died of a gunshot wound that blew off half his face. Dr. Oliver had postulated two scenarios. One was that he'd tied weights to his ankles and shot himself on the edge of the dock, knowing he would fall into the water and the weights would pull him and the gun to the bottom.

At least for a while.

A lot of people didn't realize how much buoyancy a dead body developed when putrefaction set in. The weight needed to drown someone wasn't nearly enough to keep them from bobbing to the surface within a week.

Why he would do this and why he would do it this way remained a mystery. Dr. Oliver's other scenario was that someone else shot him, used the weights to submerge the body, and then tossed the gun in after him.

The security footage from the neighbor with the great cameras would be quite useful, except for the footage obtained during the thunderstorm, when the visibility went to almost zero.

No one in the neighborhood remembered hearing a gunshot in the middle of the night, but a well-timed shot that coincided with a rumble of thunder wouldn't have registered in anyone's memory.

They were missing something. She knew it. Gabe knew it. Dante knew it. Dr. Oliver knew it.

Even Mr. Cook knew it.

"Ron didn't do this, Anissa." Mr. Cook had arrived in a pickup truck two hours in. How he'd found out, she had no idea. Although it wouldn't have surprised her if her so-called security guards had been reporting everything back to Charles Campbell. And Charles Campbell wouldn't have hesitated to tell Mr. Cook.

"I know you want to believe the best about him," she said. "But the evidence, weird as it is, points to him."

"I don't believe it. Not for a second." Mr. Cook crossed his arms, his mouth set in a firm line. "You're in danger because the person who did this is not in the morgue." He looked at Gabe. "Don't you let her out of your sight."

"Yes, sir." Gabe's response had the weight of a solemn vow.

They'd found it a bit faster than he'd

expected, but that just meant he'd be getting his hands around Anissa's throat sooner than he'd dared to hope.

He'd chosen this particular unit because the security cameras had been damaged in the storm last week. When they'd called in for a repair, he'd jumped at the chance to fix them . . . and to ensure there was no footage showing him hauling everything in. It had taken him the better part of forty-eight hours, but it had the look of a place that had been curated over several months.

It wouldn't hold up to detailed scrutiny and that was okay. He didn't need them to think Ronald Talbot was the killer for long.

Just for long enough.

21

At 2:00 p.m., Anissa stood outside the sheriff's office family meeting room where Velma Brown waited on her. After a good night's rest, some of Leigh's healing food, and a sweet reunion with her daughter, Velma was ready to speak to them about her ex-husband.

Leigh had come up with the brilliant idea to invite Brooke Ashcroft over. Not to swim, but to hang out with Liz while Velma was gone. The last report Leigh had sent was that both girls were curled up in the den watching *Singin' in the Rain* and wondering how they'd missed the classic film.

Gabe stepped close behind her, and for a few seconds she allowed herself to lean into him. To soak up some of his strength. To breathe in the essence of him. He'd volunteered to come with her into the room, but she needed to do this alone.

She'd filled in the captain this afternoon

when she returned from the storage unit. He'd been shocked, concerned, and more than a little annoyed that his homicide investigators had been off on a tangent. But he'd also been understanding of the importance of this case to Anissa. The fact that he had a fourteen-year-old daughter may have helped. More than once, he whispered, "I can't imagine."

So, he would be watching along with Gabe, Ryan, and Adam. The latter two had no reason to be there other than that they wanted to be supportive, and she appreciated that more than they would ever know.

With one final prayer for wisdom, Anissa opened the door.

Velma Brown attempted to stand, but Anissa rushed forward and took her hand before she could get an inch off the sofa. The woman looked as though a glancing blow from a squirt gun would knock her over.

"Please, don't get up. I'm Anissa Bell. We met yesterday."

"Of course. I remember." Even Velma's voice had a thinness to it.

Lord, please give her the strength to handle this. Anissa sent up the quick prayer before speaking to Mrs. Brown. "Thank you for agreeing to talk to me today."

"That nice officer, Detective St. John, he said there were some questions regarding my husband's death that you thought I might be able to help answer? I'm not sure how I could. We've been divorced nearly a decade. Well, that's not entirely true. We've been separated a decade. The divorce took a few years. Maybe three? So we've been divorced seven."

"May I ask what the delay was with the divorce?"

"I couldn't find the man to divorce him." Velma ran a hand over her face, the skin like tracing paper over her veins. "I suspect he thought I wanted child support, but I didn't. But remaining married made things so complicated, especially with the medical insurance for Liz. I needed to get the divorce finalized so I could apply for all the things she needed without everyone asking for his financial information. And I needed him to give me full custody so there wouldn't be any issues there either."

"He didn't contest custody?"

Velma's eyes misted as she picked at a knot in her sweater. "No. He . . . we . . . it's hard to explain. We couldn't have children. Decided to adopt. We were thinking about fostering first, maybe adopting a child a little bit older, when a guy on my husband's crew — he worked construction — had a niece who needed to be adopted. This guy already had five kids of his own. Couldn't take on another. But the parents had died. No will. It was a mess. He knew we had been considering adopting an older child. Said he hated the thought of her going into the foster care system."

She shrugged. "I wasn't sure about it, but then I saw her. Such a doll. Precious. A little skittish, which was understandable. Cried for her mama. I know her mama loved her. I made it my goal to love her so much she'd never remember that there'd ever been a season when she didn't have a mama. Liz knows all this, of course. I told her. Never kept it from her. I wanted her to know she was doubly loved."

Anissa's heart twisted as Velma told her story. Jillian had cried for her mama. And Velma Brown had loved her enough to tell her how much her mama had loved her.

"We'd both, Sy and I, wanted a baby so much. Liz was the answer to so many prayers. And it hadn't cost as much as it normally would have, so we would be able to adopt again. I was thrilled. But Sy, he never seemed to take to her. It was strange. It was like he never bonded with her. He'd play with her. Make her laugh. Feed her.

But it was always like she was a stranger's child. Not like she was his daughter. It destroyed our marriage. I never understood it. Still don't."

Her voice trailed off. "He wasn't a bad man. But when he left, I was relieved. It made everything easier. I quit trying to fix things with him and I could focus on Liz. She was having health issues. Turned out to be kidney failure. Several years of dialysis. Then a transplant. She's done great since. We've had a good life. But then I got sick this spring and I panicked. Liz comes across as confident and strong, but she has some deep-seated fears of abandonment that my love has never been able to completely eradicate. I didn't want her to be afraid. Figured if she got a great summer of fun at camp — she's been to Camp Blackstone before and loved it — then when she got home, the worst would be over."

Velma gave a weak shrug. "But it hasn't worked out that way. The doctors tell me I have a good chance of living another five to ten years. Maybe more if they make some awesome medical advances. I need to stay alive until she's an adult and can manage on her own. She demanded I tell her every-thing last night. Give her the worst-case scenario. She said she forgave me. I hope she has."

"I'm sure she has, Ms. Brown. She seems like the forgiving type."

"Yes, she is." Velma blinked a few times. "But I've gotten us off track a bit, I'm afraid. What is it you need to know about my husband?"

Anissa took a deep breath. "Ms. Brown, there's something I need to tell you, and I'm afraid there's no easy way to say it. We wanted to ask you about your husband because there were some irregularities surrounding your adoption of Liz."

Anissa didn't think it was possible, but Velma Brown went even paler. "Irregularities?"

"Yes, ma'am. We don't have the DNA back yet, although a judge gave us the warrant for it and we expect it back anytime, but we do have fingerprint confirmation that your daughter is a child who went missing thirteen years ago." Velma leaned back against the sofa and Anissa had to get the rest of it out. "Her name was Jillian Davidson and she was taken from a city playground in Virginia and never seen again."

Velma's eyes filled with tears. "That can't be right. Her parents had died. Her uncle . . ."

Anissa didn't try to fill the silence. She

was 99 percent sure Velma Brown had no idea that Liz/Jillian had been kidnapped, but if there was any chance she did, this would be the time she might slip up.

"Does she know?" Velma asked.

A valid question. "No, ma'am."

"Do her . . . her parents . . . her birth parents . . ." Velma paused, no doubt letting the idea of birth parents sink in after years of believing they were dead. "Do they know?"

"No, ma'am. Although those are the next steps in the process. We expect to have the DNA back by tonight or tomorrow. Once that confirmation comes through, those notifications will happen immediately."

"They'll take her away from me, won't they?" Velma rocked back and forth on the sofa. Her breath started coming in short gasps.

Anissa clung to her own composure by the thinnest of threads. "I truly don't know. The family, the Davidsons, was devastated by Jillian's disappearance. I know they will want to have her back in their lives. But she's sixteen. You're the only mother she remembers and she adores you. I'm sure her wishes will come into play, but I can't make any promises."

"I didn't know. I swear I didn't know.

But . . ." Velma's tears fell from her cheeks to her lap. "I wonder if he did. It might explain why he never treated her as his own. Do you think he knew?"

Anissa had her own suspicions that went along with Velma's train of thought but no verifiable evidence. "I don't know if we'll ever know the answer to that."

Velma hugged her own arms tight, like she was trying to keep herself from falling apart. "I have no idea what to do."

"I understand that feeling," Anissa said. "I don't either."

"What's the next step?"

"You decide how to tell Liz. And prepare her for the Davidsons. That's a phone call they've been waiting on for thirteen years. I don't imagine they will delay in coming to see her."

Anissa's phone buzzed. "Excuse me." She pulled the phone from her pocket. Dante had texted her.

The DNA is a match.

She swallowed hard. "Ms. Brown, the DNA match has been confirmed. Your daughter is Jillian Davidson."

As Gabe stood in the observation room and

watched her break the news to Velma Brown, he knew for sure that he was in love with Anissa Bell.

She took Velma's hand and told her about Carly. About Jillian. Gave her a condensed version of her own role in the story. Velma cried. Anissa cried.

There wasn't a dry eye in the observation room either.

Then Anissa gave Velma a few moments of privacy to compose herself. When she joined him and the others in the observation room, they closed the blinds so they couldn't see Velma. Not that Velma would know one way or the other, but it seemed wrong to gawk at her in this moment.

"I don't know if I did that right." Anissa directed the words to Gabe first, and then her gaze moved around the room.

"You did great." Gabe almost pulled her in close, but then he remembered the captain was in the room.

Ryan, Adam, and the captain all backed him up. "None of us could have handled it better, Anissa." The captain gave her a rueful smile. "There's a lot of winning here for the Davidsons, of course, but there's also a lot of confusion and hurt for Liz and Velma."

They all stood in silence — the air thick

with the complexity of the situation.

"Have you thought about how you want to contact the Davidsons?" the captain asked.

"I have, but I'm not sure you'll like it." Anissa's eyes darted in Gabe's direction and back to the captain.

Gabe had no idea what she was up to, but he already didn't like where this was going. He had a bad feeling that the "you" who wouldn't like it was going to be him, not the captain.

The captain didn't seem to share Gabe's concerns. He smiled at Anissa as he said, "Let me guess. You want to drive to Virginia?"

Oh no.

"It doesn't seem right to make a phone call." Anissa's voice had taken on a pleading tone. "It's a two-hour drive. I need to do this."

"I understand." The captain was nodding like this was a done deal.

This could *not* be happening. Gabe stepped between Anissa and the captain. "I hate to be the Debbie Downer here, but we still have a situation going on with that storage room. And let's not forget that Anissa's been attacked. Multiple times."

"*Attempted* attacks," Anissa corrected him.

"That doesn't make it any better, Nis." Gabe tried, so hard, not to let his aggravation bleed through.

Based on Anissa's expression, he hadn't succeeded. Adam, Ryan, and even the captain all decided this was the right moment to check their phones. Cowards.

Anissa moved closer to him, her voice calm, almost a whisper, which somehow made it scarier. "I have lived with this for thirteen years, Gabe. Thirteen years. I searched bushes and Dumpsters with the Davidsons. I manned phones. I put up flyers. I have poured years of my life into the hope, slim though it was, that somehow, somewhere, Jillian was still alive."

"I know."

"No. You don't. No one does."

And just like that, her walls were up. He couldn't see them, but they were there.

The captain cleared his throat. "Anissa, I'm fine with you going. But you need to get back here ASAP. I realize this is huge and life-altering, but you have an active murder investigation on your hands and a very messy situation with that storage room that needs to be dealt with."

"Yes, sir. I'll drive there and back. Tonight."

"Sir, permission to go with her?" Gabe

had to ask.

"Can't do it, Chavez. You leave town with the Jeremy Littlefield case still hot like it is and we'll all catch it. Bell can handle this."

Gabe wasn't giving up that easily. "Then at least send someone with her. There may be someone trying to kill her."

"Ronald Talbot is dead," Anissa said. "He can't hurt me."

"Mr. Cook doesn't believe he did any of that," Gabe shot back.

He'd made a direct hit and he knew it, but Anissa recovered fast. "Mr. Cook always wants to see the best in people. Maybe he —"

"You can't have it both ways, Anissa. You don't get to think everything the man says is just shy of holy writ one minute and then discount his opinion the next."

Anissa glared at him. Right now the only energy between them was toxic. He didn't think she could get any unhappier with him, so he finished his argument. "You're taking a big chance that it was definitely Ronald Talbot. If you're wrong and there's someone else out there, then driving to southwest Virginia is like putting a sign out that says, 'Hey, come and get me,' and I don't think that's what any of us want."

Adam looked up from his phone. "The

security team that's been with her can go to Virginia. There are no jurisdictional issues."

The captain lifted his chin and for about ten seconds had some kind of internal conversation. "Agreed. Anissa, the security team goes."

"They can follow me. I don't want them in my car." Anissa snapped the words. Then closed her eyes. When she opened them, they were turned to Adam and filled with remorse. "I'm sorry, Adam. I appreciate it. I . . ." She shuddered. "I cannot handle a two-hour trip with people in the car. I need to think. To pray. To —"

"No apology needed," Adam said. "I get it. I would be the same way. But you do have to promise to keep them in the loop and not lose them." Adam gave her a quick hug. "I'll get it set up. And I'll be praying."

"Thanks."

Ryan followed Adam's lead. A quick hug and a whispered word that Gabe couldn't hear but that Anissa reacted to with a quick nod.

When the door closed behind Ryan and Adam, the captain made quite the show of looking from Gabe to Anissa. Then back to Gabe. Then back to Anissa. "Is there something going on I need to know about?"

Gabe waited.

Anissa shook her head, barely glancing up. Had the floor tiles become that interesting that she couldn't even look in his direction? "No, sir."

The captain rolled his eyes. "Okay. I'll try that question again in a few days. For now, Investigator Bell, I expect a full report and ongoing communication this evening. I'm short-staffed as it is. I can't lose a homicide investigator. Do you understand?"

"Yes, sir." Anissa acknowledged him and went back to her inspection of the flooring.

The captain paused with one hand on the door. "Investigator Chavez, regardless of what may or may not be going on between the two of you, may I suggest that you would do well to remember that you are not in charge of what Investigator Bell does or does not do? This isn't like when you were undercover and could get her assignment changed with a phone call."

Anissa's head popped up. Her eyes wide. Fury oozing from every pore.

He'd been wrong. Things had just gotten much, much worse.

The captain punched Gabe on the shoulder as he left and murmured, "Good luck."

As soon as the door clicked closed, Anissa was in Gabe's face. "What is he talking about? What did you do? Did you call and tell them not to send me back? Because they told me they had everything they needed and that you had to change your plans for the evening so I was done."

Gabe couldn't — wouldn't — deny it, but facing her wrath, he also couldn't seem to get any words to come out of his mouth.

She took his muteness as confirmation. "How could you? I was so excited to be chosen. It was a big deal. Did you not trust me? Was that it? Did you think I would blow your cover out of spite? Or did you think I couldn't handle it? The little girl didn't need to be in over her head with the bad guys? I'll have you know I was just fine. I didn't need you to come swooping in and save me."

Gabe had never forgotten that night. Every detail was burned into his brain. He'd been undercover for months. Every so often the captain would send someone in to get eyes on him and to pass or receive information. It worked well. Usually it was a guy. He'd come in one night to observe. The next night Gabe would pick a fight with him and they'd make the exchange and that was the end of it.

But he knew that wouldn't work when the captain sent Anissa.

Gabe had been furious. As much as he'd claimed to despise her, he had to admit there was something about her, something he couldn't articulate, but something he recognized as beautiful that deserved to be protected. It wasn't just physical beauty, although she certainly had that in abundance, but beauty of spirit. Someone like her — good in a way he couldn't even begin to comprehend — didn't belong in a nasty bar. Didn't deserve to have gangbangers pawing at her.

So he'd done the only thing he could do. He'd kept her close to him all night. Given the other guys the impression that she was his and they should leave her alone. Even going so far as to kiss her in a darkened alley right before he shoved her away — in view of the others, but far enough away that they couldn't hear him tell her he was sorry.

And when she'd left the bar that first night, he'd risked a phone call to tell the captain not to send her back.

If anything had happened to her. If those guys had . . .

He would have broken his cover to protect her. It was too much of a risk to have her around.

He'd hoped never to have to deal with her again. She was too infuriating.

Too confusing.

And now, years later, it was time to explain himself. He needed to fix this.

Now.

"You're right."

"Then why?"

He closed the distance between them, and before he thought it through enough to hit the pause button, his hands were on her face, his lips pressed to hers.

Soft, tender. Nothing at all like the kiss he'd planted on her that night. It was over almost as soon as it began, and he pulled away, his face inches from hers. "Because I'm in love with you. That's why."

22

Anissa had no idea how long they'd been standing there, Gabe's hands on her face, lips millimeters from her own.

She was mad. She had every right to be mad.

But . . .

He'd kissed her.

He . . . loved her?

"Um . . ." Anissa swallowed and tried again. "Gabe . . ."

Nothing worked. She couldn't move or speak. Her body refused to cooperate. Probably because it was locked in a pitched battle between her mind and her heart. One of which was still furious. The other was . . . not.

For his part, Gabe was looking at her the way an astronaut looks at Earth. Like he could see his home but couldn't quite reach it. His thumb brushed her cheek before he released her completely.

Her heart and mind continued to duke it out.

Say something.

What should I say?

"I love you too" works.

He lied to me.

Not technically.

He doesn't trust me.

That was years ago. You didn't trust him either.

Anissa couldn't tell if the awkward silence bothered Gabe, although she was getting the impression he would stare at her until she said something coherent. She tried again. "Gabe —"

A sharp *rat-a-tat-tat* on the door sent her back three steps, but it was a full five seconds before the door opened. Ryan leaned in, holding the door in front of him. "Sorry if I'm interrupting, but, Anissa, I think you should let Ms. Brown know we have everything we need before you leave, don't you? I'm sure she's ready to see Liz."

Anissa's mind and body finally synced and she managed to say, "Yes, that's a good idea," without stuttering.

Ryan's smile had a forced quality as he looked from her to Gabe. The sigh that followed filled the space with a melancholy vibe. Whatever he'd seen as he looked at the two of them, it hadn't been good. "I'll give you a minute." He closed the door.

Maybe if she didn't look at Gabe, she'd be able to speak. "I need to go."

In her peripheral vision she could see Gabe cross his arms and lean against the two-way mirror. "Be careful."

His attempt at nonchalance was so bad she risked a glance in his direction. He wasn't looking at her but was staring a hole in the opposite wall.

She didn't know what to do. This wasn't the time or place to hash it all out. What had that even meant? That he was in love with her now? Had been in love with her then? That made no sense at all. He'd hated her. Well, maybe not hated, but strongly disliked.

But that kiss . . . it was different from their first kiss. Sweet. Tender. It was the kind of kiss lifetimes are made of. The kind of kiss a girl could imagine she'd still be getting fifty years from her wedding day.

A sharp rap on the door jolted her from her musing. She stepped around Gabe. She had to say something. Didn't she? The problem was that she couldn't think. She squeaked out a "Bye, Gabe" and got out of there as fast as her shaking hand could turn the doorknob.

■ ■ ■ ■

An hour later Anissa was driving to Virginia. She'd been following Tonya Davidson's social media accounts since the moment she suspected Liz was Jillian. The family had moved to Galax, Virginia, eight years ago. From Tonya's posts, Anissa knew the family was in town, but would they be home? She would drive all over Galax if she had to. But it would be best to have this conversation in a private place.

She made it out of Carrington and hit the highway before the tears burst from her eyes. She should have pulled over, but that would have meant her escorts — the car in front of her and the car behind her — would witness her breakdown. So, she kept her sunglasses on and the tears slid down behind them. She cried for Carly. She cried for baby Jillian and sixteen-year-old Liz. She cried for Tonya and Steve Davidson. She cried for Jillian's siblings who had lived in the shadow of their sister's disappearance and now would live in the chaos of her return. She cried for Velma Brown. She cried out to the God who she believed with all her heart had been there that day . . . and hadn't stopped it.

And then, when she thought she'd cried all she could, a fresh wave hit her.

She cried for herself. For the girl she'd been and the woman she'd become.

A girl who'd blown it and paid for it.

A woman who'd had love in her hands and walked away from it.

How had she messed up this much?

A comment Mr. Cook had made during one of their many phone calls came back to her.

"I've known you a long time," he'd said. "You have a lot of great qualities. But one thing you might want to work on is being open to the gifts God is trying to give you."

She hadn't understood. "Sir?"

"You serve a big God, Anissa." Mr. Cook's chastisement always came with a healthy dose of positive observations. "You've always known him to be the kind of God who does big things. But sometimes even people who serve a big God can make the mistake of putting God in a box. A big box, to be sure, but a box all the same."

Anissa grabbed a tissue from the box she'd put in her front seat in case the Davidsons might need it.

"Oh, Lord, what have I done?" She whispered her confession. "How have I only imagined that you work in one way, when I know you are the God of infinity? I still don't see how there could be any good from Carly's death. Any good from Jillian's disappearance. From thirteen years of pain for her family. For me. I don't understand and I know I never will. But when did I stop believing you could — or would — give me anything good? When did I stop seeing my job, my friends, my life in Carrington as a gift from you? As your plan for me? When did I get it in my head that you would only give me the minimum?"

She blew her nose.

Gabe was not the minimum. Gabe was . . . more than she could have ever imagined.

But she'd closed that door. Literally and metaphorically.

Could she trust God with her shattered heart . . . again?

The tears ran out, but the prayer, the pondering, continued. Mile after mile. An hour into the drive, she got a text from Leigh. She had the car read it to her.

Velma told her. It was . . . tense. Liz yelled at Gabe big-time, but he handled it. He's got a really good way with teenagers. Anyway, I think Liz understands now. She doesn't want to leave Velma, but she's willing to see Mr. and Mrs. Davidson whenever they want to see her. She's a very empathetic girl. I have hope that God is going to do something amazing out of all of this.

Until the moment she pulled into the family's driveway, Anissa had no idea how she was going to say what she'd driven two hours to say.

Before she'd put her car in park, Tonya Davidson stepped onto the front porch.

As soon as she opened the door, Tonya called out, "Anissa? Is that you, hon? What are you doing here? Why didn't you call?"

Steve joined Tonya on the porch and Tonya clutched his arm. "Anissa's here."

They watched her approach. Eyes wide, darting. Nostrils flaring. Heads shaking. It took Anissa a moment to realize that they'd caught her before she had a chance to fix her face or her eyes. She must look like she'd cried for hours. After all these years, they would interpret her sudden appearance to mean she had bad news.

Anissa jogged up the steps. "I found her. Alive. She's alive."

Tonya sagged against Steve. Steve wrapped his arms tight around his wife, his own shoulders shaking as enormous tears dripped from his chin into her hair.

Anissa kept talking. She knew they would need all the details, but for now, they needed to hear only the most pertinent points. "She was adopted by a family that loved her. Her adoptive mother had no idea she'd been kidnapped. She believed the adoption was legal. But you need to know that she has loved Jillian — she loves Jillian — with everything in her. Your girl has been safe and warm and fed and loved."

Steve pulled Anissa into a hug with Tonya and they all cried. It didn't take long for Tonya to recover enough to ask the most pertinent questions of all.

She looked at Anissa's car. "Is she here? When can we see her? When . . . when can we get her back?"

Anissa pulled her phone from her back pocket. "She's in Carrington. She had a bad cryptosporidium infection. But she's doing fine, and she was released from the hospital yesterday. She's with her adoptive mother, Velma, at a friend of mine's house."

Tonya's disappointment was palpable.

"I have a picture though." Anissa turned the phone around. Tonya took it from her like a sacred chalice. She and Steve studied the photograph, with awe and love and joy and confusion all fighting for dominance on their faces.

"She has your laugh, Tonya," Anissa said. "She goes by Liz. That's the only name she knows. And she's a delight. She spent the better part of the past week encouraging a young patient who'd tried to commit suicide after . . ." Anissa couldn't keep going. "She's amazing."

Steve studied the photo. "Does she know?"

Anissa nodded. "She does now."

"When can we see her?" Tonya asked. So much hope. So much emotion in those five words.

"Tonight."

Gabe paced the deck at Ryan and Leigh's house.

Liz sat on the dock below. Alone. What must she be thinking?

She'd screamed at him after Velma told her. "You knew! You knew and that's the only reason we're here! That's the only reason you care! I'm just a case to be solved!"

He'd let her yell at him because he knew she needed to yell at someone and she was afraid to yell at her mom. And when she ran back up to her room and slammed the door, he patted Velma's arm and told her not to worry about it. That he'd been accused of much worse, by much worse people.

She'd eventually left her room and they'd let her go outside without stopping her.

Maybe by now she'd calmed down.

He walked to the dock, and when she didn't tell him to go away, he slid off his shoes, rolled up his pant legs, and took a seat three yards away. He dangled his feet over the edge of the dock, cooling them in the water, and started talking.

He shared the parts of the story that were his to tell. He left out the parts that were Anissa's.

Clearly Anissa needed to fight her own battles and didn't appreciate it when he tried to fight them for her.

He told Liz about Jeremy and Brooke, and why he and Anissa had been at the hospital that day. That Anissa had recognized her immediately. That it was nothing short of a miracle that they'd been in the right place at the right time. About how he'd been taken by Liz's joy. Her zest for life.

She was listening. He knew that much. At one point, she'd pulled off her own shoes and stretched her long legs toward the surface of the water.

He kept talking.

He wished Anissa was there, the way she'd

been there the day he'd talked to Brooke in the hospital, to give him little signals to let him know he wasn't messing this up. But she wasn't. And even if she had been, there was no guarantee the message would have been positive.

After a while, Liz faced him, threw her hands in the air, and said, "How am I supposed to handle this? Can you tell me that? I'm not an idiot. I get that the Davidsons" — the name rolled off her tongue like it was a foreign word she was trying to get the hang of — "are my biological parents and that they never wanted to lose me, so I can't be mean to them. I can't leave them to be miserable. But my mom is sick. She might even be dying! What am I supposed to do about that? Leave her? Go live with my stranger-parents?"

She pulled in a shuddering breath. "No matter what happens going forward, someone is going to be hurt."

"That's one way to look at it." He couldn't argue with her on that. "There's a minefield ahead of you for sure. But . . ."

Liz cut her eyes at him like she was daring him to find a way to make any of this better.

"Maybe a better way to see it is that, no matter what happens going forward, all of us will be different. And we'll get to decide whether that change is good or bad."

She frowned but didn't argue, so he pressed on.

"We'll all be more sympathetic. More loving. More willing to forgive. At least I know I will. I watched you with your mom. I know she hurt your feelings by hiding her illness from you, but you forgave her. You recognize that she isn't perfect and she made a bad decision, but you still love her and you've forgiven her."

"She's my mom. She's not hard to forgive."

"Fair enough. But it was still a good example for me. There are people I need to forgive. For a lot of things. Some grudges I've been holding on to for a long time. And it's time to put all that aside."

"You mean about Paisley, don't you?" Liz gave him an all-knowing smirk.

"Paisley is one thing. Yes."

Liz grinned a little.

"But there are other people I need to forgive for hurting me. For messing up my life. They don't even know they did anything wrong. Or they don't care. Either way, I need to forgive them. Not for their benefit, but for mine."

"What does this have to do with the fact

that my birth parents are on their way here?"

"Because no matter what happens over the next few weeks, there are bound to be mistakes that will require forgiveness. I can almost guarantee you there will be hurt feelings and hard words and aggravations, and when it's all said and done, the one thing you have control over is whether or not you'll forgive."

Liz didn't answer. Her gaze followed a boat as it pulled a wakeboarder into the cove. The rider held on tight as the boat turned, his speed increasing with every second until the boat was straight again and he was jumping the wake on the way back into open water.

When the silence returned to the lake, Liz's sighs were easy to hear. "Even the guy who took me away in the first place?"

Why did she have to ask him that? "That's a tough one. That might be one that takes a lifetime to manage."

"Probably."

Gabe didn't try to add anything. She stared at the water and so did he, watching the random bubbles popping up on the lake from unseen fish.

"Do you think they're nice? The Davidsons?"

The fear in her voice was a vise on Gabe's

heart. "I've never met them. Anissa thinks they're wonderful."

"And you think Anissa is wonderful." Liz didn't state it as fact as much as a taunt.

"That is none of your business," he said, softening the words with a wink.

Liz laughed. A real laugh. "I think you'd make a great couple. She's gorgeous, with that long hair, and have you noticed her biceps?"

Gabe wasn't sure how he was supposed to respond to that. Of course he'd noticed Anissa's biceps. He'd noticed everything about her. But that wasn't a conversation he was comfortable having with a sixteen-year-old. Thankfully, Liz kept going with barely a pause. "She's so healthy and fit. Is she a vegan?" Liz's horrified expression pulled a laugh from Gabe.

"She is not. She eats a lot of salads. And a lot of fish. She grew up on an island and seafood makes her happy. But she eats junk food too. She loves pizza. And Coke. She's barely human until she's had a cup or three of coffee in the morning. She loves cup-cakes, but she does this thing where she breaks off the bottom and puts it on the top so the icing is in the middle, and then she eats it like a sandwich."

Liz's eyes widened. "That's a great idea."

"Oh no. Not you too. I can't have two weirdo women in my life, decapitating their cupcakes. Cupcakes are supposed to be eaten the good old-fashioned way." Gabe pounded his fist on the dock.

Liz's giggles bubbled out of her. " 'Cause you're so old? What exactly is the old-fashioned way to eat a cupcake?"

"You bite into it, and if you get icing in your nose, then that's just an unfortunate side effect."

They both laughed. "I can't see Anissa wanting to get icing in her nose," Liz said.

"Good point."

"But if she eats junk food, how does she stay so fit? She just looks strong."

Liz's words rang with admiration. Gabe got a feeling he might know where this line of questioning was coming from. Liz's skin was still pale from her recent illness and her body was thin, but not in a healthy way. "Well, she doesn't eat junk food all the time. Remember. Salads? Fish? Lots of both? But she exercises too."

"A lot?"

"Almost every morning, unless she's working a case and can't go. She usually goes for a run on the weekend. And, of course, she swims."

"Brooke said you called Anissa a fish."

"You didn't notice her gills?"

"She doesn't have gills." Liz jumped to Anissa's defense.

"Okay. Fine. But she can hold her breath for a freakishly long time and she is the strongest swimmer I know."

"Stronger than you?"

"Way stronger."

The sound of doors opening and closing and then footsteps on the deck had them both turning around. Leigh leaned over the rail and called out, "I have supper ready. I wish you would come eat something. Velma says pasta is your favorite, Liz."

"We'll be there in a minute." Gabe flashed her an okay sign.

"Pasta?" Liz rubbed her hands together.

"Are you drooling?" Gabe asked.

"Maybe."

"Well, if you aren't, you should be. Leigh makes her own pasta. It's tender and delicious. Want to go find out what version she went with tonight?"

"I guess." She stood, picked up her shoes, and squared her shoulders.

"It's not the guillotine, Liz. It's just dinner. Take it one thing at a time."

Gabe followed her to the house. *Lord, help us get this sweet girl through the next thing after dinner, because it's going to be loco.*

■ ■ ■ ■

He couldn't believe what he was seeing through the scope of the .270 hunting rifle, but there was no doubt about it.

That girl was Jillian Davidson.

And she wasn't three years old anymore.

Anissa had to be involved. He wasn't sure how, but if Jillian Davidson was hanging out with Anissa's main squeeze, then there was no way Anissa wasn't aware of what was happening. If he kept watching long enough, maybe she would show up.

But if he couldn't get his hands on her by tomorrow . . . A new idea was forming. One that was sure to get him close to Anissa Bell — and eliminate the one person still alive who could identify him.

He'd done all the time in jail he was going to do. This time he wasn't leaving anything to chance. He would get his revenge — and get as far away from here as possible. Live his life where no one would know what he'd done. Or care.

23

Anissa arrived at Leigh and Ryan's at 8:00 p.m.

Liz didn't look happy to see her, but she didn't yell at her, so there was that.

Leigh shoved a plate with a salad, garlic bread, and a ridiculous portion of baked spaghetti in front of her as Ryan asked her when the Davidsons would arrive.

Velma was taking a nap.

Gabe was nowhere to be found.

Anissa washed her hands and settled onto a stool at the kitchen island. She bowed her head over the plate. *Lord . . .*

In that moment, she had no words. She should thank him for the food. She should thank him for safety. She should thank him for restoring a lost family. She should ask him for wisdom.

She tried again.

Jesus . . . I love you. You're the best. Amen.

When she opened her eyes, Liz was standing in the space between the formal dining room and the kitchen. Arms crossed. Expression masked.

Anissa started with her salad. Two bites in, Liz moved to a stool at the far end of the island.

Three more bites of salad, two bites of spaghetti, and one bite of garlic bread later, Liz spoke. "So, you knew me as a baby."

Anissa put her fork down and turned her head in Liz's direction. "I did. You had blonde hair. It was almost white when you were an infant, but it got darker every year. And you spit green peas all over me when you were about seven months old. I told Tonya that if she insisted on feeding you slime, then you couldn't be blamed for the result."

There was a flicker of a smile, but Liz extinguished it.

Anissa went back to eating. Maybe, just like when Liz was a baby, the key to getting her to handle the less appealing things would be to give them to her in tiny bites, with lots of breaks between.

"How did you know my . . . my family?"

Anissa twirled spaghetti onto her fork. "Your father . . . birth father . . . Steve, was the youth pastor at the church I attended. That church had supported my family on the mission field for years. I'd known Steve and Tonya since I was, well, younger than you are now. So I was a natural choice to babysit."

She held the fork aloft, ready to pop the food into her mouth. "I changed a lot of your diapers."

Liz wrinkled her nose and shook her head like she'd gotten a whiff of something foul. "Gross."

"But true." Anissa smiled at her and took a bite. She needed something to keep her busy, because while she rarely felt the need to hug people, she was aching to hug Liz. No. She was aching to hug Jillian.

Lord, help us get through the next hour.

She finished her meal — well, half of it, with Liz still sitting on the stool at the end of the island. Anissa helped herself to one of Leigh's ready pile of to-go plates. She put her leftover spaghetti, more salad, and another piece of bread in the container and snapped the lid on it. She winked at Liz. "If it weren't for Leigh, most of us would starve."

She popped the container into the fridge and turned back to the counter. "What did Leigh make for dessert?"

Liz got a funny expression on her face. "Cupcakes."

"Oh. What flavor?"

"Chocolate. With different icings. Peanut butter. Salted caramel. And cream cheese."

Anissa pretended to swoon. "Salted caramel. Yes."

She found the cupcakes, guessed the one with salt crystals was the one she wanted, and put it on a paper plate. Liz watched her with an abnormal amount of intensity.

Anissa gave the bottom of the cupcake a gentle tug and it pulled away from the top. Then she sandwiched the icing between the top and bottom of the cupcake, squished it down a little, and took a bite. She'd barely put the thing in her mouth when Liz roared with laughter.

"What?" Anissa asked around a mouthful of cupcake.

"Gabe said that's what you would do. I tried it. It's a much better cake-to-icing ratio that way."

They'd been talking about her?

Anissa tried to keep things light and breezy. "Gabe thinks I'm weird."

Liz rolled her eyes in spectacular fashion. "Gabe is in love with you. Anyone can see *that*. He gets all swoony when he says your name. It's really cute."

"Swoony?" This needed clarification.

"You know." Liz attempted a sappy look

complete with batted eyelashes as she clasped her hands together and dropped her voice an octave. " 'She grew up on an island and seafood makes her happy.' "

Liz continued in what was more radio personality voice than a true imitation of Gabe's voice. " 'She isn't human until she's had coffee.' " The giggles set in and she couldn't go on.

Anissa took another bite of cupcake while Liz wiped her eyes.

"If I ever find a guy who says stuff about the food I like and how much I need coffee in the morning — and he says it like that makes me the coolest, most amazing creature in the world? I will marry him the next day."

Anissa swallowed fast to keep from choking.

"If my parents will let me." She had been laughing moments earlier, but now the tears filling Liz's eyes were not tears of joy. "Are they going to try to take me away from my mom?"

Anissa wiped her hands and mouth before answering. "The legal situation here is complicated. But they love you. I know that's hard to understand, but they've loved you your entire life. Give them a chance to find a solution that works for everyone."

Anissa's phone buzzed. She answered. "Anissa Bell."

Tonya was on the other end. "We're almost there. Is she okay if we see her? How's she handling everything? How's her . . . her mom? Should we call her Liz?"

Anissa reached out and grabbed Liz's hand. "She's expecting to see you, and I think she's handling everything like a champ. She's nervous."

At this, Liz nodded.

"And she's worried about her . . . well, her mom."

"Of course she is. How is she? Her mom?"

Anissa could only imagine how hard that word had been for Tonya to say. The grace upon grace that Anissa could sense was blowing her away. "She's been napping. She's very weak. But Leigh, my friend here, promised to wake her when you arrive. She wants to be with Liz. And I think Liz probably still wants to be called Liz, but I'm sure she'll understand if you call her Jillian from time to time."

Anissa hoped she was saying the right thing. She looked to Liz, trying to communicate her questions. Liz nodded again. Little bursts of motion.

"Okay. Oh, Anissa. I can't. I just can't. I'm so . . . I've dreamed of this for so long.

And she's right there with you and I . . . my heart . . ." Quiet sobs came through the line.

Steve's voice was the next one Anissa heard. "We'll be there in about ten minutes, Anissa. Thank you for everything."

"Of course."

She disconnected the call. "They'll be here in ten minutes. You should probably go wake your mom. Meet us in the living room whenever you're ready. Okay?"

An hour later, Anissa slipped outside to breathe.

The emotions of the day, the week, the month were overwhelming.

Gabe had been in the den with Ryan when Anissa had left the kitchen. He had nodded in her direction. Winked at Liz. Then went back to staring at his phone.

Tonya and Steve Davidson had come in ten minutes later, quiet and somber. Tonya had been trembling. Steve had appeared calm, but he kept squeezing Tonya's shoulder. They had brought their three younger children — all boys — with them and the boys had taken to Gabe like pineapple to coconut rice. Gabe and Ryan had whisked the boys downstairs to the game room. They — a bit in awe of being in the presence of real cops — had been hesitant, but within minutes the sounds of foosball and air hockey floated up the stairs.

When Liz and Velma had come downstairs, Leigh and Anissa slipped away to the screened porch to give the families privacy. They couldn't hear anything, but they hadn't been able to resist watching the reunion. The way Tonya and Steve reached tentative hands toward Liz. The hugs. The tears.

When Tonya embraced Velma, Anissa couldn't hold back her own tears. Leigh slid an arm around her shoulders and they cried together.

After a little while, Steve had called the little boys up the stairs and they had stood, shy and wondering, as they met their big sister for the first time.

Leigh had a sixth sense for what people needed, and when she picked up on a lull, she'd gone inside and offered everyone coffee. The youngest had declared he was starving and Steve had given him that death glare parents were so good at. But Gabe had jumped in and made a big deal about how he was starving too and puppy dog–eyed Leigh for more spaghetti even though he had to have already eaten.

Within ten minutes, all three boys were sitting at the kitchen counter happily eating warmed-up spaghetti and garlic bread — they had passed on the salad — and laughing at Gabe as he slurped noodles in a most undignified fashion.

Tonya and Steve hadn't been able to take their eyes off Liz. Liz had had a bit of a cornered-animal look, but the boys' antics and shared laughter had eased the tension, so Anissa had taken the opportunity to escape.

"I had a feeling I'd find you here." Gabe's deep voice set off butterflies.

Was he mad?

He should be.

Was she still mad?

She should be. Shouldn't she?

Gabe cleared his throat. "I know the timing is bad, but don't you think we need to talk? At least a little?"

Gabe waited for Anissa to answer. Waited to find out how angry she was.

Anissa stood on the edge of the dock. There was a slight breeze, the night air finally starting to cool. A little. She brushed her hair behind her ear, and her shoulders moved up and down a couple of times. Then she sighed. A soft, somewhat exasperated sigh. "I should be mad at you."

Should? Should was good. He walked

toward her, slow and steady, stopping a few feet away. "You should."

"I need to know why."

"I told you why."

"No. You said you were in love with me. That's not a why. That was years ago. We didn't even know each other."

"I wouldn't have called it love then. But I think that's what it was. I just didn't realize it yet."

"Love doesn't lie. Love doesn't get someone kicked off an undercover assignment she'd been thrilled to get. Love doesn't sabotage someone's career like that." Anissa sounded more confused than angry.

"I didn't see it that way."

She waited.

"By the time you showed up that night, I'd been undercover for a while. I'd been working at that bar for six months. I knew how those guys were. How they treated women. Had you rolled up in there as a cop, I would have feared for you as a cop. But coming there that night in that dress and those shoes. And your hair. You looked like the kind of girl they would want, and the kind of girl they would mistreat. I couldn't risk it."

He took one step closer. "You may not know this, but I told the captain not to send any women in ever again. Not just you. And not because I don't like women or don't think women should be cops. It wasn't because I didn't think you could do the job. But because it was not a risk worth taking. That op had no backup. No real safety net. But a guy could come in and be a buddy and leave and no harm would come to him. That's not how it was for a girl coming in there. You didn't hear what they said when you walked in. I had to act fast. I was a wreck all night, and I knew when you left that, as much as I had enjoyed seeing you and as good as you were at the part, I couldn't let you come back. I would have broken my cover to protect you from them. Or you would have broken your cover to protect yourself and I wouldn't have blamed you."

He took a half step closer. "I did what I did for the same reasons you kicked me off the team. Not because you couldn't do the job. But because I couldn't live with myself if anything happened to you. So, was I in love with you then? I guess not technically. But my heart was already yours. I was just waiting for the chance to get to know you. To find out that everything I suspected to be true was true."

Her arms were still crossed, but she didn't

fight him as he pulled first one hand away, then the other. They stood there, facing each other, hand in hand. "I don't know if I'll ever be able to do enough to prove to you how I feel. To show you that I'm worth taking a chance on. To convince you that no one will ever be able to make you happier."

She shifted her feet but didn't pull away. "You don't get it, do you?"

Uh-oh.

"I'm not saying that the things you do don't matter, but why do you think you constantly have to prove yourself? I'm not convinced by heroic acts of sacrifice."

She wasn't convinced. Little pieces of his heart crumbled. He could picture them tumbling down like a rock slide.

She stepped closer. "The things that convince me are the things you don't even realize you're doing. Because you aren't thinking about them. You're just being you."

Convinced? Past tense. The rock slide froze. What was she saying?

"You're a good man, Gabe. A good friend. You like the role of class clown, but when things are serious, your friends can count on you. You don't back down from a fight. You don't walk away when things get weird. Or tense. You make things better. You entertain confused little boys and you give their terrified older sister a way to relax. You're the kind of person who fights for what you believe is right. Whether that's hunting down a serial killer or . . ."

She was killing him slowly. "Or what?"

"Or fighting for me. For us."

Us?

"If you were smart, you'd walk away, Gabe. Right now. Because if you think getting me to date you has been a challenge, it's only going to get trickier from here. I have more quirks than you can possibly imagine."

"You mean beyond your pathological need for coffee in the morning or your aversion to apples or the way you get twitchy if you haven't been diving in a week or the way you like to wear your hair in a braid on the weekend but not during the week or how you wish you could live on the lake because water makes you calmer than anything else or maybe how you hate to run in a counter-clockwise direct —"

He had no idea how it had happened, but she was no longer holding his hands. Her hands were twisted in his shirt and she had pulled him closer. Her lips were on his and he lost track of where they were or what there had been to worry about ten seconds earlier. He wrapped his arms around her and pulled her closer.

When she broke the kiss, he couldn't resist whispering in her ear, "So, does this mean I'm forgiven?"

She whispered back, "It means I'm thinking about forgiving you."

If that kiss was only a thinking-about-it kiss, he couldn't wait for her to decide to forgive him completely.

"I should apologize too." She tried to step away, but he held her close.

"For what?"

"For lying to the captain."

"Oh. Yes. That did hurt." It had. No sense in pretending it hadn't.

"I am sorry."

He kissed her, soft and sweet. "I forgive you."

Anissa laughed. "He didn't believe me though."

"No doubt about it. He's on to us." Gabe kissed her forehead. "I promise to be on my very best behavior. At work."

"I don't want —"

"Want what?"

Anissa buried her face in his chest. "I don't want to keep it a secret. Keep us a secret."

"I don't think it's much of a secret as it is. I think everyone else saw it even before we did. Well, before you did. I've been on board for a while now."

She stopped him with one finger pressed to his lips. "Shh."

He didn't argue.

He ran through the edge of the woods. How stupid could he have been? So busy setting up his new plan that he failed to follow through on the original plan. It had been only a matter of time before Anissa would be back on that dock. She loved that spot. He'd been watching for her, hoping for another chance. And tonight, he had it.

He had no idea how long she'd been out there. Or how long she would stay.

Although based on what he'd seen through the camera he had pointed directly at the dock, he had a feeling she wouldn't be going anywhere anytime soon.

Still, he couldn't risk going to his primary firing location. It would take too long.

While his secondary firing location wasn't ideal, it could work. The distance was more than he wanted, but with the scope, he should have a perfect view.

If she would stay out there a few more minutes, it would all be over.

Anissa Bell.

He would have his revenge.

No one else needed to die.

It was a shame about that kid. And about that guy in the cabin. And about the guy who would soon be holding a dead woman in his arms.

But they'd been in the wrong place at the wrong time. It hadn't been personal.

But this was.

24

Anissa had no idea what had come over her and she didn't care.

Gabe Chavez loved her. Her!

He knew about her past. Her mistakes. Her general weirdness. And it wasn't that he didn't care about those things, but rather he seemed to think those very things made her the person she was . . . the person he loved.

She would have been content to spend all night standing on the dock, his arms around her, whispering and exploring this whole new idea of us and we.

But reality would not stay away for long and soon intruded. He must have sensed it, because he paused in the act of tucking her hair behind her ear. "What is it?"

"It's all the drama going on inside. I think we should check in."

"Okay." Gabe gave her a gentle squeeze and then relaxed his arms.

She stepped away, already missing the warmth of him. He grabbed her hand and laced his fingers through hers. That was better. "Are you worried about what happens next?"

"A little."

"With us, or with them?"

She rested her head on his shoulder as they walked up the hill toward the house. "With them."

But everything inside was fine.

Not normal. Definitely not normal. But fine.

Tonya and Steve were sitting with Liz and Velma as Velma, pale but smiling, told them about Liz's categorical refusal to play a mushroom in her kindergarten play because mushrooms were gross.

The boys were back in the game room with Ryan.

Leigh was in the kitchen.

When Anissa and Gabe entered, she took one look and ran to them, wrapping them both in an embrace. "Yes! I knew it would work out. I told Ryan he was being a pessimist and that love would win. I knew it!"

Anissa didn't even bother to ask how Leigh knew. Leigh wouldn't be able to explain it anyway.

When Leigh stepped back, she was radiating joy. For such a tiny person, Leigh filled up the space with her emotions. "So, while you were gone, I was shamelessly eavesdropping."

"And?" Anissa and Gabe said the word at the same time.

"I got the impression that Tonya and Steve are very sensitive to Liz and Velma's relationship and are not expecting to take Liz home with them immediately. They were going to get a hotel, which is ridiculous because we have plenty of room. Velma and Liz are in the upstairs rooms already, so I'm putting them in the downstairs rooms. The boys are thrilled. I think Tonya is relieved. You can tell she doesn't want to let Liz out of her sight. This lets everyone stay together while giving everyone a little bit of space. I haven't heard any of the truly hard conversations — like where they go from here — but I think everyone's tacitly agreed to take tonight for the joyous night it is and worry about the hard stuff tomorrow."

"Wonderful." Anissa couldn't think of a way this night could have gone any better. It wasn't perfect, but at least it wasn't a disaster.

"But that means you need to go home and get some sleep. Because Ryan asked me to remind you, if you ever came back inside, that you still have murders to solve and all sorts of unpleasantness."

The evening ended with the guys helping Velma get back to her room and the boys getting settled in what they had named the bunk-bed room. As Anissa left, with Gabe hot on her heels, the last thing she saw was Tonya and Steve wrapping Liz into a hug.

Carly was gone — separated until eternity would reunite them.

But this — the Davidsons together again — was the miracle Anissa had hoped and prayed and begged God for.

And on the same night that her heart found Gabe's?

How blessed could one girl get?

Anissa's protection crew, who had remained outside and unobtrusive while she was at Leigh's, had passed the baton to a new unit. They were sitting at her house when she arrived, and their presence was the only reason she was able to convince Gabe to go home.

She had expected to have difficulty falling asleep, but her body had had other ideas and she slept hard until her alarm woke her at seven.

An hour later, she was sitting at her desk,

staring at the photos of the storage unit she'd spread out around her and frustrated beyond belief that none of this made sense.

They were missing something. A big something.

Gabe and Ryan came in together, Ryan carrying what had better be some sort of treat from Leigh. Gabe was carrying three cups of coffee, one of which he set on her desk with a wink.

No PDA in the office.

Shame.

Ryan set down the box, opened the lid, and revealed cinnamon rolls. "Leigh said if we're all working on a Saturday, then we deserved a special treat."

Gabe took one and brought it to her, then took one for himself. "When did she have time to make these?" he asked around a mouthful.

Ryan didn't grin.

"Did something happen last night after we left? Were the Davidsons okay? Liz — ?"

"They're all fine. I think." Ryan still had that look on his face. Like he wasn't feeling well? Or —

"Do we need to talk?" Anissa waved a hand between her and Gabe. "Is this going to be a problem?"

Ryan gave her a confused look. "What?

You and Gabe? I should hope not. I've made my opinion clear on this subject. I'm all for it as long as you don't mess it up and don't bring it to the office. If you start kissing over the coffee machine, I may puke."

Gabe's obvious relief mirrored her own, but he pressed Ryan. "Then what is it?"

"Leigh couldn't sleep. That's why she had time to make the cinnamon rolls. She was up at four, mixing and baking and letting the dough rise."

Anissa glanced at Gabe. He shrugged. Okay, so neither of them knew where this was going.

"Leigh said she woke up around three and couldn't go back to sleep. So she got up, prayed for a while, then decided to keep praying while she made breakfast. She had these rolls, bacon, eggs, fruit. When I left, the entire Davidson family, and I'm including Liz in that, was in the kitchen eating."

"That sounds . . . good." Gabe took another bite.

"It is, but I've learned to pay attention to Leigh's middle-of-the-night prayer/baking episodes. It makes me think there's still something unresolved. Something we're missing."

Anissa couldn't explain how Ryan's words filled her with both comfort and concern. "I agree. I keep coming back to this storage unit. I've requested all the files from the management about when it was rented, more security camera footage, et cetera. But they've been less than cooperative. I could be wrong, but I don't think it's because they are being intentionally evasive but because they may not have what I'm asking for."

Gabe sat at his desk. "That wouldn't be surprising."

"Not to us, but it would be to the people who have rented storage units there and expect better security." Anissa shoved the last bite of cinnamon roll into her mouth.

"Good point." Gabe tipped his coffee cup in her direction.

"I'm going out there this afternoon," Anissa said. "I'm tired of the stonewalling. But before I go, I want to be sure I have a clear picture of who Ronald Talbot was."

Gabe's stomach growled. They had ordered lunch in, but it hadn't arrived yet. A knock gave them two seconds' warning before Adam poked his head into Anissa's office. "Mind if I join you for a few minutes?"

Anissa grunted. Ryan waved one hand. Gabe didn't think either of them was paying close attention because Adam didn't look happy at all. "What's up?"

Adam cleared his throat. "I may have found something."

Anissa and Ryan both stopped what they were doing.

"Define *something*," Ryan said.

Adam tapped the folder he'd brought with him. "Sabrina set up a search pattern this morning. It's been running for several hours and it's populating a spreadsheet. The idea was to see if there was any connection between Ronald Talbot and Anissa."

"I didn't put him in jail," Anissa said. "I checked."

"No. You didn't. But Sabrina looked for other connections and it turns out your dad put someone in jail — a man named Harvey Dixon, who was in jail with Ronald Talbot. Someone who is out now. In fact, he got out in March."

"Your dad was a cop? I thought he was a missionary." Ryan voiced what Gabe was thinking.

"Dad was a cop in Virginia. He was working in the robbery unit when God called him to the mission field. He hasn't been a cop in decades." She turned to Adam. "How did Sabrina find the connection?"

"I called to ask her before I came in here. She said previous searches had used Anissa's officer number. This time she didn't run it with the number. She ran it with the surname — Bell. That's how it pulled up your dad's info."

"Why would she do that?"

Adam held out his hands, palms up. "I have no idea how her mind works, Anissa. She's a genius. She thinks of things I would never think of and somehow it occurred to her to run it this way, so she did. This is proof that I will lose every argument we ever have because she'll be twenty steps ahead of me."

They all chuckled. Adam was right about that.

"This guy, this Harvey Dixon. What's his story?" Gabe asked.

"No idea. All I have is the name and that he was in the same prison as Ronald Talbot. Anissa, it might be worth making a phone call to your dad."

Anissa checked her watch. "It's the middle of the night in Yap. I'll call him this evening. Maybe by then we'll have something more to go on than a name."

Gabe waved a hand in Adam's direction. "Give me that, please."

Adam handed over the file. "The program Sabrina created is still running. If I get any other hits, I'll let you know." He headed for the door.

"Thank you, Adam." Anissa's smile wobbled, but she held on to it until the door closed behind Adam. Then it faltered.

"Why don't you want to call your dad?" Ryan asked.

"It isn't that I don't want to call him, but I can't imagine he'll remember. We're talking about something that happened at least four decades ago."

"Forty-three years ago, according to the police record." Gabe scanned the page. "Looks like your dad put together a solid case and the guy went away for twenty years."

"Twenty? Ron Talbot wasn't old enough to have been in prison with him then."

"True." Gabe searched for the criminal records of Harvey Dixon. It didn't take long to see his entire rap sheet. "Harvey Dixon went back to prison. Eleven years ago."

"When was Ronald Talbot released?"

Anissa checked some of her notes. "Ten years ago."

"Okay, the timing works. He was in the same jail as Ronald Talbot for four months. And then Harvey Dixon was released in March of this year."

"What was the crime the second time? Another armed robbery?"

"No."

Gabe studied the report. He didn't like what he was seeing and he didn't like the direction his mind was going.

"Gabe?" Anissa's tone had a sharp edge. "What was the charge?"

"Kidnapping. With intent to sell."

25

Anissa jumped from her seat and held out her hand for the file.

Gabe didn't question why she wanted to see it. He handed it over.

It was there, on his face. On Ryan's face. They were thinking the same thing she was.

She studied the mug shots.

"Does he look familiar at all?" Gabe asked.

"No."

Was it possible that after all these years, she was looking at the man responsible for Carly's death? For Jillian's disappearance? Sure, it could be a coincidence that this man had been imprisoned by her father and then happened to be out in the small window of time when he could have committed those crimes, and then tried again but got caught and put back in prison.

But she didn't believe in coincidences.

How could he have gotten out so soon?

Kidnapping with intent to sell had a steep penalty.

And if he was out and was targeting her. Why?

And could this mean Liz was in danger?

"Ryan, would you call Leigh? I'd like to know what Liz is up to right now."

"On it."

Anissa walked to Gabe's desk and looked over his shoulder at the information he'd pulled up on Harvey Dixon.

"They're doing what?" Ryan's question pulled Anissa's attention away from the computer screen.

"Okay. Listen. I don't want to alarm them, or Mr. and Mrs. Davidson, or Ms. Brown, but we've got a situation here. Are you sure they're at the theater?"

He listened.

"Okay. Have Velma text Liz and tell her not to leave the theater until she sees one of us. Okay? We're probably overreacting. You know how we are." A pause. "Okay. Love you too."

Ryan hung up.

They're at a theater?

Ryan looked at her. "Apparently things have gone okay at the house today. This morning, Brooke Ashcroft called Liz to see if she'd like to go to a movie this afternoon.

All the parental units agreed, and Paisley picked them up around noon. The plan was to grab lunch, and then she was going to drop them off at the theater and pick them up around three."

Harmless enough under normal circumstances.

Which these weren't.

Anissa looked at Gabe. "I can't believe I'm about to say this, but what do you think about calling Paisley and giving her the whole story?"

Gabe rubbed his face with his hands. "I knew this was going to happen eventually, but I think we need to talk to the Davidsons and the Browns first to get their permission. Although Liz may have already told her. Or told Brooke. And then Brooke may have already told Paisley about it."

Anissa glanced at her watch. It was two o'clock. They would be in the movie right now.

Anissa tried to pull her random thoughts together. "Why don't I go to the house and talk to Mr. and Mrs. Davidson and Ms. Brown while Liz isn't there? Bring them up to speed. Make sure everyone's aware of the potential danger. Gabe, you head to the theater and get eyes on the girls, preferably without scaring them. As soon as I get permission from the families, you contact Paisley. Tell her, um, tell her —"

"Tell her she'll get an escort from the theater to our house," Ryan said. "And you'll talk to her there."

"I like it." Gabe was already up and gathering his things. Still mostly one-handed.

"Ryan, while we're gone, would you fill the captain in and see if we can get this guy's picture circulating as a person of interest? Then talk to Adam and Sabrina. Ask them if we can make finding out everything about Harvey Dixon our top priority? Maybe Sabrina can do that thing she does with the cameras and see if she can find him."

"You got it."

Ryan left the homicide office and Gabe and Anissa were alone. Gabe pulled her close, pressed his forehead to hers. "See you soon."

Then he was gone.

Anissa grabbed her things as well as the file about Harvey Dixon. Maybe the Davidsons or Velma would recognize him. It couldn't hurt to ask.

Gabe arrived at the movie theater at two thirty. The crowd on this July afternoon was typical of most summertime days. Mostly North Carolina plates in the parking lot, but a fair number of out-of-state tags too. It was so hot outside that any activity that involved being indoors, air-conditioning, and snacks had to be a winner with locals and vacationers alike.

He went inside to the customer service desk.

The young woman behind the counter was probably in college. She flashed him a flirty smile. "Good afternoon. How can I help you?"

He palmed his badge and showed it to her. Her eyes widened. "I'm Investigator Chavez. I have reason to believe that some patrons who are here could possibly be in danger. I need to get in to the theater where they are and confirm their whereabouts. Once I know where they are, I —"

"Gabe?" Brooke Ashcroft's shouted question carried over the sounds of popping popcorn and ice clattering into oversize cups at the concession stand.

Gabe turned and Brooke ran to him with tears streaking down her cheeks. "I can't find Liz! I checked all the bathrooms. She isn't answering her phone. I —" She sagged against the desk.

He caught her, put one arm around her

shoulder, and led her to a nearby bench. "Start at the beginning. Tell me everything." Panicking now could lead to a lot of unnecessary chaos later.

Brooke gulped air. "We came to the movie. She said when it was over, she wanted to tell me something but that it could wait. She seemed, I don't know, not herself. Kind of down. And she was so upbeat in the hospital. It didn't make sense. But she was having fun. I think she liked the movie. Then she said her mom had called and she wanted to make sure everything was okay. I didn't think anything about it until I realized she'd been gone twenty minutes."

Brooke held her phone up in trembling hands. "I texted her. Called her. Nothing. So I left the theater. I checked all the bathrooms. She's just — gone."

"Okay. Brooke, this could be important. What time, as close as you can remember it, did she leave the auditorium?"

Brooke looked at her phone. "Around one forty-five. Definitely before two."

"Okay. Stay right here. Do not move."

The customer service clerk leaned over the counter. "Investigator Chavez, is there anything I can do to help?"

"Yes." He leaned close to her to try to keep Brooke from overhearing. "Do you have a procedure for putting this theater on lockdown? No one in or out?"

She blinked a few times, then fumbled through a stack of paper before producing a laminated sheet with in case of emergency boldly printed across the top. "Yes."

"Do it."

"What?"

Gabe enunciated each word. "I need you to lock this place down. Now."

"Okay."

Gabe dialed Anissa's number. No answer. He tried again.

No answer.

He called Leigh. She didn't even say hi. "Gabe, what's going on?"

"I need to talk to Anissa."

"Anissa? She's not here."

"What do you mean she's not there?" Gabe pushed back the rising fear.

"Is she supposed to be here?" Leigh's voice had an edge of alarm.

"Leigh. Listen to me. Lock every door. Turn on the alarm system."

"Gabe, you're scaring me. The boys are playing in the lake."

"Then get them inside. Someone will call you soon."

"Okay." Leigh's voice was a combination of fear and trust. Fear about the situation.

Trust that Gabe wouldn't be scaring her unnecessarily. He would have to thank her for that. Later.

Brooke was shaking all over. The doors had been locked. The clamor of annoyed patrons was growing. The manager was coming toward him. Gabe's next call was to Ryan. As soon as Ryan answered, Gabe filled him in. "Liz is missing from the theater. Anissa's not answering her phone. I've called Leigh and told her to bring everyone in and lock the place up tight. I've put the theater on lockdown. I need —"

"Sir, what's going on?" The manager, a doughy guy who could use a day or two in the sun, stood across from him, arms crossed. An obvious attempt at bluff and bluster. One that Gabe was in no mood for.

"Do you have security cameras here?" Gabe asked the manager.

"Of course, but you have no right —"

"Take me to them. Now."

A security guard approached. A kid. Couldn't be a day over twenty-two. "Everything okay?"

Gabe showed him his badge. "No one gets in or out. Do you understand?"

The guard nodded.

Gabe looked at Brooke. "You're with me, kiddo. Let's go see if we can get a glimpse of our girl." He had to give it to her. She was terrified, but she kept moving.

Through the phone, he heard Ryan barking orders. By now, Dispatch was sending units. "Parker, have the units secure every exterior exit and the security guard here" — he looked at the name tag — "Tom, will let them in. We need a full search of the building — every auditorium, every closet."

He hung up with Ryan and turned to Tom. "No one gets in here unless they are Carrington sheriff's deputies or Carrington Police officers. And no one leaves. We've got a missing girl on our hands. You got that, Tom?"

"Yes, sir."

He looked at the manager. "After you."

The manager had lost the attitude at the mention of a missing girl and now moved at a decent pace toward the right side of the concession area.

Brooke followed him, eyes wide, but her trembling had eased. Her lips were moving. Praying? Maybe.

That would be a good idea for him too.

Ayúdanos por favor Dios. Anissa . . . help her. Please.

Gabe didn't know what was going on, but he knew there were only a couple of reasons why Anissa wouldn't answer her phone. None of them were good.

26

Anissa ignored Gabe's call.

Again.

It had taken her ten minutes to get away from her bodyguards. To be fair to them, they had no reason to suspect that she would try to get away from them and every reason to expect her to want to keep them close.

She'd been a quarter of a mile from Leigh's house when she got the text.

The photograph.

Liz. In a canoe. On a body of water. Eyes closed.

Was she asleep? Unconscious? Anissa couldn't be sure but didn't think she was dead.

But the text had been enough to cause her to do what she did. What she was doing now.

Follow my instructions or this is the next

body you'll pull out of the lake.
Lose your bodyguards.
Don't call for help. I'll know.

She knew it was a trap. She knew it was Harvey Dixon. He knew the one thing that would make her come to him. Because there was no way she would risk losing this sweet girl again.

If he wanted Anissa dead in exchange, he could have her.

Gabe tried to have Brooke sit in a chair by the door, but she popped back up and hovered near his elbow. He couldn't blame her. He didn't have time to explain everything, but she was a smart girl and she'd lost her best friend two weeks ago to violence. It wouldn't be far from her mind now that something was very, very wrong.

"I want to see footage from every exterior door from one thirty this afternoon until now."

The manager held up a finger. "Which auditorium were you in, Brooke?"

Brooke rummaged through her small purse and pulled out a ticket stub. "Eleven."

"Let's check the door on the south side of the building first. If I were going to sneak someone out, I wouldn't bring them through the main entrance. I'd go out one of the side exits."

Gabe wasn't sure whether or not this guy should go on a watch list, but his logic was sound. It took a painful two minutes for him to find the right set of video files. While he started them forward, Gabe bumped Brooke's arm. "Hey. Call your sister."

Brooke grabbed her phone, then hesitated. "What do I tell her?"

"Tell her the truth. Tell her you're okay first. Then tell her where you are. Tell her you're with me and I'm not letting you out of my sight. Tell her about Liz. Tell her to bring the cameras and the chopper for all I care. Liz is missing and Anissa's not answering her phone."

He refocused on the video. "I'll watch this one," he told the manager. "You get the video from the other door queued up."

A minute later, with Brooke murmuring into her phone, he saw what he'd been hoping he wouldn't see. "Right there. Play that back."

A clean-cut man in khakis, a nice golf shirt, and casual shoes walked out with a girl. "Brooke, do you remember anything about what Liz was wearing?" Gabe could go back through and find it in the footage of the girls entering the theater, but he didn't want to take the time to do that if it wasn't necessary.

Brooke told Paisley to hold on and watched the video. "That's Liz." Her eyes filled with tears.

"Are you sure?" Gabe kept his voice steady. Even. No pressure. Nothing that might upset Brooke any more than she already was.

She nodded and sniffled. "Her flip-flops."

Gabe rewound the footage again and then froze it. They looked like basic flip-flops to him. But they did have a flower on them.

"The daisy." Brooke pointed to the screen. "She told me she's always liked daisies. That her mom loves that movie with the line about the daisies being her favorite flower."

Brooke tapped the monitor with her finger — the nail chewed to the quick. "Those are Liz's shoes. That's Liz. So, who is the man?"

Gabe had a very bad feeling that he knew the answer.

Finally.

He had an escape plan.

It would work.

It wasn't as good as his original plan. When he ran into Ronald Talbot a few weeks after moving to Carrington, he'd considered it fate. Harvey set everything in motion to blame Anissa's death on Talbot. It had been a good idea.

But he hadn't counted on Talbot coming to him and asking for a place to stay or for him to see the photos he'd taken of Anissa. When he caught him sneaking out of the house in the middle of the night, he'd had no choice. He couldn't risk Talbot blabbing to the police.

Harvey lit that pitiful excuse for a cabin on fire, hoping they'd search the debris for a body and wouldn't find Talbot for several more days.

He never dreamed they'd search the lake again.

But none of that mattered now.

He'd have his revenge on Anissa and on this entire wretched town.

He looked at the canoe bobbing in the camp lake. He hoped the girl would stay asleep. He'd gone to a lot of trouble not to kill her all those years ago. Anissa had been the target. The kid had been an accident. She'd started crying and he'd scooped her up to avoid the attention of the other people at the park.

Then he realized he didn't have Anissa after all. It only took a second to kill the girl. But the kid . . .

He'd never planned to kill a kid.

He'd done a lot of bad things, but killing kids had never been something he'd set out to do. Even today, he'd given her a drug with amnesiac properties. She wouldn't remember anything. Including his face.

He waited.

Anissa would be there soon.

27

Anissa pulled over in a gas station parking lot. She sent up a prayer as she texted one word.

Where?

Don't you recognize it?

He was playing games with her. Great. She thought about calling him by name but reconsidered. At this point, it was possible that he had no idea they were on to him. She had no certainty about what would happen over the next few hours, but she did know Gabe would never stop hunting for Harvey Dixon.

She studied the photo. Oh no. She did know that water. She knew that place.

He'd taken Liz to Camp Blackstone.

The campers were gone. Staff gone. No one was supposed to be there until they'd sorted out the water situation. The place was the stuff of the environmental guys' nightmares. Too close to Lake Porter for comfort. Too contaminated to let anyone stay.

But that meant Harvey Dixon had been in the area. Knew the area well enough to know the camp — normally bustling with kids — was closed.

On my way.

She pulled out of the parking lot and onto the highway.

Come alone or she dies. At this distance I'll put a bullet in her heart.

Anissa stared at her phone.

How would he know if she called for help? Was he watching her? Had he bugged her car again? Her phone?

He could be bluffing.

She couldn't risk it.

Lord, be with Liz. If she wakes, help her be calm. Be with Brooke when she realizes Liz is gone. Be with Gabe.

She didn't dare pray the words out loud, although she longed to. Instead, she repeated them, again and again. Not because she didn't think God had heard her, but because she needed to keep talking to him to remind herself that she wasn't alone. Not now. Not ever.

Flashes of Carly's decaying body forced themselves past the barriers she usually kept in place.

Would that be her in a few days? Rotting flesh? Family mourning? Gabe —

She shook her head. No. She wouldn't go there. She didn't have the luxury of worrying about herself right now. She had to save Liz. After that, God could take her. She certainly deserved to die to save Liz. She was willing to do it.

But for the first time in thirteen years, she knew, all the way to her core, that God didn't work that way. Yes, there were consequences for sin. But God wasn't ready to smite her. If she died today, it wouldn't be punishment for mistakes. It would be because Harvey Dixon was evil.

And she knew something Harvey Dixon didn't know.

Help was coming.

The next half hour was a blur for Gabe.

Paisley banging on the door of the theater, demanding to see her sister. Thanking him for protecting Brooke. Not that he'd done

444

anything. Promising him whatever he needed, including, heaven help him, the news chopper currently hovering over the theater.

Sabrina calling him, demanding in her most professorial tone that he send all footage directly to her and making it quite clear she would be offended if he even tried to involve the forensics team in this matter. Their forensics group was great, but no one could argue with Sabrina's superiority in skill and resources.

Adam going to Sabrina's lab to work with her from there.

Ryan taking one for the team and volunteering to tell Mr. and Mrs. Davidson and Velma that Liz/Jillian had been kidnapped — again.

The captain, the sheriff, the city police, including his buddy Claire Tollison, all converging on the theater. Every law enforcement officer in the state looking for Anissa's car.

Then Sabrina called.

"I found her car."

"What? How? Where?"

"She's at Camp Blackstone. She's been there for five minutes. Tops. Her phone is on the property as well. Adam is on the phone with Dispatch. He's sending everyone, but no sirens and no one is to approach without permission in case there's a hostage situation."

Gabe didn't ask again how she knew. He'd find out later. "Headed that way." He ran for the lobby of the theater where officers were questioning everyone inside to determine if they'd seen Harvey Dixon. It took him a minute to spot her, but he found Paisley in one corner with Brooke. "Paisley, you know how you said you'd like to help?"

"Yes! Please let me."

Gabe couldn't believe he was doing this. "I need a ride."

Anissa pulled the car over to the side of the road.

She wanted to save Liz, but the longer she stalled, the better chance she had of Gabe finding her.

She was ready to die, but that didn't mean she wanted to.

There was no way to know where Harvey was, or what his plan was. Did he intend to shoot her? Strangle her? Drown her?

Either way, she didn't plan to make it easy for him.

She slid from the driver's-side door and crouched beside the car. The car would protect her, but only if Harvey wasn't already on this side with a rifle pointed at her head.

I'm here.

Good. Come to the lake.

Anissa's legs had never felt so heavy. Not after the toughest workout, the longest run, the heaviest lift. She forced herself to walk forward. One step at a time. She kept to the tree line, taking a few steps between trees, then pausing.
Her phone buzzed.

Hurry it up. That canoe she's in has a leak. And she's tied down.

Bile rose in her throat even as her pace quickened.

Gabe had to admit the chopper pilot was good, setting that thing down in the side parking lot, landing in between power lines and streetlights like it was an everyday occurrence. Gabe settled himself in the back, right beside Paisley's photographer. Paisley scrambled into the seat by the pilot, having handed over Brooke to Officer Claire Tollison's safekeeping.
"You don't need to come, Paisley," Gabe

yelled over the roar of the rotor. "It could be dangerous. This is just the fastest way for me to get there."

"I'm not staying behind." She settled the headphones over her ears and spoke through the microphone. "I know you think I'm only about the story, but I'm not. I don't have that many friends, but I like Anissa. And Brooke loves Liz. I want to help. This is how I can."

She turned to the photographer. "No filming, Vic. When it's over, we'll have the live exclusive on the ground, but we will not risk this child's life for ratings. Got it?"

Vic nodded and set the camera he had with him at his feet. The cameras on the chopper itself were still ready to go at a second's notice, but at least Gabe didn't have to worry about having his every move recorded.

She punched the chopper pilot on the shoulder. A woman in her sixties. "Agreed, Sam?"

"I love rescue missions." Sam's gravelly voice carried a hint of defiance. "If you don't care about getting fired, then neither do I."

"Great. Let's go." Paisley settled into her seat.

"Sam, do you know where the camp is?"

Gabe asked the pilot.

"I do. And I know the perfect place to land. I can also hover this baby a few feet off the ground if you need me to, but the camp doesn't have a lot of places for me to do that. The lake's probably the only place open enough."

"Okay. For now, stay to the perimeter. We have no idea what we're flying into."

"You got it."

28

He might be lying. Anissa knew that.

But as she perched behind a tree at the edge of the lake, the canoe did appear to be riding lower in the water than it did in the picture.

Where was he? What was his plan? She couldn't bother with the ultimate question of why. Either she'd live long enough to find out or it wouldn't matter anyway.

Anissa studied the area. The canoe Liz was in was smack in the middle of the large camp lake. The canoes and kayaks stacked near the dock were tempting, but they would be impossible to get into the water without making a huge commotion. If by some miracle she managed to get in the water without dying, sitting in a kayak or canoe would make her a huge target.

There was another option.

One he might not have considered.

Mostly because it was a bit crazy. It would

leave her unarmed and mostly defenseless. But it was the only viable option she could see at the moment.

"Tick tock, Anissa!" The words came from the camp's loudspeakers, making it impossible for her to know where Harvey was hiding. "You have two minutes or I'll do what I should have done thirteen years ago. One bullet. Right through her heart."

Gabe didn't like helicopters.

But he couldn't complain about the way they were zipping over the traffic as they flew toward the lake.

A new voice came through the headphones. "Why don't we have video, Paisley?"

Paisley's voice came through the headphones. "Fred, we're just providing a lift to a sheriff's investigator."

"Again" — Fred's voice lowered, his tone overtly threatening — "why don't we have video?"

"It could get a girl killed, Fred." Paisley left it at that.

"Or it could get you fired," Fred said. "I want that video. We have anchors ready to go live and we have nothing to go on."

"I'll get it for you as soon as it's safe." Paisley wasn't backing down.

"Don't think for a second that you're irreplaceable. I can get another pretty face in a heartbeat."

Gabe had a feeling Fred wasn't kidding. "You don't work for the sheriff's office, Wilson. You work for me. You work for the people of Carrington who want to know why the theater is on lockdown and cops are converging on Camp Blackstone."

Bad news traveled fast.

Paisley shook her head at both Sam and Vic. "The good people of Carrington will boycott our station when they find out we aided a murderer because we wanted a story. You'll get your story, Fred. But you will have to wait. We're approaching the camp. Signing off."

Another new voice came through the headphones. Is this the Sky9 helicopter? Paisley frowned and Gabe could see the confusion on her face. "Yes?"

"This is Dr. Sabrina Fleming. I understand you have Gabe Chavez on board and it is imperative that I speak with him."

"Sabrina?" Gabe had no idea how she'd gotten through on the chopper's radio frequency, but he'd add that to the growing list of questions he had for later.

"Gabe. Thank goodness." Sabrina's brisk tone had a panicked edge. "Listen to me. Anissa's car hasn't moved. I was able to get a hit on her cell phone. She's not responding to any texts or calls, but she hasn't turned it off. She's on the edge of the lake."

"Okay." Good to know.

"But listen, we've also been digging deeper into Harvey Dixon. When Anissa's dad arrested him, it was for armed robbery."

"Right." He knew that.

"But we know how he did it. He blew a hole in a concrete pipe under the building and through the floor of the basement. That's how he got in."

"So we're dealing with an explosives expert?"

"Yes. And a marksman. Well, he was forty years ago, anyway. He was a sniper in the army before he was dishonorably discharged. I texted Anissa, but I don't know if she saw it or not."

Why did he get the feeling there was more? "What else, Sabrina?"

"I hacked her phone."

"That's the best news I've heard all day. What did you find?"

"There's a photo. Adam's sending it to your phone now."

Gabe pulled his phone from his pocket. The photo came through and rage followed.

"There were a few texts. He told her to come alone or he'd put a bullet in her heart like he should have done thirteen years ago. By her, I assume he means Liz."

That would have been enough to make Anissa come.

"But there's more. After I hacked her phone, I hacked his. He's been bragging to someone that he could destroy the ecosystem of Lake Porter for a generation."

"What?"

"This guy wants Anissa dead, but he's not out of control. He's not reckless. He's been careful to plan every attack. I'm not sure what it is, but I guarantee you he has an exit strategy that he believes will work. He isn't interested in dying today."

"Fine, but how does he think he's going to get out of there after he kills her? We'll go in guns blazing. He has to know that."

Paisley raised her hand like she was in school. He'd forgotten she, Sam, and Vic were hearing every word. "Paisley has something she wants to say."

Now it was Sabrina's turn to say, "Okay?"

"His text said he would ruin Lake Porter for a generation? And he's at the camp?"

"Yes," Sabrina confirmed.

"And he's an explosives expert?"

"Well, he was at one time." Sabrina was never one to avoid specifics.

"That's the connection."

"You're going to need to be more clear, Ms. Wilson." Sabrina was in full professor mode.

"Sorry." Paisley sucked in a breath. "I'm working on a report about the camp. I was so burned up about that whole situation, all those kids getting sick, that older lady nearly dying, that guy with cancer still in the hospital."

"Paisley?" Vic was giving her the look that everyone in the universe knows means "you aren't really going to say this, are you?"

Paisley twisted in her seat and made eye contact with Gabe. "Look. It hasn't been reported yet. I found out through a source, so I've been digging into it. Everyone was getting sick, yes. But the real reason they shut the place down is that one of the environmental engineers discovered a pipe that goes from the lake at the camp and empties into Lake Porter. It's sealed shut, but there were concerns about leakage. They're monitoring the spot on the lake where the pipe exits and formulating a plan to get the lake at the camp cleaned up so there's no risk."

Sabrina groaned. "If he blew the seal to the pipe . . ."

"All that filth would go straight into Lake Porter."

■ ■ ■ ■

Anissa eyed the canoe. It was definitely sitting lower in the water than before.

It was now or never.

She stripped out of her shoes, left her phone, weapon, badge, sunglasses, watch. Everything electronic and heavy. She rolled her pants above her knees. Twisted her hair into a tight bun and secured it with the hair band she kept in her pocket. She brought two things with her. The compass from her key chain and her knife.

If Dixon had access to the loudspeaker system, then he was probably watching the lake from the main house. The woods around the lake provided a natural barrier, and if he was where she hoped he was, she should be able to get to the canoes without being seen.

Lord, help me.

She kept herself low, ignoring the pain as rocks and sticks jabbed her bare feet. She weaved back and forth until she reached the stacks of canoes and kayaks near the dock.

Whew. No shots fired.

Thank you, Lord.

She darted behind the canoes and kayaks and shimmied between them, easing into

456

the water without exposing herself to Harvey Dixon.

She squared her shoulders and lined her body up as best she could with the canoe.

When she came up for air, he'd probably shoot her in the head.

Which was why she had no plans to surface until she was behind the canoe.

Another quick look at the compass.

Another quick prayer.

Father, I'm yours. Liz is yours. Your will be done.

Anissa inhaled and exhaled, pushing out as much air as possible from her body before taking one final breath and going under.

"We're approaching the camp." Sam's voice came through the headphones. She pointed to her left.

Gabe strained to see anything.

"How do you want to play this?" Sam asked. "He's going to hear us before he sees us. I can make this baby do a lot of things, but I can't make her be quiet."

The wrong decision could result in a lot of death and destruction. *Dios, por favor, ayúdanos.*

"Gabe?" This time Paisley asked the question.

Unfortunately, God didn't seem inclined to give him an answer in the sky, but there was one idea he couldn't get rid of. "Let's see if we can get a look at the lake."

A garbled voice, male, came through the headphones. Paisley shook her head at Sam. "I'm not talking to Fred again."

"That's not Fred. I don't recognize the voice," Sam said. The voice came through again, this time clear. "Hello? Can you hear me?"

Gabe recognized it immediately. "Ryan!"

"How are these people getting through?" Sam mumbled as Paisley said, "Is this Investigator Parker?"

"Yes. Do you have Gabe?"

"Yo, where are you, man?" Gabe asked.

"Just left my house. All secure. I'm almost to the camp. We've got roadblocks. The camp's surrounded. SWAT's on-site. I don't know how this guy thinks he's getting out of here."

Gabe filled him in on Sabrina's and Paisley's theories.

"Paisley, where's this pipe?" Ryan asked.

Sam pointed again and said, "I'm coming up on the lake. I'm barely above the treetops, but we won't have a line of sight until we get right over it. Which will be in about thirty seconds."

Paisley handed Gabe a pair of binoculars.

"I can hear the chopper," Ryan said.

"Let's see what we can see. Hang on, Ryan."

Gabe craned his neck, trying to get a visual on the lake. When it came into view, it came and went — fast.

But there was one thing he was sure of.

There was a canoe.

And someone was in it.

29

Anissa estimated her depth at five feet. Deep enough to keep her hands and feet from accidentally breaking the surface but not so deep that she would waste any air going down or coming up. And at this depth, she could see the compass when she held it close to her face.

Everything burned as she took stroke after stroke. Her arms, her legs, her lungs.

She was out of practice, but she'd grown up free-diving in the waters off her island home of Yap. She could survive a little burn. The dark shadow of the canoe filtered through the water. Almost there.

She surfaced without touching the canoe and tried to breathe without gasping.

Oxygen. *Thank you, Jesus, for air. May I never take it for granted.*

As her own heartbeat slowed, a new sound reached her ears.

A chopper.

She turned toward the sound.

That was the news chopper and it was flying low.

Straight toward her.

Was that — ? Gabe pressed closer to the window. Could it be?

"Someone's in the water by the canoe." Paisley's excitement confirmed what Gabe thought he'd seen.

"It's Anissa." What on earth was she doing in the middle of the lake? When this was over, they were going to have a long chat about survival tactics and how a big one was not to swim into the middle of a lake when someone was trying to kill you.

"How can we help her?" Paisley asked.

"Let's buzz the camp," Sam said. "Draw attention to us and not to her."

"He might shoot at us," Vic said.

"Yes. Yes, he might." Sam's grim pronouncement didn't change her mind though. She pointed the chopper straight at the main house. "I've been shot at before."

"Well, I haven't," Vic mumbled into his headset. "Can we film this?"

"Do you have a way to record without transmitting?" Gabe asked. He didn't want to believe that this wouldn't end well, but he didn't want to risk Steve and Tonya

Davidson and Velma Brown watching their daughter killed on the local news.

"Sure can," Sam said.

"Then do it." Maybe the footage could be used in court if needed. "Ryan, you still there, bro?"

"Still here. We have the place surrounded, but we're staying out of sight and staying quiet."

"Listen, Anissa's in the lake at the canoe. Liz looks like she's asleep. Maybe he drugged her." Gabe couldn't even consider the chance that she was dead. "We're flying over the rest of the camp to see if we can get a visual on Harvey."

"It's risky, man."

"I know, but it wasn't my idea. Our pilot is a hotshot."

"Got that right, babe." Sam dropped the chopper lower than seemed safe and aimed it straight for the main house. "Let's see who's home and give that brave girl a fighting chance."

If she survived, Anissa would find out who was flying that chopper and hug them for a week.

She pulled her knife from her belt and cut through the anchor line. As soon as the canoe was free, she reached one hand under the pointed bottom, shrugged it against her shoulder, and swam toward the beach area.

For a few seconds, she couldn't tell if she was making any progress. This was not the most efficient method of getting the canoe to the dock, but it kept her from getting her head blown off.

Lord, don't let him shoot at the canoe.

The helicopter continued to swoop around the camp and Anissa swam for all she was worth, thankful for every second she'd spent in the gym and in the water.

A moan from the canoe both soothed and worried Anissa. The noise meant she wasn't risking her life for a dead girl. But it also meant Liz might panic and sit up.

"Liz, don't move," Anissa whispered. "I need you to be still. Please." Anissa kept up the murmuring, unsure if Liz was conscious enough to understand.

A few more strokes and she would be close enough to shove the canoe onto the beach.

She allowed her body to go vertical and her feet touched the grainy sand of the beach. She paused. "Liz, honey? Are you awake? Can you hear me? Don't sit up. Just give me a little whisper."

"Mmm."

"Wonderful. Listen. We're in a bit of a spot

here, but we're only a few feet from the shore or the dock. Do you know how to swim?"

"Yes."

"Brilliant." A plan was forming. It wasn't a great plan, but it was the best she could come up with on the fly.

"Can you tell if you're tied to the boat?" Harvey had said she was, but . . .

A shot. Then another. Chunks of the canoe sprayed over Anissa.

"Liz!"

"Gabe! Shots fired. Two!" Ryan's voice came through the headsets.

Sam whipped the helicopter around and headed back toward the lake.

The canoe was now ten feet from shore. But it was tipping at a bizarre angle.

"That canoe is going down," Vic said.

When Gabe found the canoe through the binoculars, he couldn't believe what he was seeing.

Liz was still in the boat, thrashing wildly against restraints as the canoe tipped at a forty-five-degree angle. He couldn't see Anissa anywhere.

Had she been shot?

Was she on the bottom of the lake?

Sam was relaying what she was seeing to

Ryan. She had to have been a military pilot at one time. The woman had nerves of steel. Her voice was calm, but there was fury behind it. "Feel like going for a swim, Investigator?"

Gabe couldn't believe what she was offering. She'd have to hover near the canoe. A canoe that someone was shooting at. "Can you get me down there?"

The huffing noise Sam made was a mixture of exasperation and annoyance. "I wouldn't have asked if I couldn't do it."

"Then yes!"

Gabe pulled off the headset and removed everything else he could get to and handed them to Vic.

"You'll have to be ready to jump when I tell you," Sam said. "No hesitation. I'm going to put you a little off the shore so you don't break your legs on the bottom."

That was a wonderful idea.

"Open that door and get ready."

Gabe did as he was instructed. As they got closer to the canoe, Gabe could see that Liz's hands were tied to the sides of it. The end her feet were in was already submerged. Anissa's head popped up for far too brief a moment, then she went down again.

Gabe had no idea if she was injured. "Ready."

Gabe had never jumped out of a helicopter, but nothing was going to keep him from getting to that canoe.

"Jump!"

Gabe threw himself from the chopper, expecting at any moment to feel the scorch of a bullet, but it never came.

When he hit the water, pain radiated through his chest. His arm and shoulder screamed at him, but he forced himself to the surface and then to Anissa.

Anissa sawed through the last rope trapping Liz's feet to the canoe.

Thank you.

In a worst-case scenario — well, if she ignored the very real possibility of them being shot — Liz could stand outside the canoe while Anissa worked to free her arms.

Poor girl. She'd been a trouper through the whole thing, although it was also possible that she was in shock.

The roar of the helicopter was deafening, the wash churning the water as Anissa surfaced.

Her momentary irritation vanished when Gabe's head appeared only a few feet away.

She didn't bother asking him what he was doing. He shouldn't be in this nasty water. He shouldn't be swimming. His arm was not ready for this. But that wasn't stopping him.

He swam to her as she sawed at the bonds trapping Liz's hands. Without saying a word, he reached for his own knife and went to work on the other side.

The helicopter bobbed and weaved in the space between them and the main house. But no more shots were fired.

What was Harvey doing?

Harvey tossed the rifle to the side.

Nothing ever went well when he tried to kill Anissa Bell.

He picked up the 9mm and tucked it at his waist.

Then he picked up the detonator.

He was sorry it had come to this. He was. The goal had always been Anissa.

He'd never intended for anyone else to die, but he was not going back to jail.

This was all Jack Bell's fault, and he could live with the consequences for the rest of his existence.

That helicopter would fly him out of here, and then while they were all stressed out over the charges he'd placed on the pipe, he would blow the place to kingdom come.

30

With Gabe's help, Liz was freed from the canoe. Liz seemed dazed. Had he drugged her? Or was it shock? Anissa couldn't tell. She kept a hand on Liz, making sure she stayed low in the water rather than risk becoming an easy target.

"What's the plan?" Gabe asked Anissa as they pulled Liz along with them toward the dock.

Anissa didn't have a clue. She was in a contaminated lake with an immunocompromised girl and a man with a still-healing stab wound. What she needed to do was get them both out of this water. Because if they survived Harvey only to die from a cryptosporidium infection, she was not going to be able to handle that.

"Dios," Gabe said. There'd been no warning. He'd just launched into prayer. Verbal prayer, no less. "We don't know what to do, but our eyes are on you."

Yes, Lord. Show us what to do.

Anissa scanned the shoreline. If she tried to retrace her original steps from the trees to the water, they might have a chance. "Follow me."

With a quick glance to be sure Liz was behind her, Anissa swam toward the canoe rack and climbed to shore over and around the canoes there. Once Liz and Gabe joined her, she pointed to the path she'd taken earlier. "We'll have to run for it. The next time the chopper dips down, we go."

Gabe nodded. Liz nodded.

They waited.

Gabe didn't even want to think about exposing themselves, but where they were provided minimal coverage. All Harvey had to do was look closely and they'd be sitting ducks.

As soon as the chopper came between them and the house, they took off. He led, with his good arm tucked through Liz's. Anissa was right behind them.

"Going somewhere?"

A cruel voice, far too close.

Gabe had a split second to decide. Freeze. Or run.

He ran. Liz ran with him.

"Not you, missy."

Gabe hesitated, but Liz's momentum propelled him forward and he knew.

Anissa would never get over it if anything happened to Liz. She'd sacrificed herself for Liz, and right now all he could do was get Liz out of here.

When they got to the trees, he found the little pile of things Anissa had left behind, including, hallelujah, her weapon and her phone.

He grabbed the gun and spun around. Harvey was two feet from Anissa. His gun pointed at her head.

"Tell your boyfriend to have the chopper land. That pilot is going to give me a ride out of here, or you will die and this whole place will blow."

"You're going to kill me anyway, Harvey. I'm not going to risk my friends for you."

Harvey laughed. The fact that he didn't sound deranged made him more terrifying. "I don't think you'll get to make that choice. Will she, Investigator Chavez?"

Gabe didn't have a shot. Harvey was behind Anissa, and downslope slightly. There was no way for Gabe to get to him without shooting her.

"Here's what's going to happen. You're going to have that news chopper land. They are going to fly me out of here. They will not be followed. And then I will tell them where the explosives are. If you fail to follow my wishes, we all die. This place is set to blow in five minutes."

"You're bluffing." Anissa didn't know if he was bluffing, but it couldn't hurt to keep him talking.

"Oh, you wish that, don't you? But here's what I know. I know the charges I set on that ancient pipe connecting this water supply to Lake Porter will blow in five minutes. When they do, there will be nothing to prevent almost all of this lake from draining into Lake Porter. But there won't be anything you can do to stop it because this entire facility — all these lovely wooden cabins — will be in flames."

Could Harvey Dixon have done all this? How long had the camp been closed?

Anissa didn't like the look on Gabe's face. She could be reading him wrong, but she didn't think she was. Gabe believed what Harvey was saying could be true.

"Liz, could you hand me that phone?" Gabe asked in a calm, polite voice.

Liz handed him Anissa's phone. He punched in a few numbers and held it to his ear.

"Parker, we have a bit of a situation here."

A pause. "Oh? Lovely. Well, this gentleman claims he's put explosive charges all over this camp and on the pipe that connects this lake to Lake Porter. He has requested that we provide him a way to leave the facility. Specifically, the chopper —"

"Hurry up!" Harvey's angry scream startled everyone. "I'd rather not die today if it's all the same to you!"

He might be faking it. But —

Anissa lunged for him. She hit him across his chest and they tumbled into the water. She got a full breath of air right before her head went under.

He was strong. Stronger than she'd anticipated. He'd dropped the gun and now he twisted around, holding her under. He did have weight on his side. And a good grip. He got his hands around her throat. Was this the last thing Carly felt, right before she died?

Maybe. But Anissa had something that Carly didn't have.

Anissa had a knife. And she knew how to use it.

She allowed herself to go almost limp. Her arms, she hoped, appeared to be flailing uselessly when what they were really doing was trying to get a grip on the sheath.

Got it.

She didn't want to kill this man. Despite everything he'd done, all the pain he'd caused, the lives he'd taken and the lives he'd attempted to destroy, she didn't want him dead.

But she didn't want to die either.

She thrust the knife upward.

Gabe ran toward the water, but all he could see were thrashing bodies. He couldn't tell where Anissa ended and Harvey began.

Then everything went still.

Anissa! The water bloody.

For an interminable second, Gabe couldn't see anything in the silt and sand.

Then Anissa's head emerged. She stood, gasping. "Help me get him out!"

Get him out? Gabe stood beside her. "Are you sure?"

Anissa, sucking in lungsful of air, nodded. "Yes."

Together, they pulled Harvey Dixon's limp body from the lake. The chopper set down on the nearby field. Paisley and Vic ran toward them. What were they doing?

Paisley grabbed Liz and ran with her back to the chopper. Vic came all the way to the water's edge. Gasping for air, he said, "Have to go. Bomb. Real. Now."

Harvey, limp and bleeding, was still

breathing. "We'd better not die for this guy," Gabe said. It took all three of them — Gabe, Anissa, and Vic — to get Harvey up. They carried him to the chopper and shoved him aboard. As soon as everyone was on, Sam lifted off.

They had cleared the tree line when the first explosion ripped through the air. Followed by a second. And a third.

31

Christmas Eve — Yap, Micronesia

"Ready?" Anissa's excitement was contagious. Gabe was ready, all right. She had no idea how ready. They made use of their masks and snorkels as they swam toward the buoy marking the spot for them to descend in the crystal-clear water.

After promising the captain they would return, he and Anissa had arrived in Yap three days earlier. Gabe had met Anissa's parents, briefly, after they'd flown back to the States in August. Jack Bell had been overwhelmed with grief at the knowledge that someone he'd arrested four decades earlier could have harbored such a vendetta.

Harvey Dixon had survived the stabbing and the cryptosporidium that had made all of them sick in the week after the camp blew up. Dixon had gotten a plea deal after providing the names and locations of three other children he'd kidnapped and handed over to the dirty adoption attorney.

His prison sentence was still long enough that he wouldn't be up for parole until he was ninety-two. Not that ninety-two-year-olds couldn't be dangerous, but they would deal with that when the time came.

Part of his plea deal involved a full confession for the death of Carly Nichols and the kidnapping of Jillian Davidson. It had all been a case of mistaken identity. Harvey had gotten out of prison with one goal: kill Jack Bell. But Jack Bell was in Yap, literally on the other side of the world.

So Harvey had gone for the next best thing.

Anissa.

The day of the murder, he'd followed Anissa's car. Then, as she was getting out of the car, he'd grabbed her from behind and broken her neck.

His plan had been to leave Jillian alone in the park, but someone pulled into the parking area as he was sliding Carly's body into the car. Jillian was screaming her head off and he feared the newcomers would chase him down if he left her. Then he'd be caught with a dead girl in his car. So he'd tossed Jillian into the car with Carly. Only after he'd gotten to the Dumpster did he realize he'd killed the wrong girl.

Carly had been driving Anissa's car. She was the same size. Same hair color. She'd put on a ball cap and a sweater that Anissa had left in her car.

Now he had the wrong dead girl and a screaming kid. Despite the fact that he'd just killed Carly in cold blood, he couldn't bring himself to kill Jillian. He called his attorney — a man who would be in jail now if he hadn't committed suicide ten years earlier — who said he'd take care of it and could make Harvey a tidy sum.

After selling Jillian, he'd sold three other children before getting caught and going back to jail for attempted kidnapping with intent to sell.

He'd waited, biding his time, until he found Anissa again after he got out of prison. He'd cleaned himself up, gained access to money he'd successfully hidden while in prison, and rented a place on the lake near Ryan and Leigh's. He'd passed himself off as a retiree and landed a part-time job installing, of all things, security cameras for the same company from which he'd bought the cameras he'd installed at his lake house. He'd even willingly shared the footage from those cameras with the sheriff's office.

Dixon had conceived multiple plans to kill Anissa.

None of them had worked.

The real start of the end was the night he had decided to shoot her from across the cove. The lightning had blinded him. Startled him. And his shot hit Jeremy.

It had been a fluke.

An accident.

But the fact that the bullet had been meant for Anissa, that Carly's death had been meant for Anissa, that Jillian's abduction hadn't been about Jillian but about Anissa . . . the burden of it all had lain heavy on Anissa in the days and weeks that followed the revelations.

Her parents had arrived in Carrington and their presence had calmed her, but it had terrified Gabe. Not that he was afraid to meet them, although Jack Bell did have a way about him that would make any potential suitor be very careful with his daughter.

Gabe had been afraid that when they left, she would go with them. It had been obvious, seeing her with her family, how close they were. How deep the bond. How much she had missed them.

How much they had missed her.

When they reached the buoy, Gabe and Anissa paused. He reached for her BCD and held on. She did the same as they bobbed in the surf.

"It's beautiful here," Gabe said. "Are you sure you don't want to move back?"

Anissa splashed water in his face. "No. I know where I'm supposed to be."

He really hoped she meant that.

Gabe's smile sent Anissa's heart into overdrive.

It was a smile reserved for her. And her alone. It wasn't his usual quick smile, the flirty smile she'd seen a million times. This was a smile that said "you're the one," and when he smiled that way . . . she pulled him closer and kissed him. He tasted like saltwater and sunshine. Her favorite combination.

"I love you." He whispered the words against her lips.

"I love you too." One more quick peck and then she asked, "Ready?"

"After you."

They resettled their masks and this time shoved their snorkels to the side in favor of their regulators. No fancy equipment. No way to speak. Nothing but a full tank of air and crystal-clear water.

Diving in Yap was like diving nowhere else.

For forty minutes they explored. She led him to some of her favorite spots and they watched schools of fish, sharks, and sting-rays. She could stay down there forever, but a peek at her dive computer warned her it was time to head to the surface. They would need to take their time on the ascent, and she didn't want to risk running out of air during a safety stop. After her experiences this summer, she'd lost all desire to hold her breath.

Liz was doing better than anyone could have ever dreamed or hoped. She'd gotten horribly sick after their dip in the lake. Her body was simply unable to fight off the crypto in the water. The Davidsons and Velma Brown had kept a vigil, united by their mutual love for their sweet girl. Brooke Ashcroft had stayed close as well. And a collective sigh of relief could have been heard from central North Carolina to southwestern Virginia when Liz turned the corner.

When it all had been said and done, the Davidsons did something that still left everyone in a state of awe when they heard about it. They opened their home to Velma Brown, asking her to please live with them and Liz. Velma, still fighting the ravages of cancer, had been overwhelmed and had accepted. Liz was able to stay with her mother while getting to know and growing to love the family that had loved her from birth.

Anissa's beloved Lake Porter had survived the hit of contamination from the lake at the camp with minimal impact. The environmental teams had been on high alert and had spent the next several months doing extra testing, but the lake remained safe for recreational use. Engineers had determined that the pipe had caved in on itself in the explosion and most of the water from the camp never reached Lake Porter.

Paisley, Sam, and Vic had received commendations from the sheriff's office for their assistance, and the Davidsons had given Paisley an exclusive interview that had aired all over the country.

Brooke had gotten back in the pool and was well on her way to that college scholarship. She was planning to major in criminal justice.

Anissa's dive computer chirped at her and she paused her ascent. Gabe paused with her.

She couldn't get over how much she loved him. He could still make her completely crazy, of course. She suspected he always would.

And if she wanted to be honest, she knew that's what she needed. Someone to bump up against her sometimes hard edges and soften them up a bit.

Bringing Gabe home, to Yap, had filled a little piece of her heart in a way she hadn't expected. He loved it here. He got along great with her parents and her siblings. And she suspected that her grandmother had a crush on him.

She would always love Yap and part of her heart would always roam these shores, but her life was in Carrington. It was the life God had given her, and it was good.

They ascended again, slow and steady, until they reached a point fifteen feet beneath the surface. Last safety stop. Three to five minutes of breathing in and out and waiting. Some divers hated this part, but she'd never minded it.

Gabe put his arms in an *x* cross across his chest. Then pointed to her.

She laughed around the regulator in her mouth, bubbles blowing around everywhere, and held her hand up in the sign for I Love You.

Gabe reached into a pocket on his BCD and then reached for her hand. He pulled her close and then held something toward her face.

She blinked twice before she could believe what she was seeing.

A ring.

She couldn't say yes fast enough. Well, she

couldn't technically say yes at all, but she said it around the regulator and nodded and flashed the okay sign, all at once. Gabe was laughing as she scrambled to pull the diving glove off her left hand.

Gabe slid the ring on to her finger.

A perfect fit.

When her dive computer indicated that it was safe to return to the surface, they ascended the remaining fifteen feet.

Together.

ABOUT THE AUTHOR

Lynn H. Blackburn is the author of *In Too Deep, Beneath the Surface, Hidden Legacy,* and *Covert Justice,* winner of the 2016 Selah Award for Mystery and Suspense and the 2016 Carol Award for Short Novel. Blackburn believes in the power of stories, especially those that remind us that true love exists, a gift from the Truest Love. She's passionate about CrossFit, coffee, and chocolate (don't make her choose) and experimenting with recipes that feed both body and soul. She lives in Simpsonville, South Carolina, with her true love, Brian, and their three children.

The employees of Thorndike Press hope you have enjoyed this Large Print book. All our Thorndike, Wheeler, and Kennebec Large Print titles are designed for easy reading, and all our books are made to last. Other Thorndike Press Large Print books are available at your library, through selected bookstores, or directly from us.

For information about titles, please call:
  (800) 223-1244

or visit our website at:
  gale.com/thorndike

To share your comments, please write:
  Publisher
  Thorndike Press
  10 Water St., Suite 310
  Waterville, ME 04901